The Future Burns Bright

Book Two : *The Race*

(First Edition)

by

Marcus B. Shields

ISBN : (978-1-926515-09-0)

For additional information about *The Future Burns Bright*, surf to :

http://abfbook.telostic.com

For my mother, Dorothy Shields,
who prepared her kids for the world, so well;

and

For my aunt Barbara Shields,
a wise pioneer who inspired the women in this series;

and

For my cousin and friend, Carl Kohlmeyer,
who should have had the time to read the books

We miss all of you very much;
but you will live forever, in our memories

Table of Contents

Prologue

Since this book is the second volume of the sequel to a predecessor series, it is strongly suggested that you should enjoy…

Angel of Mailànkh (Book One)
Doubt Me Not (Book Two)
Angel and The Empire (Book Three)
Children of The Fire (Book Four)

Of *The Angel Brings Fire* series, and then…

Storm In The North (Book One)

Of *The Future Burns Bright* series…

Before starting to read *The Race.*

With that said, it is recognized that for various reasons, some readers will have happened upon *The Race*, without having convenient access to the preceding books of the series.

We have therefore provided the following brief synopsis of the events of *Storm In The North*, so that the reader can make sense of some of the characters and themes involved.

Marcus Shields

Author

The Future Burns Bright (Book One) – Storm In The North begins with the gang-leader "Sebastiàn" – now a super-powered confidant of the Storied Watcher – leading his nascent ghetto army, on a supernaturally-mandated quest to find a stolen, ex-Pakistani nuclear weapon hidden in the Los Angeles area.

Meanwhile, Karéin-Mayréij's second group of followers – led by the FBI team-leader, Minnie Chu – are in an alien-crafted "air-ship", pursuing the alien-girl as she bears down on the underground prison in the Alaskan Aleutian islands, where the Billings and Jacobson teams are fighting for their lives.

Enshrouded in fire and thunder, the Storied Watcher – whose mighty and devastating alien-powers have now mostly returned – blasts her way through the very bedrock, exploding on to the scene of the battle and making short work of her family's tormentors.

A rescue is in the offing, but at the last minute – with the newly-able-to-fly Cherie Tanaka in tow – Karéin-Mayréij is forced to do aerial battle against a large group of U.S. military aircraft. She is successful, but the Air Force attackers unleash a nuclear weapon, which explodes dangerously close, wounding not only the Storied Watcher but also many of her friends.

To seek temporary respite while considering "next steps", the alien-girl leads her family and friends – who now number many-score people – to a secluded campground in the Canadian Rocky Mountains. There, a meeting – entitled "The Council Of The Woods" – of all of Karéin-Mayréij's North American entourage, is held; but immediately, it is clear that irreconcilable differences about what to do with the U.S. government's brutality, corruption and repressiveness, have arisen between the Storied Watcher's first and second groups of followers.

The first ("Mars Gang") team (led by Sam Jacobson of the Mars exploration mission) plans to force the President to abandon his persecution of the super-powered "New People" and to implement reforms. The second ("FBI") team (led by Minnie Chu of the Bureau's "Red Rover" project) hopes to work inside the system, by reaching a negotiated *détente* between the Storied Watcher and the U.S. government.

The Storied Watcher herself remains outwardly neutral in the dispute; but though they know it not, her demi-godly hand is subtly guiding both groups as they reach this impasse. For the alien-girl's greater supernatural powers have set tests for the Mars Gang and the FBI team; and these can only be passed by both groups achieving their goals… which, at this point, seem to be mutually-exclusive.

Eventually, it is decided that the two "more-than-human" teams (minus some individuals, who for various reasons elect not to participate) will be transported to different, far-apart places within the United States by Karéin-Mayréij. From there, they will go forward on their respective "quests".

Thus, at the end of *Storm In The North,* there is a parting of the ways for the Storied Watcher's friends and family, with the Chu and Jacobson parties being loaded on to the alien-girl's "air-ship", heading for as-yet-unknown perils and adventures in the unstable, misruled America of the 2040's.

The Race

Now Arriving... Ellensburg, WA

When the invisible 'Magic Bus' first touched down in the United States, after having streaked stealthily around the peaks of the central Rocky Mountains, there had been a confused scene, upon the intended disembarkation of the FBI party : the Storied Watcher had, for reasons both sentimental and practical, parked the vehicle in a clearing behind the *Santa Esmerelda* Grill, just off Idaho's Route 26.

But the restaurant was now boarded-up, lifeless and abandoned, a fact that Chu only realized at the last minute, as the bus was about to take off again. She had raced frantically back and flagged down a surprised Karéin-Mayréij, who sheepishly agreed to try another drop-off-point, after the FBI team-leader had explained what had happened to Osvaldo and Karlie, shortly after, as Chu had inelegantly put it, “the crap about your arrival, hit the Bureau's fan”.

So the restaurant-owner and the waitress were added to a growing rescue-list, the FBI team trouped back on board the 'Magic Bus'.

The second *aterrissage* – which was in a secluded corner of an industrial park, just outside Ellensburg in Washington State – was, however, fully-successful, and, one by one, the FBI team, plus Kaysten, Abruzzio and her dog, stepped off the bus.

Chu, for her part, had insisted on giving Jacobson a goodbye-hug; it was a gesture which the usually-stolid Mars mission commander accepted without reservation, and the two quest-leaders exchanged a few private comments, before the FBI team finally exited the vehicle.

They slowly walked away, with several of them waving as they headed towards civilization.

“Will y'all look at *that,*” commented Devon White, as he was looking out a side-window, at the figure of a strangely crestfallen Karéin-Mayréij, who was slowly and dejectedly moving to take up her position in front of the 'Magic Bus'.

“Wow,” agreed Boyd. “She's... *crying*. Well, after all... she *is* pretty close to Minnie and all of those people, I guess.”

“I guess you must feel the same way... right, Wolf?” inquired Tanaka. “I mean, sort of like us... you guys all went through quite a lot, together. Down in L.A., I mean.”

The bounty-hunter shrugged, and with a far-off look in his eyes, said, “No... okay... yeah. Reckon you're right, there, pardner. Pups 'n me kinda got *used* to them folk... you know? Guess I'm just worried about what's gonna happen to 'em. Minnie, Otis, Will – they know their away around... but Sylvia, and especially Jerry... ah, nothin' I can *do*, anyways. Hope they'll be alright.”

The Russian, like Jacobson, had been silently studying the Storied Watcher's every move, and Tanaka asked, “What's so interesting, Misha? Something wrong?”

“No... I do not think so... although, of course, *everything* about Karéin is always, 'interesting',” he replied.

“Well then... what're you staring at?” pressed Boyd.

“She no longer has that little shield on her arm,” observed Misha.

They heard the war-song of Karéin-Mayréij – still thrilling and impressive, but this time, strangely mournful, like a silver silk sheet, edged in black velvet – as the 'Magic Bus', pitched upward, and all outside scenery, faded from their mundane senses.

Now Arriving... Lake Buena Vista, FL

It was more than two hours after take-off from Washington State, until the 'Magic Bus' again began to descend; and several of those on-board exchanged grumbling comments to the effect of, “where in the world is she taking us”, until White had observed, “Y'all assumin' that it even is on Earth.”

But, as it turned out when the vehicle came to a gentle, complete stop and the Storied Watcher, with the flame of *Vìrya Ahn'jë* tamped down to a minimum, again came aboard – being sure to close the door behind her – off-planet excursions were not to be had, on this day.

“So, Karéin,” requested Jacobson, “Where's 'here'?”

“I would have thought that you would have guessed,” she teased. “It is almost as far away as possible, from where we said our 'goodbyes' to Minn-ee and her brave compatriots. We landed in silent, hidden mode, behind a stand of trees. I checked that there are none in the vicinity to disturb our privacy.”

“Bermuda, maybe?” inquired Boyd.

“Ha – good guess… but other than for Cherie, you have no easy way of traversing a large body of water,” replied the alien-girl. “No, friends... you are now in the principality of Flow-ree-dah, near the city of Oar-land-oh. There is a large meeting-house some distance yonder, and people are participating in that sport with the little white balls and the striking-clubs, that Bob used to talk about doing, back in Too-sawn... what was it again... oh, yes, I remember... 'golf'.”

A peal of tense laughter echoed inside the bus, as White quipped, “Girl, y'all a mind-reader – I never *did* get to see Disney World as a kid.”

“But”, she replied, “Is that not the place wherein one finds a 'Magic Kingdom'? If so... send me back a report, please, because I would not venture there, myself.”

“Always *wanted* to burn that damn place down,” commented Wolf, “Just for the fun of it. Maybe I'll get my chance?”

“Just the 'Magic Kingdom' part, if you please,” answered Karéin-Mayréij, not missing a beat.

There were more broad smiles and a few chuckles. Then she went on,

“Now I have some words of great import, good friends. First off : since the time when it became apparent that Minn-ee's quest, and your own, would go in different directions, I began to ponder what preparations for each, would be fair; for I wish not for either of you to fail, let alone, be hurt or lost, in the doing of it. In thinking of this, I had to also consider the fact that while dear Minn-ee and Jerr-ee certainly *do* face some challenges of their own, these – especially if they are welcomed, at least at first, by the President's courtiers – may not be as severe as those which confront all of you. So I have acquired, and created, some items – and someone else, as well – to help you.”

“'Scuse me, Karéin,” mentioned White, “I know y'all not completely up on English, but didn't y'all mean, 'some*thing*, else'?”

“No,” she replied, with a gleam of the greatness in her eye and a few notes of her war-song, sounding in their psyches, “I meant... some*one*.”

“Okayy...” responded the puzzled black ex-astronaut.

“Now to the details,” elaborated the alien-girl. “Here,” – she announced, with an outstretched left arm, palm up – “Is a sack of many diamond-gems, as well as little gold coins, fashioned as best I could, to imitate those minted by your Ew-Nighted-States government... the inscriptions are not perfect, but the metal is nearly pure, so hopefully you can use them to purchase such equipment as may be necessary for your journey. Also,” – she indicated, pointing at a kind of footlocker near the back of the 'Magic Bus' – “I have, ahh, 'appropriated', new casual garments and foot-gear for all of you... I hope that they will fit properly, as these were the best that I could find, from the tailors of Jasper. In any event, they should make you less conspicuous, than would otherwise be the case. If you would like, I can disintegrate what you now wear, so that no trace is left behind.”

“Ahh, Karéin, you've shot down my chance for a nice little clothes-buying spree in all those tourist shops,” commented Tanaka. “But save my rags, if you don't mind... take them back with you. I'd like to have them for a souvenir, when all of this is over with.”

“As you wish,” agreed Karéin-Mayréij. “And, as regards clothing... there is one *other* thing.”

She waved her hand.

The footlocker opened, and out of it, floated six individually-sized examples of what looked like silver-shaded, subtly-sparkling, single-piece cool-water swimsuits, the area of each of which could cover the wearer's legs, abdomen, trunk and arms. With a flick of the wrist, the suits were sent to the laps or grasps of those listening.

“*Whoa*,” remarked an amazed Boyd, as he ran his hands over the smooth and light material, which, to the touch, felt halfway between aluminum-foil and silk. “You make us any surfboards to go with those, Karéin?”

"Alas, no," answered the Storied Watcher, with a pleasant smile. "Though in fact, that thought *had* occurred to me, after reading one of those 'comic-books' owned by young Kevin McGregor. Now, as to the purpose : these garments have been specially-crafted and treated, to withstand both *Amaiish* herself, as well as those elemental and other forces that may be generated by her. They are both light and easy to wear; and over time, each will adapt to your own body-form. And other subtle arts, have they, as well; for example, as they absorb your personal spirits, they will begin to augment your own powers of the *Fire*, and they have a limited ability to protect you against a wide range of perils. I would recommend that you always use these under-garments, so that you have, ahh, something to cover you up, in the event that some mishap, destroys what mundane clothes that you have on, over top. And lend them to no-one! The energies contained within them, after they are your own, will be very harmful to an ordinary human who makes the mistake of trying to use such a garment. Are you, uhh, 'with me, so far'?"

"Most definitely," offered Misha, with a wicked smile.

"Damn well beats boxer shorts," joked White.

"Oh-kay," continued Karéin-Mayréij. "And I have, ahh, 'acquired' for you, a number of other things, which may or may not be useful... I could not be the judge of it, since I am still somewhat poorly-acquainted with this techno-society. You will find these items in the locker, over yonder; among them are some mobile comm-oon-ee-cay-tors, make-up kits, shaving-razors, pens and paper, *et cetera*, plus some 'pree-paid' credit-mon-ee cards, some Canada Kingdom money and driving-license cards, the latter corresponding to your own names – please be aware that I am not sure how well these will work, as although *Vîrya Ahn'jë was* able to re-program the little crypto-chip within them to include your names, there were some details that she did not know, and thus could not inscribe – and many other needful things, as well, contained within three back-packs, taken from one of these Jasper stores. Oh, and there are a few choc-o-late candy-bars. But *only* a few. I sort of, ahh, ate the rest. Sorry."

"Oh, that's quite alright," allowed Jacobson, "Cherie told me, a while ago, that I needed to go back on the diet, anyway."

"I *did* give one each, to Tommy and young Kevin," added the alien-girl. "Which I consider to be quite generous... they *were* delicious, after all."

The former Mars mission commander bent over his knees and began to laugh, almost uncontrollably.

"*Honestly*, Karéin," he started.

"Yes?" she answered, with an arched eyebrow.

"Nothing... *nothing*," he demurred.

"Oh-kay..." she said.

"Sometimes I wonder if we'll *ever* understand you," offered Tanaka.

"I hope that you never will," remarked the Storied Watcher. "I rather *like* being – ahh – 'mysterious', you know."

There was a short pause, and then Jacobson, having more or less regained his composure, came to his feet, and announced, “Well, folks... I guess it's time we should get going. We've got a lot to do – not least, finding a place to stay.”

“Wait,” requested Karéin-Mayréij. “For there is one other thing.”

She came under the intense scrutiny of six pairs of eyes, and commented, “Ahh – I detect your minds, trying to probe my own, for the secret. Impressive... but you will need to spend more time perfecting this skill, I am afraid.”

“I'm hopin' the secret's, like, 'I stole y'all a nice luxury car, 'long the way',” quipped White.

“Ha! Not quite,” coyly responded the alien-girl. “In fact... it is someone much better.”

“There you go again, with that some*one*,” observed Tanaka. “A riddle?”

“Step forward, noble *Vîrya* Cherie Tanaka,” instructed Karéin-Mayréij, “And kneel beside me, as we face the hatch-door, at the back of this vehicle.”

With a puzzled look, the former Mars science officer slowly walked over to the Storied Watcher and complied with the order, noticing that the bounty-hunter's two dogs had also joined the scene, on the alien-girl's other side.

“Ahh,” mentioned Misha. “A pet for the Professor, Karéin?”

“Nay... a *child*,” answered the Storied Watcher.

“*What?*” protested a perplexed Tanaka. “I'm not even preg –”

“*Shh*,” interrupted Karéin-Mayréij, with a finger held in front of her mouth. “Now summon the greatness inside you, Cherie; and sing to your daughter.”

“Oh... wait a minute... I *see*,” knowingly commented the Russian.

“I'm not going to sing, *anything*,” argued the scientist. “I failed voice –”

“Use your war-song,” ordered the alien-girl. “She will know you by it.”

“Uhh... *right*,” mumbled Tanaka. From deep down, she began to hum.

A glimpse or two of the nascent might of which the Storied Watcher had spoken, appeared in the eyes, body and aura of the former Mars mission Science Officer, as she began to follow her mentor's instructions; Tanaka's *ooo–ai-ooo–ooo-ai* psycho-music, its beat electric, exciting and power-infused, echoed so loudly that for a moment or two, the others were afraid that it might attract undue attention, from the outside.

There was a thumping sound from the storage-hatch at the back of the 'Magic Bus', as if something imprisoned therein, was trying to find a way out. After a couple of seconds, the catch that sealed the compartment somehow opened on its own, and the cover swung open.

Slowly, something amazing, though unexpected – to all, that is, save Karéin-Mayréij and Misha – emerged from the storage-area, while the Storied Watcher's war-song played as a second-track to Tanaka's. Yellow-gold in hue, it bore a distant resemblance to the alien-girl's own war-child, *Vîrya Ahn'jë*; but it was more like a breast-plate, with a linked belt and abdomen-covering, akin to a short kirtle, and – mercifully – it bore none of the flaming, infernal character that made *Vîrya Ahn'jë* so forbidding, though it did have a subtle sparkle-and-glow, like the latter's own.

"*Vîrya* Cherie Tanaka, behold now thy blood-kin-offspring, whose high-born title and name is *Vîrya Sài'ymë,*" announced the beaming alien-girl. "She is of the essence of your body, taken in your sleep, and she is of mine own arts, those of *Vîrya Ahn'jë* and *Vîrya Quü'j,* too. Tell her of your love, and how you would travel together, inseparable, until the end of days. And ask her to bind to your frame."

"How do you... say its name, again..." stammered a flustered Tanaka.

"VEER-yah sye-EE-may-YEH," whispered Karéin-Mayréij, "And she is a 'her'... a girl-child. This will be immediately apparent, when you touch. *Call* to her, now!"

Both of Wolf's dogs, fire in their eyes, yipped a strange chorus; and the onlookers could have sworn that they were addressing the breastplate, directly.

"Hi... Little One, *Vîrya Sài'ymë,*" spoke the scientist, straightening her body and advancing one of her feet in front, while remaining in a kneel.

The majesty in Tanaka's voice waxed, with every word.

"I don't know how to be a Mommy... I've never had a child before... I don't even have a real boyfriend," she continued, "But I'll try to learn, and, uhh, look after you –"

"*Thee,*" corrected the Storied Watcher, *sotto voce,* with a friendly elbow-poke to Tanaka's midriff. "The blood-kin of the *Makailkh* use the formal, when addressing each other... except for verbs, that is. Do not worry about the standard as opposed to the subjunctive. In time, you will master this, as well."

"*Sorry,*" retreated the former Science Officer.

Doing her best imitation of a semi-divine, alien tutor, she went on, "Dear *Vîrya Sài'ymë,* I name thee as my own daughter... I ask thee to, uhh, adorn my body, of which thou are my flesh and blood. Thus, thou shall, uhh, feel my love, as we travel together, learning and sharing in each other's grace, until the last of my days. Will thou have me... as thy mother?"

"She's really layin' it on *thick,*" whispered Wolf, to Boyd.

"Guess the Professor's relating to the whole 'alien goddess thing', better than the rest of us," philosophically replied the former Mars mission pilot.

There was a tear in the eye of Karéin-Mayréij, as she regarded Tanaka with a loving, "teacher-with-'A'-student", glance.

How far you have come, beloved First-Of-The-Fire! she sent.

I am so very *proud of you!*

Now, the more-than-humans, and others, in the 'Magic Bus', first heard – or, perceived – a new, tinkling, trilling, weirding voice, distantly reminiscent of Elissha's hesitant, shy tone.

Tanaka Blessed Cherie Vìrya *Mother!*

In much less than the blink of an eye, the breastplate rocketed across the 'Magic Bus', encasing Tanaka's trunk, in the next quarter-second.

The scientist bent over and started to sweat. Flashes of the *Fire* raced through her entire body, making her glow as if lit up from deep inside; and a few of the energy-charges escaped, jumping like miniature lightening-bolts, as far as two or three inches from where Tanaka was holding.

"You *okay*, Cherie?" demanded a worried Jacobson.

"No... I'm... fine... Sam," breathed the more-than-a-woman, her eyes now glowing, as her war-song began to rise, "It's just... that... she's... in here... *with* me... with my *mind*... that is... hooboy, what an *experience*..."

"Young *Vîrya Sài'ymë* has your essence and substance, noble friend," counseled the Storied Watcher. "She is not only of your blood and dee-enn-ay, but also of your mind... your *soul*. Defend her with your *life*, First-Of-The-Fire, as she will do in return, for you."

"*Crazy* shit," observed White, "Bit like what I felt, back there in the camp, when Miss Angel Lady let me have a talk with that blue dagger of hers?"

"You... can't *begin*... to imagine, Devon," gasped Tanaka, with a tearful look of delight on her face, as she caressed the breastplate, back and forth. "It's like she *knows* me... I've known *her*... for my whole life... utterly amazing..."

"Ain't such a *new* thing," spoke Wolf, his eyes now glowing dull red.

As if talking to himself, he looked at his chest and said, "Sure – you can go meet her... but be right back, y'hear?"

Immediately, the bounty-hunter's darting, elfin little flame-spirit streaked from his body, impacting with, and seemingly being absorbed by, *Vîrya Sài'ymë*. The gesture was met with astonished glances on the part of everyone except the Russian.

"Ohh... *wowww*," mumbled the former Mars scientist. "I feel *another* mind... completely unlike either of us, but I still understand her... hi there... why, thanks! I don't know how to use it... but *she*... of course... come back any time..."

A dart of fire emerged from the living-breastplate. It struck the bounty-hunter in almost exactly the same place from where it had first issued.

"This is too *much*, Karéin," protested Tanaka. "It isn't supposed to be *possible* – intelligent beings *this* different from you and I –"

"Yeah, well, that's what Sylvia said, too," grunted Wolf. "Tried to argue it out with Her Nuclear Highness, over there, as I recall. Guess who won?"

"There is no 'winning', in such cases, dear friend," mentioned the Storied Watcher, with a friendly finger-wave. "Only the joy of coming to comprehend, something which one previously did not."

"So... what can she *do*," inquired Jacobson, with a purposeful stare. "Combat-wise, that is."

"*Vîrya Sài'ymë* is still of tender years," noted the alien-girl, "And thus her abilities are as yet, rather modest; but in time, they will grow, as would the strength and endurance of a human-child. Some of these arts are as yet unknown both to herself and, indeed, to myself; but, as for the others... well, Cherie – why not stand in front of us, and ask her?"

Tanaka, her eyes glowing, came to her feet; and the others realized that she had also been transformed, in some hard-to-describe way, as well.

"I'll... I'll try to translate," stated the scientist. "Here... goes. Yes? Umm-hmm? Well, *that* will come in handy..."

"*What* will?" pressed Jacobson.

"First, she can, uhh, flatten herself against me, so I can wear her underneath regular clothes... at least, some kinds of clothes," explained the scientist. "But she can also, uhh... disappear – vanish, become invisible, that is. Although she's still right nearby."

"As can my own war-children," commented Karéin-Mayréij. "They travel, out of sight by means of the light-bending art. Which is often necessary, lest my beloved *Vìrya Ahn'jë* set fire to whatever I sit or lay upon."

"Y'all must go through a lot of furniture," quipped White.

The alien-girl winked at him, with a fang-toothed smirk.

"And... *Vìrya Sài'ymë* has a lot of other abilities," offered Tanaka. "Like, right now... my Mars senses are *way* better than they were, before... I'm hearing... no, not hearing, but... it's like I can perceive stuff going by, on the airwaves... radio, TV, computer networks... have to turn it off, gets too confusing..."

"Anything else?" inquired Boyd. "Defensive abilities, maybe?"

"Oh, *yeah*," gushed Tanaka, staring off into space, as she spoke. "You think so, Little One? Well... let's hope we never have to test... oh, sorry, Brent... was just talking to her... she said that she could make my 'bubble' much more powerful... heal me, if I'm hurt... she's has some of *Vìrya Ahn'jë*'s computer-hacking ability... and if I need anything more to fight with –"

Instantly, the more-than-a-woman's left arm was adorned by a translucent, dimly-glowing, yellow-gold-and-white-tinted shield, about twice the size of the Storied Watcher's mysteriously-absent *Vìrya I'ëà'b*'. This holograph-mimicking item was accompanied by the appearance of a skull-cap, made out of the same semi-ethereal substance, on the top of Tanaka's head, not to mention that of a Roman gladius-like, gold-white-yellow short-sword, in her right hand.

"She can, uhh, make them into anything she wants," absentmindedly noted the scientist. "As long as they're in close contact with her, and me. Like... *this*."

Faster than any could discern, the sword changed into something resembling a crowbar, albeit composed of the strange, glowing material.

"Don't need a tool-kit, anymore," remarked Tanaka.

"Ha," agreed Boyd, with a wry smile. "Wish we'd had, uhh, 'her', with us, back on the *Eagle*."

The former Mars science officer blinked her eyes. The spear and arm-shield disappeared, as if into thin air.

"Can I try her on?" asked White. He sounded half-serious.

"The same warning – only more-so – that I mentioned about your new under-garments, apply to innocent and new *Vìrya Sài'ymë,*" cautioned Karéin-Mayréij. "Her essence is bound to Cherie's own, and while you can touch and speak with her, I would advise all of you not to place her on your bodies, as her new mother does. This might offend her – and as she is but a child, she might, uhh, 'react', in a forceful way. *You* would survive such an experience... an ordinary mortal, would not."

"Maybe I'll just stick with them 'undies'," carefully stated the black ex-astronaut.

"So... she supposed to just walk around with, uhh, her new offspring, on her, all the time?" asked Jacobson. "The Professor, I mean."

"It would be appropriate for you to keep *Vîrya Sài'ymë* close to your breast for at least a few hours, henceforth, Cherie," proposed the Storied Watcher. "After that, you can ask her to use the hiding-trick. But consider that she is a child, and needs her mother's love and attention. Do you understand?"

"I... sure *do*," acknowledged Tanaka. "I'm growing very fond of her little voice, already." She stopped talking and sat down, seemingly lost in a personal reality.

"Listen, Karéin," Jacobson requested, "Is there anywhere, uhh, private, where we could change into those new clothes that you acquired for us? I'd really not like to venture out of the bus, while still wearing our Air Force-issue suits... we'd stand out like a sore thumb."

"Behold," indicated the alien-girl, with a quick hand-gesture; and immediately, something similar to a bead-curtain drew across the ceiling of the vehicle, separating the rear quarter of its interior – which included Tanaka and her new, living-armor charge – from the rest of the 'Magic Bus'.

"I installed this while I set to work in crafting *Vîrya Sài'ymë*... and a few other things, as I did not want to be disturbed, in so doing," she explained. "I will wait up in the front-quarters, while you all choose the garb that you deem most appropriate. Oh... and if anything – especially, the shoes – do not, uhh, 'fit', do not despair; I can do some quick mod-ee-fee-cayshuns, on these, before you finally depart."

"Ah, Karéin," they heard Tanaka mumble as she emerged through the curtain, "Now you're a cobbler, too..."

"Another word for 'shoemaker'," offered the Storied Watcher. "An honorable profession – so I accept the compliment."

"I'll go first," proposed Boyd, stepping forward and passing the former Mars science officer, in so doing.

"Figures... he just wants the best pick," commented Wolf. "Well, save me the 'extra-larges', 'less you want to see more of me than any man should do."

After perhaps thirty-five minutes – longer than anticipated, but Jacobson insisted on many small tailoring-changes and on comfortable foot-gear, given that they'd likely be walking a nice long distance – they stood outside the 'Magic Bus', outfitted in their new clothes, with the 'special' undergarments worn discreetly underneath.

Tanaka was the most stylish, with a wide-brimmed, ribbon-bedecked, beach-hat, sandals and a flowing, flower-and-garden-motif, Kandyan *sari*-like dress that hid her undergarments, including the living breastplate, with little obvious external evidence; Boyd, Misha and Jacobson all looked like they had just stepped off the 18th hole, as they were clad in golf-shirts (light blue for the *Eagle* commander, white for his former pilot, while the Russian wore an orange shirt), neutral-colored casual pants, green driving-range-caps and canvas sneakers. Wolf gained an outfit somewhat similar to what he had first worn, with a new pair of jeans, but he had – reluctantly, and only at Jacobson's insistence – given up his prized cowboy-boots and “lucky” leather-jacket in favor of a blue-collar shirt and work-shoes, ending up resembling a garage-mechanic. White was the most formally-dressed, with loosely-fitted, khaki slacks and a plain white dress-shirt, although he had insisted on being allocated the storage-locker's only pair of brand-name sneakers. Neither he, nor the bounty-hunter, had been able to find a suitable hat; though, like all the rest, the black ex-astronaut was elated to discover that the alien-girl had, thoughtfully, remembered to purloin a pair of 'mirror' sunglasses for each member of the new Jacobson party.

“Don't we look like an odd bunch,” remarked the former Mars science officer. “Sort of makes sense, though... wouldn't you say?”

“Ah, in Eng-lish, as I understand it, 'odd' can mean 'unusual', in either a good, or a bad, way,” observed the Storied Watcher. “I prefer to believe the former, friends.”

“Nice duds, man,” observed White. “Almost makes me forget what we came here for... *almost*.”

“Yeah,” agreed Boyd. “Though we got next to no chance of actually chasing the bastard down, mind you. Any tips for us on that front, Karéin?”

The alien-girl fell silent for a second or two, as if carefully pondering her answer; then she said, “Then, it might be best, to make *him*, come to *you*... that is, to give him a reason why he must deal with you, and in person. I tried the same, and it did not work – at least, not completely – but perhaps he is less, ahh, 'scared' of you, than he was of me. That could work to your advantage.”

“Dogs 'n me'll *teach* him a reason to be afraid,” offered Wolf, with a dull, menacing red eye-glow; and the others flinched and moved away, as his vicinity became immediately too hot to tolerate, for all save the two smoking, drooling hell-hounds.

“That is for you to decide, fearsome Son Of The Flame,” commented Karéin-Mayréij, “Though I would counsel all of you, not to reveal too much of your art, until it is needful so to do. Keep them, ahh... guessing.”

“Like that idea,” mentioned Jacobson. “Well, folks... time's a-wastin'. We'd better get out of here, and find somewhere to stay for the night.”

He turned to the Storied Watcher.

"Karéin," he stated, trying to keep control of his emotions, "The thought has occurred, that this might be the last time we'll ever see each other... so is there any chance I can get one last hug, from my personal 'angel'?"

"It will not *be*," countered the alien-girl.

As she disappeared in the much bigger man's arms, she argued, "Have *faith*, Sam Jacobson; the quest which now awaits, while formidable, is less than that which first called us together. You *will* overcome! Come to me – all of you!"

As they closed in, they realized that she was weeping.

"*Liar*," gently chided Tanaka. "You don't believe a *word* of that."

"I believe in *you*," whispered Karéin-Mayréij, with a quavering voice.

"It is just... just... I did not think it would be so painful... saying, 'good-bye', I mean," she stammered.

"It is difficult for many of us," said a subdued Misha. "Oh, Karéin... if I had just taken a different assignment, when I arrived in this country, what a poorer man, I would be... but just to be back in that hotel-room, with..."

"*I love you*," she gushed, covering him with embraces and kisses.

He nodded, nuzzled her for a few seconds, and then somehow found the strength to pull away.

"Hey," spoke Wolf, "Been a *bitchin'* ride, Karéin... wouldn'tve traded it for all the tea in China, all the blow in Mexico, and all the... whatever the hell they got, up there in Canada. Thanks, girl... that goes for all four of us, over here."

The fire-spirit appeared from his neck, and it emanated a sad tone that, somehow, all around could understand. The puppies also sighed.

She embraced the bounty-hunter, almost as tightly as she had done for the Russian.

White settled for just a hug, while Boyd held the Storied Watcher close to his breast and quietly commented, "You know, I was the first to speak with you... to *touch* you... back on Mars... remember? So long ago, so far away..."

With a vulnerable stare delivered by doe-like eyes, the alien-girl said something back in her strange, trilling, warbling tongue, kissed him on the cheek, and, with slumping shoulders, backed away.

"I leave six of my dearest friends, a beloved child, and a cherished girl-cousin," remarked Karéin-Mayréij, her demeanor still wistful, though her superhuman nobility again began to leak through her human-like guise.

With folded hands, she looked upward, apparently at the bright Florida sun.

"Light of Heaven... guide their way... guard them *safe*," she prayed.

Then – with only the whisper of her war-song, its chords like the sound of a symphony, played from far over the horizon – both she, and the 'Magic Bus', were gone.

You're Missing One Ingredient, Sir

"So then we *did* get her?" was the first thing that came out of the *nouveau*-President's mouth, as – with the self-invited "Spiritual Adviser", along with National Security Adviser Bezomorton and several other close *confidantes* within the cloistered confines of the airborne command-post, who were looking closely, if silently, on – the U.S. leader interrogated his Secretary of Defense.

"All I can tell you, sir," responded the leather-faced former Marine, "Is that according to the Air Force, our confidence is high, based upon local TACEVAL reports. We had a good track on the target, shortly before detonation... it was well within lethal radius, especially considering that the weapon had been configured for enhanced initial neutron output. GrayWar – which, unfortunately, happened to have a large number of their people caught in the open, at the time – is reporting well over 75 per cent KIA... and most of *them* were actually much further from the zero point, than was the target. Mr. Duke, by the way, is about to present us with a *very* large bill, for his costs so incurred."

"Well, Mr. Duke can *wait*," retorted the American leader. "*I*... can't. What about a corpse? Did we get a corpse?"

"Sir," politely replied DeWitt, "At that distance, it should have been vaporized, so I'm afraid that we're unlikely to find that kind of positive evidence. Of course, we're still searching the area."

"So are we," interjected a ghostly, monotonous voice, coming in, without a visual, from over one of the secured communications links. "Nothing yet, but there are some contradictory, confused reports from those few fully-operative personnel that we still have on the island. I have to advise you that the Agency has lost some of our *best* Wet Ops people, in this engagement – some were with GrayWar when it went off, others were on the transports – we've only got a few, who had ingressed southbound from the Alaskan mainland, left. Mr. President, this entire thing should have been *much* better-planned and executed; as matters stand now, I've only got maybe eight to ten people experienced enough for a reliable long-range kill, left in the Western Hemisphere. Sir, we simply *cannot* continue to waste hard-to-replace assets like this –"

"Your comments are noted," interrupted the *nouveau*-President. "And for every spook that *you've* had fried, Air Force and Army have probably lost ten... that right, Mr. Secretary?"

"Sadly, yes," confirmed DeWitt. "Although for the record, Blue-On-Blue casualties as a *direct* result of the detonation were considerably lower than we had anticipated – most of the losses were incurred in the air engagement that transpired shortly beforehand, because the device appears to have gone off to the north of the planned Zero Point. Incidentally, Mr. President, we're still going over the TACEVAL from that battle, because whereas previously, the alien elected to cripple rather than destroy our fighters – that is, previously she, or it, gave some of the pilots a chance to eject – in this one, we had a large number of aircraft, including three of the transports, destroyed outright, by something that the survivors described as a kind of 'brilliantly-shining, really small point of light that flies faster than a missile and which emits a terrifying, screaming sound'... one hit from this thing is capable of downing a F-32, three or so, a transport."

"Had we seen her use this attack before?" asked the Security Adviser.

"Negative," mentioned the Defense Secretary, "But we lost *hundreds* of fine airmen and soldiers, to this accursed, new, weapon. Casualties would have been much higher, but for some reason, in the middle of the battle, the alien suddenly disengaged. Then it seemed to notice the nuke, pursued it, and, luckily, got within lethal radius when it went off."

"I think this provides as clear proof as we'll ever get, about the creature's innate cruelty and blood-thirstiness," quietly mentioned Bezomorton. "I shudder to think of what she – it – might have been capable of, if we hadn't gotten her."

"*Did* you?" spoke up the normally taciturn, "lurking-in-the-background", Spiritual Adviser.

"Beg your pardon?" asked DeWitt.

"Get it. The alien, that is." answered Brother Harold.

"Well, sir," offered the Defense Secretary, "Our last track showed it to be within two nautical miles of Ground Zero... of a half-megaton, enhanced-radiation, high-yield, three-stage thermonuclear warhead. *Nothing* we know of, can survive at that range. The heat and radiation would have melted an aircraft carrier, for example. Like I said... our confidence is high."

"That may be," continued the Spiritual Adviser, "But you're missin' one critical thing, I'm afraid."

"And what would that be, sir?" incredulously demanded DeWitt.

"You can't kill the Devil with fire, my friend," calmly counseled Brother Harold, "'Less the blood of a saint, goes along with it."

That Which Was Lost, Is Almost Found

All the mosques in America had been closed, at gunpoint, a long time ago, of course; nonetheless, "Allah's faithful" still found plenty of places at which to discreetly congregate and worship.

This – a nondescript, unmarked, apparently-unoccupied joint in a run-down, suburban Flint, Michigan, strip-mall – was one such. The prayer-rugs had been laid out to face Mecca, using an old-fashioned magnetic compass (the GPS boxes were too risky, considering that almost every piece of high-tech wizardry now made in America, had one of those special 'government back-door chips' pre-installed), and the sermon from the local *Imam*, who doubled as a car-parts-dealer during the day, was in the process of being delivered.

As the rote, fundamentalist recitals of the Holy Qu'ran's inerrancy and corresponding, indignant denunciations of "godless, infidel America" continued, and as they arose from the familiar prostate prayer-position, a stout, bearded, tan-skinned, white-robed man in perhaps his 50th decade, kneeling in the back row of the throng, whispered to the believer next to him.

"Peace, brother," he said, in fluent Arabic. "Have you any news?"

"Indeed," replied the second, tall and lean, early-thirties man, speaking equally quietly and not taking his eyes off the religious leader. "But I am not sure whether it is good, or bad. *Inshall'ah,* the former."

"Go on," requested the first Muslim.

"Well, it is about the disaster that occurred down in Texas. The one regarding the 'shipment', if you know what I mean," replied the younger man.

"Yes?" said the elder man, his tone rising with interest, although he was still not speaking loudly enough to attract attention.

"There is news about the cargo," explained the second Muslim. "As you know, only one brother survived the encounter, and – may merciful Allah grant him endless delights, in the hereafter – he succumbed shortly thereafter; but he gave the brothers in Texarcana a good description of the infidel criminals who hijacked our equipment. These turn out to have been working for a thug named 'Don Morales' –"

"None of this is new," remarked the older man. "As you will recall, we had no choice but to deal with scum such as them, just to get the materials transported to the intended transfer point. Ai! If *only* we had the resources to have imported it, just by ourselves. We could have struck a mighty blow against the Great Satan, and you and I would be martyrs by now... what a *pity*."

"Yes, it is a great tragedy, that is for sure," agreed the second Muslim, "But thanks to what was related by our late brother, specifically, descriptions of those gangsters who were present, some believers in the Houston area were able to identify these same criminals... we acted on a hunch that if those who stole our goods were there, so would be the item, itself. Allah be praised – this turns out to have been true."

"Wonderful!" exclaimed the elder man, still trying to keep his voice down. "So... we would then need to discuss a rescue operation. Who do we have in Texas, who can participate?"

"Unfortunately, it is not that simple," admitted the younger man. "The equipment seems to have left the state, entirely. But we know, in a general way, where it is going; it was loaded on to a van that was last seen heading to the west. Our faithful in the area inquired as diligently as they could – although we have only a few who have infiltrated this particular gang, and then only at the lowest levels – and they were able to determine that the destination is somewhere in the Los Angeles metropolitan area. We have no idea why it was sent there, however, other than for some loose talk about 'Don Morales has a score to settle with the Crips', *et cetera*. If we want to recover the cargo and put it to its intended use, that is where we will need to look."

The first Muslim stopped speaking for a few seconds, pondering a response while reflectively stroking his beard. Then he said,

"Then we will need to go to Los Angeles, forthwith, brother."

"But why?" argued the younger man. "It is a large city. Was something of the same type, not what we were hoping to achieve? Why not just let them do with it, what Don Morales intends?"

"Three reasons," listed the elder man. "One – given that the equipment must already have been there for some time, and given that it has not yet, uhh, *operated*... likely, the criminals do not know how to arm and detonate it, in the first place; and if, while trying to figure this out, they do not properly hide or protect it, and if it is in the meantime captured by the infidel government, the design and programming would give away almost our entire supply-chain. We would not be able to get the next two, anywhere *near* this sinful country. Two – it should not be used against a place where too many our own brothers and sisters reside... do not forget, there are Black Muslims in the poorer enclaves of Los Angeles, and though they do not exactly follow the truest teachings of the Prophet, none the less, they are still Allah's children, struggling against the filthy immorality, drug addiction and female disobedience, that plagues that city. If we cannot move the device to where we had first intended to use it, then, at least, the item should, instead, be placed in a more favorable location, like, say, Beverley Hills, or, even better, Hollywood."

He paused for a second, and then went on,

"Finally – most importantly – are we not *called* to martyrdom, in this task, brother? It would be cruel beyond all cruelty, to deny this opportunity to the fourteen select of our group… to whom I will relay the news, as soon as I can. To what *finer* purpose, could we give our corrupt mortal flesh, to the Almighty?"

"Of course, there *is* none," admitted the younger man. "With such joy, shall I accompany you, on this sacred mission, brother. Scarcely, can I *wait!*"

The elder man, a kindly smile on on his face, noiselessly nodded, as the sermon ended and they both again bent forward in humble devotion to glorious Allah, the Just and Merciful.

A Modest Update For Ms. Chu & Company

"Hello? *Hello!*" demanded a frustrated Minnie Chu, her voice rising perceptibly with each word, as she spoke into the handset receiver at the Amalgamated Kittitas County Sheriff's and Ellensburg State Patrol Office. "This is an *important* call! Is anybody *there?*"

"Hey, take it *easy*, lady," advised a burly, "Smokey-Bear"-hatted State Trooper, who was himself struggling through filling out an accident report, on one of the "seen-better-times" police office's computer terminals. "You're gettin' about the same response as we usually do, when we call up the Bureau on somethin' or other. They don't pay much attention to us, frankly... they go and do whatever they want. Local law enforcement's usually the last to find out."

"Well, they *will,* this time," muttered the woman, "Or, at least... they'd *better*. Will – Otis – you guys getting anywhere?"

"Not so far," answered the big black agent, who had draped his butt sideways across a desk. "Numbers I had previously in my book ain't workin'... I'm on hold right now."

"Zilch," added Hendricks. "I'm trying a bunch of numbers out of the Chicago office, though... maybe I'll get through to somebody who knows how to get the Director."

"Pretty stupid," complained Kaysten, from the desk-chair over which he had slumped. "Considering where we've *been,* I mean."

The FBI team-leader held up a cautionary index finger against any more loose-talk on the part of the former Chief of Staff, and then again began to talk.

"Got a District Supervisor for Western Region," she whispered, to the others.

"Hello?" announced Chu. "Yes, that's right... umm-hmm... yes... my name is Minnie Chu, and I'm with... no, I can't just come back to H.Q. and file a report... well, of course I would, if I could, but... look, this can't *wait!* I need to speak to the *Director – pronto!*"

There was a lengthy pause, in which Chu's brow furrowed, and the look of exasperation on her face became even more pronounced.

"Okay, tell you what," she bargained, "Can't you just send Ochoa a one-line message saying, 'Minnie Chu and her team are back from L.A., and –"

She again stopped speaking, and this time, her expression was one of surprise and worry.

"*What?*" warily exclaimed the team-leader. "When'd *that* happen?"

There was another long delay, as Chu remained silent and listened to what was being said by whomever was on the other end of the phone connection. Then she spoke up.

"Well, no, frankly," she stated, "We've been, uhh, out of town for awhile – special project – news didn't get through to where my team and I, were stationed, I guess... yes? Okay... we'll wait here, but you need to know that we've got to speak directly with this new Director – whoever's taken over from Ochoa, that is – *immediately*, the minute we get back to a field office. The only condition is, we need to all be together – I don't want my team broken up or sent to different locations... can you commit to that? Good... two *hours?* You *sure* you can't get somebody here in less than that?"

The voice over the phone mumbled something and then Chu concluded, "Fine... just make sure they're not late. We'll be in the lobby."

She hung up.

"You sounded surprised there, for a minute, Minnie," observed Boatman. "Anythin' goin' on?"

"Ochoa's out," she replied. "Replaced by some guy who I've never heard of – name sounds like 'Warnock', or something like that. Apparently there was a large-scale purge, in the upper echelons, back at Bureau H.Q... only one in ten of the people who we knew, above the rank of Region Manager, is still there."

"*Wowww...*" gasped the third agent. "What the hell? Why'd they do *that?*"

"Some 'national security' spy scare, and it wasn't just the Bureau," mentioned the team-leader, staring off into space. "It's affected almost every other branch of the government, particularly the military and departments like State, Treasury and also groups like Secret Service. He warned me, 'there've been a lot of changes, and you shouldn't expect business as usual, when you get back to Headquarters'."

"Well, now," said the black agent, with a wan smile, "Ain't he just understatin' the matter, by at least half."

"What about the White House?" demanded a perplexed and agitated Kaysten. "He say anything about any, uhh, 'changes', there?"

"You're not going to *believe* this, Jerry," softly remarked Minnie Chu, "But it seems we've got a new President."

Little *Amigos*, By The Thousands

Despite having 'recruited' – or, forced – over a hundred *vatos* from various ghetto L.A. backgrounds into his new gang, and notwithstanding having overrun the first Aryan Brotherhood strong-point (really, just an impromptu hangout of four former Hell's Angels adherents, three of whom had died quickly in the gunfight, the fourth who... well, even *Sebastiàn*, didn't especially like reflecting on *that* scene), with consummate ease, things hadn't been going nearly so easily for the former *Mara Salvatrucha* gangster, in the most recent encounter.

They had read the spray-painted signs indicating "WhiteMan's Sacred Territory" and "Mongrels, Niggers, Faggots, Jews and Inferior Races To Be Shot On Sight" that were all over the place, on the way in; and the morale of Sebastiàn's followers' hadn't been helped very much, by seeing the ragged, rotting corpses of unfortunate minority victims, impaled on stakes fixed onto rooftops and dangling from telephone-poles, seemingly at every major intersection.

Plus, this part of eastern Los Angeles was even more deserted than most; hardly a "civilian" of any type was to be seen, anywhere.

No extra rukas *for them* vatos *to have a little fun with,* reflected Sebastiàn... *an'* ninguna yayo por mi.

Fuckin' place is as clean as the butts on them two twelve-year-old toss-ups en mi casa.

Somethin' got *to break, soon,* cholo*!*

It was again nearing sundown, and the ex-*Mara*'s foot-soldiers were almost in a state of rebellion, by the time that the insurgent army of the new Latino gang, began to encounter really serious resistance from the AB'ers. Two *muchachos* had been shot while scouting on ahead – one died on the scene, another was left bleeding and moaning in some smashed-in storefront, a few blocks back – but at least the rest of them had the presence of mind to recover their precious guns and reserve ammunition.

"Skinheads *por alla!*" warned a huffing and puffing Ramòn, his nearly-bald, tattooed-all-over head glistening with sweat in the waning L.A. sun. "*Mucho* shootin', too. Just about got tagged myself, but I duck in time."

"*¿Quantos?*" demanded Sebastiàn.

"Don' know, *señor,*" replied the lieutenant, cringing and looking over his shoulder, as he spoke. The gesture was well-advised, since two bullet-shots whizzed right overhead.

"*Seis o siete, por lo menos,* I figure", continued Ramòn. "Can't see 'em – they got cover. Two *cholos* down up front, that I can see. What now?"

"Bueno... can't chill here, with them *putos* right 'cross the street. Gonna *do* 'em," ordered the neo-*Mara* leader. "All at once."

Immediately, though the offending parties were well out of human earshot, Sebastiàn heard the grumbling breaking out, within his gangsta battalion. And this time, one of the braver – or, perhaps, more foolhardy – of the foot-soldiers, advanced to plead his case.

"*Oyeme, jéfé,*" requested the man, a burly, squint-eyed slightly overweight guy with a mustache, extensively-tattooed like Ramòn, but bigger, almost as tall as Sebastiàn himself, and considerably heavier. "*Claro que nosotros* runnin' with *usted*... you the shot caller, we *get* that... but this *loco, señor.* I was on *otro lado* when Fuckin' AB'ers open up on *hermano* Ramòn – I see what goin' down – that place's fuckin' *fortified, señor.*"

"*¿Tienes miedo, cholo?*" sneered Sebastiàn. "*Es buen dìa para morir,* today."

"What's the *point?*" pressed the *soldado.* "We gonna get smoked before we get close enough to get a good shot off."

"I meant, 'es buen día para morir', for *them... no nosotros,*" growled the more-than-human gangsta chieftain. "*¡Vean por ustedes mismo!*"

Hey, chica demonia, silently mused Sebastiàn.

All part of the plan.

Send it to me, now!

His faith was well-justified; a strange, rhythmic, entrancing (yet foreboding) tune started to issue – it seemed – from the street-pavement and light-poles, as Sebastiàn, his eyes and body glowing with a barely-visible green aura, stepped away from his followers, clenched his fists and turned to face the direction of his entrenched Aryan opponents.

The war-song waxed, and for a second or two, the others believed that the increase was just due to sound-volume; but then, their ears perceived something new and even more ominous.

The buzzing, humming timbre of tens of thousands of tiny insect-wings and limbs, began to intermix with the ex-*Mara*'s *Fire*-song; and his human followers sprinted for cover, as, to their fascinated, apprehensive astonishment, a veritable cloud of creepy-crawly things – including but not limited to ants, termites, wasps, bees, flies, spiders, centipedes, beetles, and even a small snake or two – appeared out of nowhere, around Sebastiàn, completely obscuring his figure from view. Immediately, this fearful miasma extended a full six feet in every direction; its growth slowed, but continued by about an inch every few seconds.

"*Jesús, María y José!*" yelled Ramòn. "*¡Jéfé! ¡Que pasa!* You *okay?*"

"*No se preocupen,*" reassured the still-invisible Sebastiàn, his voice barely audible above the maddening, nerve-wracking, buzzing din of the vermin-cloud, "*No hay problema*. Got about two feet clear between where I end and they start. An' I can see *todos ustedes,* easy."

"What the fuck goin' on, *jéfé?*" warily inquired the big, mustachioed gangsta. "*Todo esto... no es normal...*"

"Told it before," shot back the more-than-human street-army-leader. "*Ustedes* runnin' with *El Diablo,* himself. An'," – he added, with an evil sneer on his invisible face – "These little *muchachos* can go forward an' do them AB'ers... or they can go back, an' do whoever behind me. *¿Ustedes lo entienden?*"

Mutely, the overawed gangsta army nodded assent.

"*¡Que vamos!*" ordered Sebastiàn.

"Captain! Klaxon Terror *Captain!*" yelled the tight-muscled, shaved-headed, spare-bodied, pock-marked whiteman, as he emptied the last two or three rounds from his auto-rifle – this time aiming randomly for suppressive fire, instead of a well-aimed shot, as he had previously been doing – and momentarily turned his head to shout a message to his superior.

"*What?*" barked back the huge, bald-headed, bearded and tattooed guy who was coming up from the basement, carrying three very heavy cans of machine-gun ammo, as he went.

"Fuckin' spics are *retreatin'!*" triumphantly exclaimed the Aryan soldier.

Indeed, the claim was true, as one Hispanic thug lay dead in front of his AK-74 replica, and three others had run back to find shelter.

"About fuckin' *time,*" grunted the leader, as, huffing and puffing, he put down the ammo-cans, during the momentary break in the action. "Wetback whores this time, right?"

"Yeah," confirmed the gunner. "Eight or ten of 'em. Dropped two so far."

"Fuckin' niggers last night, shit-eatin' spics today," complained the Aryan captain. "Least we got lots of bullets in th' bunker."

The gunner's claim of victory was premature, however; it was interrupted by the staccato *brip-brip-brip* sound of a SMG going off, from another room in this heavily-barricaded, East Whittier ex-mansion.

"More over here!" warned another warrior of the Brotherhood – this one, almost as big as the leader, but with a World War 2 Nazi-style helmet on his head, despite the blistering heat of "no-A.C.-L.A.". "Need more ammo!"

"Comin'!" shouted the leader.

"Yee-*hah!*" yelled the helmeted guy, after firing several more times at an unseen target, out in the street somewhere. "Like *that, puto?* Hope you didn't need a head!"

"Reinforce, sir?" asked the first AB'er.

"Negative," countermanded the leader, the sweat and stink of him heady, even for those so accustomed, as he raced past with an ammo-can. "Maintain position!"

For a few minutes, it appeared as if this engagement would end as many others had, that is, with superior firepower and a well-prepared position, providing the tactical advantage needed to prevail. The white warriors rested.

Then the guy with the helmet again peered out of his firing-slit, and did an astounded, wary double-take.

"What the *fuck's that?*" he gasped, "Like a fuckin' *carpet* or somethin', rollin' all over the street... comin' right *at* us!"

"Mother*fucker!*" shouted the first whiteman, eyes bulging in amazed horror. "Can hear 'em buzzin' from *here!* What the *fuck? Music...?*"

"Well don't just *stand* there, asshole!" bellowed the leader. "Open *up!* I'll get the flamethrower!"

The pock-marked Aryan soldier aimed his auto-rifle and pulled the trigger.

I Need A Car

There had been a few awkward moments at the Osprey Ridge Country Lodge – during which both Wolf and Devon White shared the unenviable quality of "looking 'out of place'" (the bounty-hunter had to use his special hiding-ability, after his male puppy-dog mischievously set fire to part of a carpet, and the black ex-astronaut got repeatedly mistaken for a golf-valet) – but the first few hours at Disney World proved considerably easier than anticipated.

Jacobson and Tanaka played the "rich tourists from New York" *shtick* with surprising convincingness, particularly after White, using street-skills learned as a youth but never since forgotten, managed to trade five of the alien-girl's little *ersatz* gold coins to one of the resort's *sous*-chefs, for the princely sum of seven hundred and fifty dollars in cold, hard, dura-plastic U.S. "paper" currency.

To preclude against a scam, the man had insisted on using one of the restaurant's electronic chemical-testing gizmos on the metal in the coins, and had been astonished upon seeing the results : the gold was over 97 per cent pure.

As he exited the scene as quickly as he could safely do, way out of human earshot, the ex-astronaut's Mars hearing had picked up something akin to, “damn, that boy's *stupid*... I can get two grand at *least* for these, back in 'Lando”.

White couldn't decide whether to smirk about counting Ramirez as a friend, or to grimace at knowing that he'd come out on the short end of the deal. In the end, he settled for a shrug, upon advising his former commander, “Well, Cap'n, just be glad that I didn't go for that synth he had to sell, or y'all woulda been hitchin' a ride... *that* shit's even more expensive than when we blasted off.”

Despite these initial successes, the party soon encountered other challenges. Avoiding the U.S. government's nearly-ubiquitous video-surveillance infrastructure proved bothersome but workable, thanks to Tanaka's new, half-sapient companion, who warned the group of most of the microphones and cameras, selectively and subtly jamming the few that they had to pass in front of. However, they had to hire two separate taxi-cabs to get them all out of the resort, and the first three that were hailed, refused to take Wolf, on account of “them two weird-lookin' dogs”, as one cabbie had sneered (although, “Boob” got the twit back by surreptitiously biting a nasty hole through his back bumper, just as he was ready to drive away).

A similar problem presented itself after nightfall, as the first motel they tried, didn't accept cash, while at the second, the dreaded “no pets” policy reared its ugly head; but finally – after being warned “don't care *how* big or poor he is, if either of his damn mutts piss in one of *my* rooms, it's an extra hundred on the bill, or I call the cops” – Jacobson, Tanaka and White managed to bed down for the night in Room Number 137 of the La Renta Inn, just off the Andersen Beachline Expressway, while Wolf, Boyd and Misha, in Room Number 138, tried to tune out the sounds of sirens, far-off gunshots and hip-jump gangsta music blaring occasionally outside. This proved easier to do for the bounty-hunter than the other two, since Wolf, it turned out... snored.

The two puppies were exiled to the Room 138 bathroom, after everything flammable had been carefully removed from it. This proved to be a wise precaution, after “Tube”, who was evidently still undergoing teething issues, left some odd-looking scorch-marks on the water-pipes underneath the vanity. Fortunately, these weren't detected by the motel proprietor, prior to the group checking out shortly after dawn, on the next day.

They were now crowded together in the wall-side booth (they had first sat down at a table in front of the lunch-counter, but had moved to a more private area, after Tanaka stated that “she didn't like the stares she was getting from that greasy-haired, bearded guy at the next table, he smells *disgusting*”) of a sparsely-visited, dingy greasy spoon off Florida Route 528.

The bounty-hunter, accompanied by his pair of lovable, though rather dangerous, mutts (even White had, somehow, grown fond of them), had decamped to the restaurant's secluded, back lawn. He could just be seen, from their current vantage-point; Wolf was stamping his feet down on something.

"Snake?" idly asked Tanaka. "Or an ant-hill, maybe?"

"Grass-fire," said Boyd, with a backward glance, as he bit into a grilled-cheese sandwich.

The former Mars science officer sighed and rolled her eyes.

"Coffee?" insouciantly proposed the Russian. "Or tea. I prefer the latter, actually. It reminds me of home."

"Could *use* one," muttered Tanaka. "I'll take it black... no crystal-creamer. He's gonna give us *away* sooner or later, you know."

"Ahh, well, madam," philosophically observed Misha, "Somehow, after what we have all been through, so far... this seems an acceptable risk."

"Ha... you *think?*" grunted White. "Don't get me wrong, I *like* them two – opposites attract, I guess – but, *dogs?* What the hell she was *thinkin'*, both with his mutts, and with Sylvia's, I'll *never* know. Pass the butter, if y'all don't mind."

Jacobson, who had been neglecting his heaping plate of pancakes while fiddling with the settings on the only one of the mobile communicators that seemed to work in this part of the country, held up a finger, in request of silence.

"Hey, Chuck – that *you?*" intoned the former Mars mission commander. "Yeah... yeah... it's me, Sam... can hardly make you out, some kind of delay, or echo, on the line... better, now... whaddya *mean*, who's 'me'? Well, who you *think* it was? Yes – but don't use my last name... I'll explain later – just a sec –"

He held a hand temporarily turned to address the others at the table.

"*Got* someone," triumphantly announced Jacobson. "Chuck Vargas... Cherie, you remember him? The car dealer in Rockledge – you know, the guy who I did that school visit, for his son, year before we left, that is. Hold on."

Tanaka looked as if she was about to swoon. Sweating, she swayed slightly back and forth, running her fingers over her thorax, mumbling something, apparently to herself.

"You *okay?*" uneasily demanded Boyd, leaning over toward the woman.

"F-fine," stammered the professor. "It's just... *Vìrya Sài'ymë,*" she explained. "Little One is telling me... she's routing your call through Sacramento... and Hartford, Connecticut. Bugger up the trace, in other words."

"So, Chuck," continued the former astronaut, speaking into the phone. "Can't talk too much over the air, right now – *what?* No, I'm very much alive, and so are the rest of my crew... it's the *truth!* For God's sake, is *that* really what they're telling people? *Figures*... what? Oh... nothing. Look... I don't care *what* they said on T.V. – if we all show up right there, would *that* be proof enough? Sure. But I got a favor to ask... umm-hmm? Well... would you believe I need a car? A van, in fact – it's gotta seat six adults. Ha, ha, yeah, I know. Well, the thing is... doesn't have to be too fancy, but it's gotta be in decent shape for the highway, and, I'm gonna need to pay in cash... sort of. Yeah?"

He paused for a second, then said, "Sure, I *know* they're tracing all the credit transactions, but that was kind of the point... why don't we make it so you keep title? No, I won't need insurance... well, that's optional, isn't it? Since the last hurricane down here... you know, when all the companies pulled out of the state, I mean... doesn't matter to me... no problem. So... would this afternoon, be good? Oh, *wonderful.* Hey, man, I owe you, big-time. See you then. Bye."

"You're not going to *believe* this," stated Jacobson, upon ending the conversation, "But for the past few days, the government has been telling the country that we're *dead.* Story's that we all succumbed to some kind of awful Mars virus, shortly after we got back to Earth – but that they suppressed the news until now, 'to avoid panic'."

"Well, don't *that* make sense," sourly mentioned White, "Considerin' that they all but *did* smoke us, back up on the island. I'm just glad that Saquina and the kids missed hearin' it, what with most of the network bein' out, in L.A.."

"Perhaps it is just one of those, how do you say, 'pre-announcements', such as you Americans have for video games, music and movies," wryly quipped the Russian. "That is... we are already dead, and we do not yet know it."

"Y'all make a *great* morale-booster, there, man," mumbled White.

"Cherie?" asked the former Mars mission commander.

For a few seconds, Tanaka did not answer; her head was bowed, as she was intently watching something on a mobile communicator.

"Still with us?" pressed Jacobson. "I'd have thought you'd be interested –"

"Oh... sorry," apologized the woman, "Couldn't connect to the phone network with this thing – something's wrong with it, not even *Vìrya Sài'ymë* could get it to sync – but she *was* able to camp me on to the local restaurant wireless, so I was using what time I've got to do a little research over Neo."

"About what?" inquired Boyd.

"Fighter-planes... missiles... weapons," she replied, not taking her eyes off the communicator's small, brightly-lit screen. "Air Force, that is. And Army."

"Y'all was never 'into' that kind of stuff before, Professor," observed White.

"Never had to *fight* them before," commented Tanaka, her voice and demeanor even and analytical. "Nor had to, maybe, withstand a direct hit or a near-miss, from several of 'em. I'm trying to figure out the number of mega-joules in a standard air-to-air missile warhead, at different detonation ranges... compare that with how things felt, up over the island... Little One is saying it's about one point three times ten to the seventh power... yeah, *that* sounds correct, since the bullets were a few kilo-joules..."

Boyd looked up, lightly chuckled and did a half head-shake.

"You *do* know," he muttered, "How bizarre it sounds, to hear you saying something like that... more so, that you'll probably survive, if you get it right?"

"Thanks for the compliment," said the woman, with a wan smile, "But 'probably' doesn't sound too good, from where I'm sitting."

"Well, anyway, about Chuck, and the car," persisted Jacobson, "Not sure he's going to go for the gold, so to speak... so we'd better try to find somewhere that we can change as much of it as we can, into cash. Anybody know how we could work that?"

Boyd shook his head. "I got shipped to the Cape late, after completing pre-flight training, like Devon," he said. "Family's still in North Charleston... I *hope*. Don't really know a lot of people around here. Listen, Commander... any chance I can talk you into letting me call home? Now that you've got the phone working, I mean."

The former Mars mission commander's lips pursed, and he replied, "We went over that, before bedtime last night... remember? Even with Cherie's new little, uhh, friend, working her tricks –"

"*Daughter*," corrected Tanaka. "Did you know I can hear her crying, when she gets upset?"

"Well, 'least y'all don't have to change her diapers," taunted White.

"Okay... daughter... whatever," continued Jacobson. "Anyway, what I meant was, we gotta be *very* careful, here. I'll bet the government thinks we really *are* dead – God knows, we certainly *deserve* to be, what with everything that went on, up there – but one way or another, NSA will undoubtedly be monitoring voice and video traffic directed to our families... mine too, of course. I feel the same way about it, as you do. But it's too high a risk."

"Yeah," dejectedly remarked Boyd. "But do you have to make so much goddamn *sense*, all the time?"

"If I may express an opinion," commented Misha, "I think we would have to assume that Ms. Chu *will*, at some point, inform the American government, about us. What we cannot know, of course, is how forthcoming she will be, in disclosing this information. She may simply say that we are alive... or... well, you know."

"I didn't have a lot of time in which to get to know her," observed Tanaka, momentarily looking up from her NeoNet surfing activities, "But I've got a lot of respect for Minnie. I don't think she'll sell us out... she's not a bad person."

"What if they try the same stuff on her – or them other folks – that they was doin' routinely, up in that shithole in Alaska," countered White. "*Anybody'd* crack, under pressure like *that*. 'Specially that Kaysten guy."

Tanaka allowed herself a wicked-looking smile, and riposted, "Well, that's true, I suppose; but as I recall, it didn't work out too well for the Agency, when they first tried it on us. I'd really *love* to be a fly on the wall, when they try it on Minnie... and she whips out that 'dirty look' of hers, at them. Oh, that is... as long as I'm not on the wall, in the direction in which she fires it."

"What's the *matter*, Professor," maliciously noted Boyd, between mouthfuls of toast and cheese. "Her death-ray better than yours?"

"Don't *think* so," parried the woman. "*Sure* don't want to find out. That goes for yours, as well."

"Thanks," said the former Mars mission pilot, "I feel more important already."

"Okay," pressed on Jacobson, "So what I'm proposing, is, basically, that we get established – car, house to hang out in, maybe even some fake or part-time jobs – until we can figure out how we're going to achieve the, uhh, final objective."

"Ahh," remarked Tanaka, "Just your average American super-human family, with a nice little bungalow in the Cape Canaveral suburbs... right?"

"Actually," proposed Jacobson, "I was thinking more of somewhere more central... Kansas City, maybe, or St. Louis... actually, I think I'd prefer St. Louis, though it's still damaged from the comet... it'd be easier to sneak in there, maybe help with the cleanup, make some friends who'll cover for us... *et cetera*."

"I *do* have a few friends in Missouri... Kansas and Oklahoma, too," noted Boyd. "But a move of this type might put back our, uhh, plans, by a month or more, if you count travel, time to get settled in, and so on. Not sure that's a good idea, all things considered. What if we're being hunted, right now?"

"Well," patiently argued the former Mars mission commander, "You got a *better* plan? I mean, as matters stand, we don't have the foggiest idea as to where he really *is*. We might as well find a place where we can do the necessary research, where we can make ourselves as comfortable as we can, until the, ahh, right opportunity, presents itself. At least, that's how *I* see it."

"Captain," agreed Boyd. "You *do* know – don't you – that we'll be confronted, and hunted, by all the resources that the government can muster, starting the minute after we, uhh, take our best shot, whether or not we're successful? They'll *never* relent, until we're cornered and either have to surrender – I don't think I have to explain what kind of a trial we'd get, in that case – or are simply overwhelmed and annihilated right on the spot –"

"We *won't* be," growled Tanaka; and she had to immediately give up her network-surfing and spend a second or two in deep concentration, to prevent the sudden surge of her war-song from becoming loud enough, to attract third-party attention. "There's *nothing* they can throw at us – at me – that I can't handle. I had a discussion about this, with Karéin, back at the camp... the gist of it was, 'be merciful with them, Cherie – they're only *humans*, after all', kind of thing. Frankly, I feel sorry for them... they'd better not even *try*."

"Professor... your *eyes*," cautioned an alarmed Misha.

"Sorry," muttered Tanaka, looking down. When she again regarded them, the glow was again merely latent.

"I'll take your word for it," said Boyd, with a friendly wince, "But even assuming that you can, uhh, simply pulverize anyone or anything that they throw directly at us... it still doesn't really address the question of what happens next. What do we do... set ourselves up as the new aristocracy, in charge of the 'More-Than-Human Kingdom Of America'? How would we get anybody to execute our orders?"

“But who among us would be the *Tsar* or *Tsarina?*” insouciantly asked the Russian. “Unfortunately, I fear your country would not be, ahh, as well-suited as is mine, for such a change in system of governance.”

“Like the idea, though,” quipped White, “'Long as I get a nice big castle, somewhere. Gotta have a moat, though... 'case wife 'n kids want to go skatin'.”

Smiling broadly, Tanaka added, “Ha – you'd be one to set it up... right?”

White gave the woman a frosty-fingered “thumbs-up” gesture.

“First off,” interjected Jacobson, “I'll state, for the record, I don't *have* a 'Plan B' – that is, 'what happens if we don't get the target'. I'm assuming that we *will* get the target, no 'ifs', 'ands' or 'buts'... it's 'do or die trying', folks. So on to Brent's question, which is a good one... namely, 'what do we do, after those responsible, have paid for their crimes'. I haven't thought this completely through, but here's what occurs to me.”

Four pairs of more-than-human eyes trained intently on the former Mars mission commander, whose judgment Tanaka, White, Boyd and, latterly, Misha, had learned to trust.

“If we're to have any chance of getting back to a normal life afterwards,” elaborated Jacobson, “It's vital that the country knows two things : one, that this is *justice* – not just blind revenge. The moment we've, uhh, prevailed, we call a cease-fire and go right to the media, laying out the entire story about what's happened since we got back to Earth... not to mention, about what the Agency's been doing, up in Amchitka –”

“I will have something to say about this later,” interrupted a skeptical-sounding Misha, “But *do* go on.”

“Okay... so, two – the other message that we need to communicate, and in no uncertain terms – is basically the same one that our alien friend has also tried to convey. Namely, 'we *can't* be defeated, and we'll only be bound by the law, if it's fairly applied, in an open court, with *all* the facts on the table'. The government *must* understand that it can't use its usual tactics of delay, dissembling and treachery, supplemented by lethal force where necessary, against us – we must show them that they're up against an opponent that they can't beat... otherwise, they'll just keep trying to kill us until they get a lucky shot in. If we first demonstrate our abilities by eliminating everyone who was involved in the plot against us, Bob's friends and Karéin, then honestly explain our reasons for doing so, and only *then* ask for clemency... I'm hoping that when the facts come out, public opinion will end up on our side.”

He paused for a second or two, then concluded, “So... there it is. Maybe not all that workable – but other than high-tailing it off to Mars for the rest of our lives, I don't know what else we could do. Comments, anyone?”

“I appreciate your position, Commander,” offered the Russian, “But you are correct... this plan *seriously* lacks plausibility. Consider, for example, the fact that if we are to properly defend ourselves, there are bound to be fatalities on the defending side. It is *very* unrealistic to assume that the American political elite, never mind public opinion, would treat us as anything other than 'terrorists', in circumstances such as those. I doubt that whatever remains of the U.S. senior command structure would *ever* compromise with us, after that point."

"Well," suggested Tanaka, "There *is* an alternative, you know."

"What?" requested a startled Jacobson.

"*Do* inform us," said Misha.

"Like I said... back at the camp, I had a couple of long talks with Karéin, about the whole 'alien goddess' thing," continued the woman. "One of her beliefs is, 'if you are sure that you can win a battle without the element of surprise, then it is shameful to strike without warning... give your foe a chance to avoid bloodshed'. So what we could do – like *she* apparently did, in trying to get the President to reveal where Bob was being imprisoned – is to issue an ultimatum. We could demand that the President make a full, honest accounting of the government's misdeeds, by 'x' time and 'y' date, in person... or *else*."

"You neglect to mention," advised the Russian, "That by her own account, Karéin was singularly *un*successful in issuing these types of 'ultimatums' to the American government... the President ignored every one of them, and went about his business. There is no reason at all to believe that the stance of your government, will be any different, this time."

"*Maybe*," evenly replied Tanaka. "But I've been carefully scouring Neo for information on *that*, as well... as you might expect, the government's censors have been trying hard to suppress the news, but it looks like Karéin's little gambit *has*, indeed, had quite an effect... it just took more time than she was willing to wait –"

"Now *that's* interestin', Professor," remarked White. "What y'all mean? I was gonna ask some folk 'round here – since we got dropped off, that is – 'bout all that, but I figured doin' it might attract too much attention."

"You got *that* right," commented Jacobson.

"It sure *is* interesting," acknowledged the former Mars science officer, with a pleasant smile. "The, uhh, 'events' at Rushmore and then in D.C., in particular, seems to have thrown the chattering classes into a complete panic, especially since Karéin, from their perspective, just disappeared thereafter... a 'story without an ending', in other words. It was *too* spectacular for the government to *completely* cover up, so they've concocted some nonsense about 'this was all done by a rogue Air Force officer using a secret nuclear-powered battle-suit, which seems to cause mental problems in those who wear it... so the program's now canceled, there's no reason to worry', yadda yadda yadda. Oh, and there are some reports on Neo, about a 'suspected nuclear detonation, somewhere in the North Pacific'. Of course, the government's blaming it on 'aggression by the Chinese'."

"The public can't *possibly* be stupid enough to believe such an obvious pack of lies, about the Washington incident... *can* they?" complained Boyd. "On second thought... don't answer that."

"I think the jury's still out on that," elaborated Tanaka, "But there *are* a few Democrats left in the Congress – and even some of the mainstream media outlets, who we all know are pretty tame, are starting to ask questions... there's a lively debate going on. My bet is, if we went directly to the media, beforehand, and spilled the beans about what the government's been doing – not just to Karéin, Bob's people and us, but also their many other crimes – we'd be able to get our message out to a large audience. How it'd be received, is anybody's guess."

"This entire *strategy* is questionable," argued Misha, "Since it would give up whatever element of surprise that we might otherwise have. None the less, even if we *were* to adopt your proposal, madam... what, exactly, would we do, if the President either refuses these demands outright, or simply refrains from commenting, at all? The U.S. government – like my own – receives hundreds of vague, unauthenticated threats from terrorist and opposition groups, not to mention just from mentally ill persons, every month. Most never are acted on. He would likely ignore this one as well."

"Man's got a point," offered White. "President probably thinks we're dead, 'less Minnie tells him otherwise. He gets some kind of 'ultimatum' from us, it's just gonna go in the trash-can... unless we *do* something to get his attention. In which case, 'out comes the dragnet'. We'd better think both outcomes through."

"What if," slowly stated Jacobson, his eyes staring purposefully off into space, past the others, "We were to take control of some completely irreplaceable government economic asset – Fort Knox, the Manhattan Federal Reserve Bank, the White House, Wall Street, an ICBM base, the Supreme Court, the Houses of Congress, that kind of thing – and then I were to show up – alone – on TV, stating our case?"

"Kinda like the idea of Fort Knox," remarked an interested White. "We could tell Mr. President that if he don't get his ass out there, we'll get Her Angel-ness to dump all that gold out into, I don't know, maybe the Sun or somethin'. Fuck up the currency system *real* good, and we wouldn't have to risk killin' too many folks. Be pretty hard for him to ignore, I'd say."

"Yeah, but isn't there a big Army base right beside Fort Knox?" warned Boyd. "An attack there would be immediately met with heavy firepower. We'd probably have to knock out the local military assets before attacking the vault, and in so doing, we'd lose the element of surprise."

"Unless, of course," suggested Misha, "We attack both points simultaneously. I doubt that we are strong enough to do so now, but perhaps in a short while..."

"Sam," softly remonstrated Tanaka, "Apart from all this, you can't be *serious*. If the government finds out ahead of time – which it very well might – they'll set a trap, with as many cops, spooks and soldiers as they can find in the six surrounding states. They'll kill you the *moment* they get a clear shot."

"Cherie," countered Jacobson, "I appreciate what you're saying, but... while there's certainly some risk to this... I'll be okay."

"Don't want to burst your bubble, Cap'n," stated White, "But... how y'all so sure of that? We're talkin' about *hundreds* of cops, not to mention heavy-duty firepower, and y'all would be trapped inside a buildin'. How you gonna escape, let alone get past the army they'd have set up, outside?"

"Let's just say," smoothly replied the former Mars mission commander, "Cherie and Sylvia aren't the *only* ones who the 'voices' have been talking to."

He looked hither and yon.

"Can anybody around here see us?" queried Jacobson. "No? Good. Let me show you something, then."

He held his left little finger low over the table, so as to be visible only to the other four. Instantly, to the tune of a couple of war-music-notes, it was encased in a dimly-glowing, translucent, multi-faceted *something*, as if enclosed in some kind of half-polished quartz crystal.

"Whoa!" gasped an obviously-impressed White. "Looks like y'all wearin' the mother of all diamonds on your pinkie, there, Cap'n."

"Good comparison, Devon," answered Jacobson. "And every *bit* as tough. First came to me in a dream, while I was back at the camp. I was practicing it when I went of hiking by myself, although a couple of times, Karéin gave me some pointers about the, uhh, fine points of how to use it. I'm pretty sure it'll stop *anything* that they throw at me... and I can see perfectly, right through it."

A malicious smile now appeared on Boyd's face, although Tanaka still seemed worried.

The former Mars mission pilot laughed out loud, while taking note of a similar grin on the part of White and the Russian.

"She did the same with *me*, you know," offered Boyd. "Said 'it should be our little secret, since it is appropriate that all warriors should have arts known only to themselves, until the time is needful for use'... or some-such blather."

"So what's *your* new trick?" inquired Tanaka.

"*Bunch* of 'em," said Boyd, with another evil-looking smirk. "Did you know that my kind of energy can be invisible, even when I deploy it as a force-field, around me? And that it can screw up electronics? Including guidance systems, needless to say. She told me that 'your arts are alike to those of Sylvia, as is the kinship of one brother to his sister'. Let's *hear* it for gamma-rays!"

By now, even Jacobson was chuckling.

"Devon?" demanded the woman.

"Well," lazily disclosed White, "Confession time... our little guidin' angel's been doin' quite a bit of work behind our backs, I guess. In my case, she tested firin' some beams of, uhh, tell you the truth, I got no *idea what* that shit was, but whatever it was, when she zapped me with it, at first – low voltage, don't you know – it hurt plenty; but eventually, after a few tries, I learned that my little encirclin' Sno-Cone can deflect 'em away, and sometimes, it feels good when they hit, like I'm absorbin' the energy. 'Top of *that*, remember, Professor, how y'all got your new little, uhh, kid, to be makin' up just about anything you want, out of the *Fire?* Well, seems I can pretty much do the same thing, with ice.

Can't make y'all anything with a lot of movin' parts... but short of that, well, I'm gettin' pretty good at it. Maybe even win one of them ice-sculpture contests, one day."

"Ah, if only we doing that could make us a steady income," smartly responded Tanaka. "Misha?"

"I would prefer to comply with the Storied Watcher's instructions, and leave some of my new, uhh, 'arts', private... just in case one or more of you are taken prisoner – 'need to know', as it were," demurred the Russian. "But I *will* tell you this : do you recall those two fighting-daggers – I believe their names are *Ksé'l'ch*' and *Ss'éth'ch*' –"

His explanation was interrupted by the woman's making of a "shussh" sound, directed at her lower-body, and then her warning, "*Væran Ss'éth'ch*' and *Væran Ksé'l'ch*', if you don't mind... Little One is complaining that you're, uhh, 'insulting' them... and she thinks of them as her, uhh, 'cousins'."

"Oh... sorry," apologized the Russian. "Please tell *Vìrya Sài'ymë* that no offense was meant. And that, it should be said, goes also for *Væran Ivan* and *Væran Pyotr* – my two throwing-knives, which were made for me by Karéin herself, albeit with the assistance of Mr. Hendricks – and no, I am not sure why he was called upon to help, or what he did. They are somewhat smaller and easier to hide than those used by the Storied Watcher, but they are very effective, as I believe you saw in the engagement on the island... although at that time, they had benefited only by my own craftsmanship."

"Are they, uhh, 'sentient', Misha?" inquired a fascinated Tanaka. "Like *Vìrya Sài'ymë*, for example?"

"How would I describe it, madam?" rhetorically asked the Russian. "I suppose the best analogy would be like with Wolf's dogs. I can communicate with them... hear their thoughts... which, as yet, are mostly of a superficial nature. I cannot, for example, have a conversation with them, but I can order them to attack, to defend me, and so on. They have powers of homing, armor-piercing... shock and acid, too. I would trust my life to them, I suppose."

"Let's hope that neither you nor any of us, have to," remarked Jacobson. "Because –"

His commentary was cut short by the sound of a small bell on a pull-string above the door, followed by the appearance of Wolf in short order afterward.

"Hey!" exclaimed the bounty-hunter, "Any of you tourists bother to save me somethin' to eat?"

Five pairs of eyes stared sheepishly back and forth at each other, while Wolf gave a "come hither" gesture with his right arm and then demanded, "Fine, then... you can damn well come help me pick up after the pups... and make sure you bring a *big* bag."

Despite being sorely tempted, he had waited for almost thirty seconds after the group of "tourists" had paid their tab and left the booth to which they had moved after he had looked them over, first out of idle curiosity, but then, for a more serious purpose.

The bearded, greasy-haired, twentysomething Caucasian guy, dressed in dirty cut-off jeans, a "Real Men Don't Mow Weed" logo t-shirt that hadn't been washed since one of the Tuesdays last month, and the cheapest flip-flops that you could buy down at the beach second-hand store, shuffled over to the door of the restaurant, stuck his head out of the portal and caught a glimpse of the Jacobson van, just as it exited the parking-lot.

The slacker fumbled around in his pocket, retrieving and enabling a mobile communicator. He powered it up and began to enter a lot of numbers, into the keypad; so many, in fact, that he might as well have been writing a short story.

If you were "in the know" and looked closely at this guy's prized toy – and you'd normally never get such a chance – you'd have noticed that the otherwise stock, Re-Amalgamated AT&T device had had a few, apparently-modest "modifications" made to it; certain chips had been removed, others had been subtly tampered with, and the little box's software, though perfectly mimicking a "legit" operating system to the network, had been re-written from top to bottom.

The slacker spoke as softly as the excitement would allow him.

"Yo," he started, "Gator-Boy here. You in the dark, man?"

"Copy," came a metallic, ghostly voice. "Redwoods here – we're on Dusk Channel 7529-3F, symmetric keys good for ten at least. Haven't heard from you for awhile... which I guess I can't blame you for, after the Man busted the Atlanta Ring, poor dudes. What's *happenin'*, bro?"

"You're not gonna *believe* who I just saw!" gushed the slacker.

Anything To Add, Ms. Chu?

Much to Minnie Chu's surprise and displeasure – not to mention Kaysten's, the latter voiced too frequently and loudly for comfort – the next day-and-a-half dragged on with frustrating tedium.

All five of them, including even Abruzzio's cloying-cutesy dog (which had an alarmingly-bright twinkle in its eyes when it rolled over, hoping for a belly-rub : the former JPL scientist had to spring to the rescue on several occasions), had, fortunately, been kept together, and had been relatively well-treated; they were put in a good hotel, albeit with limited access to the computer-networks and without permission to go wandering out of doors.

Each member of the group was, however, dragged through a seemingly-interminable set of repetitious de-briefings, although, sometimes, interrogations were conducted individually. But strenuous entreaties both on the part of the Chu herself and from Kaysten, to the effect of "we've *got* to speak with the President, *immediately*", resulted in nothing more than bored shrugs and vague promises to "escalate your request through the standard channels".

This doesn't add up, the FBI team-leader had mused, in more than one quiet moment.

A sanely-run government would want to know everything there is *to know about us,* tout de suite.

What's wrong *with them?*

After being shuttled first by car-convoy to a Bureau field-office just outside Las Vegas, then by air and dark-windowed bus, to a large one in downtown Pittsburgh, they had finally arrived in the location in which – or so they had been told – she'd have a chance to "speak with someone higher up"; so Chu and the others fell asleep, with high hopes.

Relishing the opportunity, the team-leader spent the whole morning ensuring that her dress – a conservative, blue-and-white, businesswoman's garb, with the hem below the knees, not to mention her dress-shirt and blouse – were, along with her makeup (actually, since recent events, not much need for anything artificial, on that front) and hair... immaculate.

She even, atypically, wore earrings.

Now, without the presence and moral support of her subordinates and friends, who for some reason hadn't been invited to the meeting, Chu walked, escorted by two big, physically-fit, male Bureau agents, one on each side of her, through the sun-drenched, chrome-and-marble main hall of the office. The place, which had also served as accommodation for the team-leader and her compatriots over the last day, was apparently a converted five-star luxury hotel, so the roof of its foyer and waiting-area was nothing but skylights; and it she noted with interest that even the bottom-floor was brimming with activity, with glimpses of rooms filled with agents immersed in meetings and doing investigative work, available as she passed by.

She was ushered into the elevator. The doors "whooshed" shut.

Up went Chu and her two escorts – both unusually taciturn, even for Bureau types, though chit-chat among agents unfamiliar to each other wasn't common, anyway – as level after level flashed its arrival and departure on the LED display over the inside elevator-portal. At length, the floor-display showed "60" and the elevator came to a gradual stop.

The elevator-doors opened, revealing what had previously been a penthouse suite : brilliant sunshine came through multi-directional, cobalt-tinted glass windows, casting a strong reflection from the polished-marble floors. The area was strangely barren, however; where, in other times, there would undoubtedly have been fine furniture, *objets d'art* and all the other accouterments of upper-upper-class-living, now, all that Chu beheld was a simple, European-modern-style, silver-and-black desk and chair, with its back to one of the glass outside walls; everything else was simply empty.

And there was a man waiting at the desk.

This guy – who sat impassively, staring forward and not saying a word as, on her escorts' prodding, the team-leader slowly advanced toward him –

impressed Chu as nothing more than your average, garden-variety, middle-management accountant.

Caucasian, thin and in reasonable shape, though not muscular-looking, he wasn't especially tall, and he had a bland, clean-shaven, utterly-forgettable, forty-something face. This was made only a bit more notable by a pair of thin-rimmed glasses (their lenses slightly darkened, likely to auto-adjust for the sunshine) and dark, slightly-thinning, conservatively-cropped hair.

The man was dressed in a well-pressed, unspectacular dark-gray business suit. He had an unpatterned blue tie over the standard white shirt, and the woman noticed that his fingers weren't adorned by a ring, but there was a mobile wrist-communicator just visible on his left wrist.

Chu took a couple more steps forward and the man held up his left hand to motion “stop”. She complied. Another hand-gesture sent the two guards to the far parts of the room, presumably out of earshot.

“I'm given to understand that you're Ms. Minnie Chu, of the Red Rover Project,” said the man in a curious, flat monotone, his lips making the minimum movement necessary to emit a sound.

“That's correct,” replied the team-leader. “Who do I have the pleasure of addressing today, sir?”

“That's on a 'need-to-know' basis, but let's just say, 'you wanted to speak to someone higher-up... and now your wish has come true', Ms. Chu,” he evaded. “You're pretty far up the food-chain, right now. As I understand it, you said that you had something regarding the Red Rover project, that had to be related directly to the President... fair enough. I report, and have personal access, to him... I'd be happy to tell our Old Man, as it were, whatever you have to say. You have my word that I won't omit or misrepresent anything.”

Is this dweeb, that 'Warnock' guy? wondered Chu.

I hate *this kind of two-step.*

But fine... we'll do it your *way.*

“Sir,” she stated, “You'll appreciate that without understanding the, uhh, entire context here, I *do* have to be succinct, and exercise some discretion –”

“I don't think that would be advisable,” he interrupted, his voice not showing any sign of emotion.

The man's weirdly stolid, inscrutable stare would have unnerved Chu, or any normal human being... *before*. But now, it just made her wary.

“Well, perhaps I should just say my piece, sir,” politely responded the team-leader, “And you can be the judge of it. Obviously, I can't control what measures that you feel it appropriate to undertake, after that point – but I'd urge you to entrust what I say, *only* to the President, until he decides to make it more widely known.”

“Indeed... and... do,” he requested, never taking his cold eyes off her.

“Okay,” she offered. “So here's what I think the President should be told. My team and I – acting with authorization from Director Ochoa, I should point out – has made direct contact with the alien being calling herself 'Karéin-

Mayréij', also known as 'the Storied Watcher'. We had extensive discussions with her, and, I'm proud to say, were able to discourage her from fully executing on a series of threats that she had made against the United States, in the dispute that she had with the President regarding the disposition of certain individuals – the 'Bob Billings' group, that is – who Karéin-Mayréij felt had been kidnapped and were being held against their will. With me so far?"

"Yes," replied the man. "Not a lot of 'net new' information there, Ms. Chu."

"Shortly after our initial meeting," continued Chu, "The Storied Watcher elected to, uhh, remove our group, which at that point was in the Grand Canyon, to downtown Los Angeles; she felt that the government would have more difficulty targeting her, in that location. However, while we were in L.A., which was in a highly lawless state due to uncontrolled gang activity, we discovered that there was – as far as I'm aware, still is – a terrorist nuclear device, hidden somewhere within that city. Shortly thereafter, Karéin again moved us, this time to a place in the Rocky Mountains, and while we were there, she, uhh, 'heard' – that's the best way to say it – the cries of Mr. 'Billings' and his friends, who were being held captive, and were being severely abused, apparently by the Agency, that is CIA, in an underground prison, located on Amchitka Island in the Aleutians. Sir... I don't see you taking notes... are you recording this conversation?"

"Oh, you can be sure that every word will be captured," smoothly answered the guy behind the desk. "Please go on."

"Very well," said Chu. "At this point, the Storied Watcher flew off to Amchitka and rescued the Billings group, who, though badly traumatized by the treatment they'd had to endure, were still all at least, alive. All of them are now being held, and defended, by her. The point, sir, is that from Karéin's point of view, the 'war' – if it ever *was* a 'war', as opposed to a one-sided-battle – is over. Although she's still quite upset at recent events, she's no longer a threat to the President, or to the nation."

"You quite sure of that, Ms. Chu?" coolly responded the man. "And is that all you had to relate to the President?"

"Pretty much," evenly answered the team-leader.

"*Really?*" pressed the man.

"*Really,*" she persisted.

"That's... *interesting,*" he commented, his voice revealing the hint of sarcasm. "Because... we have good reason to believe you're leaving out some rather... *important,* details. Would you care to fill us in?"

"Not sure what you mean, sir," evaded Chu.

"Well," indifferently offered the man behind the desk, "You see, Ms. Chu... as you'd no doubt have expected, the... Bureau, had to keep track of your, uhh, 'comings and goings', after you were able to convince the former Director to let you undertake this somewhat... unconventional, mission. In so doing, we received a number of... anomalous, results. Such as, for example, having you opening an communications channel to former Director Ochoa, while apparently at an altitude of several thousand feet over Los Angeles. I suppose you've learned how to fly?”

For the first time in the conversation, Chu found her mind racing.

I should be so lucky, she ruefully pondered.

Maybe later I will... but how'd he know*?*

Unless Ochoa told *him – and that's why he got turfed –*

“Like I said, sir,” answered the team-leader, “In the interest of brevity, I've omitted a few details... in this case, I was carried aloft by the Storied Watcher – it was *her* who was flying, not me. And the purpose of the call, which you're probably aware of, if you have access to a recording of it, was to warn the Director and the President, of the nuclear device in the city.”

“The alien was observed to use a suit of armor that's surrounded by fire,” noted the man at the desk. “If she – it – were carrying you, how'd you avoid being incinerated?”

“She can instruct *Vîrya Ahn'jë* – that's the name of the armor-suit, by the way – to turn off the flames,” parried Chu. “I should also point out that *Vîrya Ahn'jë*, like Karéin's other 'war-children', the sword, the daggers, the shield, *et cetera*, is, uhh, *alive*... I have no idea how she did it, but they have minds of their own, independent personalities, and so on. I mention this because they're part of a very long list of highly advanced abilities that she has at her disposal... sir, the country came very close to total annihilation, when, for reasons that neither Karéin nor I understand, the government kidnapped the Billings group and then repeatedly tried to kill her. The President *must* take this opportunity to make amends with the Storied Watcher and permanently ensure that we won't end up at odds with her, ever again! She's *far* too powerful for us to safely antagonize... I can *personally* attest to that. If we, to put it bluntly, sir, 'screw up', a second time... utter *disaster* will result!”

“So the alien's prepared to surrender and stand trial for her crimes?” idly proposed the man.

You stupid son of a bitch, stewed Chu.

No. I take that back.

There's something... else*, going on here.*

Who are *you?*

“I'm not sure how to respond to that, sir,” she remarked. “Except to say, issuing ultimatums to Karéin-Mayréij, especially if done under threat of force, should, in my opinion, be considered treason against the vital interests of the United States... and should be an 'impeachable offense'. *Sir.*”

“Interesting choice of words,” offered the man. “'Treason', I mean.”

“Not following you there, sir,” demurred Chu.

“Well,” he lazily and unctuously slurred, “I think that label might apply a lot better to a Bureau agent who's himself – or, perhaps, *her*self – fallen under the undue influence of an opposing power – of this Earth, or, maybe, from somewhere else; like, for instance, an agent who seems to be on a 'first-name basis', with said, enemy alien being. Oh, and add, 'someone who's divulged all sorts of *highly* confidential Bureau and government information, to the same, hostile power'. Don't you think?"

Any lesser being would have been paralyzed with fear, upon hearing this; because the penalty for 'treason', in modern-day America, was savagely demonstrated to the masses on live TV, every month. But Chu stood firm.

I can make you take that back, she thought.

I can bend your pathetic little human mind into a pretzel.

But not just yet.

And you, my personal Fire – *tamp down.*

You call... I hear... you'll get your chance.

Patience, patience...

She hoped that nothing was glowing, and, luckily, her interrogator's demeanor did not indicate that anything was amiss.

"If you're accusing me – or any of the members of my team, not to mention the others who accompanied us back from L.A. – of that, sir," defiantly answered the team-leader, "I'll first say that any such accusation is absolutely, completely false, and it will be vigorously contested by every legal means at our disposal! And under Bureau rules, my team and I have the right to independent counsel and a formal hearing. Not to mention, that I have to be informed in writing of being charged, or of the likelihood of being charged, with the complaint clearly listing each accusation and the evidence supporting it. Do you have such a document prepared, sir?"

"Oh... that *depends,*" teased the man behind the desk, his poker face hardly showing a twitch.

"On *what,* sir?" prodded Chu.

"Nothing's been decided, so far," he stated. "But if you forced me to say, I'd note that failure to divulge critical information about a field operation, could well be considered as disloyalty. Like, for example... a team-leader who conveniently omits any mention of the so-called 'Jacobson' group... that is, the Mars mission astronauts... when she's *obviously* been in contact with them. Anything to add on *that* front, Ms. Chu?"

"The news reports are saying that the astronauts perished due to a dormant Martian virus, which somehow became active when they arrived back on Earth," evaded Chu. "A great tragedy, to be sure."

"Oh... *please!*" he retorted, with the first sign of genuine irritation in his tone. "Would it help your memory to know that we can place these so-called 'astronauts', down in the Amchitka facility, along with the alien? And that we have reports of you and your two Bureau friends, physically on that island... specifically, in a bunker being used by the GrayWar organization? You were claiming to be doing an audit, apparently; and for the record, I can't *believe* the local authorities, *fell* for it! Proves the difference between the 'professionals" and the 'amateurs', I suppose... but how'd you *get* there, and then get back, Ms. Chu? It's *thousands* of miles from the continental United States."

MacGammon... you fucker! furiously mused Chu.

Should have 'done' you when we had the chance...

How much does this S.O.B. know?

"Is that *right?*" deadpanned the team-leader. "Well, sir, if you need elaboration... I think I'd prefer to give it directly to the President."

"Might not be possible," he diffidently commented. "Oh... and we also have some... *strange* reports, about the goings-on, up there, associated with the three of you... that is, yourself, Mr. Hendricks and Mr. Boatman."

"Again," she parried, "Not sure what you're talking about... *sir*."

"Well," he said, "After all the, uhh, *business*, on Amchitka was over with, we had our forensic teams on site – standard procedure, as you're aware. Found enough to keep the lab boys busy for *years*, but a few things *really* stood out."

"Fill me in," disingenuously requested Chu. "Sounds... *interesting*."

"Oh... it *is*," he offered. "A lot of it's classified, of course; but for example... we found the locking-mechanism on one of the bunker's outside egress doors – this is a big, steel-reinforced thing, mind you – just... *disintegrated*, is I guess how you'd describe it. And you know what's *really* odd?"

Chu casually shrugged and shook her head.

"The thing is," he commented, "We're used to seeing all sorts of physical damage – thermal, blast, impact, that kind of thing – but *this* one, well, it's kind of got us stumped. Near as we can tell, the damn thing – sorry, please forgive my language, I get *excited* when there's something brand-new... you know?"

I bet *you do*, thought the woman.

Like if there's somebody new to torture.

At least I know who's running the show, now.

"Anyway," he continued, "We found quite a bit of dust at the bottom of the door, and back at the lab, it checked out as steel – but its molecular properties, well, we're not sure *what's* going on... but it doesn't seem to melt, or behave as we'd expect it to. Oh, and we have reports of you and your team, having exited through that doorway, shortly before the, uhh, 'action', started. Anything you can tell me about that?"

"I'd *love* to, sir," countered Chu. "In the presence of the President."

The guy behind the desk let out an unconvincing sigh.

"Ms. Chu... Ms. *Chu*," he *faux*-wearily argued, "I thought better of you... of your *judgment*, that is. You can make this *so* much easier for everyone concerned, if you'll just stop playing games and fill us in, fully and completely. Your failing to do so will likely end up badly, not only for you, but for Mr. Hendricks and Mr. Boatman, and also... what were their names again... ah, yes... this 'Abruzzio' lady, as well as the former White House Chief of Staff. You really should think of *their* best interests; what we need to find out, we'll get from them... *eventually*. All you're doing, is needlessly prolonging the process and setting yourself up for a fall... a very long, hard and unpleasant one."

If I were to do what I easily can, she tried unsuccessfully to stop herself from speculating,

There wouldn't be enough left of your body to stain the glass on the window, before it, too, got blown to bits.

How's that *for a 'fall'?*

"Sorry to disappoint you, sir," she answered, "But get me in front of the President, and you'll hear everything I know; and I believe that statement goes for Will and Otis, too. As for Jerry and Sylvia, I *implore* you to leave them out of this! They're just *civilians* – they don't know anything that my fellow-agents and I, don't. They got tied up in all of this largely by accident, after the fiasco at the Hotel Tucson and then us calling Karéin down in the Canyon –"

"What about that 'Ramirez' guy?" interrupted the man. "Where's *he?* We know that *he* was down there, as well... not to mention the bounty-hunter and the Russian spy, who you casually let out of custody, in this misguided adventure. *That's* also a summary dismissal offense, by the way."

"My team and I were proceeding under orders of the Director," she protested. "On *his* authority, which was fully valid at the time. As to the others who you speak of, as far as I know, they're with Karéin, wherever she's now at – which of course probably isn't where she was, when I left her company – and in any event, it would be *highly* inadvisable to make any move against them, or her, until I've briefed the President and he's had a chance to negotiate a final settlement with her. That's about it... *sir.*"

"I... see," he smoothly observed. "Too bad, you know."

There were a few seconds of tense silence, and then Chu requested, "Am I free to go, sir? If you're planning to put me into custody, or charge me with something, I have the right to know that, now."

The man's face showed a thin, insincere half-smile. He shook his head.

"Find your own way out, with the help of our two friends over there," he unctuously suggested, pointing to the two guards, who were off in the distance, on either side of the elevator-opening. "Oh, but Ms. Chu..."

"Yes, sir?" she answered, trying to maintain her composure.

"We'll get *back* to you... be sure of *that,*" he stated.

Riders On The Storm

It's gone amazingly well so far, reflected the former mission commander, as he reflexively tapped his fingers on the van's steering-wheel, inched the vehicle a yard or two further forward and tried to shut out the sounds of the winds and torrential downpour, outside.

Traffic on I-22's almost at a complete stop, he mused, *but, after all... into every life – human or otherwise – a little rain must fall.*

Man... it's sure dark out there... only 2:35 p.m.... strange... Mars eyes can see stuff pretty well... but still a challenge, what with how the windshield-wipers can hardly keep up with that rain...

The last two days had been the proverbial blur, as events – mostly positive ones – occurred almost too rapidly to safely handle.

White, with surprisingly able assistance from the bounty-hunter, had managed to fence about half of the Storied Watcher's mother-lode of gold and diamonds to various shady characters in and around Melbourne and Titusville. The group had been pleasantly surprised at how many "New Issue U.S. Dollars" the exchange had bought; since recent economic crises, paper currency didn't seem to be worth that much, and the Florida street-hustlers were only too glad to accept something whose buying-power wouldn't degrade by large percentages, each month.

A "sweetener" of a fairly-large diamond had been necessary to convince Jacobson's car dealer pal to part with the dated, but fully-functional, '29 Patriotic family-van, in which the group was now riding; even better, they had been able, albeit with some extra cajoling and trickery, to transact both this acquisition – and several others conducted in the area, to pick up everything from "genuine" forged identity-cards, to new changes of clothes (including smart-looking business-duds for everyone except the bounty-hunter, who had only reluctantly consented to anything more up-class than denim), to the three cases of beer that Wolf insisted on having available – on a "cash-only" basis.

Half the battle, idly thought the more-than-human driver.

And at least we've agreed on the plan to get the President's attention – though how we're actually going to implement *it, well,* that's *another subject...*

Let's just hope that Cherie's new little 'kid' has done the rest of the job, and kept us off the radar-screen of the cameras, not to mention of the drones...

Jacobson's semi-reverie was interrupted by an accost from a bored and somewhat frustrated Tanaka, who squirmed a bit in her passenger-seat, to reposition the loose-fitting track-suit that she'd taken to wearing.

"Sam..." she started.

How can she can go for hours... days, even – with that suit of armor on, underneath, silently considered the man.

It sure must get a little, uhh, confining...

Uh-uhh, came a familiar mental voice.

She's like silk... satin... bunny-fur, sent Tanaka.

As easy as can be.

Although Sensei assured me... no bunnies were harmed, in her coming into this world...

"Remind me to pull up the drawbridge, when I daydream," muttered Jacobson.

"*Told* you we should have taken the Corinth bypass at Tupelo," complained the woman, out loud. "At this rate, we might get stuck in the State Park by nightfall. Traffic's hardly *moving*. We'll be lucky if we get past New Albany."

They heard a yawn from Misha; the Russian had been asleep, but was awoken by the discourse.

"Tell me something I *don't* know," answered Jacobson, over the incessant din of raindrops pounding on the vehicle-roof. "Don't blame *me* for driving into a thunderstorm... yeah, it *was* my decision to turn off the weather warning computer, but for a good reason... remember?"

"Yeppers," agreed Boyd. "We've been very lucky they don't seem to have a track on us... yet. Turn on the wrong network interface, especially if it's got face-recognition rigged up with the on-board, and we could end up wearing a drone missile, *real* fast. Not a risk that *I'd* like to take."

"Well, I could use a chance to stretch the legs," yawned Wolf, "I was gonna say, 'pups could probably gotta do their business, as well'... been two hours since the last stop. But all this shit goin' on outside got 'em a bit spooked, I reckon... probably couldn't get 'em out from under the seat."

It was true. Both of the bounty-hunter's two hell-puppies – animals which had proven very capable of taking care of themselves, under the most rigorous conditions – were now cowering at Wolf's feet. Only an occasional nervous whimper issued from them.

"Yo, Boob," spoke White, who had turned his head to peer backward into the vehicle and address the female puppy. "What's *eatin'* y'all?"

"Hmm," observed Boyd, his brow furrowing. "They *worry* me."

"What you mean?" responded Wolf.

"Didn't they start fidgeting, or something, when we were up on the island – just before those robot-saucers attacked?" noted the former Mars mission pilot.

"*Think* so," confirmed the bounty-hunter. "But I'm pretty sure it was 'cause they could *see* them little flyin' fuckers – if it's drones, or somethin' like that, they got no line-of-sight, here... maybe they're usin' one of Little Miss Alien Angel's weirdo powers? Either way... Jacobson! Better pull over... get out and see what's goin' on. If anythin' *is* goin on, that is."

"Hear you," sounded the voice from the driver-seat. "Still pouring out there, but if you don't mind getting soaked, might be a good idea to do a little reconnaissance... and the traffic's hardly moving anyway – not much to lose."

Jacobson carefully steered the van to the road-shoulder and came to a gradual halt, noting with interest that his vehicle wasn't the only one that had done so : two cars up ahead, and at least one behind, had also stopped, with those inside cautiously stepping out, while hastily sheltering from the downpour under whatever could be held above their heads. They appeared to be apprehensively staring at something in the distance, ahead and to the right.

"Holy *shit!*" came a shout from one of the parked vehicles. "It's goin' right 'cross the *highway!*"

"Look over there – *'nother* one!" yelled a redneck Southern voice. "Comin' right *at* us! We gotta get the fuck *outta* here!"

"*Where?*" came a plaintive query, from a female voice to one side of another car. "No cover, 'cept for those trees on the side – can't turn 'round neither – road's jammed!"

By now – though they were all getting thoroughly drenched, since the one thing they'd forgotten to buy back in Florida, was an umbrella – everyone in the the Jacobson party van, save the two cowering dogs, had clambered out.

And the cause of the commotion was immediately, frighteningly, visible.

As the already-brisk wind began to markedly pick up, propelling rain to a stinging velocity, seemingly from all directions at once, they adjusted their special sight, looked forward and to the north, and saw, under a churning, gray-to-black, malevolent cloud-ceiling, two huge funnel-clouds bearing down on the Interstate.

The warnings were accurate, indeed : one of the tornadoes was already almost at the right-hand side of the road, perhaps a mile or so ahead, while the other was about the same distance from this part of the highway, heading south and closing the distance rapidly.

"Good advice," offered Misha, his voice rising to be heard over the howl of the storm. "We should find shelter, quickly, and head back to the south-east, at a right angle to the tornado's apparent path. If I invoke my power I can easily get far enough away, Commander – so can the Professor and yourself, but what about Brent and –"

"If we use our telekinesis all at once, we might be able to get the van far enough out of the traffic to drive back on the shoulder, but we'd better do it quick... see, some folks are already –" interjected Boyd.

They all had to shout, now, just to be heard.

"O my *Lord,*" gasped White. "May Y'all rest their souls, up there – look at *that* –"

The first tornado was now crossing I-22. A sickening feeling swept over all around, as their heightened senses brought home the ugly reality of cars, trucks and other vehicles being swept up into the funnel-cloud, with the sounds of crashing metal, accompanied by the final screams of crippled and dying human beings, accosting their ears.

"*Horrendous!*" remarked an aghast Jacobson, "But if you don't want to end up like that, come on, let's all put our minds together, and –"

"*No!*" countermanded Tanaka.

"What the hell you *mean*, lady?" incredulously asked Wolf. "We're gonna get fuckin' torn *apart* by that thing!"

"*Stop!*" yelled Tanaka. "You've got a *job* to do here – we *all* do!"

"Yeah, and that's to get the fuck *outta* here!" shouted the bounty-hunter.

"Cherie," argued Jacobson, "Time's running out – two minutes at most –"

Now, the woman's eyes were glowing, and her war-song – somehow audible over – no, *within*, the howl of the winds – began to reverberate, from everywhere and nowhere.

Sam, she sent,

Don't you see?

It's a test.

A test of... what? he mentally replied.

Of us, psychically answered Tanaka.

Of whether we're worthy *of having these powers... if we're capable of using them for good, as well as –*

Remember your vow?

For a second or two, the former Mars mission commander stood transfixed, as if coming to an overlooked, yet obvious, revelation. Then he shouted,

"Goddamn it, Professor, do you always have to make so much *sense?*"

"What the fuck you *doin'*, just *standin'* there?" bellowed Wolf.

"They are... *communicating,*" offered Misha.

"Getting my marching orders from above, I suppose," answered Jacobson, who cast a glance at Tanaka. "Fine, then, but how the hell do we *fight* it?"

"Leave that to me, Devon and Little One," vowed the woman, with charges of the *Fire* – now bright enough to draw astonished stares and shouted comments from the humans who were milling confusedly about – now racing up and down her body.

"Uhh... Professor... I hearin' y'all right?" nervously inquired White. "That damn thing's gotta be a half-kilometer across... and I don't have to remind y'all 'bout how much energy's caught up in it. Ain't no *way* we can overpower it – prolly be a tough job for Karéin herself. Maybe I can ice up a shroud over some of these cars, but I can't protect *all* of 'em –"

"Too bad Ramirez ain't here," grumbled the bounty-hunter. "This'd be right up his alley."

"We're not going to 'overpower' it, Devon," explained Tanaka. "We're going to *extinguish* it – that is, *you're* going to."

"But them winds gonna tear us *apart* –" he tried to protest.

"Professor – we're being observed – you'll give us *away,*" warned Boyd, to Tanaka's clear indifference.

"Good luck, my friend," advised the Russian, with an impressed, knowing smile and a pat on White's back. "Remember to aim your power as wide as you can – try to envelop the accursed thing, if you can. Thermodynamics will do the rest."

"Come here and grab on!" demanded Tanaka, giving a forceful "come hither" gesture with one hand.

The black ex-astronaut ruefully shook his head, but he complied, placing an arm over the woman's shoulder, as if needing her support to walk.

His eyes began to glow a dim blue and his own *Fire*, along with his rhythmic, choral-quality psycho-music, now energized.

"Well," sighed White, "After a fuckin' H-Bomb... how much worse can *this* be? Don't answer that question, if y'all don't mind."

Despite the onrushing danger, a number of the onlookers stopped, momentarily, to gape in amazement at the scene unfolding by the Jacobson van; a translucent, soap-bubble-like *something* enveloped Tanaka and her more-than-human passenger, as – her eyes glowing bright, her echoing voice infused with a song of majesty – she cried,

"*Vìrya Sài'ymë*, hear thee now thy mother – full *power!*"

Ooo–ai-ooo–ooo-ai, called her war-song, as upward they rocketed, in an arc toward the tornado.

Three terrified, yet fascinated, onlookers, rushed up to the Jacobson party van. One of these – a portly, good ol' Southern-boy, whose baseball-cap had blown off, revealing a balding head – accosted Wolf.

"What the hell was *that?*" incredulously exclaimed the guy.

All the vehicles on the road were now starting to rock ominously, back and forth, as the tornado's edge-winds began to reach the area of the highway.

"Angel, or somethin'... maybe the Tooth Fairy – I don't *know*, man," evaded the bounty-hunter. "What I *do* know is, if we hang 'round here, we're gonna get lifted to Kansas, without Toto or no fuckin' Yellow Brick Road... *Jacobson!* Dogs 'n me are *outta* here! Boob! Tube! Get yer asses out here!"

But there was no movement from inside the van; the puppies had flattened themselves under a seat, and they steadfastly refused to move, despite Wolf's increasingly frantic entreaties.

He clambered aboard, swearing a blue streak, trying to dislodge his pets.

"He's *right*, Commander," shouted Boyd. "Godspeed the Professor and Devon, but if they fail – damn thing's still coming *at* us! Abandon the van – it's not worth our *lives!*"

"We've got to at least *try* to protect these people!" argued Jacobson.

"How would we do *that*, Commander?" complained the Russian. "Our powers are not effective in a situation like this – all risk, no gain –"

"What y'all *talkin'* 'bout, mister?" inquired another bystander, this time, a young girl.

"Maybe *yours* aren't," countered the Mars mission commander, with his eyes and body beginning to give off a blue-green aura, "Mine... *are*. I'm going to clear the cars out of the storm-path –"

"There are *hundreds*," protested Boyd. "You'll never have *time!*"

"Holy *shit!*" gasped the good old boy. "Wish I had my vid-cam –"

"*Watch* me!" purposefully vowed Jacobson.

His war-song – a thundering, exciting, percussive tune, like a herd of elephants stamping to a rock beat – started to carry over the gale, as the big man, to yet more unbelieving stares, braced himself and then jumped clean over the van, coming to rest beside a small car, two or three lengths back.

Which he picked up and put to his shoulder, as easily as would an adult grasping a child's inflatable backyard pool... and carried off to the southeast, leaping hundreds of feet, again and again.

Boyd – worried sick at the futility of it all, but wanting to keep up appearances – used his own mind-powers to levitate to the top of the van; more use of telekinesis was immediately needed, as the howling winds almost lifted him skyward.

He held out his arms and invoked his power, causing a brilliant light to radiate from his body, illuminating the entire area like mid-day in the Sahara.

"Listen, everybody!" he yelled, pleasantly surprised that somehow, his voice had been boosted to be easily audible over the storm. "Situation's under control – get back in your cars!"

As they streaked upward, racing through the dense, obscuring clouds (both Tanaka and White had to turn on their 'Mars eyes', which, fortunately, showed the scene perfectly) and then made a gradual downward arc, approaching the twister – Tanaka tried mightily to hide the fear in her gut.

The freight-train-cum-jet-takeoff roar of the mighty storm, not to mention its towering, debris-suffused size, took her quite aback; and it was very difficult to maintain a stable course against the sheer power of these cyclonic winds.

It also quickly became obvious that spoken communication would be useless; words simply vanished into the din. Especially, when – as had already happened – the more-than-a-woman's force-field was struck by the lightening-discharges that abounded, up here.

You with me, Devon? sent Tanaka.

Whew!

Last one felt... good!

Well if I ain't... I know where I'm goin', rocket-speed, Professor, sourly responded White.

Prefer to do it inside this-here force field, if y'all don't mind.

Might be more left for the open-casket viewin' that way, don't y'all know.

There's *the spirit,* she cheerily broadcasted.

Mommy dear me help Devon brother too, came an odd, child-like thought, to both Tanaka and White.

Damn, Professor – that her? he sent.

You're her 'uncle', you know, answered the more-than-a-woman.

Well, 'hi there', honey, mentally commented the former Mars navigator.

Uncle Devon's hopin' y'all – 'scuse me, 'thou' – gonna get his ass out of this in one piece... okay?

Oh-kay, Uncle dear Devon, chirped a weird little mind-voice.

I'm going to dive and fly a cork-screw pattern, advised Tanaka.

When I tell you – I'll open a breach in my bubble... stick your hands through it and freeze the whole damn thing... remember what Misha said?

Yeah, I took climate science too, Professor, acknowledged White.

Not sure if I can kill all that hot air it's feedin' on... but I'll give it the ol' college try.

His mind flinched. It was a surge of concern that was felt by both Tanaka and her living-armor.

Shit carried up by that thing's goin' at hundreds of miles per hour – my hands is gonna get cut to shreds! worried White.

I'll go with the wind... and I'll give our velocity a small positive Delta, argued the super-woman.

Easier job of flying, and relative velocity will be lower. Can't you, uhh, ice up your hands, or something?

Yeah, I guess, came White's mental response.

Better'n nothin', I s'pose.

But watch out, Cherie – it's gonna get cold *in here, y'understand?*

Little One, can you help? queried Tanaka.

Ss'éth'ch'Væran Ksé'l'ch' Væran me and things small teach, advised the intelligent-armor.

Best my try Mother noble.

The black ex-astronaut tried not to let his mind wander, but all the same, he couldn't help pondering,

So here I am, flyin' into a tornado on the back of Professor Cherie Tanaka, trustin' my life *to her and a suit of armor that seems to have a mind of its own.*

'Scuse me... her *own.*

I hate *this job!*

Oh, come on, Devon, came Tanaka's friendly chide.

Surely *you didn't want to just be a boring old space-hero...* did *you?*

Here we go...

As the more-than-a-woman put the plan into action, diving and turning into the maelstrom, White began to get a taste of the ferocious G-forces that others, over a different part of the United States, had already encountered. Tanaka had to fly at a speed of hundreds of kilometers per hour to slightly out-pace the velocity of the tornado's gusts, and the accumulated centrifugal forces so generated, would have knocked an ordinary human being quickly unconscious; but to White, the effect was merely, though thoroughly, unpleasant.

Jaysus, complained the former Mars navigator, *this what y'all used to doin', while y'all flyin' back and forth after Miss Angel Lady?*

Oh, I can fly, and turn, much, much *faster,* serenely replied Tanaka.

Would you like to see?

No, Professor – quite alright now, if y'all don't mind, he beseeched.

Open 'er up, and 'Little One' – do that 'thermal underwear thing'... now!

Tanaka complied, and it became her turn to react, as, in one motion, White thrust his arms through a small cleft in the force-field, brought his own alien-abilities to full strength and in so doing, encased his forearms and hands in a thick shroud of ice; the gesture was very necessary, as he felt the buckshot-like impacts of hundreds of tiny bits of airborne grit quickly eroding the protective ice-armor.

He then concentrated again, energizing the "cold-wall" trick that he had been taught back on Amchitka; this worked better, easily deflecting the debris-cloud, although Tanaka immediately complained that the frozen-*Fire*-shield made it difficult for her to navigate (its essence appeared to be largely opaque, except to White's own "Mars eyes").

Though the former Mars mission navigator tried his best to direct his cold-power exclusively outward, a small fraction of it still leaked inward, causing the super-woman and her weirding child to shudder with shock, as – with two-and-a-half war-songs reverberating both inside and outside Tanaka's bubble – *Vîrya Sài'ymë* bent her nascent skills toward protecting her parent.

Omigod, Devon, wailed Tanaka's anguished mind,

Far worse – way more powerful – than back in that jail... like it's draining the very life *out of both me and Little One... can't you keep it on the outside?*

Pouring Fire *into airspeed and trying not to fly off on a tangent, but I'm freezing to death – hardly can stay airborne –*

I can dial it back a mite, he responded,

But I can't control it like that – a bit's bound to get through, 'fraid there's nothin' I can do there... don't want to let up, though... 'specially if I got no idea if we're havin' any effect...

All my Mars eyes's tellin' me, is that we're in a damn scary big twister... had to shut down my ears or I'd go deaf... damn, this G-force shit... feels like my ribs is bein' pulled out of my chest*!*

Suck it up, o my noble brother, counseled Tanaka, her wincing eyes meeting those of Devon White in an alien-powered glow, as the improbable threesome held on for dear life and spiraled slowly downward, dodging wind-borne debris while racing through the tempestuous north Mississippi sky.

I didn't say, it would be easy.

Will you look at that*?* she added, casting her senses – those which would still function, thereby – to scan just outside the bubble.

I think your 'gift' is creating a snowstorm!

Well, then, Professor, he ruefully sent,

Merry fuckin' Christmas*!*

One or two of the beleaguered human 1-22 travelers had stopped, for a second or two, and had amazedly remarked that "somethin's flyin' rings 'round that twister – and where's that damn music comin' from?"; but most of them, prior to former Mars mission pilot's light-show display, had merely been milling about in a state of utter panic, with a few (in a gesture that pleased Jacobson, since it made his job that much easier) abandoning their vehicles and sprinting to the south, in a naïve hope of outrunning the storm.

Boyd, from his vantage point on top of the van, was only barely able to brace himself against the still-inexorably-approaching tornado's outer winds and stinging, driving rain, by intermittent use of his telekinetic abilities. He strained to make his voice audible to the surrounding crowd.

Well, at least I got their attention, he realized.

I guess glowing like a 1,000-Watt bulb, would *do that...*

"Everybody!" he implored, "Back in your cars! The Commander can get you all to safety, faster, if he can do each family together!"

But as fast as it came, his audience was now rapidly diminishing, as the terrifying sight of the dark, towering, howling pillar of destruction – advancing seemingly faster and faster, toward a point a few car-lengths ahead of Jacobson's van – unnerved even the most stoic (or fool-hardy) of the bystanders. The situation wasn't helped in the least by the appearance of Wolf, one squirming, cowering, whimpering puppy under each arm, stepping out of the van's side door, looking up aghast at the tornado, and then turning to the right and starting a dash for cover.

Boyd was about to accost the bounty-hunter, but he was beaten to it.

"What the hell you *doin'* up there, *hombre*?" incredulously yelled Wolf, who took only a momentary pause in so doing. "Fuckin' thing's almost at the tree-line! Get your ass down here – we'll run together!"

He wasn't kidding; at just that moment, Boyd had to dodge with alien-martial-arts-endowed agility, to avoid something large – at least the size of a bread-box – that had been flung into the air, by the swirling winds. The debris crashed into the windshield of a car behind the van, smashing glass everywhere, although fortunately the other vehicle had already been abandoned.

"He is right, Brent," called Misha's voice, from somewhere that the former Mars mission pilot strangely couldn't see. "It is so close that if we stay for even one more minute, even I might not be able to outrun it – let us go, now!"

No fool he, Boyd took another wary look at the frightening maelstrom, turned off his glowing-power and jumped to an unusually-difficult landing beside the bounty-hunter.

"My *God,*" he remarked, with a sinking feeling, "I can't see the Professor, anymore –"

All three of them had to duck another large missile, which, to Boyd's distress, impacted with a family that had been trying to get out of a car, about a hundred feet behind them. There were screams as these unfortunates huddled around the crippled, prone figure of a family-member.

"Look for them two later, pardner," advised Wolf. "Let's hoof it!"

All three men now began to race to the southwest.

"Shit!" complained Boyd, as he rounded the rear end of the van and held a hand against a painful bruise on the side of his neck. "I'm gettin' *hit,* big-time... that felt like a bullet! Wetter than normal – am I bleeding?"

"Luckily, no – but what did you *expect,* Major," answered Misha. "Closer to the vortex, that thing can propel debris at *hundreds* of kilometers per hour – oww, I see what you mean – wait –"

"'Wait', yer ass!" grunted Wolf. "No time to lose... damn, don't remember it bein' *this* cold, when – what the hell's *that!*"

With no other warning, a cumulus-like cloud of something dense and white, suddenly surrounded the tornado-column, all the way from its top near the clouds to its base; then, no more than three or four seconds later, this improbable phenomenon billowed out in all directions, quickly enveloping the three more-than-human men, not to mention everyone and everything for a half-mile in every direction.

Near-instantly, they were in the middle of a blizzard, but no ordinary winter-storm, this : heightened senses complained of weirdly-low temperatures, which put the former Mars pilot's teeth to immediate chattering, though Wolf was able to offset the freeze with both a literal and figurative *Fire*; for his part, the Russian seemed to take it completely in stride. Fortunately, this extra-cold effect seemed to last only five or six seconds.

The rain stopped, and the wind quickly abated to the point where they could actually speak, and be heard, in a normal tone of voice.

"A *blizzard?* Oh, right... Devon," offered Boyd. "Well, thank God, that means he and Cherie are still alive –"

"Whoa," exclaimed the bounty-hunter, who had cast his glance up in the direction of the tornado. "Ain't seein' *nothin'* – 'cept a lot of thick clouds... hey, what's those sounds, over there, where it was comin' at us –"

Just to the northeast of them, airborne detritus – some of it very large, much more small to tiny – was coming back to Earth under the influence of gravity.

But there was only a light incidental breeze.

And there was no longer, a... tornado.

"Damn! They did it... *they* ***did*** *it!*" joyfully shrieked Boyd.

He looked behind and to the southwest, and observed Jacobson gently lowering a SUV, which he had been carrying, to the ground. He stared skyward, gaping in disbelief.

"Now I've seen *everything*, folks," called an obviously awed Jacobson, who, in this emotion, was joined by the large number of ordinary highway-travelers, who had already begun to congregate around him. "We – I mean, they – just overcame one of the most powerful forces that Mother Nature has put on the planet. Words... are so... *inadequate*."

As the more perceptive of those on the Mississippi Interstate this day, realized that history was being made, they raced for mobile communicators, video-cameras, flexible-surface-computers, or just anything that could capture the moment.

They were just in time to hear an odd, yet exciting and uplifting war-song combination, echoing from the skies above; and a half-second thereafter, the music was followed by the advent of a godly-looking, super-human, Eurasian-American female, accompanied by an equally-regal African-American man, the both of them cocooned in some kind of shimmering, barely-visible encasement, streaking out of the sky.

The duo landed next to Wolf, Misha and Boyd, in the midst of an astonished throng that must have numbered in the hundreds. Oddly, for a few very long seconds, there was complete silence, as if no-one dared be the first to raise his or her voice.

But presently – with her eyes glowing incandescent-yellow-white and with her *Fire* and war-song adorning the very fiber of her being, the woman planted her feet, crossed her arms in front, raised her head high and pronounced,

"I'm *Vîrya* Cherie Teruko Tanaka... First Of The *Fire*."

Our Little Box Is The Best One

The abandoned, almost completely-trashed former truck-stop, just within the "Greater Los Angeles Prohibited Zone", was anything *but* luxurious accommodation; but they *had* been able to hide the two long-wheelbase jeeps that had transported them here, in the facility's rather spacious garages. Similar privacy was available for the group of male true believers, as they relaxed a bit and tended to the expected duties, such as cleaning gun-barrels, counting available grenades and rounds of ammunition, and ensuring that the triggers for the *plastique*-belts and -vests, were all still in the "safe" position.

"How many did you say have survived, brother?" inquired the tall, early-middle-age, olive-skinned man dressed in a ragged t-shirt and dirty track-pants, as he resentfully stroked his chin.

He felt naked, without the beard; but there *was*, at least, some scant comfort from the fact that every other one of his infiltration force had to suffer the same indignity, for the sake of passing themselves off as "nothing more than another group of Latino gang-bangers".

"Other than the six in our group," quietly replied the other guy, who was a bit younger, though similarly-dressed, "Five... I believe, out of those who were advancing down the coast, from the northern part of the state. After Mokhtar's brethren reported that they had run into that police checkpoint in Mission Viejo, we lost contact. I fear that we must assume the worst."

"Not worst," patiently observed the first man. "Martyrdom is far from that. Let us hope that they were not captured, however."

The younger man mutely nodded.

There was a prolonged pause in the discourse, and then the elder man again spoke up.

"So is the remote arming-box still functioning?" he asked. "We had a rough ride back there, first in outrunning the police-vehicles, and then in escaping those, what were they –"

"'Crips', I believe," offered the other, "Judging from the blue headscarves."

"Criminals... decadent scum... worse, maybe, even than the government," scoffed the leader. "But of the box...? It is *very* delicate, you know. And if it does not work, we may have to make our way in and accomplish the task manually."

"Well, brother," commented the younger man, "The self-test system is still showing 'O.K.', for whatever *that* is worth. However, I suppose we shall not know for sure, until we try it. Personally, I am not worried... after all, did you not provide duplicates to both of the other groups?"

"Yes, *yes,*" countered the leader, as he tried unsuccessfully to avoid a hint of worry sounding in his voice, "But those are earlier models – remember, unlike our one, they were not meant specifically for use with this device. The teams led by Brothers Mokhtar and al-Sabah were only meant to be a diversion, in any case. It falls to *us*, to do Allah's work, in this matter."

"So?" responded the younger man, with an arched eyebrow. "Brother, you never said anything about that, to me. What difference does it make?"

"I was told," explained the leader, "That unlike our own controller, the range of the other ones is very limited – no more than a few-score meters – and they may only be able to set the time-fuse, as opposed to achieving the desired effect, at once. This is even more a problem, because in contrary fashion to our unit, the, uhh, 'boxes' possessed by Brothers Mokhtar and al-Sabah must be within about two kilometers of the device, in order to detect its presence. And last, their controllers do not have the kind of, oh, what did my contacts in the League say it was –? Oh, yes... 'encryption', that our remote control, has. The signals that their equipment sends out, could theoretically be intercepted and decoded by the American government."

The younger man laughed out loud; it was a gesture that was met with a quizzical look on the part of the elder man.

"What is so funny?" demanded the leader.

"Well, then," offered the follower, "Let the government, listen in; and let them – as many as they can send – come hither. Would this not please Almighty Allah?"

A broad smile appeared on the face of the leader.

"Yes, brother," he said, "Perhaps it would."

Guerrilla Interview On I-22

The small, surrounded group of more-than-human co-travelers – particularly Tanaka, after her spectacular return to earth – was, predictably, immediately inundated by a thousand questions. Most of these were shouted by eager guerrilla-reporters, who were simultaneously pointing video-cams, or mobile communicators, or just anything capable of doing a recording. Bedlam broke out, with Misha and Wolf, the latter carrying a squealing puppy under each arm, retreating post haste inside the van, hoping that its tinted windows would afford a measure of privacy.

Jacobson, Tanaka, Boyd and White, however, stayed outside to face the madding crowd, awkwardly pushing through it to the southwest at the more-than-a-woman's insistence. After a determined effort, shrugging off persistent inquiries, they had reached a damaged car and its crippled, bloodied male driver, who had been hit by what was now revealed as the crumpled remains of a refrigerator.

The man's face was a ghastly white, and he was only barely conscious : the debris-impact had struck the drivers'-side door, causing this to smash against his chest, which had blood all over it. Bleeding slowly from the mouth and moaning, he was propped up against the car's rear tire.

As a light rain again began to fall, Boyd bent down to examine the unfortunate.

"Broken ribs, for sure," he warned. "Internal injuries, probably. Anybody got a first-aid kit? Think there's one back in the van... can somebody get Misha to bring it?"

"Let *me*," offered Tanaka.

She joined Boyd and began to examine the injured man.

"Yeah... okay," acknowledged the former Mars mission pilot. "But he's, uhh, *human*... you know? You sure you won't just make it worse, Professor?"

"What the hell you mean?" asked an elderly white guy who was, along with all-to-many others, crowding dangerously close. "'Bout bein' human."

"Nothing... *nothing*," parried Boyd. "Listen, everybody, I know you must find this interesting, but there might be more twisters around here... can a few of you please stand guard, east, west, north and south, so we get a bit more warning, if and when?"

He couldn't tell if his request had been honored, as the throng surrounding himself, Tanaka, Jacobson and White was much too thick to see through, even with Mars eyes. But the onlookers *did* gasp and step back momentarily, upon hearing a graceful, down-tempo variant of the super-woman's war-song begin to play, as a gentle, white-and-purple glow began to emanate from Tanaka's fore-body, enveloping the injured man in a comforting embrace.

"This is *priceless*, man!" enthused a teenager with a wrist-recorder.

"My subscriber count's gonna *skyrocket!*" happily added another.

"Wait – wait – what y'all *doin'* to him?" came the anguished cry of a stout woman, obviously the injured man's partner, who was about to intervene.

"It's alright, Ma'am," reassured Jacobson. "The Professor's trying to heal your husband."

"She don't look like no doctor to me, and what's *that* – oh, *my* –" protested the woman; but then, at once, her voice fell silent, as a measure of the crippled man's color returned and he stopped bleeding. The whimpers of agony ceased as well. He closed his eyes and began breathing more normally.

"I, uhh... read Bobby's condition," commented Tanaka, as she arose, to address the woman from the car. "He's stable now, but you should get him to a hospital, as soon as you can – I think that my, uhh, 'arts' can only heal soft tissue, and your husband has at least two broken ribs... maybe a fractured clavicle, as well."

"Well thank you, thank you from the bottom of my *heart*, missy," gushed the grateful woman. "Can't y'all hang 'round here a bit more, 'case he needs y'all again? Oh, and by the way, I ain't his wife... we're common-law. Kids in the car's his, though. How'd y'all know his name, anyway?"

"Long story, and, that's, uhh, good to know," politely replied the more-than-a-woman. "But we can't hang around here too long – Sam, we'd better head up the road, to where that other tornado hit, I mean. There's *terrible* damage about a mile forward from here – Devon, Little One and I saw it, while we were, uhh, 'dealing with our tornado'. The people up there *need* us... the road's so jammed that the emergency vehicles probably can't get through."

"Yeah, she's right 'bout that," agreed White. "Most of them poor folk that was in the way of that twister, they're beyond our help... but there's a lot more of 'em that are buried under debris and such. We could at least dig 'em out."

"Understood, Professor," acknowledged Jacobson, "And I can undoubtedly carry the van that far – might be some huffing and puffing, with everybody except yourself in it, due to the extra weight – but be advised, we have to limit our effort here... I don't want any confrontations with the government, when the police get there... you understand?"

"Hey," called an African-American, male onlooker, "Why'd y'all be afraid of them – the po-lice, that is? They should be givin' y'all a *medal!*"

"You done saved our *lives!*" enthusiastically added another. "How'd you do it? Don't tell me you stopped a tornado – no man can do somethin' like *that* –"

Jacobson straightened up and stepped forward to address the crowd; to add to the effect, he allowed his eyes to glow ever-so-slightly, as he spoke.

"Listen, everyone," he announced, "The Professor's quite right; we shouldn't waste too much time here, since the folks up the road have been badly hurt – we, and by 'we' I mean not just us, but all of you, too – need to get up there and lend whatever assistance that we can. There'll be ample time later for us to explain fully, but for now, please pay careful attention to what I say; it's of the *utmost* importance."

A hush – offset only by the subtle timbre of Jacobson's personal war-music, playing softly in human psyches – fell over the throng.

"You are now looking," he explained, "At the crew of the *Eagle-Infinity* space mission. My name is Commander Sam Jacobson, and with me here, are Science Officer Cherie Tanaka – she's the flying one, by the way – and also Majors Brent Boyd and Devon White. It is us who traveled all the way to Mars and who freed the alien being named 'Karéin-Mayréij', a.k.a. 'The Storied Watcher', who, in turn, destroyed the 'Lucifer' comet, and in so doing, saved this planet from total destruction. For reasons that none of us can comprehend, although we're going to get to the bottom of it, mark my words on that, the government has been trying to kill both her and us, since the 'Lucifer' episode –"

"*Wait* a minute," interrupted one of the more self-confident onlookers, "Y'all the *Mars* astronauts? *Can't* be! They say, few days 'go, that y'all was *daid* – like, in quarantine, 'cuz y'all got sick from some Mars bug, or –"

"That's just the usual bullshit comin' from the government," remarked White. "If every fifth word they tell y'all's true, that's a *good* day, y'understand?"

"Anyway," continued Jacobson, "They *did* imprison us, but as you've noticed, we're alive and kicking, and we plan to remain that way. So's Karéin, incidentally; and here, I have a very important message for our illustrious President, and everyone within the government – particularly the intelligence agencies and the military – who seem to want us dead. Are you recording?"

"Damn right!" sounded several voices, answering almost in unison.

With his war-song increasing in exciting, growling power, the former Mars mission commander looked straight into one of the video-cameras, and defiantly warned, "We have inherited some of the Storied Watcher's powers; you've seen a small demonstration of these here, today... but be advised, there's much, *much* more of it, where *that* came from. You repeatedly tried to murder Karéin-Mayréij, and us along with her... *that* didn't work so well... did it?"

"Why'd them Feds want to kill you?" incredulously asked an onlooker. "Don't make no *sense!*"

"You're right – it's totally insane," confirmed Jacobson, "And we have our own theories about what's behind it... in the interests of time, however, I'll skip that for now, and instead explain of our three, non-negotiable demands."

"Demands?" inquired somebody. "*What* 'demands'?"

"First," continued the Mars mission commander, "The President must stand down from office, then make a full, public confession of the disgraceful crimes that he has so far instigated against Karéin, her friends and family, not to mention, ourselves. Two, that he must surrender himself, and all those also involved in these crimes, to stand trial in a neutral, objective court, on charges including, but not limited to, murder, conspiracy to commit murder, kidnapping, forcible confinement, torture and high crimes and misdemeanors. Three, that he does *not* order anyone under your command – particularly, members of the Armed Forces or the police – to try to harm us, or to take us forcibly into custody. We don't want to hurt anyone, but, as you've no doubt seen, we're more than capable of defending ourselves; if the President and his cronies are callous or stupid enough to order police officers or Army soldiers to attack us, then the blame will rest *exclusively* with him... not, us. Got that?"

"No kiddin', man," offered one of the youthful video-recorder onlookers. "But what if he just don't answer you? Like, with them on-line petitions that everybody signs on to, but then nothin' ever comes of it?"

"The administration has a *very* short amount of time in which to demonstrate an honest effort to come clean and confess to the American people," brusquely responded Jacobson. "We're talking a matter of hours to days... not, weeks. If the President chooses to delay, we'll begin undertaking some measures – the nature of which I'm not at liberty to disclose – which will make it clear that we mean *business*; and no power on Earth is going to stop us."

“Well, Commander,” phlegmatically observed White, “Actually, there *is* one 'power on Earth' that *could* stop us; but she's on *our* side, don't you know.”

A malevolent smile appeared on Tanaka's face as she commented, “I like how you put that, Devon. And, to everyone who'll be watching this statement... to those who thought that the government was just too big, too powerful, to resist... to everybody who just kept their heads down and hoped that they'd leave you alone, even though one of your friends 'disappeared' last month... please understand, we're here, fighting for *you*. We mean to set things right – to restore human rights and the rule of law to this country – but we need your support. We can bring that son-of-a-bitch President to justice... but we can't oppose the American people. The decision about continuing to live under tyranny, or to choose freedom, will shortly be up to *you*. Choose wisely.”

“Anything to add, Brent?” inquired Jacobson.

“No... okay, on second thought... I *do* have something to say, to the President,” requested the former Mars mission pilot.

Boyd's eyes began to glow and his war-song intermixed perfectly with Jacobson's, as he spoke.

“We're only too well aware,” he growled, “That one of the government's favorite tricks, is to threaten or punish the friends and family of people who it's taken a dislike to. So let me be very clear about something : leave my wife, my children, my in-laws, my friends and acquaintances, alone. This dispute is between the four of us and your gang of White House criminals... full stop. Touch one hair on the heads of my loved ones, and as God's my witness, *I'll kill you*. I'll destroy you so thoroughly that there won't be enough left to put into a fucking *thimble*. Is anything unclear about that?”

Gravely, the other three super-humans nodded agreement.

“One other thing,” quietly stated Boyd. “Laura... kids... if you can see me... hear me... I just wanted you to know... this'll all be over with, soon. In the meantime, if anybody from the government – or anybody, no matter *who* they are – comes to bother you... make sure to tell them what I said a moment ago, you understand? I love you all *so* much. I can't *wait* to be with you, again.”

He hung his head and looked away from the cameras, as his compatriots moved in front, to afford Boyd a few seconds of relative privacy.

There was a shocked silence within the crowd for a moment or two; but eventually, one of the onlookers said, “Cool! Anythin' else?”

“No,” commented Jacobson. “And please... hold the questions for now. We've got work to do. If you want to know more, head to where the other tornado hit... a few more hands would really help, I'd bet.”

“Wait!” shouted multiple voices.

“Interview's over,” countered the big man with a pleasant smile, as he extended an arm around both Boyd and White.

“Ready?” he insouciantly asked of Tanaka.

“*Very*,” she answered, with an enthusiastic grin and gut-flashes of the *Fire*.

"See you up the road," loudly announced Jacobson, as – in nearly-exact synchronization with the woman – his legs first tensed, then propelled him and his super-human cargo over the crowd, toward the van.

Packin' For Bouvet

Although, by his own admission, Robert K. Billings, former floor-tile and custom-kitchen-assembly salesman from Tucson, Arizona, had "seen it all", by now – and even though he had been allowed, from time to time, into the underground-cavern that his erstwhile alien girlfriend had hollowed out, underneath the second campsite (this one, much further north in the Canadian Rockies, than the first; it was actually cold outside, most of the time) – he still reflexively dashed for cover behind the trees, when her exciting, beautiful war-music began to roar, when the ground began to heave, earthquake-like... and when, a half-second later, the *thing* emerged, being thence transported by the Storied Watcher's unbelievable telekinetic abilities.

In doing this, he was joined by well-nigh everyone else from the McGregor family, the Compton refugees and the other stragglers; the display was nothing if not spectacular.

"Holy *Jaysus*, Sari," gasped the more-than-human man, with a reflexive whistle, as soon as the forest-and-dirt-debris had more or less settled back into place. "You did all *that* just with, uhh, your *head*? I can hardly lift a bucket!"

The slim, teenager-lithe, golden-haired figure of Karéin-Mayréij, still clad only in mufti, dropped down in front of him, from her former vantage-point of perhaps three meters above.

"*Patience*, my love," she counseled, with an entrancing smile. "I have had many thousands of your years, in which to build my mind-pulling-arts. Your own shall flower, soon enough... as will those of all our friends. And the time for it, is opportune : behold the ark, which will protect you, as we travel."

What was now in front of them was unlike almost anything that any had previously seen, or anticipated. As near as they could see from casual observation, the Storied Watcher had completely dismantled almost all the major components of both the original 'Magic Bus', as well as the McGregor recreational vehicle, then reassembled these – plus, as she had mentioned, after 'foraging' trips hither and yon, over the past few days, "a few other items discreetly-borrowed from airplane-hangars, auto scrap-yards, com-pu-ter-stores and other places" – into a thoroughly alien-looking contraption.

The thing was oval-shaped, like a squashed, elongated flying-saucer; with an almost perfectly-smooth exterior skin, it was half again as wide and a bit less than twice as long as the original 'Magic Bus', with only two small, circular windows on its sides (though there was a larger, perfectly-flush, glassed-in area, like the cockpit-windows of a jetliner, up front, except these were both on the top part of the oval and underneath). And its color – or, rather, colors – were distinctive; while the base-coat was apparently dull gray, the vehicle's surface had a measure of the same ever-shifting, semi-translucent, kaleidoscope-effect previously seen on *Vîrya Ahn'jë*.

"So much for my RV," ruefully muttered Jim McGregor. "Can't even tell where you put the parts from it. Maybe I should have just packed 'er up and gone off to Vancouver, while I still had something to go *in*."

"Ahh, you will still feel 'at home', when you climb on-board," cheerily countered the alien-girl. "And the soul of your arr-vee – all the happy memories held therein – is preserved, dear friend. My war-children and I have made this ark as self-sufficient as possible, and that extends not only to preserving your arr-vee's former comforts, not to mention being sealed against very low or high outside pressures, but many other things beside. For example, *Vîrya Quü'j* and *Vîrya Ahn'jë* have coöperated in providing much better flying-controls and navigation-instruments than were previously available. They have also safe-proofed her against all manner of evils, ranging from the President's electro-spying-eyes, to the high-en-er-gee particle-shine... to hostile magic –"

With a bemused smirk, one of the Compton parents interrupted.

"Magic?" he remarked. "Y'all mean wizards 'n witches 'n ghosts, 'n such?"

"Umm-hmm," confirmed Karéin-Mayréij, with a nod of acknowledgment.

"Everybody know, ain't no such *thang*," argued the Compton woman.

"Maybe not here... not... *yet*," solemnly advised the Storied Watcher. "But it is prudent to take precautions, none the less... is it not?"

"Whatever y'all *say*, Angel lady," grunted the interlocutor.

"Now, as to propulsion," continued Karéin-Mayréij, "Some explanation is appropriate : this ark can, unlike our last 'Magic Bus', travel on her own, albeit at a relatively low speed; my war-children and I have, ahh, 'rigged up' a system of turbines, particle-shine ree-actors and batteries – the latter, as well as the internal structure, having been modified by both myself, and by kind Hector, so thank you very much, my brother –"

"Gratitude's all mine, Karéin," demurred Ramirez. "I've been taking notes on this crazy metallurgy you've been teaching me... it's *priceless* stuff... like, a hundred, maybe a thousand, years of learning, in a couple of days – I just wish Sylvia were here to see it, you know?"

"Soon, shall we all be reunited," reassured the Storied Watcher. "Though not an hour does pass, in which I do not pray for the safety of Sylvia, Minn-ee, Sam, Cherie and the others. Enough of that sad matter... about our new traveling-ark, her ability to keep you aloft should be more or less self-sustaining, as long as you do not attempt to fly too fast, travel very far underwater, or load too much weight. Moreover, if you can call upon the *Fire*, you can directly pour her into the ree-actor, so as to supply any en-er-gees that may be lacking. My war-children and I have calculated that the ark should be easily able to accommodate all of those here, plus provisions and other similar cargo, before the strain is too much; but be warned, she cannot make an abrupt take-off or landing, so expect a gradual, slow rise or descent. Perhaps that is for the best, considering that many of you are not yet accustomed to the great pulling-forces that would otherwise be risked. Is everyone, uhh, 'with me', so far?"

There were enthusiastic cheers from most of the children in the audience, followed by the inevitable "can we see what's inside?"

"In a few moments," directed Karéin-Mayréij, "For first, with this campsite as for the last one, we must gather those belongings which we brought here, and then remove all traces of our stay. When that is done, then I will open the folding-doors – there are now three of them – and you can all go inside and prepare for the trip."

"The... uhh... trip?" hesitated Billings. "What you *mean*, sweetheart? I don't think that Tucson would be a good –"

The Storied Watcher waved her finger, with a schoolmarm, tutorial demeanor. "Bob, you are off by a small bit," she answered, "For we will shortly be going somewhere that is, ahh, somewhat further away."

She wheeled to address the audience of Compton refugees, former GrayWar mercenaries, Canadian tourists and others.

"In my travels to acquire the necessary materials to produce the flying-vehicle that you now see before you," she explained, "I have tarried long enough to use the various com-pu-ter networks for research purposes, and in so doing, I have become very familiar with the geography of this planet. Have any of you perhaps heard of a place called 'Bouvet Island'?"

The alien-girl drew the proverbial blank, as bewildered stares from everyone except Ramirez faced back at her.

"Hmm," he mumbled... "Isn't that in the Arctic? No, wait a minute... the *Ant*arctic... right?"

"Aye," confirmed Karéin-Mayréij, with a pleasant smile. "It is described in several your map-books as 'the world's most remote place'; an island in the Southern Ocean, it is so remote and desolate – hardly a few paces' worth of solid land are found there, since almost all of the place is covered by a thick sheet of ice – that its only inhabitants are sea-birds and the occasional marine mammal. No human can survive for long in the open there, since the gales of winter beset forlorn Bouvet, well-nigh year-long. A perfect place for a 'Destroying Angel' who wishes for privacy... would you not agree?"

"Y'all *got* to be kiddin' us, Karéin," loudly protested Saquina White. "*Please* tell me, y'all ain't fixin' to take us all to some crazy-ass place like that!"

"Well, *ah* wants to go," exclaimed Jermaine Kingsley. "Ain't never seen none of them seals, since they drained the L.A. 'Quarium, that is... an' it be *wicked* cool to go hikin' on some glacier!"

"'Cool' is right, kid," complained Billings.

"Would you have preferred, say, the far side of yonder moon?" insouciantly teased the Storied Watcher. "I *did* consider such, but thought that it might be more risky... in case my, ahh, 'wall-sealing job' would be less than perfect, and the air transported there, should escape. At least *that* would not be a problem, on, ahh, 'fair Bouvet'."

"Fine... *fine*, Sari," muttered Billings, "By now, you should know, glutton for punishment that I am, I'll follow you to the Moon, the Sun, the stars, or some goddamn rock out in who knows where... but why do you need to haul all these other folks along with us?"

"And leave you sitting out in the open, here, Bob?" firmly responded Karéin-Mayréij. "You would be, ahh, 'sitting ducks', for the first bomb that the President chose to send your way. Later, when your own powers fully evolve, my continued protection may not be as necessary; but for now, you must stay with me, if at all possible. That includes going to this new place – and the several others that I will construct, in locations near-equally-remote, so that should an assailant attack them, hoping to catch me off-guard... they will need to do so, in coordinated fashion, lest I be absent from any particular one. And besides... I *need* you there."

"What could *we* possibly do, that you can't already, Karéin?" inquired Ramirez.

"In addition to exercising your own nascent powers, in crafting the structure of our hidden fortresses," she proposed, "You can help me, ahh... 'decorate'."

"Uhh... Missy," commented Atasha Jones, "How you 'spect us to 'decorate' a glacier?"

"Not that," serenely answered the alien-girl. "Rather, you shall assist in setting up the cavern-dwelling that I shall presently blast out underneath the ice – indeed, deep below the very rock, itself. Large and grand, shall this be; and furthermore, I shall approach from below the waves of the Southern Ocean, so as to be covered from these spying-satellites, that the American President seems so fond of. We shall have everything that we need... a redoubt which is safe from all but the most potent attacks, one that is completely hidden from detection, and, since this island was built on a sleeping-volcano, there is a natural source of energy, which we can use to our advantage. Oh... I *will* need to stop in a few places, to, ahh, 'pick up' additional equipment, that may be useful, for a long-term stay in our new dwellings. I promise not to leave you for more than a few moments, in each such case."

"All the comforts of home," quipped Billings, "That is, if you think of the North Pole, as 'home'. You gonna steal us a TV, by any chance, Sari?"

"It's the *South* Pole, Bob," corrected Ramirez.

"Still a bit less warm than what I'm used to," parried the salesman.

"I will put that on the, ahh, 'shopping-list', my love," remarked Karéin-Mayréij, with an affectionate wink. "And, for the record... I do not 'steal'; I... *borrow*. Like, for example, all those expenses on your charging-card. They will be paid back, in the fullness of time. Even the cost of those choc-o-lates."

She gave a half-shrug, and three entrances – two at the front, on either side of the vehicle's fuselage, plus a ramp at the rear – opened, revealing a dimly-lit, shiny-white-and-silver interior.

"Only one other thing remains to do, after you have cleaned up," advised the alien-girl. "Namely... to name our new ark. Atasha, I shall leave *that* project, to yourself. Choose wisely, as it is said that knowing a good and true name, is sometimes supremely important... right, Bob?"

"Don't *remind* me," ruefully mentioned Billings.

"Well, Missy," asked Jones, "How we gonna decide? You all got any good Mars names, that we could start with?"

"Lamentably, none come immediately to mind," parried the Storied Watcher, "But I *can* offer you one modest piece of advice."

"Yeah?" asked the teacher.

"'Boob', 'Tube' and 'Rainbow', are already taken," said Karéin-Mayréij.

Wolf Drinks It In

They had observed the other tornado crossing I-22, about a mile ahead of them; but the ugly reality of the scene that confronted Jacobson and his friends, upon arriving there, still left them more than horrified. A gap of at least five hundred feet in the tree-line had been torn on either side of the highway, and within the path that the twister had clearly taken, the ground had been scoured clear of everything larger than a grass-blade. Slightly further out, many-score trees had been reduced to the proverbial match-sticks, and all that remained of cars was twisted metal; but further still – up to another few hundred feet – there were the bent shapes of heavily-damaged cars, trucks, and... *people.*

"*Jesus,*" gasped Boyd, as he surveyed the damage. "Where do we *start?*"

"I can't heal *everyone* who's hurt," commented a heartbroken Tanaka. "Far too many of them... but, listen – do you hear – sounds like people, trapped, all over the place –"

And indeed, she was right – even without "Mars ears", the moans and pleas of wounded, terrified ex-motorists could easily be detected from every direction. There had evidently been a large number of commercial vehicles trapped in the traffic-jam on this part of I-22, when the tornado had hit; most of these were just panel-vans, pickup-trucks and tractor-trailers, but there were also several tankers carrying various types of inflammable substances. Three of the latter had overturned and had begun to burn brightly, contaminating the air with a foul chemical smell, although this was partly offset by occasional storm-gusts and a persistent, light rain.

"I will scout out the area," offered the Russian. "We must find out how many victims there are, around here."

Before there could be an argument, he was off like a gazelle, darting between overturned vehicles, tree-trunks and other detritus.

"I'll try to pry as many as I can, out of –" started Jacobson; but the moment he spoke, he was interrupted by the thunder of a sizable explosion, issuing from one of the tanker-trailers, less than a hundred feet down the highway, to the northwest. Immediately following on this was an even larger conflagration, the heat of which was unpleasantly felt by everyone except the bounty-hunter (and his two dogs, which had, somewhat reluctantly, now ventured forth from inside Jacobson's van). As the fireball mushroomed upward, it left a pall of flame igniting everything flammable in the vicinity, causing even more panicked screaming from that direction.

They heard someone shouting from the direction of the inferno. Though loud and clear, the call was oddly straightforward, certainly not as if from a human being about to be roasted alive.

"Hey!" yelled a far-off male voice, "Need *help* over here! Three of 'em trapped in there – I can't git at 'em!"

"Devon – can you –" hastily requested Tanaka.

As the ex-astronaut's war-song started to play, he was pre-empted by Wolf.

"You freeze out the smaller 'uns, pardner," directed the red-glowing-eyed bounty-hunter, whose own, entrancing, portentous melody began to reverberate from everywhere, "'Cause this – *this* shit... it's what *I* do."

"Come on, Devon," proposed Boyd, "For once he's thinking straight."

"Huh?" stuttered the more-than-a-woman, while White began to follow his fellow ex-astronaut, off to the south.

Wolf was already away. Flexing his hands into and out of fists, he strode confidently toward the overturned tanker-trailer, accompanied by his two puppies, which were already drooling something that sizzled and evaporated, as it hit the ground.

Tanaka and Jacobson also rushed forward, but stopped soon thereafter, dissuaded by a sudden flare-up that shot multiple jets of flaming fuel, streaking skyward.

"I can handle it, Cherie," shouted the former Mars mission commander, over the din of the repeated explosions and other general mayhem. "Fire... the normal kind, that is... not fun, but I'll raise my shielding –"

"Don't think you need to, Sam," remarked Tanaka. "Holy Toledo, look at *that* – he's *breathing* it in, *absorbing* it, or something –"

And she was right. The bounty-hunter, standing tall and walking steadily forward in long steps, had formed a roaring, howling curtain of fire around him and his hell-hounds; and, as he got to a point about thirty feet away from the accident, the flames issuing from the wrecked tanker converged on his body, drawn there like iron filings attracted by a powerful magnet.

The heat emanating from the scene was terrifying, even to the likes of Jacobson and his super-human distaff companion.

"*Ohhhh,*" loudly half-moaned Wolf.

"What the *fuck!*" shrieked the male voice, from the direction of the wreckage. "You're on *fire*, man!"

"You hurt, Wolf?" shouted Tanaka. "I can block it, with my –"

The bounty-hunter held up a big hand and lazily responded, his voice becoming more easily audible as the roaring energy of the fire was, little by little, being drained, "Peace, sister... was slightly more to eat than Little Miss Hottie counted on. We're five by five, over here. Hey, whoever you are, in there – how come you're not, like, done on both sides? Bit warm out here, even for yours truly, you know."

"No fuckin' *idea*, man," yelled the voice. "Hurts like hell, but I'm copin'... don't ask me how. Things've been fuckin' *nuts* for a while – 'splain later. Can y'all git over here and help me pry 'em out?"

Wolf was saying something about "Got to keep suckin' it up", while Tanaka, encased in her force-field, and Jacobson, enshrouded in his diamond-like *Fire*-armor-suit, raced over to the periphery of the charred, jumbled, tangled metal.

Just inside it, they saw a handsome, muscular, mid-thirties Caucasian guy dressed in what had, before having been burned in many places, been standard truck-driver-garb – a mini-Wolf in some respects, he was somewhat shorter and leaner than the bounty-hunter, and his long, dark-brown, hippie-rock-star hair accented mutton-chop sideburns and a mustache – frantically trying to open a path through the debris, with bare hands.

"*Helllppp!*" came a screech, from behind the pile of smoldering metal.

The guy's jaw dropped as he momentarily took his eye off his appointed task, and wheeled to regard the three more-than-human beings behind him.

"Jaysus, Mary'n *Joseph*," he whistled, taken completely aback by the impressive presence of the three shining-eyed, *Amaiish*-energized beings. "Who the hell're *you?* Like, Army, or somethin'? Uhh... don't matter, anyways – listen, there's folks behind all this shit – can't get a good grip on it, too fuckin' *hot* –"

For a second or two, Tanaka, her eyes watering and joy on her face, stood transfixed; she tarried so long, in fact, that Jacobson had to use an elbow to get her attention, saying, "Professor...?"

"Of *course* we'll help... *brother*," breathed the former Mars science officer.

"Huh?" replied the confused newcomer. "Well get over here, then – but watch out, that metal's *boilin'*, you'll need somethin' to lever it with –"

Tanaka partly dropped her bubble, enough to take hold of the guy's arm.

"Don't worry," she counseled, while – to the man's astonishment – charges of the *Fire* arced within her body, "We don't need anything like that. Sam?"

"On your mark," confirmed Jacobson. "I'll pull from the middle to the left – you do the right."

"3... 2... 1... *go!*" intoned Tanaka.

Though the wreckage was intertwined and interlocked in devilish, Gordian Knot-style, the combined telekinesis unleashed by the two ex-astronauts made steady progress; the tangled, smoking metal was being dismantled, bit by bit.

"I could easily slice through this, with my 'Sword' – the lightening-bolt, that is," offered a sweating, wincing Tanaka, while the hippie-haired guy looked on in amazement.

"Not a good idea," warned Jacobson, as he stared forward, with his war-song humming over the surroundings, "You might hit whoever's in there. Same reason I can't just charge through it – too unstable... it might collapse."

"*Save us!*" screamed a young, female voice, from the other side of the metal-wall. "Fire's getting close!"

There was another big fire-burst, to Tanaka's right, and she flinched from a painful surge of heat – which disappeared almost as quickly as it had appeared, thanks to being drawn instantly into the inferno still roaring around Wolf, who was holding at a point about thirty feet behind, his eyes glowing a sinister red.

"Got it," he purred. "Damn, and part of me don't *want* you to put it out... if *that* makes any sense. I ever tell you how pretty a fire can be?"

"Absorb as much as you can!" shouted Jacobson. "*Humans* in there!"

The three of them at the wreckage noticed that the bounty-hunter's dogs were doing their own part to abate the fire-surges, for they were also – as near as could be determined – breathing in the flames, albeit in smaller quantities than was their master.

"*Thought* I'd seen 'hot dogs' before," commented the newcomer, "But I guess I ain't. Who the fuck *are* y'all?"

"Introductions later, noble brother," answered Tanaka, as she continued to apply her telekinetic powers to the metal. A duly-impressed Wolf and Jacobson noted that something – undoubtedly, her living-breastplate – had created a pair of dimly-glowing, crowbar-like appendages attached to Tanaka's forearms. These she used to pry apart some of the twisted wreckage between herself and the trapped accident-victims.

"*Amazing,*" observed the former science officer, her attractive, Eurasian face – complete with yellow-glowing eyes and her shifting, almost-enveloping bubble – turned to regard the hippie-haired guy. "It's got to be 65 Celsius or more, here – that metal burns to the touch... oww. Your denim's burned through, all over... how are you *surviving* in here?"

"*You* tell *me*, lady," grunted the new guy. "Damn hot, I'll admit... but I ain't leavin' 'till they're out."

"*Helllppp!*" implored the remote voice.

"We're coming – hold on!" shouted Jacobson. "Crouch down, hands over heads, like in a plane-crash... debris might shift when we punch through. Just a few seconds more..."

With embers and sparks flying all about, the last few pieces of damaged metal gave way, opening a breach large enough for a good-sized adult to climb through. Inside – within the almost-crushed confines of what must have, at one time, been a large car or SUV – there were two Caucasian children (a boy of about 10 and a younger girl) and their mother, although the woman was lying, motionless, between her offspring.

"Come here – we'll take you out!" requested Tanaka.

"Too hot!" protested the boy. "I can't touch it!"

"Here," reassured the super-woman. "I'll get the three of you."

She flew forward, dropping her bubble only long enough to position herself in the middle of the refugees. The glowing pseudopods faded into nothingness.

"Don't be afraid," explained Tanaka, as her appearance had, if such a thing were possible, frightened the children even more than they already were, "You'll feel something strong, pulling on you, and your Mom, too... let's see... oh, thank God, she's still breathing. Don't resist... it will feel like you're being carried on the wind. My bubble will protect us. Ready?"

Wide-eyed, the two kids nodded, and were, in the next two seconds, transported – along with the somnolent adult woman – outward, along with the former science officer.

"Nobody else?" asked Jacobson, as Tanaka and her charges floated by.

"Don't sense anyone – at least nobody, who's alive," she sadly agreed.

The children quailed and struggled upon seeing the foreboding sight of the red-eyed Wolf and his hell-hounds, encased in a roaring tempest of flame; but the youngsters could go nowhere, as they were securely held by Tanaka's mind-forces.

"Don't worry," she reassured, "He's on *our* side... I believe."

The bounty-hunter, his eyes still glowing a deep, ominous scarlet, turned to look at the four within Tanaka's bubble and quipped, "Welcome to Mars, kids."

To push the merely bizarre to the edge of the surreal, Wolf's two dogs turned their heads to the sky, bayed in hound-fashion and snorted a few embers.

"*Mars?*" stammered the hippie-haired guy.

"Let's get out of here," suggested Jacobson, as they bolted out of the wreckage, about six seconds before another explosion sent its pieces flying.

Sensei's Old Flame

None of them had much time to talk, in the chaos unfolding on this part of I-22. Tanaka spent only a short while in making the unconscious woman (who, mercifully, didn't seem too badly hurt) that she had dragged from the auto-wreckage, comfortable; then, the former science officer turned her attentions to the many other crippled people – many, unfortunately, beyond even Tanaka's ability to help – who lay strewn all about.

Luckily, most of the other fires had by now been tamped down by White's icy skills, so *that* danger had been mitigated; and the scouting-trips undertaken by Boyd and the Russian not only established that no more tornadoes were on the way, but also that, happily, the highway just to the north of this point, was relatively free of traffic-jams.

However, just as Wolf and his hell-hounds finished off the last flares from the overturned tanker-truck, as the last of the trapped motorists were freed (at the cost of three sets of license-plates being discreetly "liberated" from various wrecked vehicles) and as a semblance of order was being restored, the first few of the mob of fascinated, publicity-seeking civilians from the southern tornado, began to show up at the far edge of the clearing wrought by the northern one.

"Uh-oh," grunted White, who was shaking a patina of frost from his upper-body, as he walked up to an impromptu meeting including Jacobson, Tanaka, Wolf, and the new, hippie-haired guy who they'd encountered beside the burning tanker, "Here come them gawkers."

"Only place we'll have any privacy's in the van," proposed Jacobson. "Cherie, you finished? With the wounded, I mean."

"As I'll *ever* be," answered the more-than-a-woman. "I had two of them use their communicators to call for help... not sure how long that'll take, though. I *could* do more for some of these people... but I'd likely have to hang around here for a few hours more."

"Well, for obvious reasons, *that* wouldn't be a good idea," noted the former Mars mission leader.

Seemingly by itself, the catch on the van's side-door disengaged, and the door slid to the left, opening up the entrance-way into the vehicle. A second later, with the crowd rapidly approaching from the south-east, Jacobson clambered aboard, followed in rapid succession by Tanaka, Boyd, White, Wolf and his two dogs, and, finally, the Russian.

But the hippie-haired guy stood by himself, outside.

Eventually, he said, "Well, y'all... thanks a lot for the help. Gotta get goin', I guess... *how*, I don't know – my rig's on its side, and I reckon it's gonna be a while before any tow-trucks show up. Might as well head into town on foot..."

"Get your butt *in* here," ordered Jacobson. "Another minute, and we'll be surrounded by those nosy civilians and their video-cameras."

"So?" countered the hippie-guy. "What's it to *me*? Besides – I don't *belong* with y'all, anyways. I'm sure y'all got some really, like, important government super-spy shit to do –"

He didn't understand the barrage of guffaws that came from inside the van, but was able to make out a wry comment from Boyd – or someone – to the effect of, "Boy have *you* got a wrong number there". Notwithstanding this, he saw Tanaka's shapely and somehow, supernaturally-attractive feminine figure, appearing in the van's side-doorway.

With her eyes and body dimly glowing, she gave a slight head-toss and began to hum; instantly, her exciting, empowering war-melody began to echo from raindrop to raindrop.

"This is *my* song, dear brother," she cooed, in a tone both tutoring and entrancing. "What will *yours*, sound like? Take the first step to greatness and power, by coming in here with us. Or... walk away, and regret doing that, for as long as you shall live."

What the hell? he thought. *Jaysus, I* hate *riddles such's this.*

And what's that damn other *voice, comin' from this lady – no, ain't comin' from her, she ain't* sayin' *nothin' – not in American, but it's in my head, or... somethin'... 'He is Mother noble also us one of'... WTF?*

For a few seconds, he hesitated; but then, he cast a glance over his shoulder and saw that in another five seconds or so, he'd be caught in the surging crowd, coming fast upon the van.

"Okay, fine," he muttered, stepping aboard, with no more than three seconds to spare, before – to the dismay of the throng, which immediately started to shout demands from outside and to knock loudly on the van-doors – the onlookers finally arrived.

Boyd stuck his head out of a rolled-down passenger-side window.

"Hey, everybody!" he shouted. "Back *off*, please! We're discussing some important stuff in here!"

But the pounding continued, and the van started to rock back and forth.

"Want me to give 'em a reason to stop?" growled Wolf.

The hippie-haired guy noted, with immediate consternation and apprehension, that there was that same, familiar dull red glow in the eyes of the bounty-hunter. The air-temperature seemed to jump by twenty degrees.

"Appreciate it, Wolf," parried Jacobson, "But I think Major White may be able to do it, without the same, uhh, risks to these folks outside... Devon?"

"No problem," offered White, with a slight smile. "Give 'em a Popsicle."

He stuck one arm out the driver's-side window, and immediately, even within the van, they could feel the wash of an Antarctic chill.

White kept it up for perhaps five to ten seconds, causing the vehicle to be encased in a shroud of ice and snow.

"Nothin' too thick," he said, with a bright grin. "Good'n cold, though."

They held their breath for a few seconds, and, to their encouragement, it did seem as if the madding crowd had retreated to a safe distance.

"Look," warily interjected the hippie-haired guy, "Don't mind sayin'... I'm feelin', uhh, like, a bit out of my depth, in here, with y'all doin' all this crazy-ass, 'super-hero' shit. I need some explanations, or I'm *outta* here... understand?"

"Sure," pleasantly replied Tanaka, whose war-song and other *Fire*-characteristics had abated, by now. "But perhaps we could start, with some names. I'm Cherie Tanaka, and these here are Sam Jacobson, Brent Boyd and Devon White... all of us, we're from the Mars exploration mission –"

"Damn!" interrupted the new guy. "*Thought* I marked y'all... like, from TV, I mean. *Wait* a minute... y'all's *dead* –"

"Fill you in later," continued the more-than-a-woman. "Since I have a feeling that we'll have some time, as we travel together. Now, and over here, this guy – with the two lovely little doggies that breathe fire – he's Darryl –"

"*Wolf,*" peevishly objected the bounty-hunter. "*Nobody* calls me, 'Darryl'."

"Sorry," sighed Tanaka. "'Wolf', he is. His friend there, is Misha, formerly of the Russian foreign espionage service –"

"Unfortunately," mentioned Misha with a half-smile, as he extended a handshake to the hippie-haired guy, "My commission in Mother Russia's SVR has been, 'suspended'. As the several assassins who now hunt me, will attest."

The new guy flinched a bit, upon hearing this.

"And *you* would be...?" inquired the former science officer.

"Who... *me?*" replied the hippie-haired guy.

"Umm-hmm," confirmed Tanaka. "And, while you're at it... how is it, that you've come here, and that you have the *Fire,* within you... brother?"

"What's all this talk about a 'fire', or somethin'? And I don't think we're related, no offense meant," complained the newcomer. "Oh, but since y'all asked... name's 'Donny'... Donny Wade, that is. Trucker, by profession, 'though I ain't been makin' too much money lately, what with them roadblocks up everywhere, and hardly any cargo to carry that's worth the cost of fillin' my rig. As to what I'm doin' here, well... nothin' particularly special 'bout *that...* just delivered a quarter-load down to Macon and I was headin' to Vegas – nothin' at all on this leg of the trip, though, I'll be damn near broke when I get there – got a job waitin' for me there... *if* I can make it in the next two days, which looks unlikely now that my rig's on its side, and maybe damaged beyond rollin'. Shitty luck I've been havin' these days... but no worse than most, I s'pose."

"No, brother," corrected Tanaka, with more than a figurative gleam in her eye, "In fact... today's the most lucky and important day, of your life. But what I can't figure out is, 'how did you become one of us'. Have you had any, uhh, odd *experiences*, lately, Donny?"

"What y'all *mean*, 'odd'?" he retorted. "Like, maybe, bein' ready to kiss my ass 'goodbye', with that 'comet' shit goin' down? Yeah, *that'd* do it, I guess. Good enough for y'all?"

"We've *all* had to deal with that," commented Jacobson, "Though some, uhh, more... directly, than others. Has anything else, out of the ordinary, happened to you over the past month or so, Mr. Wade?"

A suspicious look showed on the man's face. He cast a glance at the floor, then rose his head to meet their glance, and slowly offered, "Okay... I s'pose y'all's got yer own, uhh, 'issues' to deal with, kinda makes us even... so... 'long as it don't go past these walls, y'hear?"

"*Promise,*" committed the former science officer, with fingers crossed.

"Well... don't know *what* the hell's goin' on," explained the hippie-haired guy, "But I first noticed it few weeks ago... delivered a load to Wichita, headin' out of Seattle, had to detour big-time 'round Spokane – bad scene there, as I'm sure y'all heard – finally got paid, ended up in a cheap beer-can with too much time on my hands... y'understand?"

"Been there... done that, pardner," knowingly drawled Wolf. "Many times."

"Yeah," said Donny, "So... this is kinda hard to explain... stepped outside this place and had a few smokes – *know* it ain't good for me, but last few days, I dunno but can't seem to stop puffin' on 'em, I feel better'n fine when I take a drag... went back in, beer tasted good, but I wasn't gettin' the usual buzz from it – I was, like, completely sharp, even though I'd knocked back six or seven, by the time that these three guys at 'nother table, well, they'd had a few themselves, and, bottom line, they see me sittin' by myself, decide to pick a fight... and then, that's when the really *strange* stuff started to go down."

"I feel a thrill, brother," eagerly remarked Tanaka, "In waiting to see what your blessing has turned out to be."

"Huh?" stammered the newcomer. "Not readin' y'all too good, there, lady... but, anyways... they take a run at me – these is three pretty big, strappin' farm-boys, mind you, wouldn't be 'fraid of one by himself, but *three*, well, *that's* not a fair fight... is it? Should've been scared, somehow, I wasn't... but I *was* cornered, couldn't get to the door, and before I knew what was happenin', we was goin' at it. Now, I've never been too bad at brawlin' – did some tours in the Army and some middleweight boxin', few years ago – but *this*, well... what happened next, I hadn't been countin' on."

"Wager you, *they* hadn't been counting on it, either," commented Boyd, with an evil grin.

"So all of a sudden, this damn *music* starts playin', country-rock stuff, never heard the band but it was *good*, man, loved the beat... I get a clean punch at the first of 'em," continued Donny, "And would you believe I crack his jaw, right away... lucky hit, I guess, although... don't know how to describe this, but, even though I could see other folks dashin' for cover as you'd expect they'd do, these guys who was fightin' me, they were, like, movin' awfully *slow*... I could hardly *miss*... *know* it sounds crazy..."

Now it was the Russian's turn to smirk.

"Not at all, my friend," he counseled. "It will be good to have a sparring partner – one who can, ahh, 'keep up with me'."

"*Whatever,*" cautiously parried the newcomer, "So... this asshole drops, but his two bum-buddies come at me, and one of 'em's got a busted beer-bottle. Had to grab that one by the forearms – I was tryin' to keep the fuckin' thing away from me, because he hit home with it, right at the start, we was so close I couldn't dodge – and, then, the *real* weird shit goes down."

"*Do* tell us," requested an obviously-amused Misha.

"See," elaborated Donny, "This joker tries to get a grip on me, but the minute his hands touch my bare flesh, there's, like, a loud poppin' sound, then there's this bad smell and a flash of light, so bright and hot that for a second I could hardly see, neither... he yells a blue streak and staggers back, screamin' and cryin' like a baby, shoutin' some shit about 'fucker Tasered me' – of course, *that* was a lie. I noticed his hands 'n fingers had these red marks, almost like he got burnt or scalded or somethin'. Spent a bit too much time starin', I guess, because the third farm-boy, he sneaks 'round behind, and all of a sudden, he just *creams* me with this chair, brings it down right on top of my head, and I sure felt *that*... but somehow – and don't ask me how or why – when I get back to my feet, with little bits of smashed wood lyin' everywhere 'round me, and even with a pretty bad slice from that bottle, on my right arm, bleedin' all over the place... I'm not really hurtin' that much... I'm just, like, really pissed... you know?"

"Oh," mordantly observed the former Mars mission commander, "You could say, 'we know all *about*, being in such a frame of mind'."

As the others in Jacobson's team chuckled with rueful acknowledgment, Donny concluded, "Can't figure out how I didn't end up with a skull-fracture from *that* one... I turned and was fixin' to deck this fucker... then, the room lights up, like, with really bright colors I never *seen* before – yet another thing I got no clue about, but I wasn't on drugs, I *swear* it – and I start hearin' folks, like, in the back of the room, they were only speakin' normally, but they were clear as a bell – they're starin' at me as if I was a ghost or somethin'... thought I heard one or two sayin', 'look at his *eyes*'... right after *that*, this last farm-boy turns white as a sheet and he skee-daddles for the door. I left twenty bucks on the table and high-tailed it out of there, before the cops got there... don't think they got my license. That's it."

"That's everything?" inquired Boyd.

"Everything," stated the new guy. "Okay... maybe *one* more thing. 'Member how I told y'all, I got a good big gash from that beer-bottle?"

"Yeah," spoke White.

"Well... didn't pay much attention to it, in the heat of the moment... then, I was concentratin' on gettin' the rig back on the highway," noted Donny. "Got about a mile down the road and thought to myself, 'Jaysus yer stupid, man, gonna bleed half to *death*'... but when I looked at it, damn thing was bone-dry... and when I next pulled over, it was gone altogether. I can *not* explain that... should have a nice ol' duellin'-scar, where he landed home with that thing. Not to mention at least a bruise on the top of my head... nothin' there, neither."

"Hmm," observed Tanaka, her voice professorial and analytical, "Let's see... enhanced strength, *Amaiish*-based electrical and maybe heat discharge on hostile contact, rapid damage regeneration, the ability to slow enemies in physical combat, and the usual sensory enhancements; plus the war-song. I miss anything, Sam?"

"Nope... pretty good summary, I'd say," said Jacobson, with a wan smile.

"Mind tellin' me what the hell y'all talkin' about?" demanded the new guy.

"Donny," calmly answered Tanaka, "*Brother*. What I'm referring to, is the power of the alien being called the 'Destroying Angel', a.k.a. the 'Storied Watcher', a.k.a. Karéin-Mayréij... who we freed from a stone tomb on Mars, and who is our *Sensei* – that's Japanese for 'teacher', by the way – which has been granted to you, like it has been granted to us. You're no longer a member of the species, *homo sapiens*; you're now *homo superior*... like us. Congratulations – but there's *still* something I can't figure out."

"This's all Greek to me, lady," grunted the hippie-haired guy, "But I *saw* what y'all were doin' out there... okay, maybe y'all got it, but... *me*? Don't make me *laugh!* I ain't met no 'angels', 'destroyin' ones or any other such thing, for that matter. No 'aliens', neither. Just got lucky in a bar-fight, is my guess... and I s'pose I should be goin', so's I can get workin' on the rig –"

"You ain't met no 'angels' or 'aliens'... that what you're sayin', pardner?" spoke up Wolf.

"Got *that* right," agreed Donny.

"Okay," said the bounty-hunter. "Mind if I show you something?"

"No," assented the new guy, "But let's get it over with... oh... how'm I gonna get through all that snow out there?"

"Peace, *amigo,*" answered Wolf. He held up a mobile communicator, one with a small video-screen on it, fumbled with some buttons on the device for a few seconds, and then held the screen in front of Donny's face.

"Ever meet *this* cute little *señorita,* pardner?" inquired the bounty-hunter.

The hippie-haired guy studied the still-picture of a comely, golden-haired, late teenage girl with mischievous, elfin smile, dressed in track-pants, a T-shirt and a red baseball cap with the letter "A" on its front, displayed on the communicator-screen, then, slowly and hesitatingly, stated, "What if I *did?*"

"She's pretty hard to forget, once you get to know her," prodded Wolf.

"Look," defensively retorted Donny, "Y'all ain't gettin' me on no charges, if what yer plannin' to do, is call the Feds... I *know* the law, and I ain't stupid enough to take *any* of them girls, 'cross state lines... that's the *truth.*"

"What, 'girls'?" asked Tanaka, with a bemused smile.

"Come *on,* lady," replied an exasperated Donny, "You ain't been born yesterday... man gets on the road for weeks on end, needs a little *recreation...* you know?"

"I bet she was *good,*" maliciously suggested White.

"*Devon,*" tut-tutted Tanaka. "You're a married man, you know."

"Just married... not dead," said the former navigator, not missing a beat.

"Well, y'all want the *truth?*" offered the new guy.

"*Do* tell us," requested a smirking Boyd.

"Truth is," laconically noted Donny, "Picked her up on a state highway back in Idaho; she was thumbin' a ride, and boy was she glad to see me, like, as if she'd do *anythin'* to get out of the cold... guess them workin' girls was havin' a hard time gettin' tricks, what with everythin' bein' still crazy, after that 'comet' business. She was the best I *ever* had, by a country mile. And only forty bucks, too! Could've asked for five hundred, and I'd have paid it, no questions asked. Now, mind you, she *was* a bit... *strange...* like, fer instance, she had a real thick accent of one kind or another, and she was wearin' some beat-up Army surplus clothes with a lot of burn-marks on 'em... must have been in an accident or somethin', I guess. And she had this thing for fire... like, at one point I dropped a cigarette-butt in her hand, but she didn't flinch – didn't hurt her none. Honestly, it was one of the hardest things I had to do, to let her go, at that state border checkpoint... but she didn't have any ID, and I couldn't take chances... them soldier boys was awful trigger-happy back there... they still are."

He couldn't understand why, all of a sudden, the others in the van, collapsed into gales of laughter.

“A 'thing for *Fire*',” observed Tanaka, with an arched eyebrow. “I suppose you *could* say that. Ah, Mr. Wade... how does it feel to be in the history-books? Oh, and by the way... that was *my* uniform, that she was wearing. Which had been given to her, while she accompanied us in the *Infinity* spacecraft, on the way back from Mars; and it was the one she wore, when she destroyed the 'Lucifer' comet and saved this planet for utter, complete annihilation. I don't suppose you had time to say, 'thank you', after you... well, *you* know?”

“Honestly, lady,” complained Wade, “By the time we was, uhh, done, I was way too zonked to say much of anythin'. And okay, she *did* whimper' 'bout bein' scared of that comet, but hell! So was everybody... nothin odd 'bout *that*.”

“Forty... forty bucks,” barely managed Boyd. “That's *too* funny.”

“Yeah... talk about a cheap date,” muttered Jacobson. “For God's sake...”

“Well, I had her for free, Commander,” unhelpfully added Misha.

“What y'all findin' so amusin'?” demanded the perplexed trucker.

“How's it *feel*, pardner,” offered Wolf, rolling his eyes and shaking his head as he spoke, “To've been the first person on Earth, to fuck an angel?”

Rightin' The Rig

After the hilarity had died down, despite a flurry of as-yet-unanswered questions on the part of the befuddled Mr. Wade, decisions and actions on the part of Jacobson's small more-than-human party, followed in rapid fashion.

The bounty-hunter and his two dogs quickly melted a pathway through the shroud of ice and snow that White had surrounded the van with; then, Wolf, with a contrived “halo” of fire over his head to ensure that he was the focus of interest (the gambit worked doubleplusgood), played Pied Piper to the crowd, leading the onlookers off to the north of I-22, with an impressive, if carefully-restrained, *ad hoc* fireworks-display.

While this was going on, and while Misha played day-watchman inside the van, Jacobson and his three Mars mission companions crept away with Donny to the south side of the highway, where they found his 18-wheel semi-trailer, lying forlornly on its side. To the truck-driver's amazement, it proved relatively easy for the telekinetic abilities of the four more-than-human ex-astronauts to return both the tractor and trailer to upright position, at least once Donny had disengaged the lock between these two major parts of his rig.

Even better, once the cab had been re-connected to the trailer, Wade's 18-wheeler started up perfectly when he put the key to the ignition.

“Good to go?” requested Jacobson, who walked calmly to the driver's-side of the rig, so as not to attract undue attention.

“*Think* so,” confirmed Donny, his voice half-shouting over the din of the big diesel engine, “But where we goin'? Y'all gonna follow me in that van?”

"Got a better idea," proposed the former Mars mission leader. "Cargo-hold inside the trailer's empty... right?"

"Yeah," said Wade. "Don't get my next load 'till 'Vegas... 'member?"

"Works for *me,*" stated Jacobson. "Open the rear doors... I'll put the van inside, then I'll climb up into the cabin with you... make it up as we go, from there. Devon – can you ice up Donny's license-plates, please? It'll help if nobody gets a good photo of 'em, by the time the cops show up and confiscate all the communicators, *et cetera*. We'll switch them for the ones that Brent and I swiped from those wrecks, as soon as we get a safe place to stop."

"*Wait* a minute," protested the trucker, while White went to work obscuring the plates, "I hear y'all sayin', you're gonna, uhh, 'put your van', in the back?"

"Yep," answered Jacobson. "I'm a good judge of dimensions – I'm pretty sure it'll fit, with space to spare on each side. To answer your next question... there are a lot of pictures circulating by now of all of us, outside the van, but so far none that I can tell, about your rig. Best of both worlds if we simply take our vehicle inside yours."

"You'll have to let me get the loadin'-ramp set up," said Wade.

"Oh, no," demurred the former astronaut, "That won't be necessary. I'll just pick it up and deposit it, in there."

"That van gotta weigh a couple thousand *pounds!*" argued Donny.

"Your *point?*" insouciantly countered Jacobson. "Nothing I haven't done before. Now this big rig... *that*, would be a challenge. But my *van?* Easy-peasy."

The truck-driver sighed, rolled his eyes and muttered, "Whatever y'all *say*, Mister Space Man, but... where we goin', anyways? Vegas?"

"Honestly got no idea, at this point... but, likely, not there," mentioned the former Mars mission commander. "Too easy for them to track us down."

As Jacobson spoke, he noted, with suppressed alarm, the sound of sirens, far off in the distance.

Five or six miles away, he reflected. *We got, maybe, a few minutes...*

"I could argue, but I won't," grunted Donny. "Okay... get 'er aboard."

As quickly as they could, Jacobson and his three companions returned to the van, approaching it on the south side, away from where Wolf's light-show was entertaining the crowd.

With their war-songs as tamped-down as could be managed, Jacobson, White, Tanaka and Boyd pulled the van slowly over to a spot just behind Wade's 18-wheeler. Although this did attract a few curious onlookers, the fact that the ex-astronauts' hands were on their vehicle as it was being moved, successfully hid the fact that it was actually being dragged telekinetically.

At length, the former Mars mission leader simply picked up the van by a firm grip on its under-frame, gently dropped it in the truck's cargo-hold, then braced its front and rear tires with metal debris scrounged nearby.

“Any volunteers to go in there with Misha?” he inquired. “Donny's back-cabin, behind the front seats in the cab, won't hold *all* of us.”

Boyd and White raised reluctant hands and hopped aboard.

Jacobson swung the rear doors shut, secured the latch and then headed around the south side of the 18-wheeler, with Tanaka in tow. Both of them chuckled upon hearing White muttering, “Sure glad y'all decided to come in here with us, Brent my man, 'cause it's fuckin' pitch-black... 'cept for, well, them ears of yours.”

After the former Mars mission commander and his science officer clambered aboard, with the both of them ensconced in Wade's messy, beer-can and pizza-box-littered sleeping-cabin, Donny revved up the engine and the rig slowly began to move to the northwest along I-22, pulling toward the highway-shoulder while carefully navigating past omnipresent road-wreckage.

Just before the 18-wheeler was about to leave the scene entirely, it stopped, and the passenger-side door flipped open.

At first, Wolf, who had been thoroughly enjoying the spotlight – in fact, he had been giving out autographs, had made contact with one guy claiming to be a 'NeoNet publicity agent', with another offering to enter him into the next AKC show, and already had two offers of marriage – didn't notice the gesture. This was partly because the crowd surrounding him had gotten uncomfortably close, with several of the hangers-on (in particular, one shaggy-looking, retro-hippie guy who smelled like he hadn't had a bath, in six weeks) actually groping him, possibly to see if the bounty-hunter was a living, breathing, “real” being.

However, a few seconds later, thanks to the intervention of his female hell-puppy, which playfully got his attention by chewing (and burning) a silver-dollar-size hole in the bottom cuff of his denims, he did a double-take, saw Wade's tractor-trailer, and loudly announced, “Show's over for now, folks – but stay tuned, 'cause we're comin' to a White House near *you!*”

There was a disappointed groan from the audience, which would have closed in on the bounty-hunter; but they were well-deterred by the jet of fire that appeared when he turned his back, propelling him in rocket-fashion right to the 18-wheeler's open door.

The truck pulled away, gathering speed as it returned to the highway just past the wrecked tanker-trailer from which the two children and their mother, had recently been rescued. And as it did, Wolf reflexively ducked, upon seeing three ambulances, accompanied by two State Patrol cop-cars, racing past, in the other direction.

“Well,” he offered, upon again raising his head and leaning back in the passenger-seat, “Ain't it a bitch, to be famous.”

The Chief Makes Everything, Clear

It wasn't that unusual to see the Old Man – as denizens of the nomadic, usually-airborne White-House-In-Internal-Exile had universally come to call him – angry; but *this* time, he was visibly, really, hyperventilatingly, mad.

He had roared out of private sleeping-quarters in the mountain-retreat log-cabin complex without his tie done up, and, uncharacteristically, neither was his morning shave, complete. Instead, the *nouveau*-President came barreling out of the place (his face was flustered, not just from choler and the hang-over, after a few too many yesterday afternoon, but more from having to race up the two flights of stairs, below; most of the hide-out was, of course, deep underground, with only the semblance of a nondescript cabin, above), shrieking at the top of his lungs, "what the fuck's *this* – why am I *always* the last to know!"

None of the hulking, battle-geared Marine guards had really known how to respond, but luckily, the Security Adviser happened to be within earshot, and he, too, came racing out into the cold, clean mountain air.

"What's up, sir?" inquired Bezomorton.

"*I'll* tell you what's 'up'," answered the former Vice-President, his voice only slightly less agitated, as he spoke, shaking some kind of print-out – undoubtedly a bulletin or something akin – like a weapon, in the Security Adviser's direction. "Any of you bothering to pay attention to the 11 o'clock news, these days?"

Bezomorton could still smell the remnants of fine Bourbon, on the man's breath.

"Definitely, sir," hastily responded the National Security Adviser. "You mean about the Mars astronauts? We were preparing a situation analysis, for our morning briefing."

"You should have *told* me, and right away," angrily countered the *nouveau*-President. "How the fuck are we going to keep a *lid* on this? It's fucking all over the networks! I thought I was *paying* you idiots to shut down shit like this, before anybody knew about it!"

"Sir," replied Bezomorton, choosing his words carefully despite an urge to talk back, "NSC has already gone over it, but the consensus of the council was that news containment measures would likely be ineffective in this case, given the sensational nature of the story, and the number of underground media outlets to which it has propagated. We're working on an alternate strategy."

"Yeah?" challenged the former Vice-President, his beady eyes glaring. "And what would *that* be? What could you possibly *do?* You even know what I'm *talking* about, Bezomorton? Seems I've now got some swaggering jackass of a Mars astronaut, publicly demanding that I stand trial for what I don't know, and, even *better*, there's some crazy-ass talk of these 'astronauts' saving the lives of a bunch of dumb-ass motorists, who didn't have the brains to get off an Interstate, with a tornado bearing down on them. That's, of course, on top of the fact that according to the Agency, somehow, the fucking alien's still alive, and still gunning for me. *Jesus!*"

"Well, sir," stiffly responded the Security Adviser, "Obviously, we're trying to get law enforcement, the agencies and the military organized to close in on these, uhh, people, and try to round them up; but on the PR front, we're already seeding a story that these 'astronauts' – the Jacobson team, that is – actually caused all the deaths on I-22, by changing the course of these tornadoes, and making them head toward the Interstate... kind of like the one where we blamed the alien itself, for sending the comet, you know?"

Blanshard, his own military garb still in the process of being properly buttoned-up, had by now rushed up to participate in the impromptu meeting; he was only a few steps ahead of a large number of other mobile White House courtiers, who had been alerted by the commotion. As he approached, Bezomorton noted with relief that the flush in the Old Man's face was abating, somewhat.

"Sir?" cautiously inquired the Army general.

"The fucking *astronauts*," spat the *nouveau*-President. "Anderson's guys... remember? The ones he wanted to protect... right? Well?"

"They were Air Force, sir," evaded Blanshard, "So... not *my* guys... not exactly. But, uhh, yeah... we're aware of it, sir. We're on it."

"Yeah?" retorted the former Vice-President. "And just *what* have you got planned, General?"

Blanshard pursed his lips for a second, then replied, "Well, we're working with the Agency and local law enforcement, Mississippi State Troopers, that is –"

"Oh, for *Christ's* sake," bellowed the *nouveau*-President, rolling his eyes for effect. "You're planning to *arrest* them?"

"Uhh... yes, sir," uneasily mentioned Bezomorton. "After all... these people might have some very valuable intelligence... about the alien, I mean..."

"Look," complained the U.S. leader, his voice sighing with feigned exasperation, "What we have here, is a 'failure to communicate'. I've got a bunch of swell-headed little space cadets down in Dixie somewhere, and they're openly threatening the life of the President of the United States – that's *me*, by the way, since I seem to have to spell everything out for you people, in triplicate, these days. Screw the arrest, screw the trial – I want those fuckers dead, dead, *dead*, the sooner, the better – is anything unclear about that?"

"Quite clear, sir," offered a cringing Bezomorton.

"Okay," stated the *nouveau*-President, "Now... Blanshard... what you got down there? *Surely* this can't be very hard – I mean, yeah, so we had a problem with the alien itself... but *these* twirps are basically a bunch of ordinary human beings on alien steroids... right? Snipers... Army's still got lots of 'em, doesn't it? And drones... yeah, you know, those 'stealth' ones that we got airborne, all over the country – pop 'em with a quick missile and blammo! Problem solved. You want to explain why you didn't already give the firing order?"

"Well, sir," stoically answered the Army general, "According to the rules of engagement, an action like this, at least if undertaken by DoD as opposed to one of the agencies, has to be authorized directly by yourself... I'll assume that permission has just been granted. And yes, we *do* have some snipers available, but the best of them are tied up on the L.A. front, with many of the rest stuck up there on Amchitka – we can redeploy our resources, but that may take a few hours to a few days. As for the surveillance drones and the spy-balloons, it's the Agency that owns most of them, but they aren't armed; the continental U.S. is a big place, so we need a positive target fix, say within a radius of fifty miles, to get our own, lethal-capable ones deployed in good position to strike. Incidentally, even if we *had* had a few in the north Mississippi area, I think you can imagine how long they'd have survived, with the tornadoes, everywhere."

"Excuses, *excuses,* General," growled the former Vice-President. "They're starting to sound really stale, over here."

His angry, hard-eyed glower was met by Blanshard's own, battle-hardened, cold, impassive stare.

"I want a scalp," spoke up the U.S. leader. "Correction : *four* of 'em."

"Intel suggests that there may be as many as eight in the Jacobson party," unhelpfully commented Bezomorton.

"I thought there were only four – ?" replied the puzzled *nouveau*-President. "That's all of 'em that landed on Mars? Isn't it?"

"NSA's now got a few of the hi-res satellites up again, but due to the climatic conditions, and the fact that the targets were already on the move, results of a demand-scan of the area weren't very good," explained the Security Adviser. "So we've had to use some of the viral videos, as a substitute. We're trying to get a make on three others that were seen in or around the van... there's a big white Caucasian with long hair and a beard, another, shorter, clean-cut, white man who they think might be Israeli or something – both of them late 20s to mid 30s in age – and there's also a red-haired Caucasian woman, described as having a Southern accent. She had a kid, about eleven years old. But as yet we don't have names or positive IDs. We're pulling out all the stops to identify them, of course, sir."

"Don't worry too much about precision, here," icily counseled the former Vice-President, his teeth baring as he hissed out the words. "I want at *least* seven scalps, then... and if you get me eight, or nine, or ten... so much the better. People hang around with enemies of the state like these pompous little traitors, they get what they *deserve* – is that clear?"

"Very," evenly remarked the Security Adviser.

"You're dismissed, then," directed the *nouveau*-President.

Both Bezomorton and Blanshard silently nodded, then turned and slowly walked away.

Passing The Key On Myrtle Beach

The tall, clean-cut young Caucasian man reclined on a wooden beach-chair and gazed, absent-mindedly, out over the Atlantic. Holding his hand over his eyes for extra shade (over and above that afforded by the baseball-cap), he tried as hard as he could to remember his prayers, and to avoid looking over-long at the hundreds of nubile, barely-clad young female beauties, illuminated in glorious flesh-tones by the late afternoon sun, on Myrtle Beach's famous sands.

Temptation... he thought. *All part of the plan.*

But if the Lord could say "no" to the Devil... then, so can I.

Just as his resolve was about to wash away with the outgoing tide, he felt a tap on the shoulder, and reflexively turned his head.

"Oh – Brother – *so* good to –" he started, as he immediately arose from the chair; but his voice fell silent, at the sight of Brother Harold's index finger held up in cautionary fashion.

The Master certainly *did* look different, today; but then, if he had shown up in his normal, Southern-preacher business-suit and tie, he'd have stuck out around here, like the proverbial sore thumb. Instead, he was dressed in upper-middle-class golfer-garb, complete with mirror sunglasses, a white Panama hat, a short-sleeved, a blue-and-white thatch-patterned, cotton shirt, off-while semi-formal slacks, and a pair of gray-and-black loafers.

His leathery, severe face and Brylcreemed hair, however, gave him instantly away, at least to this particular acolyte.

"Mind if I pull up a chair beside you, son?" asked the elder Christian.

"Oh... of course... here, I'll get one –" stuttered Brother Martin.

"That's okay," reassured the newcomer. He took a vacant seat and reclined beside his understudy.

"Beautiful day... isn't it now?" said Brother Harold.

"The best, sir," replied the younger man, trying to keep his voice down.

"Relax, son," said the elder. "What with my new position, well, I got a security detail of them White House boys followin' me all over the place, these days; but I got 'em to wait up there on the boardwalk. They can see us, but not hear us. And anyway, sound of them ocean-waves will make it hard for any long-range mikes. Little trick I learned back in the Army, you know."

"That's *great*, sir," offered Brother Martin. "Especially as it's so dangerous for us to talk over the phone, or over the network."

"Indeed it is... indeed, it is," confirmed Brother Harold. "And because of that, I s'pose I should get right down to the point – I got some updates for you and the elect, and timin' will be *crucial*, here. You takin' notes?"

"Sure am, sir," eagerly replied the younger man, as he fumbled for his pen and notebook. "Paper copies only, of course. Is the plan still on track, sir?"

"I'd say so," remarked the Christian leader, "Although bein' where I am, now, I can see that actually deliverin' the goods, well, *that's* going to be a challenge, no doubt about it. Thing is – as you were already aware – the biggest issue was, 'how do we lure the creature out into the open, or somewhere, where I can fulfill the destiny that the Lord's put upon me –"

"Don't remind me of that, sir," interjected Brother Martin, "Because you *know* how I, and the trusted few, feel about it... we aren't going to defy the Lord, of course... but we're not looking forward to that day, none the less."

"Well, I appreciate that, son," came the fatherly acknowledgment, "But you're bang-on about it, pardon my choice of words, there," – he allowed himself a muted chuckle – "Since if Isaac could lie down on the altar before Abraham, and if our Savior Himself could go to the cross and offer up His holy blood – who am *I*, to deny my dirty, undeservin' flesh, in holy sacrifice?"

"Amen," reflexively spoke the younger man, with eyes momentarily shut.

Brother Harold looked straight ahead, nodded and continued, "Alright. Now, as to the plan... listen carefully. I've sat in on some of the President's meetin's on this 'alien' thing, and I can tell you, he's mighty angry 'bout all of it, especially what we all saw on the news, a short while ago... you know, them so-called astronauts?"

"It was only on the standard news channels for a short time, then they pulled it," noted Brother Martin, "But yes... I got a good look. I can't *believe* that this 'Jacobson' guy and the rest of them, are publicly boasting about being polluted by the touch of the Devil! 'God help their souls', is all *I* can say."

"I think it's too late for that... sympathy, I mean," stated the severe man. "They've *made* their choice, and they'll soon enough find out how nice a place Hell is – but it's *our* job, to git 'em down there, sooner rather'n later. Their arrival on the scene, however, has created an opportunity for us."

"How so, sir?" asked the acolyte, his voice telling of surprise.

"I have," elaborated Brother Harold, taking a deep breath, "Recently come into possession of information, suggestin' that these 'astronauts''s rather near and dear to the Devil-Girl's evil little heart. Kinda makes sense, if you think about it for a minute, son... after all, Satan looks after his own underlings, like – may the Lord forgive me sayin' this – He and our Savior, care for God's pure angels. What *we* need to do, is to lure these 'astronauts' – or, really, *anybody* that the Devil-Girl thinks is a member of her Satanic army – somewhere near the, uhh, package, capture 'em or otherwise keep 'em there long enough for the alien to show up, and then... God's will be done."

"A great plan, sir," offered Brother Martin, "But... how are we going to let the alien know, that its followers are in danger? Didn't you say something about it having disappeared?"

"Yeah," sighed the Christian leader. "That's true. From the briefin's I've seen, even the President's got no idea where it is now... they *thought* they got it, while it was up, Alaska way – unfortunately I can't tell you a lot 'bout that, 'need to know' sort of thing – but their error was, they didn't wait until they could see the red of its beady little hellish eyes... they had the right *idea*... they just didn't execute properly. But there *was* one very useful thing, observed from that whole episode – namely, that the Devil-Girl *will* show up, if its demonic lieutenants are threatened. Not sure how it knows, but somehow... it knows. We can turn that to our advantage."

"Hallelujah!" spoke the younger man. "So... what should we do, sir?"

"First," resumed Brother Harold. "I take it that you all have made the necessary preparations, for the package? I need the final details."

"I feel a bit, uhh, uneasy, about talking of such things, out here in the open, on a beach, sir," quavered the younger man. "You *sure* you want me to –"

"Time's short," interrupted the severe man, with a cautionary finger.

"Very well, sir," complied Brother Martin, "On your authority. We've got it down to just over 400 pounds; it's about four and a half feet long and a foot around –"

"Couldn't those boys've made it any *smaller?*" testily demanded the Christian leader. "That's big and heavy enough to get the folks who I travel with, askin' *questions*."

"We had the engineers working for almost a week as it was, sir," apologized the younger man. "It was a *tremendous* challenge for them to re-wire the firing system – we never could have done it in the first place, had it not been for Brother Lazlo, who spent twenty-six years in SAC before seeing the Light of God. But there's some good news to this as well, sir : since the device had to be dismantled and put back together anyway, it's now *much* better-shielded... we ran it against the best detectors we could find, military-issue every one, and they had to get *real* close – like within thirty feet or less – to get a clear reading. Some of the better gear will give warnings a bit further away but we have explanations for all of those."

"*Excellent,*" opined Brother Harold.

"The only thing is," cautioned the acolyte, "About the trigger – we had some technical difficulties with the re-build, that you need to know about, sir."

"What you *mean?*" demanded the elder man, his voice immediately upset.

"The original, uhh, 'item', had barometric-, radiometric-, proximity- and impact-fuses," elaborated Brother Martin, "Obviously, those are unsuitable for this, uhh, use-case... so our engineers had to bypass much of the circuitry and rig a substitute. They were only partly successful, though – the re-wire job *did* manage to disable the proximity-fuse but the others are still working, as far as they know."

"Fine... *fine,*" grumbled the Christian leader. "But how do I... *you* know?"

"Oh, well," explained the other man, "The way it works is, the device has to be prepared by plugging in a little key that's got a digital chip inside it, and turning that to the right – I brought two with me, I'll give the other one to you – then this thing locks in place and there's a delay of between six to twelve minutes, before you can turn it again, to the right, to – uhh – 'finalize' the operation. There's a small LED on the top of it whose display will change from "SAFE" to "ARMED" when it's ready for the key to be turned. Sixty to a hundred and twenty seconds afterwards – they couldn't be more precise than that, since they obviously had no way to test it – 'bang'!"

"Six to twelve *minutes?*" incredulously repeated Brother Harold. "And another two *minutes* or more? What in Tarnation? Why'd it have to be such a long delay? Why can't I just – you know – hit a button, like we've always done in the U.S. military, and –"

"They tried to explain it, sir," evaded the understudy, "There was a lot of really complicated physics-talk that I didn't understand, but from what I gathered, they had to do it that way to prevent it from firing prematurely... something like 'without the original PAL-codes, we can't be sure the primary won't pre-detonate, unless we first inert the spark-plug HE-charges and the tritium reservoir, then move them into position really slowly, until it's show-time' – I'm not sure if I remembered it right... but that's the gist of it. They said if they had more time to work, they could have made it a little – uhh – simpler."

"But what happens if nobody does that last step?" inquired Brother Harold. "Turn they key to the right the second time, I mean."

"Well," stated the understudy, "If you *don't* do the second key-turn, it'll eventually abort – it won't go off – *unless,* or so they told me – it's 'attacked' by an ABM-explosion... like, it's got some kind of defense-mechanism that can detect radiation and, uhh, 'auto-fire the primary'... whatever *that* means. The same thing will happen, by the way, with the barometric and radiometric fuses, once the key's first turned... like, it was meant to be dropped from a height, sir, so if it detects enough of an increase in air-pressure, or gets too close to the ground after having been up in the air... kaboom! They tried to disable those, but they're built-in and can't be removed without junking the entire thing. Oh – and they warned me... a side-effect is, once you prep the device, it starts giving off so much radioactivity of its own, that if you hang around, you'll be dead in less than an hour. Which I guess doesn't matter in our case... right, sir?"

"Well," muttered the elder man, with a half-sigh of resignation, "If that's what we've got to work with... *that's* what we've got to work with. Nothin' that Job or John the Baptist did was easy, either, I s'pose."

"Oh, and, sir," added Brother Martin, "Brother Lazlo and the others who did the rebuild... they're not expected to make it more than another couple of days, sir. We've given them something to dull the pain, since of course we don't dare send them to a hospital."

Brother Harold looked upward.

"Lord," he quietly spoke, "We beg Thee, in Thy endless mercy, to receive in grace, the souls of those whose duty has led to martyrdom; and make this poor, unworthy sinner, to not be afraid, when he must shortly follow in their faith-guided footsteps. In the name of the blood of Jesus, this we pray... Amen."

"A-*men,*" solemnly inveighed the Christian follower.

"Make sure they're properly buried, in hallowed ground," instructed the severe man, "And make sure it's a good deal more'n six feet, in case some of my Federal friends happen to come 'round with that detection-gear, y'understand?"

"Got it, sir," agreed Brother Martin.

“Okay,” went on Brother Harold, “Now, we need to get our orders straight here. My big issue is that obviously, I can't carry the device along with me all over the place – that'd attract *way* too much attention. Therefore, we got to find a way to get it into position, at the right time. Listen up – *carefully!*”

The younger man drew very near.

“What I've noticed,” whispered the Christian leader, wagging his finger for effect, “Is that while these Secret Service 'n Army 'n Marines that they got tailin' 'round with the Big Man's team – and, of course, that includes me, bein' as I'm now on the 'ins with him – are very, very good at keepin' things locked down in general, they aren't that good in dealin' with a fast-movin' situation... and *there's* our openin'. If we arrange things right, we'll have a window of no more than twenty minutes minimum, an hour or so at most, to get the device where we want it... and after that, there's *no* goin' back, because them boys *will* find it, sooner or later, 'specially with it bein' so big.”

The acolyte nodded in acknowledgment, as Brother Harold elaborated, “Now, there's gotta be two parts to all this : one, 'how do I let you all know that it's time to get your butts, and the cargo, over to the general area where everythin's gonna go down'; and two, 'how do I tell you exactly where, when and how, to deliver the goods to yours truly'. So here's what we're gonna do. No more than 24 hours ahead of time, you're gonna see me makin' some kind of public statement – might be in the newspapers, might be on TV, or maybe even on them pansy-ass computer-networks – 'bout 'I'm prayin' for God to give His blessin's to City X'... like, for example, if the event's in, say, Chicago, it'd be, 'I'm prayin' for the Lord to bless the Windy City'... somethin' like that. The *moment* you hear it, you get the thing loaded up and be on your way to the designated location.”

“10-4, sir,” cheerfully confirmed Brother Martin.

“But just remember – 24 hours, not a *minute* more,” advised the elder Christian. “Could be less, and could be *anywhere* in these-here Ew-Nighted States... so you're gonna *hustle* – you understand?”

“We'll get it there, intact and on time, sir,” earnestly pledged the understudy. “While we're waiting, we'll hide it somewhere right in the middle of the country, so we can get where we need to, as fast as possible. Luckily, it looks like a lot of the highway checkpoints are being dismantled... so we should be able to make good time on the Interstates.”

“Okay,” said Brother Harold, with a nod of his head. “Now, this next part's *very* important. Obviously, it wouldn't be smart for me to just phone you all, with the final delivery instructions... them spook-boys's listenin' to just about *everythin*' these days – you'd have a lot of company when you showed up, heh, heh. So what I'm gonna do, is write the instructions out in longhand, on paper, that is... and I'm gonna have them sent in a sealed envelope, to the attention of 'Mister Chris Lever' – that's you, of course – couriered to the front desk of the biggest ho-tel in that city. If there's more than one such place that could be considered the 'biggest', then I'll send it to all three of the most likely contenders. With me so far?"

"Yes, sir," echoed Brother Martin. "I'll have the fake ID made up immediately, but... 'Chris... Lever'? Any particular reason for that name, sir?"

"His first name's 'Christian' and his middle name's 'Bart'," explained the severe man. "Get the idea?"

The younger man pondered for a second, then allowed himself a half-suppressed laugh, and remarked, "Christian B. Lever... that's *inspired*, sir!"

"*Thought* you'd like it," said the Christian leader, with a smile. "Exact instructions about where, and when, and to whom, to deliver the goods, will be in the note... but there's one more thing."

"Which would be...?" inquired Brother Martin.

"How many of them little key-thingies, is there?" countered the severe man.

"Two, sir," answered the acolyte. "The primary and a backup, in case the main one stops working, for whatever reason."

"I want you to keep the other one – other'n the one you give me – on you, at all times," instructed Brother Harold. "'*Specially* when you are in the process of deliverin' the cargo."

"Sure, sir," complied Brother Martin. "But... why?"

"This is a somethin' I don't anticipate, and will do my utmost to prevent, son," explained the Christian leader, "But, if it looks like things's goin' wrong, and the government – or anyone, 'cept *our* people – might end up in physical possession of the device, or of yourself... I want you to put in that key, and turn it to the right, 'soon as you can. Then, open your Bible, fall to your knees and lift up your eyes to Heaven; start prayin', son, and don't *ever* stop. Chances are, in that scenario... I'll already be up there, waitin' to walk you home to Jesus."

A look of shock first appeared on the younger man's blanching face; but it was quickly replaced by something that might have been contemplation, or, perhaps, resignation.

"I... *see*," nervously gulped Brother Martin. "Well... I guess it's quite an honor, to even be *considered* for such a, uhh, important task, sir. I don't know what to *say*."

"We're all in this together, son," counseled the elder man, "God's Holy Warriors, each and every one – it's Jesus' blood that binds us, and which, in the end, which will redeem us... *whatever* may befall us, down here on this sullied, dirty, perverted, sin-toleratin' Earth. I'll tell you frankly – I can't *wait* to leave it behind and get up there, to stand proudly beside our Savior... and if you know what's good for you, it's the frame of mind that you'll have, too."

"Oh, uhh... certainly, sir," fumbled the younger man, "But please try to forgive me, sir – I *know* my faith's not as strong as your own... I admit that, I confess it, as God's my witness. I can only say... I hope the Lord will take away my fear, when and if the time comes... you know?

"He will... He will," came back the fatherly, reassuring answer. "Don't you worry for a *minute*, 'bout that."

"You know, sir," quietly observed Brother Martin, "This may be the last time when we meet each other... down *here*, I mean."

"Yeah... I reckon you're right," acknowledged the Christian leader. "Voice of the Lord's been tellin' me that everythin's gonna be happenin' *real* soon, now.. and that we should be joyful – not afraid – when it comes to pass."

Again, there was a pause, during which both men cast their gaze to the sea.

"A last one, for the road, sir?" hopefully asked the acolyte.

Brother Harold nodded, closed his eyes, clutched his hands in front (a gesture mimicked in perfect synchronization, by the other man), bent forward and began to pray.

"Blessed and Terrible Warrior Lord Jesus," he intoned, "These two unworthy, sinful, cowardly mortals now say their final 'goodbyes', knowin' that shortly, they'll face Thy ultimate test; make us all fearless and utterly without hesitation or weak-kneed, false feelins' of mercy, when we must strike the final blow, against the accursed lib-ral, Jew-, Muslim- and atheist-toleratin' forces of Thy damn-ed enemy, the Princess of Darkness, as he tries to pervert Thy Chosen Select Few, and lead them away from the One True Religion."

"Amen," interjected the younger man.

"And Lord, in humility, we ask for only one thing," concluded the severe man, "That, in that last moment here on Earth, as our dirty, polluted mortal flesh is about to be purified in Thy Holy Fire... we see the shining face of our Savior, beckoning us upward, to the reward that filthy sinners such as us in no way deserve – but can claim as Christians, only by the beautiful, cleansing blood of Jesus, poured over our souls in a joyful waterfall of holiness and redemption. Make us unafraid to take that final step, Lord; and we'll be Thy happy slaves and soldiers in Heaven, for ever and ever, universe without end... Amen!"

"A...*men*," added Brother Martin, his voice hesitant and almost inaudible over the waves.

"Well," remarked the Christian leader, as he rose from his beach-chair, with an air of weariness that might have genuine, "I bet it's gettin' a mite warm for them bodyguards that's waitin' for me up there in their nice black suits, and I gotta get back to the airport... I'm catchin' a mighty important flight on the most exclusive plane of all, if you get my meanin'. Time for us to be on our separate, appointed paths... and may the Lord light our way."

The younger man was now also standing; he solemnly nodded.

Brother Harold turned and began to slowly saunter off. But – as he reached a point about five feet distant – he turned, arched an eyebrow and asked, "Haven't we forgotten something?"

The understudy's face showed that "deer-in-the-headlights" look for a second or two; then, sheepishly, he reached into his left pocket, briefly put his palms together, stepped forward and offered his master a handshake.

"There it is, sir," said Brother Martin.
"God be with you, son," answered Brother Harold.
He walked away, while the younger man tried to hide the tears in his eyes.

Two Nasty Little Pets

"Ms. Chu?" barked the big, burly, crew-cut Caucasian government agent, on the other side of the door leading to the hotel-suite in which the FBI team-leader had been stuck, for the last full day. "Ms. *Chu!* Come to the door, right now... *please.*"

Nothing to do except watch the boob tube and stare at the ceiling... at 10:35 a.m. there's nothing worth watching anyway... I'm going stir-crazy in here, she thought, fastening the string on her kimono and hurrying to the portal.

So it'll be a blessing in disguise, if the let me out to do something... anything. Though that stuff about Commander Jacobson and his people, was *fascinating – for as long as I could get access to it.*

More power to you, Sam... go get 'em.

"It's me... Minnie Chu," she spoke, regarding the man through the seeing-hole, and not opening the door. "What do you want?"

"Management has a requisition for your presence, along with that of Agents Boatman and Hendricks, down in the lobby, in fifteen minutes," explained the messenger. "Pack your belongings – you won't be coming back here."

"I... uhh... fifteen *minutes?*" stammered the team-leader. "I'll barely have enough time to do my *hair!* Can I call Will and Otis –"

"They've already been told, and those are my orders," he indifferently replied. "I'll be waiting with one other agent, out in the hall."

"Well, thanks for the loads of advance notice... you're just lucky I had a shower this morning," muttered Chu, as she frantically set about to locating clothes, personal effects and paperwork, and stuffing these as rapidly as possible into her single, FBI-regulation suitcase, while making herself look presentable.

Miraculously, with precisely thirty-eight seconds left to spare, she was dressed and ready to go, in a conservative, albeit flexible and functional, dapper blue pant-suit, as well as comfortable, low-heel shoes. The make-up had been been skipped – since having met her alien-angelic companion, she'd noticed, she really didn't need any – although Chu did relent a bit elsewhere, and used a bit of rouge and eye-liner.

She opened the door, only to be confronted by the expected two hulking, male and muscular government (something in the back of her mind told the more-than-a-woman that they didn't "smell like" being FBI) agents, each of them in dark black suits.

"Let's go," said Chu.

Silently, one of the men pointed down the hall, toward the elevators.

At least initially, a similar scene played itself out at the separate hotel-rooms that accommodated Jerry Kaysten and Sylvia Abruzzio, though both of the two had handled the isolation and complete lack of response to barrages of questions, less well than had Chu, Boatman and Hendricks.

The former White House Chief of Staff had protested bitterly about not being able to contact anyone within the West Wing, but had reluctantly backed off when curtly advised by one of his handlers, "you talk too much, mister".

When he got his own fifteen-minute notice of departure, Kaysten had complied eagerly, and had actually asked if he could leave early. The request was, of course, denied, leaving him stewing for several minutes, until being ushered out into the corridor, down to the sunlit, glass-and-chrome-decorated lobby of the former hotel.

About thirty feet distant, he saw the familiar figures of Chu, Boatman and the third agent, surrounded by a group of five big, tough-looking, dark-suited government operatives. Oddly, Hendricks was standing off to one side, with one hand touching the small amulet that hung from his neck-chain. He seemed to be mumbling something apparently to himself; but he soon returned to join his compatriots.

"Hey, *Minnie!*" happily waved Kaysten, as he made ready to walk over to greet his friends. But before he could leave, he felt a strong grip on one arm.

"Stay here, until you hear otherwise from us, sir," admonished an agent. "And no talking."

By now, even the affable Jerry Kaysten was starting to be pissed off; but he had little time in which to really get angry, or to consider his next move.

Instead, just within earshot, he perceived an exciting, rapid-beat melody.

Only heard that song once or twice, back at the camp, he mused, noting with interest, an equally-nonplussed look on the faces of his FBI friends.

It's coming from above me, way *up there... what the H... Sylvia?*

All of a sudden, there was a loud crashing noise outside; it must have been around a corner, or something, because Kaysten couldn't see anything out of the ordinary, at street-level, in front of the building.

Several of those inside hurried out the front exit, disappearing to the left, while small groups of the same black-suited twerps that had been man-handling him, disappeared into the elevator, and also up the two nearest sets of stairs.

Something big's *goin' down, Jerry old boy,* he realized.

Back at the lake, didn't Her Alien-ness say something like, "either you seize the Ghost Of Fate by the shoulders, Jerr-ee... or She, will seize you"?

Maybe... it's... decision-time.

For her part, Abruzzio's dissatisfaction mostly had to do with having had to repeatedly clean up after her dog, since neither she nor the animal had been allowed outside the hotel-suite since being deposited there; "the damn room's starting to smell like a zoo – I can hardly *breathe* in here, anymore", she had repeatedly complained, to deaf ears.

She didn't tell them, of course, that her use of the "particle-shine", had managed to kill off the bacteria hiding in her pet's droppings; what was left over, after all, still had a ripe odor.

Despite this hardship and the small, confined size of her suite – just one double bed, a washroom and a single window in parallel with the hallway-door, at the far end of the room – the former JPL scientist treasured the companionship of little 'Rainbow', and the bond between master and puppy became ever-stronger, during their mutual captivity.

Finally, Abruzzio heard a loud knock on the door, and she hurried over to respond.

"Yes?" she spoke.

"You're ordered to pack your belongings and prepare to leave... fifteen-minute warning," requested a brusque, male voice.

"Well... I... okay," stammered the scientist, "It'll take a few minutes to prepare, but honestly, I'll be glad to get out of this gilded cage you've stuck us in. Listen... did you people get the traveling-case that I requested? For my puppy-dog, that is. I've got her leash, but she's become, uhh, pretty good at giving me the slip... you know? She always comes when I call, but –"

"That's not an issue, Ma'am," interrupted the voice from behind the door, "Because the animal stays behind. You'll be going without it, anyway."

"*What?*" shot back an alarmed and immediately suspicious Abruzzio. "You can't be serious – she's my *baby!* Either she goes with me, or I don't go, *period!*"

"Those are my orders, Ma'am," warned the agent in the corridor. "You're wasting time... I'd suggest you start preparing, now."

"Wait a minute, *wait* a minute," argued the more-than-a-woman. "Not only is this unfair, but... what are you going to *do* with her? Where are you taking her? When do I get to see her again?"

The puppy, which had come to sit beside her master, looked up, with big, subtly multi-spectral eyes, and let out a heartbreaking sigh.

"There, *there,* sweetie," consoled Abruzzio, as she crouched down to give the animal a motherly hug. "We ain't goin' *anywhere,* except together... right?"

'Rainbow' let out an enthusiastic "yip" and licked the scientist's cheek.

"You're not entitled to ask this kind of question," countered the agent, "But I can assure you that the dog will be kept in a secure government facility; it *may* be returned to you, once the appropriate tests have been completed. That will, of course, depend on your cooperativeness, from this point forward."

"What the hell you *mean,* 'tests'?" warily prodded Abruzzio.

I bet I know, already, she furiously mused. *Same kind as on Amchitka?*

"The people to whom I report, have noticed a few... *anomalies,* in the animal's appearance and behavior," indifferently replied the man in the corridor. "Apparently there's a concern that it may be carrying a disease, or something. Beyond that, there's nothing I can tell you. Would you open the door, please? You can dress in the washroom, but we'll need to secure the dog, prior to leaving... what's its name, if you don't mind? It will be easier to get into the cage that we've brought, if it can be called by its own name."

"'Rainbow'," breathed the scientist. "She's called... 'Rainbow'."

The door-handle shook, as if someone was trying to twist it open.

"Ms. Abruzzio," demanded the voice from outside, "We need you to open this door, right *now.*"

"This is unacceptable," shot back the scientist. "I'm requesting an escalation. Can you please either get your bosses here to talk this over with me, or, failing that, give me the phone number of someone to whom I can appeal?"

"You're wasting *time,* Ma'am," growled the voice.

"Look," stammered the more-than-a-woman, "What if Rainbow and I accompany you to wherever you want to take me, and we then discuss this with your superiors? I'm *sure* I can explain –"

"You're in preventative detention and you have no rights of escalation, or appeal, or anything, in this matter," interjected the government agent, his voice rising with obvious frustration. "I'll give you a last chance to open the door and surrender the dog, or, I must warn you, operational rules entitle me to use whatever force is necessary, to execute my orders. You have ten seconds."

What a fool I was, to think I could deal with these bastards, in good faith, thought Abruzzio.

I won't make that *mistake, again.*

She again bent down, looked the puppy right in the eyes, and noiselessly sent a message to it.

Sweetie, narrow-casted Abruzzio, *We're on our own, now... and we may have to do some bad things, that you and I both hate doing.*

Will you stay with Mommy... no matter what?

The dog let out an enthusiastic – but, somehow, also defiant – bark.

"You know," spat Abruzzio, whose eyes were now beginning to twinkle in kaleidoscopic fashion as her mind locked on to the portal's lock-handle and hinges, while flashes of energy raced beneath her under-garments, "I think you'll find that door's a lot more difficult to break open, than it appears to be. Call your masters and tell them that I'll go with you, but I'm not leaving Rainbow – *period!* You want a confrontation, mister, you'll *get* one... and it's one you'll *lose* – mark my words!"

She heard another voice – also, husky and male – further out in the corridor.

"Can't get a signal, sir," remarked the other man, "All I'm hearing is some kind of pop-rock music, or something. Must be interference... probably one of those damn pirate Neo wireless stations."

"Well, if you can't raise them on the intercom, get downstairs and tell them, we have a *situation* here," ordered the first voice. "We'll need restraint gear."

"Understood, sir," argued the second voice, in a volume low enough to have escaped human eardrums, though not those of Abruzzio, "But shouldn't I assist you, up here? I mean, she's *resisting...* protocol's two agents, for each captive –"

"It's just one damn civilian woman, and a small dog," whispered the first voice. "I can handle it. Mutt goes for me, I'll kick it into next week."

"10-4," agreed the second man.

Abruzzio heard his footsteps heading away, down the corridor.

A second later, the door shook mightily, as it had evidently been hit by a charge from the first agent. There were two or three more similar impacts, each of which would otherwise probably have sent the door crashing down into the hotel-room; but they had zero effect, since the scientist's telekinetic powers easily negated the man's increasingly angry, determined efforts.

"I'm *finished* playing games!" he bellowed. "Whatever you've got jamming the door, remove it *immediately* – or I'll *shoot* the fucking lock off!"

"Don't *do* this!" shouted Abruzzio, as she moved backward and to the side, positioning herself between the wall that separated the bathroom and the bed. "You have no *idea* who you're up against – don't make me defend myself, because it won't be *me* who ends up getting hurt... or worse!"

A queasy, horrified realization raced through her mind.

God help me, she reflected, *I might really have to unleash it, on him.*

How did things get this far out of control?

But he just said he was willing to kill me and Rainbow!

And he's just a... human, *after all!* Fuck *him!*

"Stand *aside!*" shrieked the man outside the door.

No – what are you saying, *Sylvia,* she self-castigated.

You don't do murder!

With her eyes now sparkling at full, multi-colored potency and her exciting, intricate war-song rising in psychic volume, Abruzzio braced her feet and concentrated on a spot just in front of the sealed window leading to the outside, several tens of stories above ground-level.

Studying the reflection of herself in the mirror above the desk and dresser on the opposite side of the room, the scientist began to silently pray.

Make an image of me, Fire, she implored.

Make it just like me. Over there. By the window.

And – just as the *crack-crack* sound of multiple pistol-shots, followed by the crash of the hallway-door being overpowered – assailed her ears, it... *came.*

It was all an amazed and grateful Abruzzio could do, to avoid gasping out loud, at the sight. A holograph-like figure, the exact duplicate of herself in every way (other than for being completely stationary and except for a very slight, prism-like color-blending at the edges, where the outside-light silhouetted the image), had appeared, at a spot about a foot from the inside pane of the window.

Thank God, she thought. *Rainbow – when he gets past us, when he's tied up looking at it – that's when we make our break! Get ready to run, honey!*

"On your knees – hands over your head!" growled a gruff voice from just inside the room.

I can't believe it, mused Abruzzio. *He* fell *for it!*

"Three seconds, and I *fire!*" warned the man in black.

Gripped by apprehension, the scientist tried to comply by kneeling in her unseen hiding-place, hoping that the holograph would mimic this action. But it didn't; instead, it just silently and impassively stood there.

"Three – two – one!" shrieked the agent.

Without another second of hesitation, he opened fire, and let fly with so many bullets – Abruzzio thought she counted six – that the gun must have been on semi-automatic, at the very least. But, to the spook's astonishment, each round simply passed through the mirror-image, instead impacting against the window, which shattered with the last couple of shots, ejecting glass-shards downward. A strong breeze suddenly entered the room, sending paperwork and other small items floating about.

Shaken with disbelief, the government agent slowly stepped forward, his eyes never leaving the simile, while his actual quarry, trying to make as little noise as possible, crept cautiously with her back to the bathroom-wall, hoping to get behind her assailant with a clean route to the hallway.

As the man, one hand still with his pistol at the ready, extended the other to try to make contact with the holo-image, Abruzzio, in a brief fit of absent-mindedness, allowed herself a quick look at the hallway-door, to ensure that nobody else was standing in the way. But upon doing this, the simile began to shimmer; its colors became translucent and desaturated, with the gaping, broken-open window immediately visible, behind it.

Goddamn! she furiously mused. *Oh no – he's on to me!*

As the holo-image in front of him flickered and disappeared, the agent looked over his shoulder and noticed the scientist, who was stepping backward, trying to avoid tripping on the remains of the shattered entranceway-door.

He wheeled and began to raise his gun.

A frightened Abruzzio energized her telekinesis, tossing her head slightly in a gesture intended to knock the weapon from the man's grasp; but she missed, and instead of striking her intended target, smashed a lamp near the window.

A shot went off, but somehow, it went off-mark. Again, she unleashed her mental powers, cursing her luck, as her opponent moved, and her crushing, pulverizing invisible fist, blew out what little remained of the window-frame, sending wood and drywall flittering Earthward.

Dare not turn my back, she realized. *Can't aim my power without seeing what I'm trying to hit – and if he gets a good shot, without being off-balance –*

As her assailant braced himself and was almost ready to fire again, this time with an angle that could hardly miss, given that Abruzzio was in a narrow hall with nowhere in which to dodge, both the protagonists heard a weird, high-pitched sound, halfway between a snarl and a squeak.

A half-second later, the spook, his arms waving wildly, like a crazy-man, staggered awkwardly backward, screaming in pain. Rainbow, her fangs bared in a savage way that her master had never before seen, had latched on to the man's lower right leg; and no ordinary dog-bite, was this : along with a clearly-visible, multi-colored shine coming from the animal's mouth, Abruzzio instantly felt a powerful surge of ionizing radiation.

The agonized, enraged man grabbed the puppy with both hands, and managed to rip it from his leg.

Abruzzio caught a glimpse of the wound, through a gash in his pants.

His flesh is turning gray... and it's... melting, she grimly noted.

The spook was obviously trained in hand-to-hand combat against canines, because, though still very much off balance, he now positioned his big, muscular arms, so as to break the snarling puppy's neck; it was a maneuver, the scientist assessed, would likely work, given that her pet was far from fully-grown.

Another burst of the "particle-shine", as the Storied Watcher had termed it, issued from Rainbow, washing over both the black-suited man and Abruzzio herself; the little dog, obviously terrified and fighting for its life, also peed all over its unfortunate enemy.

Dead Man Stumbling... he's got maybe a week, now, if he's "lucky"...But now that you're tied up with my little companion, she resolved, pursing her lips, *I've got a good fix on you.*

Believe me – this is an act of mercy. Much better to go quickly.

God rest your soul – and may He forgive me, for what I'm about to do...

"*Rainbow! Jump to Mommy!*" shouted the more-than-a-woman.

Almost the last thing that the man in black saw in *this* life, was the image of Sylvia Abruzzio, her eyes glowing with a weird, multi-chromatic shine, as one side of her mind took a firm grasp on the puppy – tearing little Rainbow from his hands – while the other smashed into him with the force of a pile-driver, propelling him, rocket-like, out of the window.

As his screams died away, being followed by a sickening crash after a few seconds, a crying, aghast Abruzzio knelt, holding the puppy close to her breast.

Mommy hates herself, she silently wailed, *But she can't stay here, and neither can you.*

We're on our own, now... just you, and me. And we gotta out-think them, little lady.

The former JPL scientist quickly donned her jacket and grabbed a few key belongings, dashing out of the room with Rainbow under one arm, and her purse under the other.

The lobby-cum-Agency-ingress-area descended into chaos, with black-suited, mostly Caucasian men (there were only a very few non-whites and females here, other than Chu herself), dashing about in a state of alarm.

The FBI team-leader, her two companion agents, and some distance away, Kaysten, noticed a group of five of the men in black, quickly jumping into an elevator, with two racing up the stairs on one side of the building and another three doing likewise on the other.

While Chu, Hendricks and Boatman were exchanging theories as to what had happened, with one eye on Kaysten and his "handlers" all the while, after a delay of no more than perhaps twenty more seconds, Sylvia Abruzzio, with her cute little dog held tightly, appeared out of one of the stairwells – the same one which the dark-suited agents had entered, only a trice, beforehand. She began briskly walking over to Kaysten, who was closer to the stairs than was Chu and the two other FBI agents.

"Guys," whispered Chu, "Something's... *wrong*."

"How you know that?" asked Boatman.

"I just... *know*," persisted the team-leader, pointing a finger at her head.

"Oh... I *see*," nodded the big, black agent. "Yeah. The damn *music*."

"Well I don't need anything like that," offered Hendricks. "To have guessed the same. Like... isn't it S.O.P. 'round here for us all to be escorted? But there's nobody *with* her."

Abruzzio walked, eyes straight forward except for a quick sidelong glance at the former Chief of Staff, right by Kaysten, and had made it almost to the checkpoint separating the lobby-area from the street outside, when she was challenged by one of the pasty-faced, flabby, male rent-a-cops who were manning this security station.

"Excuse me, Ma'am," he accosted, leaving a half-eaten donut down on his desk as he rose and sauntered over to the woman, "But we're on partial lock-down, here. I'll have to see your papers, before you can leave."

A pained look appeared on Abruzzio's face, as if she was faced with an unpleasant choice, or was pondering something especially difficult.

"I... think I left it up in my room," she prevaricated. "But anyway, I've got a very important, uhh, appointment uptown, in ten minutes. Can't I just –"

"I need to talk to that woman," requested Chu, to the group of three handlers who were standing uncomfortably close-by.

"No," countermanded one of the black-suits. "I don't recognize her... we'll need to check her credentials. Stay here with us."

Hendricks elbowed her, directing her attention to a bunch of Agency types at a central computer-console, a few-score feet away.

"One of those assholes just pointed at Sylvia... they're discussing something." he warned. "Minnie, this might be gettin' real hot, real soon."

"Well what do we do... just stand here, and watch 'em *beat* on her?" uneasily remarked Boatman. "We got no idea what's been goin' on, though."

"One moment," requested Chu, with an uplifted finger-gesture.

Not the full business, she resolved.

Just a little something to make him relent, if for only a minute or two.

"Sir," she purred, staring intently into the eyes of one of her escorts, "I think I can deal with this. *Please* let me try."

The man-in-black blinked his eyes and hesitated for a second, but then said, "Fine... don't leave my sight. We're watching you."

"Oh... *absolutely*," spoke Chu, as she hurried off to join Abruzzio. In no more than a few steps, she was within hailing range.

"Sylvia," started the FBI team-leader, "What's going *on*? They give you permission to leave? Where are you off to?"

A pained, hunted expression on the former scientist's face – plus something *else*, subconscious and indescribable, a shared feeling, or whatever – alerted Chu to the situation.

As she quickly looked around for signs of impending trouble, she noticed that Kaysten, off in the distance, was studying what was going on; he seemed to be looking right into Abruzzio's eyes.

They felt his *presence*.

"I've got to get *out* of here, Minnie," whispered Abruzzio, "Right *now*. Bad scene upstairs – they wanted to take Rainbow for 'experiments', and then tried to kill *me*... had to defend myself. I used a few 'tricks with mirrors', to get past them on the stairs... made it look like there was a wall in front of the puppy and me. Don't stop me, and don't let *them* try... you *know* what might happen –"

Shit, reflected an instantly-panicked Chu.

At the very least, this is going to blow our cover... and at worst –

The team-leader tried to invoke the perceived-time-slowing thing, to get a few more precious seconds to ponder next moves; but this was to no avail.

Damn thing probably only works in a fight, she thought.

Okay. Best I can come up with...

"Hey, *you*," she requested, to the gate-attendant. "Let Ms. Abruzzio go."

"On whose authority?" he challenged, his vapid chin flapping in the wind.

"On mine," she said. "Minnie Chu of the FBI. Here's my badge."

She held it up.

The man gave it only a cursory glance, shrugged and pointed his thumb at the door. Abruzzio, with the puppy firmly secured under one arm, stepped briskly outside.

The last words that Chu heard from her friend were, "Thank you *so* much, dear sister... I owe you a *billion*. I'll be in touch."

The ex-scientist disappeared around a corner to the right, while the team-leader, trying hard to maintain her composure, walked back to the vicinity of Boatman, Hendricks and the black-suited handlers shadowing them.

One of the men addressed her.

"Who was *that?* Who went out the door, I mean," he inquired, in an absent-minded tone of voice, as if asking a question whose answer should be self-evident.

"Oh... that was Professor Sylvia Abruzzio, of the Jet Propulsion Laboratory," diffidently responded Chu.

"But we're on lock-down," he argued.

"Yes?" she said, with feigned ignorance.

"Why'd he let her out, then?" the guy demanded, pointing at the door-guard.

"You'd better ask *him,*" replied Chu, "But to save you some time... it was on my authority. Sylvia has an, uhh, urgent family matter, that she needs to attend to. She promised to return when she's able."

"*What?*" exclaimed the nonplussed, immediately-blanching black-suit. "You aren't allowed to do that – you're being held yourself –"

I could make you grovel in front of me, mused the team-leader, *but I won't.*

You're not worth so much as a spark of the Fire.

"Well, I still *do* have management rank within the Bureau... but, sorry if you believe that I, uhh, exceeded my authority," disingenuously apologized Chu. "Lately, you know, things have been so... *confusing*, around here."

It was all that Hendricks could do to avoid laughing, but the mirth was quickly cut short by the sudden appearance of two of the agents who had gone upwards within the building, getting off the elevator, obviously after a trip back down.

"*Escape protocol!*" shouted one of the men, a big, hulking, bruiser of a guy. "*Agent down – shots fired!* Watch out if you go up there – we've got a Rad-Haz situation, in the fugitive's room!"

Shit, shit... ***shit!*** mentally cursed a frustrated Chu.

If Sylvia hit him with what she's capable of – "accessory to murder, after the fact" – let's see you talk your way out of that, *Minnie...*

Now, events started to happen in very rapid order. Two of the FBI field-team's minders raced over to the main console, evidently to get new orders, while pandemonium erupted, with guns being drawn and a seemingly endless supply of black-suits, running back and forth, especially toward the exits.

"Hey," exclaimed Boatman, "Lookee *there* – what the hell's Jerry *doin'* –"

The big black agent's concern was well-founded; Kaysten had broken the grasp of his own handlers and was dashing, with weirdly-accelerating speed, for the main exit. But the inside gate had already been shut, and the big glass doors that actually separated the lobby from the street, were slowly closing as well.

"Jerry!" yelled an aghast Chu, "*Stop!* They'll *shoot* you!"

Surely *he can't outrun a bullet* – can *he?* came a grim thought.

Immediately, three or four black-suiters raised their guns and, without even a warning, began to fire.

Kaysten's back, though he was making clumsy attempts to dodge, was so exposed that his assailants couldn't possibly miss. But, in fact, he reached the glass doors completely unscathed.

Just as the triggers began to be squeezed, a circular, dark-gray-and-silver *something,* about the size of a child's Hallowe'en arm-shield – giving off an odd, chiming, yet profoundly exciting war-song, one which immediately overwhelmed whatever spoken communications was going back and forth over the local wireless – appeared out of thin air in the blink of an eye, perhaps three feet above and behind the former Chief of Staff.

The saucer-like device rocketed downward, interposing itself between Kaysten and the gun-users, effortlessly deflecting all the pistol-rounds, including a hail of bullets directed against it by an increasing number of black-suits, who had added their two cents'-worth to the fusillade.

"Where the hell *she* come from?" whispered an astounded Boatman, to a bewildered shrug on the part of the third agent.

The song emitted by the little flying saucer now had a more ominous, growling tone. It began to spin and vibrate, end over end, at rapidly-increasing speed. Charges of something akin to lightening, appeared all over it.

"*Cease-fire, you idiots!*" frantically shrieked Chu, at the gun-firing spooks. "You don't have a *chance* – she'll slice you in *half,* if you keep *this* up!"

Wheeling with unnatural speed, in mid-step, she addressed the saucer, imploring, "*Vîrya I'ëà'b*'! I *know* they're bad people – but leave them to *me!* Help Jerr-ee get away!"

The flying shield held in place for a second, as if pondering its options; and, luckily, this was the same moment when the black-suits had evidently run out of ammunition, although they immediately fumbled to find spare clips. Then, to the FBI team-leader's immense relief, the saucer initiated a circular movement-pattern, gradually backing up, ever-ready to deflect and retaliate against a second attack... which, thankfully, appeared not to be forthcoming, at least for the moment.

As the guns were reluctantly being lowered, *Vîrya I'ëà'b*' wheeled so as to present her sharp edge to the building's locked, sealed outside access-doors; then, in a motion too fast for human eyes to follow, with a shower of sparks flying about, she sliced an "X" pattern in the portal, causing the resulting component pieces to come crashing floor-ward, under the influence of gravity.

Hendricks stepped out into the open and called to the flying shield.

"Hey, hun," he said, with a friendly grin, "You done *good,* there. Mom's gonna be real proud – I'll make sure to tell her, next time I see her."

A weird, chiming, but happy, sound came out of *Vîrya I'ëà'b*'.

"Agents," announced one of the black-suits – evidently a more senior one, or a leader – "Pursuit and capture protocol! Get the gas and the darts!"

Boatman spoke up, grabbing this guy by the arm, a gesture that was clearly not appreciated, judging by the scowl on the black-suited man's face.

"Listen, my friend," cautioned the black FBI agent, "You all try somethin' stupid like that, you gonna end up in a bunch of little pieces, all over the place. Minnie ain't *kiddin'* – that damn thing could slice a *skyscraper* in half, if it set its mind to so doin'. Let it *go*. Anythin' you all need to know, you can get from us."

A gruff expression showed Boatman that his counsel hadn't had much effect, but Kaysten made the debate, a moot point.

With tearful, genuine affection on his face, he looked upward at the little shield and said, "Don't mind saying... I love ya *so* much, kid. Think ya can keep up, while I try and find Auntie Sylvia?"

Another non-verbal, but clearly enthusiastic, shudder and sound, came from the flying-shield.

His final words to Chu, and the others, were, "Wolf was right! Take care of yourselves, guys. Catch me if you can... but... you *can't*."

There were a few hard-to-see flashes of the *Fire* in his body, and his war-song sounded for a split-second, before he sprinted out of the building, faster than a Maserati on Race Day.

Planning For The Big Push

The Combined U.S. Army -GrayWar bivouac, sprawled all over the pavement of the Mountain View Middle School of Beaumont, California, as well as out into and over Cougar Way, just south of the school-grounds – thereby preventing all traffic, which in fact had been roadblocked all the way out to the junction of Beaumont Avenue – was now buzzing with activity, even though up to very recently, the attention of the Army's top brass had been directed to some other, very "hush-hush" project, up Alaska way.

A young, male soldier, dressed in regulation U.S. Domestic Command fatigues, stepped quickly up into a mobile command-post, located almost in the middle of the parking-lot. The thing was at least the size of the trailer on an 18-wheeler, and, indeed, had been converted from the latter, since, after the Pakistan *débacle*, most large-scale operations had been, well, domestic.

The oppressive, oven-like heat affecting those outside was immediately offset by the pleasant interior temperature; after all, nothing less than the latest HVAC would do, given that the vehicle was crammed from stem to stern, with high-tech electronic gear.

"Close the door," complained a guy who was sitting at a video-console. "You tryin' to cool off the whole Basin, soldier?"

"Oh... sorry, sir," apologized the messenger, as he reached behind and found the door-handle, swinging it shut in one motion.

He saluted and then presented a flexible, electronic-paper manifest, to a jut-jawed, leather-faced superior officer.

"Here's the latest, sir," he offered. "As you'll notice," – he moved beside the senior officer, and pointed at a spot on the shimmering, dynamic-text display – "*This*, is where they think we should direct the drones. Quite a few engagements going on around there, more than normal... and the numbers involved seem to be *way* more than what we usually see."

"*Hmm*," mumbled the commander, "Which of the fuckers are goin' at it?"

"Some Latino gang – we're not sure exactly which one, their colors aren't familiar – and the Brotherhood," replied the enlisted-man. "Heavy casualties on both sides, but the AB'ers are standing their ground... they're fighting bitterly for each street and building – much more so than we'd have expected."

"Why?" asked the senior officer, with a slightly arched eyebrow.

"Not sure, sir," stated the understudy. "Especially as they're in what's normally, uhh, 'minority' territory... it's *puzzling*, sir, that's for sure. They're even calling in reinforcements. Battle's going back and forth, 'push-and-shove' kind of thing – Brotherhood loses a building or two, bodies lyin' all over the place, they retreat for a few hours, then counter-attack... Latinos seem to be having trouble gettin' enough foot-soldiers to hold the ground they took, and the TACINT has them playing weird Mariachi music with a rock beat – sorta like *La Bamba* on steroids – every time they go at the AB'ers... we're not sure what to make of that. From the looks of it, this Hispanic gang's short of ammo, too. Of course, that's not a problem for the Brotherhood."

"Yeah," grunted the commander. "Well... good news for us, I suppose. HQ told us to leave 'em alone – some damn political strategy – and as long as those nut-case skinheads are tied up with the taco-asses, makes *my* job easier. Position the drones here, and here – north and south... we'll make two incursions... outflank 'em. We got enough of those things to keep a continuous watch?"

"Unfortunately, sir," apologized the enlisted man, "A lot of 'em got sent back to the Midwest – that business with the 'astronauts'... you know? We should be good for most of the time, unless, of course, any of them malfunction or get shot down... which *is*, unfortunately, a possibility, since the Brotherhood has some MP-SAMs and knows how to use them. I'd advise that we should keep the track well off their turf, just in case."

"*Chrissakes*," complained the senior officer, "We're the effin' U.S. *Army*, they're a bunch of goddamn *bikers*, and we can't... okay. I suppose we got to make some allowances, since three-quarters of the grunts under my command these days, are GrayWar. Let's set up a perimeter *here* – just enough heavy weapons and strongpoints to stop the Brotherhood from retreating back east, if they start losing the fight with these Latinos – so we can keep as many as we can, for the big push. Got that?"

"I'll pass it along immediately, sir," eagerly agreed the soldier, "But as it'll have to go through both chains of command, it might take a while. I think the GrayWar Commandant for the Greater L.A. Front indicated that he'd only be ready to go, for tomorrow morning. Shall we proceed on that basis, sir?"

The commander shrugged wearily and remarked, “We'll have to... but how we're going to clear the rest of the city, with a force like *this*... don't ask *me*.”

The enlisted man saluted. He was about to exit, but then turned and sheepishly added, “Uhh... sir... one more thing...”

“Yeah?” replied the commander.

“Forgot to mention,” explained the soldier, “That just before I left for here, we were getting reports of *another* big fire-fight, this time on the south side of the city. Seems like there was a large group of Latino criminals – apparently a different gang than the one we've been talking about – that was on the run for some reason... they were in a convoy that stumbled right into Blood territory. Well, you can *imagine* what happened next. At least a city block was leveled in the battle... there were numerous, powerful explosions. Looks like this Latino gang fought to the death – 100 per cent casualties, as far as we can determine. Don't really *blame* 'em, of course... considering what'd likely happen, if they got taken prisoner. AB'ers aren't the *only* ones to be dismembering captives.”

“Does it look like this encounter has changed the military balance in that sector?” asked the senior officer, with mild interest. “Maybe... opened an avenue where we could send an incursion force, and not have it come back in body bags?”

“Hate to disappoint you, sir,” replied the soldier, “But the consensus of opinion in the tactical teams is, 'no such luck'. Bloods consolidated their positions quite rapidly... we'd likely hit the same defenses, if we probed in that area.”

“*Shit*,” muttered the commander, “Just my luck. Well... if we let 'em at each other long enough... one or the other's *bound* to get killed off. *My* problem is, I don't know how long that'll take – and my higher-ups aren't in too much of a mood to be patient. Alright... dismissed.”

“Yes sir... very good, sir,” said the junior soldier, as he again saluted and exited, making sure that the door was shut on his way out.

Dinner With Donny's In-Laws

Despite severe misgivings on the part of the man behind the driver's-wheel, by means of a circuitous route – staying off the main highways for the most-part, and with some additional stealth-tricks, courtesy of Tanaka's weirding demi-child – the Jacobson troupe had arrived at the sprawling, isolated Corn Belt farm owned by Wade's tall, wizened, elderly uncle Callum, off State Highway Ab, somewhat to the southwest of West Plains, Missouri.

It had taken all of Donny's years of experience to maneuver his big rig over the relatively tight turn needed to get off the highway, on to the quarter-mile-long driveway, leading to the farm's front-yard, and, initially, there had been considerable surprise; Wade's uncle, his weather-beaten, suntanned face squinting in disbelief, had commented, “we don't get too many 18-wheelers out here, son"; but, none the less, he had generously provided temporary accommodation, and a free meal, for the entire group.

The offer was gratefully accepted, and while the aunt and uncle were distracted by Jacobson's request for an impromptu tour of the farm, several of his fellow-travelers stole aboard the van in the truck-trailer, removing suitcases and duffel-bags of personal effects.

Even in the approaching dusk, it was easy to see that the farm-house was huge – almost the size of a full-scale mansion, with individual beds for each person – and the overhang on one side of the barn, was almost enough to hide the rig, once Wade had pulled out all the stops to cajole his uncle to move his tractor and combine, out from the same space.

"Well, what you worried about, there, son," the curious farmer had inquired, "Like, maybe, some damn bird takin' a crap on top of your truck?"

Donny had gulped uncomfortably and muttered something unconvincing about "new paint job on top of the cab", while trying to mask his nervousness about exposing his beloved in-laws – Uncle Callum and Aunt Marie were like a second father and mother, to him – to the danger of being associated with his new "friends".

It was now just after sunset, and, with a light breeze coming in over the plains, Callum had just re-entered the farm-house, after, with his nephew's assistance, returning the horses in the large, fenced-in paddock in front of the building, back to the barn; they had also, with considerable puzzlement on the farmer's part, helped Wolf deposit his two puppies in a barn-stall that, at the bounty-hunter's assistance, had been completely cleared of loose straw and anything else that was remotely inflammable.

"Why you sprayin' all that fire-retardant on the walls, son?" Callum had asked the bounty-hunter, while the latter man was calming down his dogs and coaxing them to drink from a water-dish. "Just stinkin' up the place, and you'd need a blowtorch, to burn through that wood... it's at least a half-inch thick," observed the farmer. "Stood up through every wind-storm since '19, you know."

"That right?" mordantly replied Wolf. "Well, pardner... let's just say, 'if they get too hot under the collar, you're gonna wish them walls was made of, I don't know... maybe, like, steel, or something'. Don't *think* they will, though. Got 'em settled down, I reckon."

"'Fraid I'm not followin' you," queried Uncle Callum. "How'd steel be any better? And, 'sides... they ain't too bad. Had a dog that looked like 'em, once."

"Take 'em longer," cryptically muttered the bounty-hunter, until Donny wisely jumped in and changed the subject, starting a long conversation with his uncle about local soil and weather conditions.

Now, all were seated at the farm-house dinner-table, which was covered with 'special occasion' china plates, place-mats, and silver cutlery. The table was filled to overloading with redolent, Midwest cuisine – roast beef, spuds, broccoli and cheese, fresh-from-the-oven cornbread, a garden salad picked in the last hour, and Aunt Marie's "secret recipe" succotash – and all, save Tanaka and the Russian (who respectfully remained silent, with bowed heads), repeated a standard, pre-meal Christian thanksgiving prayer.

"A-*men!*" enthusiastically concluded White. "And pass the potatoes, if y'all don't mind."

There were tears in Boyd's eyes, which he tried, clumsily, to hide; but the homesick man was quickly consoled by a tight hand-grasp on the part of Tanaka, who was sitting alongside. White also whispered something about "I know what y'all feelin', bro... but don't worry – y'all be home, real soon now."

The smiling, matronly, white-haired, almost-retirement-age Middle American hostess, happily complied with the African-American ex-astronaut's request. As she handed over the plate, she caught a glimpse of the farm-house's large, flat-screen TV display in the living-room, which was still on, with the sound of whatever was currently playing, barely audible to human ears.

"Hey there, Papa," she hectored her spouse, "You want to turn that thing off? We got *guests*, here, at the table."

"Soon as the weather report comes on," demurred Callum Wade. "Was an advisory last night... you remember. Hopin' for some rain, too – crops could sure use it. Don't want another damn summer where we got to irrigate too much... that water's costin' me a *fortune*. And I ain't gettin' any younger; since our younger son went off to college, I'm findin' that the less I have to do myself, the better. Haulin' tanks 'n spreaders out to the fields, ain't my idea of fun."

"Sure is," agreed Marie Wade. "And by the way... didn't I hear Donny say, you all came up I-22... that direction? Hope you didn't get caught up in all that bad weather they had down there. Land's Sakes, we've been havin' a lot of tornadoes 'n such, lately – thank the Lord, we haven't been hit 'round here, but I suppose it's just a matter of time."

There was an awkward silence for a few seconds. Then Jacobson, between heaping mouthfuls of roast beef, remarked, "Well, truth be told... we *did* run into some, uhh, nasty weather, down there on the Interstate; but we, uhh, were able to cope with it. 'Where there's a will, there's a way'... you know?"

"Oh, for *sure,*" agreed Aunt Marie, while Tanaka and White tried desperately to avoid laughing out loud.

"So... where you all headin' off to, folks?" inquired Callum. "'Fore you answer that – just wanted to say, you're welcome to stay here for a few days, 'least until the grand-kids show up... that's next week."

"Sure are," chimed in the farm-wife. "We could use the company. Gets kind of *lonely* out here, now that Mike's off to Truman State."

As his team looked anxiously back and forth, Jacobson again took the lead.

"Oh, well, we've just got to, ahem, make a few phone calls... then we'll be on our way," he promised. "Won't take more than a day or two. Could you pass the corn-bread, please? I just *love* that stuff... but my waistline doesn't, ha ha..."

"Oh, pshaw," gushed Marie Wade, with a wave-off gesture, "Ain't bad for you, and 'sides, you look just *fine,* there."

"*See?*" quipped Jacobson, to Tanaka, who sighed and rolled her eyes.

“'Reckon that's about right, given that Donny here's gotta get back on the road... keep earnin' money, that is,” observed Callum Wade. “Say... I never *did* find out what line of work you folks is in?”

Three of the travelers answered at once.

“Scientist,” said Tanaka.

“Air Force,” said Boyd.

“Catchin' bail-jumpers,” said Wolf.

As the puzzled look showed on the farmer's face, Jacobson intervened.

“We've actually got a lot of different backgrounds,” claimed the former Mars mission commander. “But right now, we're on a, uhh, business trip. Lobbying the government – oops, shouldn't have said that, probably a dirty word around here – but, we're trying to get the government to do a few things, on behalf of our, uhh, boss.”

“Shouldn't that be, '*not* do a few things', Sam?” unhelpfully asked Tanaka.

“Yeah... I suppose,” grudgingly confirmed Jacobson.

“This 'boss' of yours... anybody I'd know?” pressed Callum Wade. “Like, one of them big businessmen, who's always jackin' up the price of seed?”

“Oh, none of them,” hastily reassured Boyd. “And... it's a 'she', actually.”

“Now you all got me right confused,” politely mentioned Marie Wade. “So what kind of 'business', is this? Better not be nothin' *illegal* – we don't go for that kind of stuff here, you know?”

“Well,” drawled the bounty-hunter, leaning back in his chair and flexing his biceps while so doing, “I 'spose you could say, lady, that nothin' we're doin' – or fixin' to do – should be 'illegal'... that is, if you assume that just tryin' to stay alive, without a bullet comin' our way at any particular time of day, shouldn't be against the law –”

“Oh for *God's* sake, Wolf,” complained a visibly-upset Tanaka, “We *promised* Donny that we wouldn't *scare* these people! Can't you just keep that big trap of yours *shut*, for once?”

Wolf shrugged nonchalantly, as the farmer and his wife shared a concerned glance.

“Mind passin' the corn-bread?” interjected White, with a wide, faked smile.

“Okay, look, Uncle Callum,” spoke Donny, “The truth is, these people, and me... we're sorta on the run from the government –”

“Whoa,” exclaimed the farmer. “Son, you never told us *nothin'* 'bout –”

“I can *explain*,” stammered the truck-driver. “See, it was –”

“You may not have to,” interrupted Misha, who had up to now been quietly consuming large helpings of succotash, potatoes and salad. “Look at the television.”

Multiple eye-pairs implemented the suggestion and turned their attention to the screen in the next room. A second or two later, all of the Jacobson party mumbled a few polite words to the effect of “may I be excused”; the more-than-humans hurried into the living-room, to see what was being presented.

The local Disney News affiliate, KOZK-TV Springfield, had interrupted its nightly news lead lineup, in favor of a “Special News Bulletin”, and what was displayed in vivid, high-definition, pseudo-3D color (albeit, not to the same standards as regular network fare : this had clearly been shot by a hand-cam, or something similar), was immediately familiar to the travelers; it was from the northernmost, second stretch of I-22, in which they'd encountered Donny.

“Ladies and gentlemen,” intoned the blow-dried, business-suited male announcer, “This is Bart Westlake of KOZK Disney News, bringing you a special, late-breaking news story. Tonight, we have some extraordinary footage from part of Interstate 22, in Mississippi. What you're seeing now,” – he briefly turned his head and pointed at the video-images, rolling behind him – “Is an astonishing scene that apparently unfolded earlier today, at a place on the highway that had just been crossed by a Class 3 or 4 tornado. As you can see,” – the camera seemed to pan to the right, stopping with a clear line-of-sight to Wolf's back – “In the wake of the tornado, the area was visited by a group of individuals with some, ahem, unusual characteristics.”

The screen-display now showed the bounty-hunter's fire-and-light show, as Callum and Marie Wade got up and joined the television-viewers.

“The previously-unknown group of emergency-assistance workers, the number of whom has variously been set by onlookers, as being between three and ten,” elaborated the newscaster, “Is said to have appeared 'out of nowhere', and then to have disappeared, just as quickly. Eyewitness accounts have these individuals – two women and several more men – as having rescued and saved the lives of many of the victims of the tornado, which had passed through this part of I-22 a few minutes before, causing immense damage to vehicles trapped on the highway at the time. According to these accounts, the mysterious group of Good Samaritans are said to have 'extinguished a huge and dangerous gas-fire, with their bare hands', and also to have kept the badly-injured alive, 'just with a kiss'. Obviously, KOZK News has been unable to independently verify these rather improbable claims.”

“Thank God,” muttered Boyd. “Finally, some *good* press, for a change.”

The farmer and his wife shared another perplexed side-glance.

“And,” continued the announcer, while the background cut to a completely different scene, showing a raincoat-bedecked news reporter standing on what appeared to be a sidewalk in the downtown of a small-size city, with a microphone in the face of a sodden, baseball-cap-toting average-man, “We have some reports of even *more* incredible events today, further south on I-22, where a different group of motorists, were menaced by a second tornado from today's storm system. Ralph? What you got for us?”

“Hi, Bart,” responded the reporter, “I'm here today on the streets of Pine Bluff, Arkansas, with Mr. Frank Shepherd – do I have that right? Yes, good, I do – of Mabelvale. Mr. Shepherd, I understand that you've got something to tell us, about the amazing events that allegedly occurred on I-22, earlier today?”

"Yeah," said the man – an unkempt, 'white trash' type of guy – as he awkwardly shuffled his feet, looking down and obviously trying to avoid fully showing his face to the camera, "I seen it."

"And what did you see, Mr. Shepherd," persisted the reporter.

"Well, I'm not shore," uneasily responded the interviewee. "But I'm darn glad whatever it was... happened. See, I's drivin' my pickup truck up I-22, comin' home, Little Rock way, after landscapin' job down south... and traffic stops dead, all jammed up. Get out of th' truck, look up and there's this scary big tornado bearin' down, but there's nowhere really to run, no cover for miles, and it's comin' wicked fast, anyways. So along with a lot of other folks 'round there, I'm sayin' my prayers, and then... it happens."

"*What* happens, Mr. Shepherd?" pressed the man with the microphone.

Again, Tanaka whispered, this time to White.

"Devon," she asked, "Do you hear a phone ringing? Far-off?"

"Sort of," he replied, *sotto voce*. "Must be Mars ears playin' tricks on us. Like maybe some phone in a farm-house, a mile from here, or somethin'?"

"Yeah," agreed the more-than-woman, keeping her eye on the TV.

"Like I said, I'm not shore," parried the guy on the street, "But, see... all of a sudden, there's, like, this thing – it's shiny, like a flyin' saucer or somethin', it just shoots up from the ground, ahead of me, and there's this weird noise, or singin', I guess, kinda like one of them rock bands, but I ain't never heard it before – and then, this flyin' saucer starts whizzin' 'round the tornado... a few seconds later, or minutes, I don't remember, there's this big white cloud that just covers that twister from top to bottom... and a few seconds after that, the tornado just... *vanishes*, that's the best way I can put it."

"What do you mean, 'vanishes', Mr. Shepherd?" incredulously demanded the interviewer. "A tornado can't just 'vanish', you know."

Boyd whispered to Wolf, "You hear a chime, an alarm, or something?"

The bounty-hunter shook his head.

"Well, *this* one did," argued the baseball-cap guy on television. "Just, 'poof', and like it was never there in the first place; stuff started fallin' out of the sky, must have been carried up there when it was, like, you know, bein' carried on the winds. I just 'bout got hit by a 2-by-4 that landed two feet from where I was. Oh... 'cept, there was a blast of real nasty cold air, for a minute or two, felt like January out here on the Plains... and would you believe there was snow all over the place?"

"*Snow?* Are you sure, sir? At *this* time of the year?" disputed the reporter.

White looked down at his feet, hoping that the Wades would miss his grin.

Tanaka whispered to Jacobson, "Sam, I'm *sure* I'm hearing a phone ringing. Sounds like it's upstairs, somewhere."

The former Mars mission commander nodded in agreement.

"I'm only tellin' you what I saw, mister," repeated the TV interviewee. "I *know* it don't make no sense... but I *saw* it, and I ain't the only one – *hunderds* of other folks did, too. What I *can* tell you, without the slightest doubt, is that if that thing – whatever the hell it was – hadn't, like, shut down that twister, there'd be a lot of dead people, includin', quite possibly, me, on that part of I-22, right now... it was goin' right for the highway. So I'd like to say, to whoever, or whatever, did that... thank you. I *owe* you, and I'd love to say it in person."

"Maybe you'll get a chance to do that," proudly remarked Tanaka.

White gave her a high-five.

"So that's it," concluded the field-reporter, "Looks like something quite unusual, occurred down on I-22, earlier today; and, from reports that are coming in, it appears that the highway is now closed for much of the New Albany, Mississippi, area, as government authorities undertake an investigation; traffic's being re-routed at Tupelo. That's all for now – I'm Ralph Kravchuk for KOZK News. Bart, back to you."

The TV display returned to the announcer.

"It should be noted, ladies and gentlemen," smoothly spoke the anchorman, "That KOZK News has, as yet, been unable to verify these claims, so we're making no guarantees as to whether they're true, or just some kind of hoax made in very poor taste. None the less, we've assembled an expert panel here in the studio, to discuss what we've seen and offer some possible explanations. With me today, are –"

Suddenly, the picture and audio disappeared, leaving nothing but a silent, blue background.

"Not *again!*" complained an obviously frustrated Marie Wade. "Callum dear, didn't you say the repairman had *fixed* that blessed thing?"

"Sure did," answered the farmer. "Cost us two hundred bucks, remember?"

"I don't think that's the problem here," gently corrected Boyd. "It's just lost the signal... that's all. No doubt, because the government threw a switch, somewhere. Somebody higher up, doesn't want this story being told. I'm surprised we got to see so much of it, before they were able to squelch it."

Just as abruptly as it had disappeared, the KOZK video-feed re-appeared, but this time, instead of a news-show, the channel appeared to be in the middle of coverage of a Minor League baseball game.

"Where'd the news go?" asked a befuddled Callum Wade.

"Welcome to your friendly U.S. Federal Government," wryly noted Boyd.

"Listen, Mr. Wade," interjected Tanaka, "Have you got another phone, maybe a mobile communicator, around here? Because I'm hearing ringing –"

"Nope," answered the farmer, shaking his head. "Just the one we've always had... although they made us 'upgrade' it two years ago, not sure why. I mostly don't go for all this new-fangled technical stuff, like televisions that switch the show without askin' me."

"I'm hearin' it too," commented Donny. "Sounds like upstairs... other side of the house, maybe?"

He rushed up the stairs, and, after a few seconds, called down to the farm-house's main level.

"Yeah – it's comin' from Mike's room, and it's a phone, alright," called the trucker, "But Mr. Bounty Hunter's stuff is in there, and it sounds like it's in his coat or somethin'. Okay if I grab it? They been ringin' for *minutes,* now."

"Huh?" stammered Wolf. "I ain't got no communicator or nothin', I lost mine in... uhh... well. Here, I'll help you look for it."

He, too, sprinted up the stairs.

After another two or three seconds, it sounded as if the bounty-hunter was talking to some as-yet-unknown, third-party. Then he appeared, walking slowly down the staircase, with a small, box-like thing held to one ear.

"Yeah?" he mumbled. "Well, I don't know you from *shit, amigo,* and –"

"*Wolf!*" shouted an alarmed Boyd, "What the hell you *doing?* They can *trace* us with something like that!"

The bounty-hunter held up a hand in a "calm down" gesture.

"Peace, pardner," he countered, "Dude says it's on a 'secured channel', or something. You want to talk to him? No video, but it's got speaker on it – this button here – I *swear,* I ain't never seen this thing before. Got no idea how it got into the pocket on my jacket."

"What we got to *lose,*" dejectedly sighed White. "Might as well find out where them Agency pussies want us to show up, with a big bulls-eye, on our backs... hey, want to cook up a tornado or two, Wolf my man? I'll shut it down soon as their asses off to Kansas, don't you know."

The bounty-hunter winked at the black ex-astronaut and held up a thumb.

Well, thank God, at least they're getting along with each other, thought Jacobson.

"Here," he instructed, "Hold it up where we can all hear it, and put it on speaker-phone."

With a shrug, Wolf complied, and the rest of them could see that, unusually for one of these new-fangled devices, there indeed, was no video display – not even the default still-picture – showing on the screen of the communicator. The sound part of it was, however, operational, even though the voice that they now heard, had a weird, metallic echo, as if it was being digitally modified.

"Hello?" spoke the voice, "Am I talkin' to, like, the astronauts, man?"

"Yeah, those'd be them," laconically drawled the bounty-hunter, while several of the former space expedition, cringed.

"This is Commander Sam Jacobson," evenly replied the Mars mission leader. "Who are *you?* I'm very concerned that this call may be intercepted, as we speak, so if you don't properly identify yourself, I'm going to drop the connection and throw away this phone, in a very short time from now. Oh, and while you're at it... can you explain where the device came from, in the first place? We have no recollection of having acquired it."

"Hey, *hey,* man," hastily answered the metallic, remote, voice, "Chill out! I'm – we're – on your *side...* you gotta *believe* that... let me *explain.*"

"Go ahead – make it fast," demanded Jacobson.

"Okay... well, you see, man," elaborated the mysterious other, "My handle's 'Buddha-Boy', and, like, I'm one of the sys-ops of the NRA –"

"Huh?" interjected a confused White, "Y'all with them gun-nuts? What y'all doin' callin' us on some damn mobile communicator? Why don't y'all just send us one of them membership invites that's good for six free clips, or somethin'?"

"No, *no,* man," protested the remote voice, "Not the 'National Rifle Association'... the 'Neo-Net Resistance Army', man... that's us –"

"I *heard* of those guys," whispered Boyd, to Tanaka. "Bunch of shaggy, undisciplined, counter-culture hackers and cyber-punks... government's been trying to shut 'em down for *years,* with little success."

The more-than-a-woman nodded, knowingly.

"Okay... *stay* with me for a minute, man," continued the remote voice. "First off, this channel's got our best, custom megabit symmetric on it – we're good for a half-hour, at least, before the Man can break the key... and even then, he'd have to notice us, and we're on a side-steago band, we're reverse-endian, quantum-muxed into the slack bits, within the Weather Service's streaming bulletins –"

"*Ingenious,*" commented a wryly smiling Misha. "I shall have to tell SVR of this technique – one minute before they kill me, that is."

"Yeah, I get it... I had to take basic crypto for the Mars mission... so, assuming I *believe* you," countered Jacobson, "Which, needless to say, I have every reason *not* to... what do you want from us?"

"Papa... I don't think these people are just a bunch of businessmen," whispered Marie Wade, to her husband.

Tanaka took hold of the woman's hand, looked up at her and whispered, "No, Mrs. Wade... we're not. We're followers of an... *angel.*"

"So here's the thing, man," explained the hacker-dude, "See, we been following what's been going down with that crazy-sexy 'angel' lady that you all dug up on Mars, and then with you guys, when you surfaced down in Florida – lucky hit there, man, one of our feet on the street just happened to notice you – since all that shit went down at Rushmore, and then, the Washington Monument... hey, did she fuck the Man around, or *what*?"

"That was *my* idea, to get her to do that, *amigo,*" proudly remarked Wolf. "Well... the Rushmore part of it, anyway. I told her she should have written, 'Fuck You, Mr. President' –"

"Can we stick to the *subject,* please?" requested an irritated Jacobson.

"Whatever," shrugged the bounty-hunter, as the remote voice went on, "*Awesome*, man! But, anyway... see, like, we tried to keep track of you dudes, and dudettes, up from Florida, but it was wicked *hard,* man... you sure had us foxed! But eventually, one of our mobile LAN repeater mules – got 'em all over the country, you know, keeps the Man from zeroing in on a fixed modem – he happened to be on the scene when that 'tornado' shit went down... he took a mucho big chance, in droppin' his personal, modded 'cator into that big dude's coat... you know, the one with that freakin' fire show –"

"Okay," said Jacobson, "That explains how we got the damn thing. But you *still* haven't said what you want of us. I don't know if you were aware of this, but it's extremely dangerous for you to be talking to, or associating with, us – the government is *after* us, and we've already survived numerous assassination attempts, up to and including having a hydrogen bomb detonated against us, at very close range. If you have any brains, you'll forget about us and go back to hacking celebrity bathroom-cameras... or whatever it is that you do."

"We know about most of that... a *H-Bomb*, man? What the *fuck?* How'd you –" incredulously replied the remote voice.

"Let's just say," confidently purred Jacobson, "That we're nothing like the group of human astronauts, who left for Mars, many months ago; we're now far more powerful than any other mortal men. We're on a mission to make the President pay for the crimes that he's engineered... and woe betide anyone who gets in our way. You can certainly have your friends spread *that* message. Anything else, before I hang up?"

"Wait, *wait*, man!" anxiously pleaded the hacker-dude.

"Sam," intervened Tanaka, "We ought to listen to what he has to say. We need all the friends we can *get*, right now."

"And what if this guy is really CIA, trying to keep us on the line, long enough to get a good enough fix to drop a bomb on?" retorted the commander.

"Okay, *look*, man," stammered the remote voice, "I know you're busy, so I'll give it to you straight – we got a business proposition for you... *capiche?*"

"Go ahead," neutrally allowed Jacobson.

"See, the way we figure it, from listening to the tapes of what you said down on the highway – those are all over the Darknet, by the way," offered the hacker-guy, "Is that you dudes are, like you said, like, wicked 'powerful', or something... but you gotta keep the Man guessing, you don't want to take him on, like, all at once, or whatever – you're in consciousness-raising mode, know what I mean?"

"Yeah... that'd be fair," interjected Boyd. "Without getting into details, we're pretty confident that we can defeat any small-to-medium-scale confrontation with the government. It's the larger-scale ones that we're worried about... especially because of potential collateral damage."

"*Perfect*, man," agreed the remote voice. "So what you need, is a way you can reach a lot of people... tell 'em your story, you know? You sure as fuck aren't gonna do it on the MSM – the Man's got *that* locked down, six ways to Sunday. But we're all *over* the place... we got drops in just about every neighborhood. We can get your message out any time, any day. And with that box you got in your hand, you can chat with me, or any of the other NRA sys-ops, any time you want... 'long as you got the key... which is, BTW, your voice, and a few other things we got in our 'secret sauce'. You with me, man?"

"Understood," said Jacobson. "And what do *you* get out of all this?"

"What do we get *out* of it..." sighed the obviously frustrated hacker-guy, his voice rising with emotion, as he spoke. "What do we... okay. For better part of thirty years, yours truly, and folks like yours truly, we've been fighting a fuckin' endless war, first over the old Net, and now over Neo, tryin' to get the voice of the people, back into this damn country. For all that time, it's been a pretty thankless struggle, since the Man's got all the money, and he owns the physical level, *et cetera*... all we've got to fight back with, is our wits, being fast on our feet, and being smarter than him... but it's been a hard fight, man, and we've lost some good friends – they just 'disappeared'... you know?"

"Yeah," softly commented Tanaka, "We sure *do*. Sam... we've *got* to help these people."

"Just a minute," cautioned Jacobson. "I'm making no promises... go ahead."

"Let me lay it on the line, man," forthrightly proposed the hacker-dude, "And if you all don't want to take us up on it, that's your decision... it's the last you'll hear from us, but in that case, I'd ask you to squash up the box you're now holding... it's got some custom mods on it."

"Is it hardened against EMP?" asked Boyd.

"Not really... it's got a bit of shielding, but, like, just Tempest-grade," stated the remote voice. "Why?"

"Oh... don't worry about it," said the former Mars pilot, with an evil grin. "In that case, I'm sure we can render it... *non-functional*... if we have to."

"Excellent, man," answered the hacker-guy. "So here's the deal : we got the comms, but we got no, uhh, firepower – we're basically zero-level, on the physical side; whereas, *you* dudes, you got the magic-powers act, down –"

"*Amaiish*," corrected Tanaka. "Alternatively known of as, the '*Fire*'. It's the Storied Watcher's power, now invested in us. Nothing 'magical' about it."

"Fuckin' *ay!*" gushed the remote voice. "Can't *wait* to meet you, lady – never met a super-hero, I'll show you my comic-books – but where was I... we figure that you guys need a safe way to communicate... we can give you that. Marriage made in *heaven*, man. What you *say?*"

Jacobson looked at Tanaka and, his lips never moving, sent to her,

I don't know about this, Cherie... it sounds like a trap. Exactly the kind of thing that the Agency would try to pull.

Maybe, she returned. *But the risk can be managed... right?*

"Understood," said the former Mars mission commander. "I need to put you on hold, for a second – that the orange button, here on the hand-set?"

"Yeah," confirmed the hacker-guy, "But not too long... okay? Dead air screws up the key-randomizer. Makes it easier for the Man to break in."

Jacobson hit the aforesaid button, and the hacker's voice was replaced with a low, buzzing sound.

"I'm prepared to give him a chance – one chance – to prove that he's legit," offered the commander. "Does anyone here, object?"

"Yeah," interjected Callum Wade. "*I* do. What the *hell's* goin' *on*, here?"

Jacobson held up a hand in the farmer's direction, and, as politely as he could manage, deferred, “Later – don't blame you for being a bit, ahh, 'concerned', and, frankly, sir, the less you know, probably, the better-off you'll be. Any of the rest of you want to veto the idea... that is, of us interacting with this 'NRA' outfit? I don't have to point out what might happen, if we let them know where we are, and they're either a front for the Agency... or have had their communications, intercepted.”

“For what it is worth, Captain,” offered Misha, “SVR evaluated the group, some time ago... we found their security to be highly effective. We even used some of their covert channels, to, uhh, get information back to Mother Russia. Please do not mention that, to our friend at the other end of this conversation.”

As Boyd muttered something and ruefully shook his head, there appeared to be no other commentary, so Jacobson re-enabled the voice-box.

“Okay,” he stated, addressing the mysterious guy at the other end. “Here's the deal. We'll go with you – once – as a test... then, evaluate results. If things work out as you've described, then we'll continue the relationship. If not... well, in that case, there's something you'd better understand, right up front.”

“Oh... *sure*, man,” quickly replied the hacker-guy, “What'd *that* be?”

“What I mean,” icily explained the former Mars commander, “Is, we're on a mission to get the President – at least, that jerk who's calling himself 'the President', even though he doesn't legitimately deserve that title – and, 'heaven help anyone, who stands in our way'. Double-cross us... and *you'll* be next on the list. Got that?”

The more-than-human ears of Tanaka, Donny, Boyd, White, Misha, Wolf and Jacobson, heard a “gulp” at the other end, though this subtle sound was lost on the farmer and his wife.

Eventually, though, everyone heard the remote voice say, “That's... uhh... cool, man... we've been livin' on the edge for a long time, you know? Don't think you could track us, anyway... but you won't have to – I *promise*, man. If it's worth your knowing, the NRA Council's already met to approve this whole thing, and it was a close vote – a lot of dudes were worryin' that you might take us down with you... but in the end, we figured that we're never gonna have a chance like this – fight the Man on anything like even terms, I mean – again. So we're in it with all our chips... let 'em fall where they may.”

“Fair enough,” allowed Jacobson.

He turned to the rest of the local crowd.

“Anything else you want to say?” he asked.

“Yes,” spoke up Tanaka, as she somehow directed her voice in an unnaturally-accurate manner, right at the communicator-microphone. “And that is... 'thanks, dear friend'. My name is 'Cherie', and my title, of which I'm very proud, is 'First Of The Fire'. When this is all over, I'll introduce you to Karéin-Mayréij herself... and when I do... be prepared for a life-altering experience.”

“Uhh... that's great, lady... but what you mean, by –”

"You'll find out," purred Tanaka, after which Jacobson stoically continued, "Anyone else?"

"Just one thing," requested Misha.

"Yeah?" impatiently queried Jacobson.

"I would like to ask our friend on the line, if it would be possible for him to pass a message to the Russian Embassy in Washington, D.C., on my behalf," said the former spy.

"Uhh... *maybe,*" uneasily responded the hacker-dude. "The Man's got every feed goin' in or out of there, real-timed 'till the cows come home... it'd be risky, and we'd have to burn a one-time channel. What you want 'em to know?"

"My name is 'Mikhail'," neutrally explained Misha, "And tell them that if they have a SVR liquidation team following me – as no doubt they *do* – they should cancel that operation. All that will come of it, is the needless deaths of some good agents, with whom I have worked in the past. A spy never has true 'friends', of course; but I had liked and respected those of whom I am thinking... I would not want them to be harmed, if I, or my new, super-human 'brothers' and 'sisters', are forced to defend ourselves. Can you tell them that, please?"

"And," interjected Tanaka, "That goes also for Sergei Chkalov, wherever he is now. Tell the Russian government that if they try anything stupid against him, like the President's done to us... we'll come looking for *them,* next."

"We'll... *whaat?*" protested White. "Why don't y'all just declare war on the whole United Nations, Professor? Just to be *consistent,* I mean."

"If I *have* to," answered the former Mars science officer, with a far-away, steely look in her eyes. "After all... us space-aliens got to look out for each other... right?"

"I can see it's gonna be, uhh, a *trip,* workin' with you guys," commented the hacker-dude.

"You don't know the *half* of it, son," offered Jacobson. "Listen – we've already been on the line, quite a long time. We'll have to hold other discussions, until later... understood?"

"Roger that," agreed the remote voice. "We're gettin' near key-exhaustion-time. Just to be on the safe side, try not to call us again in less than 24 hours, unless it's an emergency – and don't do it at regular intervals, that makes it too easy for the Man to read our pattern. Talk to you soon, man... and, 'good luck'. It ain't just *us* who's rootin' for you – there's a lot of folks out there who are fuckin' fed up with the way things are... they're countin' on you to rattle a few cages... you know?"

"You can be sure," responded the former Mars commander, "That we'll be doing a bit more, than 'rattling' them. Jacobson over and out."

He pushed a button and the session appeared to terminate. Then he turned to Callum and Marie Wade, winced a bit, and sheepishly remarked,

"I guess we have some *explaining* to do, sir."

Four On Their Own, In Steeltown

"Jerry! *Jerry!*" shouted a mostly-familiar, anxious-sounding female voice, from somewhere behind him, two blocks from the glass-encased prison that he had just exited; but Kaysten was going so fast, that wherever the call had come from, he had already raced past.

He had been going purely on instinct, following the direction in which he had seen Abruzzio head off, and had almost caused a car-accident, while streaking across the intersection, to the right of the converted former hotel.

Though he knew that he could easily do much, *much* better, the White House Chief of Staff had been consciously trying to hold his velocity to something as close as possible – as far as he could guesstimate – to the maximum speed of the most proficient human sprinter. Also, it seemed that the annoying, "in-the-back-of-your-head" war-music, could be suppressed, as long as he didn't push his bionic gas-pedal, too far down.

So, when Kaysten stopped for a second or two, powering his enhanced senses to detect the slightest signs of pursuit, he got only a few strange looks from people within the downtown Pittsburgh, just-before-lunch-hour crowd.

Damn, he mused, *these 'Mars eyes' sure* do *come in handy. I see different, new stuff when it's bright and sunny outside – like today – compared to when it's pitch-dark. She sure wasn't kidding about "how much you were missing"...*

"*Jerry!*" persisted the voice. "It's me – Sylvia! *Behind* you, in the alley!"

He took a few reluctant steps, not more than six or seven, backward, and peered down a back-alley, one that had loading-docks at regular intervals, all the way to its other, north-east end, along with a sheer, brick wall extending as far up as the eye could see, on the side opposite the docks.

But other than for a couple of bored-looking workmen who were unloading food-crates of some sort, at one of the loading-docks, there was precisely... *nothing,* in the alley.

Kaysten rubbed his eyes and tried to "concentrate" as his alien mentor had so patiently tried to instruct him to do, back in that uncomfortable, grubby Canadian campground.

He blinked, again and again. There still was nothing, except for a slight discoloration – no more than something looking a tiny bit "off" – perhaps, a very slight shimmer in that weird, 'more-than-purple' tint that he'd lately taken to being able to see – in a part of the brick-wall standing about a foot out from its building, butting up against the nearest of the unoccupied loading-docks.

"Sylvia?" he spoke, trying to hold down his voice.

Kaysten felt a shove against his left shoulder, turned his head to catch a brief glimpse of the Storied Watcher's animate arm-buckler, which then "blinked" again out of view, only to reappear, a second or two later, over by the "not-quite-right" wall-section.

"*Vîrya I'ëà'b'!*" sounded Abruzzio's incautiously-loud call, from... he couldn't tell, where. "Thank God – am I *ever* happy to *see* thee, honey! But...

uhh... wait a minute... where's thy Mom? Can thou ask her to get us out of here?"

"*Sylvia?*" demanded Kaysten, just as the suspect wall-section first became desaturated, then disappeared entirely, revealing Abruzzio and her dog, where the illusion had been, not two seconds previously. She had timed it perfectly; the workmen were all either inside their van, or were inside the building.

"I wish Miss Nuclear Angel *was* here," explained the former Chief of Staff, as he nervously looked back and forth. "But, no such luck – I think Karéin asked her to protect me. Looks like the two of us – err, the *four* of us – are out here by our lonesomes; far as I know, Minnie, Otis and Will are still stuck back there. Honestly... I got no idea how *Vîrya I'ëà'b'* stayed with us, all the way from back north – but I'll take her – she saved my butt, back there, no doubt about *that*. Listen, Sylvia – we *got* to get moving. They weren't chasing me right when I followed you out of that Agency jail a couple of blocks back, but I think that was because they were afraid of my round little companion, and her 'slice-and-dice' trick. If I know the government, they'll be calling an APB on the both of us, any minute now."

"Agreed," said the former JPL scientist. "In my mind, hearing a lot of, uhh, 'chatter' on the police bands... but no hue and cry... yet."

Just then, a police-car, its lights flashing and wailing, roared by; but it neither stopped nor, apparently, took note of them.

Kaysten quickly put on the sunglasses that he'd had in his breast-pocket, a move that was reciprocated by his distaff companion, who turned to address the flying shield.

"*Vîrya I'ëà'b'*," requested Abruzzio, "I know thou can, uhh, 'hide' thyself, darling... can thou do so if Rainbow's riding with thee?"

The buckler responded with a happy, whirring sound.

"I'll take that as a 'yes'," offered the more-than-a-woman, as she scooped up the puppy and placed it on the buckler's concave interior side. "Here, baby – Mommy wants you to lie down with *Vîrya I'ëà'b'*, and –"

She stopped talking for a second or two.

"Now, *that's* interesting," observed Abruzzio, while intently studying the dog and the living-shield, which seemed to be communicating, via a series of soft "yips" and barks on the part of Rainbow, matched by odd vibrations coming from "Daughter Tornado Diamond-Curtain".

"What...? Oh," replied Kaysten. "They're... *talking*. Wow. That's great, I suppose... but we need to get going."

"Yeah," affirmed the former JPL scientist. "*Vîrya I'ëà'b'*, thou need to accompany us wherever we go, but keep thyself and Rainbow completely hidden, and silent, until Jerry or I, request otherwise. One exception – if there's any way that thou can block some of the video-cameras, without becoming visible, please do that. Oh... and please try not to hurt any of the, uhh, 'bad people', unless it's absolutely necessary to save our lives... or thy own. That goes for *you* too, sweetie – nothing more like what went on, back in the hotel, unless... well, *you* know."

The flying-shield and its canine passenger immediately disappeared from view, although, as both Kaysten and Abruzzio quickly realized, if they "squinted" their Mars-eyes in just the right manner, and knew what to look for, the shield's approximate location *could* be detected by a flicker in the air, within one of the ultra-violet light-bands. This was followed by a subconscious vibration on the part of *Vìrya I'ëà'b'* and a subdued bark by the puppy.

"Let's hope they got the message," remarked Abruzzio, as she began to briskly walk to the north and east, toward the far end of the back-alley. "Let's play 'man and wife, out for a downtown shopping-spree'. We've not a care in the world, we're just down here to pick up some stuff... then it's back to the 'burbs and a nice little roast waiting in the oven... you know?"

Kaysten now strode beside her, taking hold of the woman's offered hand. Though he gamely tried to play the part and appear to be calm, inside, he was scared half to death.

"Listen, Sylvia... this, uhh, *feels* kind of weird," he said, awkwardly looking her in the eyes, "You, uhh... *know* about me... don't you?"

"Of *course* – we *all* do," compassionately replied the former JPL scientist. "I *do* love you, but as a sister loves her brother, Jerry. Nobody gives two hoots, who you – or Minnie, for that matter – prefers to sleep with. What I *do* care about, is getting both of us – excuse me, *all* of us – out of here, in one piece."

He looked down at his suit-top, which had been his favorite blue, when he had donned it, earlier in the day. But now the thing was green, and the colors of Abruzzio's garments were unlike anything that he had yet seen her wearing. Furthermore, her hair, normally black, now appeared to be light brown.

"What the...?" he stammered. "This is one of my best jackets – it's supposed to be color-fast – paid a *thousand* for it –"

"Just a little light-trick, to make us a bad match for that APB of yours," murmured the former JPL scientist, with a momentary, multi-chromatic twinkle in her eyes. "And if it looks like they're on to us, I'm working on a bunch more of 'em. Problem is, I'm not yet very good at making 'em move, along with me... anything more elaborate than a chroma-shift, starts looking phony, *real* fast."

As they passed the busy loading-dock, paying no attention to the work-men and receiving none back, the former Chief of Staff asked, "So... what, exactly, went down, back there, Sylvia? I decided to follow you because, well, it just seemed like the right thing to do, at the time – maybe it's one of those 'voices' that her Angel-ness keeps talking about – but what made you want to bolt?"

"Agency sons-of-bitches wanted to take Rainbow for 'experiments'," stated the more-than-a-woman, staring directly ahead. "I tried to discuss it with them, they wanted to force the issue... it ended badly. One of 'em got ejected out the window, after Rainbow had already gamma-rayed him into 'dead man walking' status. He was lucky to go that way – a lot less painful than the alternative."

"Jesus, Sylvia... that's... *murder*," gasped Kaysten.

They turned a corner and began to head almost straight north, down another back-alley.

"I feel sick about doing it, brother," admitted the more-than-a-woman, "But it was self-defense, and, frankly, I'm getting awfully tired of being used for target-practice, by our ever-loving government. What'd you *expect* me to do – just let them take Rainbow, and dissect her in some CIA lab, somewhere?"

There was a sudden "yip" from an unseen point behind and above them.

"There, *there*, sweetie," said Abruzzio, apparently to no-one. "Mommy was just *explaining*, to Jerry. She won't let you get hurt. Keep it down... okay?"

Thankfully, no more noise came from the invisible mutt.

"Yeah," muttered Kaysten. "After what went on up there on the island, I can't really blame you for thinking that way. Well, thank God, all *I* can do, is run away. I'm not really 'in to' the whole 'killing' thing, you know?"

"Neither am I, unless it's forced on me," echoed the former JPL scientist.

They had now reached the northern end of the narrow alley that they had been traveling. Immediately in front of them was a multi-lane boulevard carrying moderate amounts of traffic, with the broad expanse of the Allegheny River somewhat further off.

"There's a bridge there, and there," commented the former White House insider. "Want to hoof it?"

"Hmm... we *could*," agreed Abruzzio, "But remember : I can't do 'moving illusions', very well. We'd be right out in the open for a very long way, and they'd likely suspect that we'd try – wait a minute, *there's* an idea –"

A few vehicles, luckily not including any police-cars among them, roared by; the local speed-limit was posted as "40 Miles Per Hour", although this constraint seemed to be honored more in the breach than the observance.

"Jerry," inquired the more-than-a-woman, "How's your telekinesis, these days?"

"My, uhh... *what?*" uneasily responded Kaysten. "If you *must* know... 'little to none'. She tried to teach it to me while we were back up at the camp, but I'm just a slow learner, I guess – I can hardly move a paper dinner-plate. Why?"

"Pity, but I can compensate," pledged the former JPL scientist, her voice steadfast and determined. "Here's what we're going to do... see that big, four-way intersection, about a block to the left – the one with the stop-lights?

"Yeah," confirmed the former Chief of Staff. "What's the plan?"

"We'll walk to the north side of the boulevard, ending up on the north-west corner of the intersection," proposed Abruzzio. "And stand there, until the right vehicle comes by – one that looks like it's about to turn and go over the bridge, and which has enough free space in the back, for us to hop aboard for a ride. I'll propel myself on to it... then grab you and haul you up there, with me. The trick is, when you feel my mind taking hold of you – it will feel uncomfortable, like you're in an invisible, very tight straight-jacket – don't resist, since if you do that, you might temporarily break my grasp and fall. You got that?"

"Uhh... yeah... I guess," gulped Kaysten. "But once we get aboard... what happens then?"

"Then I make it look like we're not there," explained the more-than-a-woman. "By the way, it will look very dark, almost like midnight, from inside one of my illusions – but tune your eyes to see ultra-violet, I'll let enough of that in, so we can at least be warned of someone approaching, *et cetera*. And we ride it as far as it'll go... hopefully out of Pittsburgh, altogether. If it doesn't go far enough, we hop another one."

"And *then* what?" demanded the former bureaucrat. "Where the H, exactly, are we going?"

"The H *out* of here," calmly replied Abruzzio. "Then – hopefully – to my friend Moira's place, which is in Kentucky, just outside Cincinnati. *That's* where we're going. *Humor* me, Jerry – I'm making this up, as I go. You got a better idea?"

"'Fraid not," he admitted. "Okay... let's go."

It had taken no more than about another minute to reach the intersection, but the next few passed with both of the more-than-human escapees cooling their heels in waxing frustration; many vehicles passed by, but almost every one either continued straight to the west, or was unsuitable to their purpose (there was a close call with an inner-city bus, which Abruzzio had moved toward, only to be shooed off by Kaysten, when he realized that he'd have to stand on a narrow bumper, for as far as it would take them).

The fugitives also had a close call, as three police-cars, their sirens a-wailing, flew through the intersection, heading to the east; but the former JPL scientist had simply stepped demurely backward into the shadow made by a nearby advertising-kiosk; and Kaysten noticed that in doing this, she became almost invisible, even though she was clearly "hiding in plain sight".

Well, he mused, *we've all got our "gifts", but I might very well trade mine for hers... "you can run, but you can't hide"... isn't* that *how it goes?*

Finally, after an eternity that was actually about five minutes, they both noticed a large, but rather dilapidated, pickup-truck approaching from the east; and – unlike the last three "potential targets" – there was no other car directly behind it. Though the available hand-holds and resting-places on this vehicle or in its flatbed were all either marginally-useful, or were overflowing with various junk, it was towing a decent-sized, loose-tarpaulin-covered trailer, which looked to be substantially empty. The sides and back-gate of the trailer, however, were too high for someone to jump over, at least from a standing start.

"Okay, Jerry," whispered Abruzzio, as the truck pulled up to the curb, turning slightly to the right, while waiting for the traffic-light to change and for the volume of northbound traffic to abate, "Here's our chance. We walk behind it, calm as day, crouch down – then I flip myself in, yank you after me, and down comes the curtain. You ready?"

“No,” grimaced Kaysten, “But let's get it over with.”

“Three... two... *one,*” counted the former JPL scientist. She briskly stepped into the street, just behind the pickup-truck, bent her knees in “springing-upward” position, so as to deny the driver a clear line-of-sight, and leaped only a few inches into the air, before her figure flickered and vanished from normal sight, altogether. There was a low “thump” and a muffled curse from inside the trailer. The tarpaulin shook momentarily, as something hit its rear end but then, apparently, fell downward, releasing tension on the covering's fabric.

The pickup truck revved its engine, and Kaysten's gut sank with fear.

Shit, he thought. *She's knocked herself out – I'm stuck here, all alone –*

As the truck turned the corner with Kaysten running at “maximum-somewhat-normal-human-speed” to keep up behind it, he saw Abruzzio's head, shoulders and arms peek out from underneath the tarpaulin.

A second later, he was yanked off his feet by the vice-like grip of a frighteningly-powerful, invisible, grasping force.

Oww – feels like my ribs are being crushed, reflected his panicked mind.

Don't fight it, don't resist – but I can't breathe –

So this *is what it feels like to fly,* realized Kaysten, as his feet left the pavement, and he streaked forward; but in the next blink-of-an-eye, everything around him went black, though his other senses told him in no uncertain terms that he was still in the middle of a large road, with traffic whizzing by in the other lane.

His belt caught on something hard and unyielding; and the unfortunate former Chief of Staff's forward momentum, combined with this fulcrum, caused him to tumble, arse-over-teakettle-style, into the back of the trailer.

Glimpses and extra-violet outlines of objects – including a half-complete, out-of-focus parody of the former JPL scientist's plain, elongated, yet not unattractive face – appeared to his eyes, while his lips tasted and his nostrils smelled, something soft, crumbling and unpleasantly... *earthy.*

“Welcome aboard, fellow hobo,” whispered Abruzzio. “Keep your voice down – and... would you mind cleaning up all that potting-soil?”

Home Sweet Cave

Billings could still see his exhaled breath, and – despite a stupendous remodeling job that exceeded anything yet seen, on the third planet from this particular star – the place's cavernous, echoing majesty, somehow, didn't feel like *home.*

Well... that, *would be the understatement of the Century,* reflected the salesman, as his eyes swept over the huge, artificial cave that his alien “girlfriend” had sliced, shattered and melted, out from underneath the crust of this most-isolated of all Godforsaken specks-of-island, anywhere on Earth.

The trip to get there had taken hours upon hours, due to the need for slow speed and a circuitous route to baffle the prying sensors of the world's military powers; and then – even though he certainly hadn't been the only one to have complained out loud, in no uncertain terms – the Storied Watcher, after assuring everyone "do not worry, you are all quite safe here... after all, I *am* leaving this vessel only a few-score boat-lengths below the wave-tops", had exited the "*Mailànkh Express*", as the successor to the "Magic Bus", had been named, *en route*, thence to work her will against the insides of the island.

The subsequent wait, with Billings, Ramirez, the Claremont family, most of the White family, the two ex-GrayWar mercs, the McGregors, the rest of the Compton refugees and various other hangers-on, languishing in this watery prison, had been an unusually long and enervating one, for which their super-human tour-guide had profusely apologized, upon finally returning.

"Matters did not go completely according to plan, dear friends," she had sheepishly apologized, "For this island is, in fact, the top of a volcano, and in opening up a place for us, I caused a, uhh, 'teensy, weensy, little, lava-eruption'. But this was turned to our advantage, as I have channeled the hot-rock, so as to provide a nice source of warmth for you all. Be sure not to put your cooking-pots too close to where this flows... else they might, uhh, melt away."

After Billings had muttered the obligatory "I don't know whether to laugh or cry," the Storied Watcher again exited the *Mailànkh Express* and then – contrary to their expectations – dragged it still further downward, an action that was later explained to have been necessary because, although she had blasted out four different, hundred-meter-wide entrance-ways, all of these were located deep underwater (there *was*, as it turned out, a much narrower, circuitously-winding, "emergency" exit which *did* terminate above-ground, albeit, underneath a very thick glacier, as well as a large number of carefully-hidden, topside ventilation-shafts, each too small for a human-being to enter). The claim seemed to be true, because after a plunge to a point well below safe human diving-depth, the *Mailànkh Express* abruptly leveled out and then went upward, at a steep angle.

When the weirding-vessel's motion stopped and its entrance-hatch was unsealed by a triumphant Karéin-Mayréij, they could but gasp at the magnitude of what had been accomplished, in such a short time.

The alien-girl, along with her "war-children" (particularly the sword, which they later discovered, had done much of the work), had created a gigantic, Cyclopean, east-west-oriented living-space that had to have been more than a kilometer long, at least half as wide and hundreds of meters high, with innumerable semi-circular side-tunnels, each of which led in turn to a complex, interconnected maze of secondary rooms and open-spaces of differing sizes and geometries, branching from all sides of the central, perfectly-smooth-floored, open main area.

The side-tunnels were not all accessible from the main-space, which was itself about thirty meters above sea-level; instead, there were at least five distinct upper pathways, each perhaps wide enough to accommodate a car, arranged at regular intervals on the cavern-side walls, and these ledges – except the topmost – could be reached by a series of long, gently-sloping stairways, which had been cut right from the rock. And in the precise lengthwise center-point of the cavern, where the *Mailànkh Express* had surfaced, was a kind of artificial lake, large enough to accommodate an ocean-liner, whose depths connected to the underwater exit-tunnels, thence to the world outside.

Scarcely less astonishing, to the wide-eyed stares of the first-arrived onlookers to this marvel of alien engineering, was the overall ambiance of the place. Despite being far underneath Bouvet's thick crust (which, according to her estimates, the Storied Watcher had assured them, could "save you proof against all but the most potent of those hateful, atom-smashing bombs"), with no entrance-point for natural lighting, she had put some of the molecular-rearrangement-trickery formerly taught to Ramirez, to excellent use.

The main areas of the place had, in fact, been made as bright as any underground shopping-mall, since large parts of its roof had been transformed into some naturally-luminescent substance, which gave off a steady, slightly blue-tinted light. The same treatment had been applied to selected parts of the rock-walls at regular intervals along the various side-corridors, though, not within all of the secondary-rooms, "since, perhaps, you shall want the ability to have darkness, when this is fitting". It was explained that "this brilliance comes from the particle-shine bestowed within the living rock, and it shall last seven times seven human lifetimes, ere it need refreshment".

Furthermore, the alien-girl had evidently spent a little time doing some impromptu decorating, by carving a few rococo, curving inscriptions, into the walls and floors, hither and yon.

"A poor imitation of the great vaults of the Dwellers Under the mighty *Nolan Oblé*," she had inscrutably remarked, "But even such as *these*, were not hewed, in a single day."

But – as Billings realized, after he, along with the others, had stopped to pick their gaping jaws off the finely-polished, basalt cave-floor, and had then spent an hour or two, just exploring – notwithstanding the magnitude of Karéin-Mayréij's architectural handiwork, the cavern was not yet ideally-suited for long-term human habitation.

True, it *did* have a reliable source of fresh water, via underground run-off from the glacier, and she had created a rudimentary system of toilet-holes and sewer-shafts. However, there was nothing that really resembled conventional indoor plumbing. The ambient temperature was certainly bearable (if not completely comfortable; the atmosphere had a clammy, "Seattle-in-March", maritime scent), but there was no combustible fuel of any kind, nor were there any other accouterments of human civilization, other than what they had brought along with themselves in the *Mailànkh Express*. The individual living-quarters had no furniture, and were little more than bare-floored spaces, though the Storied Watcher had, thoughtfully, created hidden closets and other storage-alcoves, in most of the larger rooms.

Finally, of course, the place was far too large for the group's immediate needs. It could easily have accommodated a small city's-worth of inhabitants, but all of the weirding-vessel's passengers, fit comfortably together into the rooms accessed by one small side-tunnel at floor-level, nearest to the central, salt-water lake.

Now, after having unloaded the "flying squashed cigar", as some of them had affectionately termed it, and after having spent a day and a half in a futile attempt to explore the cavern (they had managed to survey perhaps a sixth of it, and that was all done only at sea-level; only Ramirez had reached the uppermost tier of the cave-apartments, by lifting himself up and down on a whirlwind), Billings and the rest of the expatriate group stood in front of Karéin-Mayréij, who was dressed fetchingly only in the shimmering, body-curve-tight, deep blue-purple-black undergarment-portion of *Vîrya Ahn'jë*, without the adornment of her other war-children, who were evidently secreted somewhere nearby.

"Sari," said the salesman, "Like I mentioned when we first got off the, uhh, plane – this sure *is* an incredible job you've done here. When are we going back home, though?"

A look of genuine hurt appeared on the alien-girl's face.

"But... *Bob*," she pouted, "I thought that you *liked* it... do you not?"

"Of *course* I do, honey," cajoled Billings, "And I'm sure it's going to make a *wonderful* little, uhh, 'home away from home', in the long-run. But you gotta be *practical*... there's nothing *for* us here –"

"Bob," countered the Storied Watcher, "You *do* have something extremely important here, which you totally lack, in this 'America' empire : namely... 'safety'. There is little chance that your cruel President-Emperor could have tracked our path to this place, and still less that he could effectively attack it, for the warships and submarines of the China, India and Brazil empires patrol almost unchallenged by those of the American navy, in this sea; thus I noticed on the way in, and, indeed, I had to detour for some distance, to avoid being detected by these other flotillas."

"Well, that's just *wonderful*," complained one of the Compton parents. "We's all in some big cave who knows where, an' we cain't be smoked... that is, until we die of boredom. There ain't nothin' to *do* here, Angel Girl!"

"Yeah... ain't no TV, no vide-o... not even none of them board games," added Jermaine Kingsley, "'Cept for that 'Tunnels 'n Such' thing that Kevin's playin' all the time. It's dead dull here, lady."

"I *will* concede the point, that the, ahh, "creature comforts" here, are perhaps not up to the standard to which you all are accustomed," argued Karéin-Mayréij, "But it should be easy for me to retrieve what may be needful, from the South America continent. Let us make *this* place, our refuge – at least, until brave Sam Jacobson, dear Minn-ee Choo and their stalwart companions, not to mention grim Sebastiàn, have made good on their current quests. After that, and after the situation in your 'United States' hopefully settles down, we can re-visit the issue. Does this not make sense?”

There was a murmur of tentative approval from the crowd.

“Hey, Hugo,” called Billings. “You and me... we're supposed to be the best there *is*, on the home reno front... isn't that right?”

“You *got* it,” confirmed Szabo. “So what's the deal?”

“Think we're up to it?” asked the salesman.

“Up to *what?*” countered the sales manager.

“*This* place,” said Billings. “Get her to bring whatever we need. Real 'ground-floor opportunity'... you know?”

“Well, for God's sake,” stammered the nonplussed sales manager, “It's kinda a bigger job than I ever done... 'ground-floor' around here's a mile long!”

“Afraid of a 'challenge'?” persisted Billings.

“Fine, fine,” retreated Szabo, “I'll see what I can do, on one condition.”

“What would *that* be, my brother?” inquired the Storied Watcher.

“Beer,” demanded the sales manager. “Six cases per week. minimum. More, if she wants a discount on the tiles or on the design. Fair *is* fair... you know?”

“Right... a quick little side-trip to that 'Africa' continent, then,” patiently responded the Storied Watcher. “Hector – have you finished that trans-mew-tay-shun job? I fear that I will need many more gold coins, in the near future.”

Ramirez sat down and sighed.

“Yo, an' they got Her Highness runnin' errands to the store for 'em,” incautiously whispered one of the Compton refugee children (apparently, Julio Arellano), to another. “Quick, think up somethin' we can ask her to –”

“Remind me to teach you how to fly – and to dodge a swarm of rockets, all the while – on your own, young man,” smartly riposted Karéin-Mayréij, “Thus I can have you, ahh, 'run some errands', on *my* behalf. In the meantime... let all who stand here, tell me what they would have me procure, on their behalf.”

“You're *on!*” came back the enthusiastic answer.

A peal of laughter went through the crowd; it was followed, shortly thereafter, by a throng of pleaders surrounding the alien-girl, each with his or her individual wish-list.

Despite having seen it before, they were still duly-impressed, when, to keep the many demands fully-remembered, Karéin-Mayréij ordered *Væran Fàiagàryuu* to cleave a small writing-tablet from the very rock, and then began to inscribe the consolidated “borrowing-record” upon this, with the burning, scintillating gaze of her super-human eyes.

The alien-girl had deliberately left the last requests to the members of her own family; Billings (despite having been warned that “this poison will no longer work on you”), had insisted on being provided with a case of Bourbon, a large, flat-screen TV, and “all the movies you can carry, and don't forget the 'Best Of Major League Sports' series”, while Tommy had asked for a baseball-set, a bow-and-arrow and a lengthy list of video-games.

It was now Elissha's turn. The Storied Watcher held out a hand in a “come-hither” gesture, and the little girl, giggling profusely all the way along, was gently floated off her feet, coming to rest in a close embrace by her adoptive mother.

“What would you like me to, uhh, 'acquire' for you, sweetheart?” inquired Karéin-Mayréij.

“There's a dolly I saw on TV... she can walk by herself, after you,” chirped the child, “And she can do everything that a real baby can do. Her name is 'Blaine Maine The Cyber-Brat'. *That's* what I want.”

“And you shall have it... err, her,” quickly promised the Storied Watcher. “Where would one find this, uhh, 'Cyber-Brat', darling?”

“In better toy and department stores everywhere,” replied Elissha, to a round of laughter from the crowd.

“Thus it shall be,” said Karéin-Mayréij.

“And one *other* thing, Mommy,” demanded the little girl.

“Of course,” patiently responded the Storied Watcher.

“I want Korey back,” solemnly asked Elissha. “I... *miss* him.”

A gasp was heard and the throng fell near-completely silent, except for Saquina White commenting, *sotto voce*, to Atasha Jones, “Welcome to bein' a mom, Karéin... they always ask for the one thing you can't give 'em.”

“Oh, my beloved daughter,” half-whispered a choking Karéin-Mayréij, “How much do I wish to fulfill that request.”

“But you're an... *angel*,” said the child. “You can do *anything*. Can't you?”

Now the Storied Watcher's face approached until she was very close to the little girl's own. With a glowing aura and powerful, graceful *Fire*-music magnificently illuminating the surroundings, Karéin-Mayréij explained,

“Elissha... what you now see and hear, is the Eternal Light of Heaven, which lives and burns within me... within *you*... within all those, who love truth and justice and peace and charity. I swear by that very Light – your brother's spirit lives on, in the gentle dream-world from where none can return, ere they finally embark. It would be wrong and dangerous for me – or for anyone – to use weirding arts to overcome the fate of mortal people... like your brother. Powerful and great though I am – though you, shall soon be – it is a path that must *not* be taken.”

“Does that mean... I'll never see him again?” whimpered the child.

“No, of *course* not,” consoled Karéin-Mayréij. “What I believe is... those who we love – but who have passed on to the dream-world – *we* keep them alive, in *here*.”

She pointed to her heart.

“You can call to him every day,” elaborated the Storied Watcher, her voice soft and compassionate, “And if you listen very carefully, in a quiet place where the noise and bustle of this world trouble you not, after praying for the Holy Light to touch his spirit... you will hear him, and he will say, 'it is alright, dear sister... it is alright'. Thus has it been since the first days of mortal beings."

Holding the child close, the alien-girl tried to hide her watering eyes and whispered to Elissha, "Dear little one, there are some things which not even *I* can do... *should* do. But there is a balance to the universe, which was upset when your brother was so cruelly-taken; and perhaps, it can be put right, in a different way. Do you trust me to try?"

"Yes, Mommy... I do," innocently responded the child.

"Oh, I have spent *far* too much time away from you, noble daughter... it plagues me to leave," said the Storied Watcher. "When I come back..."

Her voice trailed off, as the child sent,

Don't worry, Mommy... I will be right here, in your *heart. All the way there, and all the way back... oh-kay?*

"Oh-kay," managed Karéin-Mayréij, her pained voice barely audible.

At length, the Storied Watcher took Elissha, Billings and Tommy – all three, unperturbed by the flames coming from *Vìrya Ahn'jë* – into her arms, murmured some soft words, provided her family with an affectionate hug, and said a perfunctory "goodbye, brothers and sisters" to the others. Then she plunged downward into the central cistern with the *Mailànkh Express,* in tow.

Though the removal of the traveling-vessel had engendered strenuous objections from almost everyone – but especially from Jim McGregor and the two former GrayWar mercs – it had been explained as being necessary, "elsewise, some of the smaller items, might fall by the wayside, in my travels".

They were now completely isolated deep within Bouvet, under hundreds of feet of solid rock, with (except, perhaps, for Tommy, Ramirez and Saquina White) no way to leave the island.

"Hey, Mista Billins'," joked Curtis Claremont, "Ah guess we's stuck all by ourselves, way down here... jus' like befo', you know?"

"That was *different,* kid," replied the salesman. "Night and day."

"What y'all mean, Mista Billins'?" inquired the boy.

"Simple," vowed Billings. "*This* time... I'll get her name right."

One On The Rocks, One Straight-Up

"*Really,* Crowford," grumbled the *nouveau*-President, over the steady background hum of four high-bypass turbofans, "I don't know why you think it's such a good idea, giving this uppity little FBI agent, a personal hearing. She's already been de-briefed, and re-de-briefed, and so on and so on... if she's still refusing to talk, the Agency's assured me that they'll loosen her tongue."

He leaned back into his captain's-chair aboard the unmarked Air Force One duplicate, and began to pour himself a Scotch-On-The-Rocks.

"Drink?" he offered.

"Oh... no, sir," demurred Brother Harold, reflexively straightening his tie-clasp. "Only liquor *I'll* have, is the trans-substantiated blood of our Lord and Savior, at Communion-time. But you all go ahead – don't feel uncomfortable 'bout it. Truth be told... I'm not shy of sayin', back in my Army days, I could drink most men under the table; but then I found Jesus, and... well, *you* know."

"Thanks, and you can be *sure*, I won't feel 'uncomfortable'," replied the former Vice-President, as he re-stoppered the fancy-cut, thousand-dollar crystal decanter. "Never have been... never will. Now about this little 'Chu' popsy – she's locked up good and tight, after that prison-break they had down in Pittsburgh... Agency Director's taking it *personally*, as I understand it. Why don't we just leave her, and those two hangers-on she's got, to –"

"But, Mr. President, *sir*," persisted the Spiritual Adviser, using his unctuous best in persuasiveness, "Didn't you get my briefin' 'bout what she's been up to?"

"I've been *busy*," answered the nouveau-President. "I don't have time to read things. What's so special about this case?"

"Here... I'll *show* you, sir," offered Brother Harold.

He took out a file-folder, complete with many pages of fine-point printout, accompanied by good-quality photographs of the three FBI Red Rover Team agents, and opened the folder in front of his boss, on the table.

"Hmm," commented an obviously-impressed *nouveau*-President, "Not bad-looking, not bad-looking at *all*... I *like* 'em slim and professional-looking, nice long hair, pretty eyes, too, but no *tits*... ahh, if I was thirty years younger, and I was into chinks... *well*. But about the other two... I thought we'd purged most of the nig... uhh, blacks, from the Bureau? Anyway, like I said, 'I don't have time to read reports'. You got five minutes to fill me in – then I got another meeting... some shit about 'the latest currency reserve depletion crisis'."

"Okay, sir," argued the Spiritual Adviser, as the U.S. leader began to knock back his drink, in customary record speed. "Here's what I think – don't mind tellin' you, I've been prayin' mighty hard, for the Lord to guide me in this. Now, by her own admission, this 'Chu' woman's been hangin' 'round with the alien –"

"Who's dropped off the radar-screen, entirely," reminded the former Vice-President. "And who, if your Lord's any friend of *mine*... is already dead."

"Wish I could support you there, Mr. President, sir," politely countered Brother Harold, "But by this 'Chu's own claims, the accursed Devil-Girl's still unfortunately with us... that's the whole point. As you'll see if you read the report, and I sure had to turn the screws with them CIA boys to get access to it, by the way, Chu's refusin' to talk, quote, 'unless and until, I can tell the President to his face, about the danger that's facing him, and everybody 'round him'. She's also demandin' that her two Bureau friends be there, for the discussion."

"So what?" belched the U.S. leader, the alcohol on his breath very evident, though the Spiritual Adviser tactfully did not react when it washed over his face. "She's not in any position to bargain."

"Well, sir," smoothly continued the Christian man, "We *could* have the Agency give her the once-over, and of course I wouldn't have any problem with that – 'wages of sin', and such – but why not do it the *easy* way, and just listen to what she's got to say? Once our little talk's over with, we can kick her pretty little butt over the side. I guess what I'm tryin' to say, sir, is, when I was in the Army, I used to do interrogations myself... and the first rule was, 'start out nice, and then only use the car-battery, when you think you've got all you're gonna get, by bein' friendly'. So we get her up here with us, and –"

"*What?*" challenged the nonplussed and immediately-suspicious, *nouveau*-President. "Secret Service'll *never* go for anything like that. Bezomorton said that she's been in contact with the *alien!* The risk –"

"Is *completely* manageable," argued Brother Harold. "What *is* the risk... anyway? You'll notice, in the report, that she ain't got any of these fancy-ass 'alien powers' that the Jacobson team had, or was claimed to have; she's just some little gook popsy with a swelled head. Frankly, *that* shouldn't be a surprise, considerin' that from the alien's perspective, Chu and the other two, *are* part of the government, and were sent out to catch the Devil-Girl... only makes sense that it would keep her at arms'-length."

"Yeah... I suppose that *does* make sense," guardedly said the U.S. leader. "So what, exactly, are you suggesting?"

With 'shark-circling-for-the-kill' intensity, the Christian man elaborated, "Get the Service to handcuff her, that black boy and his red-haired friend, leg-shackle 'em too if they want, have 'em escorted by a bunch of Marines... and tell 'em, 'first false move, you get a bullet between the eyes, honey'. Have a nice chat with 'em... then you can open a door on the plane and kick 'em out at thirty thousand feet – fair punishment for cavortin' with the Spawn of Satan, after all. And, Mr. President, sir, I can *assure* you... the Lord ain't gonna let harm come your way – He has told me this, in dream after dream. As the President of God's Chosen Nation, you're under His care and protection. You just got to *believe*."

Finishing off his drink and looking longingly at the decanter – which was dangerously-close to empty – the *nouveau*-President took discretion as the better part of valor, and, for the time being, refrained from pouring the last of it.

Instead, he wiped his lips on the top of his hand and commented, "You *do* know... if I go for this, CIA's gonna go *apeshit* – Director regards those three, as his personal property, still thinks he can use them to bring down the alien, but we've been down *that* path before... haven't we? Don't forget how I ended up in this chair, in the first place; my predecessor made the mistake of crossing the Agency, and that's a mistake that *I* can't afford to make... not if I don't want to wake up dead, someday soon. I'll have to go slowly on this... see if I can get CIA to agree. That may require some horse-trading... you understand?"

"Yes sir," answered Brother Harold, "I appreciate your situation... but don't worry – remember, sir, when the Lord Jesus Himself is your bodyguard, ain't *nothin* – no aliens, no traitors and no Agency hit-men, gonna harm so much as a, uhh, hair on your head... on the *side* of your head, I mean. And if the Director wants his own people in on this thing, well, I s'pose *that* can't hurt, can it? This 'Chu' girl said she'd only tell you whatever she's got to say, to your face, Mr. President... but I'm sure them Agency boys can rig up a way to listen in, from the next room. After that, we're done with 'em. Whole thing shouldn't take more than an hour or two."

The U.S. leader got up, took a stride for the door separating this Air Force Secret One conference-room from the corridor outside, and said, "I'll see what I can do. If the Agency goes for it, we'll take them aboard on one of the refueling stops. But... my inclination's not to have them, ahh, 'with us', as of the next time we put down; just like with that asshole Jacobson – who, I'm being told, has vanished, after publicly threatening me, but we'll get him *eventually*, mark my words – anybody who's been palsy-walsy with that fucking alien, well, America do *without* them, thank you very much. That work for you?"

"For *sure*, Mr. President," enthusiastically agreed the Christian man. "Those who are tainted by playin' footsie with Satan – the Good Book says, 'all we can do is send 'em to the next world, and say a prayer that the Lord should have mercy on their souls'. Will you tell me, as soon as the plans are made?"

"I will," confirmed the *faux*-President. "I gotta go."

With that, and a peremptory hand-wave, he left the room.

A contented – though, as always, restrained, controlled – smile, was on Brother Harold's face, as he stopped for a second or two, pondering his options.

He looked at the decanter, while reflexively retrieving a small, snap-shut pill-box, from his trouser-pocket.

The Christian leader opened the box and took out one pill.

Need somethin' to wash it down with, he mused.

For a sinner about to offer himself up as a blood sacrifice... what's the Lord gonna care, about just one little drink?

"He ain't, I reckon," he softly said to himself, pouring the excellent whiskey into a clean glass, popping the tablet into his mouth, and knocking it back.

God Of The Little Ones

With the sun going down and his dragooned army of Latino gangsters simmering somewhere just below the level of a full-scale revolt, a frustrated, exhausted Sebastiàn, finally called a halt to the push forward.

Espero que sea *just a temporary one*, he mused.

Because I got *to go on.* No sé por qué... *but I got to.*

I can smell *'em... smell...* it. No sé lo que es... *but I want it.*

Them fuckin' voices... ¡la mierda!

He had exulted in his new, weirdo alien-powers, which seemed to be growing in manners both subtle and obvious, with each skirmish; and, truth be told, *without* these abilities – which were the 'force-multiplier' that decided the outcome, in all but one of the recent battles – he and the *Ejército Del Nuevo Diablo*, would have been routed, a long time ago. As it was, he'd had to fight viciously for the approximate third of East Los Angeles, of which he now was the undisputed ruler.

But the hated Aryan Brotherhood had defended every square inch of the run-down, urban-merging-to-suburbs district, with unanticipated ferocity; and as Sebastiàn's impromptu army advanced, the resistance had become correspondingly more desperate.

Furthermore, the AB'ers were fighting back with more firepower, than even the hardened ex-*Mara* had anticipated. He'd lost six foot-soldiers when the Brotherhood had unleashed a rocket-launcher of some type, on the building from which Sebastiàn's unfortunate under-studies were providing covering fire, and, more ominously, in a couple of the positions that *El Ejército Del Nuevo Diablo* had managed to over-run, he'd noticed military-grade gear – complete with issue dates indicating very recent manufacture – indicating that either the Brotherhood had become unbelievably good at stealing weaponry from the government, or the fuckin' *Federales* were...

Basta ya de eso, he resolved. *No me importa.*

There was an apparent lull in the battle, and, with members of his rag-tag gangsta army ensconced in buildings all around, Sebastiàn had taken up residence in an abandoned, smallish burger-joint restaurant just off Clemente Street; he'd decided on this location because the place had over-sized glass windows (two of them still mostly-intact!) on all four sides, providing a commanding view not only of the surrounding parking-lot, but also of most of the several city blocks in every direction.

As he rummaged around in what had been the greasy-spoon's spoiled-food-stinking kitchen, the former *Mara* momentarily amused himself – as he'd discovered he easily could do – by ordering the multitude of cockroaches, maggots, flies, ants, termites and so on, around here, to line up and do a conga dance, at his unspoken command.

Esto es muy extraño, he mused.

I'm almost thinkin' of them like hermanos y hermanas pequeñas. *Hate to see 'em die, while fightin' for me. But better them, than...*

Hey... there's *an idea. I need it – bad – an' if* anybody *can find it... they can.*

A sickly-sweet, exciting, yet all the while ominous, Mariachi-music-infused tune, began to sound at the edges of human consciousness, as Sebastiàn's subtly-green-glowing, squinting eyes stared at the multi-legged, collectively-conscious creatures swarming within the abandoned food-preparation area.

Oyeme, muchachos... muchachas, he sent. *Where's it hidin'?*

There was a low, humming, buzzing sound, one that would have alarmed any ordinary human, and sent him or her retreating rapidly away. But for *this* more-than-*homo sapiens*, the noise was merely reassuring.

It felt like... *home.*

The buzz sounded louder and different, from a spot near the bottom of a poorly-sealed barrel of what, at one time, had been white cooking-flour, though this substance was now so spoiled as to be well past safe use.

Fuckers, mentally cursed Sebastiàn. *Well... what'd I expect. They ain't too smart, I guess... wait a minute –*

He looked closer, turning on the weirdo ability where the hot things appeared in that crazy, "darker-red than red can possibly be" tint, and noticed that the little buggers were streaming in and out of cracks in the floor-tiles, directly below the barrel.

The ex-*Mara* sent another command – *¡fuera de aquì!* – and tried as hard as he could, to avoid squashing any of his minuscule *amigos,* as he moved the container out of the way, revealing a large floor-tile whose outline, in the special sight, was sharper – more distinct – than the others.

The same long, sharp fingernails that had sent a long list of human victims to an early grave, grasped the tile and pried it loose. Underneath, inside a hollowed-out cavity under the kitchen-floor, was a sealed plastic-bag, with something like a back-pack inside it.

Sebastiàn lifted out the bag, opened it and then did the same to the rucksack. Inside, were eight carefully-taped-shut, smaller packages, of something that looked very much like baking-powder; but, even through the seal, he could *smell* what the substance *really* was.

¡Me saqué la lotería! exulted the more-than-human gangsta leader.

As the index fingernail on his left hand sliced a gash in one of the packages, releasing some of the precious *yayo* to his nostrils – causing an instant rush of strength and confidence, far beyond what would have been bestowed on even the most hardened human addict, Sebastiàn emptied at least a handfuls worth into one of his palms, and then showered it over the ants, termites, beetles and cockroaches, which were waiting, patiently, at his feet.

Esto es para ustedes, mis pequeños amigos, he benevolently sent.

And there will be more... much more... when the sun rises, and we fight again, side by side.

He propped himself up beside the grease-encrusted side of a fry-table, closed his eyes, and smiled, as the little ones thronged all around him, worshiping their new-found god.

A Call To Collect, Not A Collect Call

He had stolen away from the farm-house around 1:30 a.m., using every power, both human and otherwise, within his possession, to avoid detection; and it appeared that he had succeeded, because he was now standing underneath a tree in a cow-field several hundred feet away from the nearest road, not to mention at least six miles from the Wade property, in the outskirts of some small, now-somnolent Corn Belt town.

I could easily zap all these damn mosquitoes, or shield myself against them, he thought, *but if I did that, I'd probably be visible, ten kilometers from here.*

Reluctantly, he settled for the time-tested hand-slap – albeit, one expertly-guided by infra-red vision – against the annoying little blood-suckers.

The trip had taken much less time than he had planned for, because – to Boyd's delight – his telekinetic abilities were improving. Recalling Tanaka's fateful encounter with the Storied Watcher in the now-forlorn, abandoned *Eagle* spacecraft, he had been able to propel himself rapidly forward, by imagining a "burst of wind" at his back. Some of the leaps and bounds thus engendered, had sent him as much as seven meters high, each time, fortunately, resulting in a safe, soft landing.

Is this *how the Professor first learned to fly?* he excitedly ruminated. *Whether or not true...* that's *a hypothesis I'll have to test, as thoroughly as possible.*

Well, this far from the Wade place, ought to be out of even Mars earshot, thought Boyd, as he used a glowing finger to illuminate the control-panel of the rigged-up communicator.

The box powered up in satisfactory manner; but when he attempted to make a connection... nothing happened. He tried every trick under the sun (okay... the *moon*, ruefully admitted the former Mars pilot) to get the damn thing to work; but although he had carefully memorized the activation-pattern that had been used yesterday in the conversation with the hacker network, and even though he had exactly reproduced the phrases used at that time, the device refused to give him a dial-tone, or an IPv8 address, or a "network-ready" code, or... *anything.*

Sonofabitch, mentally cursed a frustrated Brent Boyd. *It's probably locked to Jacobson's voice... or maybe Wolf's.*

Well, I sure can't ask them to set up this *call for me,* he grimly reflected.

Okay – time for Plan B.

The former Mars mission pilot reached into a pocket. He retrieved the first of the three "burner" mobile communicators that he'd managed to buy for cash, during the only time that he'd been able to shop without "the team" being right by his side, in one of the roadside convenience-stores where they'd filled up the van's gas-tank, during the trip north-west from Florida.

Three strikes, I'm out, he realized, as he activated the small box and prayed that he wasn't too far from a tower to get a signal.

For once... some luck, exhaled the ex-astronaut, as the "6G" light came on.

Rapidly, he typed in the most familiar of phone numbers.

There were a lot of ringing-beeps – Boyd counted at least eight – before his eyes started to tear up, upon hearing the gentle, so-long-unheard voice, at the other end of the line.

"Laura? Laura? It's Brent here, darling!" he spoke.

"Brent? *Brent!*" came back the excited, relieved reply. "Oh *God,* I can't believe it's *you!* Where *are* you? Oh, Brent, if you only knew how we've been –"

"I know, I *know,* honey," stammered the more-than-a-man, though at this time, he felt far the less. "I don't have a lot of time to talk, because they'll be tracing this call... it's dangerous for me to stay around here, too long. How are the kids? Are you all okay?"

"We're fine, all fine... although those men in the black suits have been around here twice, now – they showed up a few weeks ago, then again yesterday... they were threatening us with being thrown in jail and were asking all sorts of stupid questions, like 'you have to tell us where he's hiding'... stuff like that. Brent, I'm *scared,* but I don't know what to do –"

"Okay... I want you to listen very carefully, sweetheart," cajoled Boyd. "First off – did you see what I said on TV the other day... at the tornado scene, that is?"

"Of *course* I did – so did everybody!" quickly replied the wife. "They tried to yank it off the networks, and we had our TV feed cut off about a week ago, but there's copies everywhere, I went over to Marjorie's and saw one there – but it doesn't make any *sense!* What's all this talk about you being some kind of, uhh, 'alien'?"

"It's, uhh... *true,* Laura," forthrightly stated the ex-astronaut.

"What do you... *mean?*" uncertainly inquired the wife.

"It's very complicated, darling," he tried to explain, "But, basically... along with Cherie, Devon and Sam Jacobson – plus a lot of others who you've never met – I've inherited some of Karéin's abilities. It's come at quite a price, though, because the government's trying to exterminate her, and us along with her. It isn't going to work, but a lot of people might get hurt while we put an end to the President's little witch-hunt against all of us. Right now, my only objective is to make sure that you and the kids stay safe. Am I making any sense, here? I know it's probably a lot coming at you, all at once."

"My God, Brent... when you volunteered for NASA, I never *thought...*" she offered, her voice quiet and, for Laura Boyd, unusually cool and detached.

"Honey," argued the ex-astronaut, "You've *got* to believe me, on two things : one, that this sure isn't the way I wanted everything to turn out; and two... alien-powers or none, I still love you. As soon as I can, I'll prove it, but in the meantime, there are some things you to do for me... for *us.*"

"Yeah... sure... what?" she said.

"First – the next time that those assholes from the Agency – that's CIA, by the way – show up at your doorstep, tell them the party's over, and that you aren't taking orders from them. If they don't react well to that, which no doubt they won't, tell them," – Boyd paused for a second, drawing a breath – "That I'll *personally* track them down and *kill* them, just like I've done to the dozens of other spooks that the Agency has sent to murder Commander Jacobson, Professor Tanaka and good old Devon White. I'll eradicate everyone who was involved in kidnapping you or the kids, down to the last clerk who types up the report at their H.Q. No power on this *planet* will save them – and if they don't believe you, ask them to check with their asshole boss, who'll certainly know the score... he has a few, uhh, 'vacancies' to fill, by now. With me, so far?"

"You mean you've... *killed* people?" gasped the horrified woman.

"May God forgive me," carefully answered Boyd, "Yes – I *have* had to kill people... a *lot* of people. So have Sam, Cherie and Devon, but you've got to *understand*, it was self-defense... the government was trying to torture and murder us, and they had already done so to many, *many* others, including helpless children. We did nothing to cause the situation, but got dragged into it, anyway. Honey, I need your love and support on this one. I *really* need it."

There was a prolonged silence. Boyd felt his gut dropping, and the sensation was far worse than having been shot.

"Laura...?" he pleaded.

"It's... okay," she finally, and mercifully, replied. "I... *understand*. No, I don't. What you're asking me to do – to *believe* – is crazy, Brent. But I'll stand with you, darling. I owe you at least that much, for the sake of our marriage and the kids. What do you want me to do? And what if those guys in the black suits, don't take kindly to your threats? They were pretty scary... they said things like, 'we can put you and your brats in a prison that nobody knows about, and nobody ever gets out of'. They slapped me in the face, before they left, by the way."

"They'll *pay* for that, and you can't know how much I want this all to be over... to be back home," remarked the ex-astronaut. "And as to the prison, well, let's just say, I've *been* there, along with the Commander, the Professor and Devon... there's not much of it left, nor of those who they sent after us; and if they want a demonstration of what we're capable of, well, they'll be *getting* one, real soon now... can't tell you a lot about that, unfortunately. But you're right – they have *dozens* of these damn places, and they might try to use you as hostages, just to get back at me. So I'm going to send someone to rescue you and the kids... take you to somewhere that's safe."

"'Send' someone?" answered a confused Laura Boyd. "But if the government's listening in on this conversation... won't they just set a trap for whoever that is? And where is this, uhh, 'rescue party' going to take us? The borders are all closed, you know."

"*Believe* me, sweetheart," confidently observed the former Mars mission pilot, "Anyone insane enough to attack the person who'll be coming for you and the kids, deserves what he or she's going to get. Here's what I want you to do : pack up as much stuff as you can get into the car, pack Roofer and his dog food in with you, drop Mr. Whiskers off with Marjorie, and then head up north to that nice little B&B... you know, the one where I proposed? Pay the room rental in cash using an assumed name – let's agree on one, how about 'Mrs. Wayne' – take your communicator, connect to the local NeoNet, and wait for a message –"

"But that's almost a day's *drive* from here!" protested the woman. "What if we get pulled over, *en route?* And the kids are in school –"

"Laura, your *lives* are in danger," advised Boyd. "I can't take the chance that the spooks will try to do to you, what I've already seen those bastards do to others... no *way*. I'm going to have to terminate this call soon, so the next part is extremely important for you to remember. You listening?"

"Yes," weakly responded the wife.

"If it ever looks like you're about to be captured, or if you're just in some kind of danger," explained the ex-astronaut, "Or, if you've got to the motel and you haven't heard from me in two days or more, I want you to start chanting a name – and have the kids all do it, too. Don't stop until something, uhh, unusual, happens. If you're somehow not able to speak out loud, just go over the name in your heads. Concentrate on it and on nothing else."

"I'm totally confused," complained Laura Boyd. "*Whose* name?"

"You're going to say, 'Karéin-Mayréij', over and over again; pronounce it exactly as I told you when I was on the *Eagle*, and don't ever stop, until you hear some exciting music that seems to come from all around," ordered the former Mars pilot. "You got that?"

"Uhh... I think so," answered the wife. "I'm 'Mrs. Wayne', and... the *alien?* The one from the space ship, and the one they're saying was behind what went on at Rushmore, and the White House? You've *got* to be kidding! Oh... and, what happens then?"

"Easy," replied Boyd. "You tell whoever's causing you trouble, to back off, unless they want to be immediately blown to bits. Then... get ready for the ride of your life."

"Brent, dear... you're not making any *sense*," she demanded. "I can't –"

The headlights of a car raced by on the road, and Boyd reflexively ducked, although after a few seconds he realized that he couldn't have been seen.

"Honey, I've *got* to go," he warned; though, if the truth be known, he wanted desperately not to. "Any more time here and they may be able to get a target-lock on me. Tell the kids, Daddy misses them to pieces. I love you."

"Brent – wait – *wait!*" cried the wife.

"I love you *so* much," he barely managed, before his lead-heavy finger was somehow induced to depress the "off" button on the communicator.

The box was then crushed into a shattered mass and thrown, with super-human strength, far off into the field, as Brent Boyd wheeled, invoked the *Fire,* and took a soaring bound into the Midwestern night sky.

Missouri Fightin' Words

I'm in luck, thought a satisfied Brent Boyd, as he stole into the Wade household, via the back-door whose lock he'd craftily jammed just prior to leaving. *They're none the wiser.*

And, damn – near the end of it, I was a hundred meters off the ground, at least! Just a bit more "push" – something I can't put my finger on, to unlock it, and... damn, if I had only done this back on the island... oh, well.

Better late than never, I guess...

After closing the curtains on the double-paned window, looking out over the farm-fields from the house's second story, he *did* get at least a half-hour's worth of genuine rest, when – to his own surprise – he had somehow been able to unwind and fall asleep.

He was trying to feign somnolence, as his special senses picked up the presence of Cherie Tanaka, creeping into his bedroom.

"Brent?" she softly addressed.

Shit... maybe not so lucky, after all, he realized.

What's with her? he mused. *Just a shirt and those sexy, scant panties – God, you're cute, Professor... keep it under control, soldier, you've got a wife at home – but it's like there's something invisible holding the shirt off her body?*

Though wide awake, Boyd tried to fake being groggy.

"Yeah?" he mumbled, squinting while rotating in place, slightly throwing back the nicely-crafted home quilt and sitting up, with his tightly-muscled, slightly-hairy chest supported by his forearms. "What's up?"

"I was hoping *you'd* tell *me,*" she said, while taking a side-saddle position at the end of the bed.

"What you mean?" he evaded.

"Oh, come *on,*" prodded the former science officer. "*Vîrya Sài'ymë* noticed you, both coming and going. She was actually halfway out the door, trying to follow you, when I called her back."

"Well, thanks for *that,*" he grumbled. "You can tell that, uhh, whatever-it-is... she reminds me of my mother-in-law – a little thing about 'minding her own bees-wax', if you know what I mean."

"I don't have to," responded Tanaka. "She's here with me now... she heard it. There, *there*, sweetheart; Uncle Brent didn't mean anything by it."

Boyd worked his gums with his tongue and shook his head.

"And I thought *Wolf* had his hands full, with those two mutts," he offered. "Can I get back to sleep? Been a long, busy day and night, you know."

"'Busy', doing what?" pressed the more-than-a-woman.

“'Busy', doing none of your business,” he re-evaded. “What's it to *you?*”

“Let's not play games, Brent,” she countered. “You *went* somewhere. Where? Why?”

“*Look*, Professor,” testily replied Boyd, “I like you, we've been through a lot together, and I don't want to get into an argument, but, to put it bluntly – I don't report to you, and I'm not accountable to you, either. But if it's so important that you know, I was restless; I just went off for a walk, out into the prairie... clear my mind, get a little fresh air, *that* kind of thing. Nothing you should worry about.”

“Really?” challenged Tanaka. “I find that a little hard to believe. Why didn't you invite anyone along? And why did *Vìrya Sài'ymë* feel surges of the *Fire*, as you returned back here?”

Boyd shrugged, noncommittally.

“You can believe whatever you want, Cherie,” he said. “And, okay... I *was* practicing – just the telekinesis, not my main power... which, obviously, would be a bit too, uhh, attention-getting. But I can assure you that –”

A percussive 'thump', the reverberation of which was slightly perceptible even through the walls of the house, stopped Boyd in mid-sentence.

“Just a second,” requested Tanaka, as she hurried over to the window and threw back the curtains.

Far off in the distance – much further than human eyes could have detected, but within their eyesight – were the dim shapes of multiple flying objects, going back and forth. After a couple of seconds, a small, glowing object fell from one of the flying-things, causing a momentarily-brilliant explosion upon impact with the ground.

“*Shit!*” cursed Tanaka. “I think it's the military, the police, or maybe both of them – Brent, have a look at this... can you make any of it out?”

An intensely frustrated and alarmed Boyd, clad only in tight-fitting men's jockey-shorts, sprang out of the bed and came rapidly up to the window. He pushed his Mars vision and hearing to the limit, concentrating on the distant scene.

His brow furrowed, as he observed, “Hmm... hard to tell... IR sig's too small to be fighters, or even helicopter gunships, and they're very close to the ground, only a few hundred meters high... drones, maybe? But what're they attacking? It's just empty prairie over there.”

Fuck, he thought, trying with all of his might not to allow his deliberations to leak out. *That's right where I was... no... where I threw, what was left of it...*

Tanaka, her eyes glowing ever-so-slightly, turned her exotically-pretty, Eurasian face to stare directly at the former Mars mission pilot.

“How would *you* know so precisely, what's out there?” she interrogated.

“Lucky guess,” he parried. “And I study the surroundings everywhere we go... military tactics 101, Professor. Anyway, I think we had better –”

Again, his commentary was abbreviated, this time by the appearance of a blinking, night-shirt-clad Jacobson, in the doorway leading from Boyd's room to the upstairs hall.

"Heard something going on, a ways out," he commented.

There were the sounds of several others, either coming up the stairs or stepping through the hallway.

"Yeah," confirmed Boyd. "Some kind of operation, probably military, going on, several miles from here."

Jacobson came up to the window and carefully studied the far-off conflagration.

"*Interesting*," he remarked. "Whatever they were going after, must have been neutralized... no more explosions. But what's this... hmm. Listen, Brent, Cherie – does it look to you like they're just circling, or..."

The former Mars mission commander's observation was apt; the flying-things had broken off the attack, and had taken up a rotating pattern, centered on the point upon which they had unleashed their fury. But there was something more : gradually, the circular paths involved, were becoming wider, more spread-out.

"Looks like a search-pattern," mentioned Devon White, who had come through the door and had stolen a glance or two, through the window. "Scannin' for anything – or anyone – who did the jet. Sure hope whoever *that* was, ain't tryin' to escape in *our* direction."

Jacobson cast the African-American ex-astronaut a worried glance, and said, "Yeah... that would not be a good thing... not good, at all. Bloody hell, wouldn't you *know* it... just our luck, to have some damn LEA operation start up, no more than a few miles away. Listen, everybody – we'd better think this through. We can lay low and wait it out, but if the authorities show up here sooner or later, it would be *extremely* unfair to the Wades to drag them into our little war with the government, if we got detected and had to fight. Callum and Marie might be k–"

"What's goin' on?" spoke the farmer, who had appeared in the doorway. "What you all doin' up? Three hours 'till daybreak, at least."

"There appears to be an, uhh, military operation, underway, several miles from here, Mr. Wade," stated Tanaka. "Remember what we told you downstairs, after the thing on TV and the call from that hacker-guy? We're considering our options, because we're worried about being caught up in whatever's going on, out there. We don't want you or your wife to get hurt, on account of us, sir."

"Well, I '*preciate* that," offered Wade, "But like I told Donny, 'family 'n friends is more important than anythin', even country'... you all are welcome here, fair weather or foul."

"Thanks," gratefully spoke Jacobson.

“We're awe-struck by your hospitality, Mr. Wade, but – wait – *uh-oh!*” shouted an alarmed, glowing-eyed Tanaka. “*Everybody away from the window!*”

As they dashed so as to be out of the line-of-sight into the room, the window-curtains closed by themselves.

There was the sound of something mechanical, swooshing overhead. Through the most narrow of openings between the right and left window-curtains, the former science officer took a quick glance outside, wheeled to face the hastily-arrayed crowd (which now included everyone, except Wolf's dogs, which were baying incoherently, from inside the barn), and warned,

“That was one of Brent's drones – or, at least, some military thing; *Vîrya Sài'ymë* detected it just before it flew right over us... she's trying to make sense of the communications traffic that she intercepted from it. Sam, we've *got* to get out of here. This whole part of the state's probably under some kind of dragnet, and –”

“'Veer-ya?'” inquired a perplexed Marie Wade, who had joined her husband in the doorway. “Who's that?”

“Later,” parried Jacobson, with an up-held index finger.

There were more flying-machine-sounds – at least two – one that over-flew the house, and another that went above the barn.

“I would tend to agree with you on that, Madam,” commented the Russian, who, clad only in an ill-fitting pair of pajama-bottoms, had entered the room and was sitting on the bed. “But where do you propose for us to go?”

“Away from here,” answered Tanaka. “And then, we... *what?*”

She stared off into space, for a second, after which her tone of voice became even more stressed.

“Little One's telling me that this whole thing's no accident,” accused the former science officer. “The military's referring to *your* name, Brent, as 'the target'... what on Earth did you *do* – call them and offer a deal, or something?”

“No, *no!*” quickly countered Boyd, who began nervously pacing back and forth, while trying to avoid looking any of the the others in their eyes. “This is all *bullshit!* If you *must* know, Professor, all I did was call Laura, and yes, that *was* on an unsecured line, but I threw away the phone, afterwards... I've got no idea how they traced it, since I smashed the damn thing to smithereens, before I got rid of it. I was *miles* away. *Fuck!*”

“That was pretty damn stupid, Brent,” complained Jacobson. “You've led them right *to* us.”

“I just wanted to *talk* to her, for God's sake,” defended the former Mars pilot. “And good thing I did – Laura's been getting escalating threats from the Agency, all the time. I told her to take the kids, head off and call for Karéin. Hopefully my family will be safe, by this time tomorrow night.”

“Oh, now *there's* a great idea,” sighed Tanaka. “Getting *her* right back in the middle of this whole thing. Assuming, of course, that she helps us, instead of doing the same for Minnie. I thought we'd decided on all of this, hadn't we?”

"You know, *I've* got a family too," mentioned Jacobson. "And I'm scared to *death* about what might happen to them. But I'm not so bloody selfish as to risk jeopardizing the entire mission, just because of my own –"

"I've got *nothing* to apologize for – *nothing!*" angrily protested Boyd. "And if you don't want to risk your ass and your precious 'mission', to protect your kids and wife, that's *your* business... but then, we all *know* why you don't really want to go home to face her... *don't* we, Commander?"

Jacobson's eyes were flashing both actually and metaphorically, as his war-song began to sound and he took a step toward his former pilot, who stood his ground while his own powers started to energize.

"God *damn* you, Major – how *dare* you –" he hissed.

"Hey, *hey*, y'all *chill!*" stammered a shocked White.

Instantly, Tanaka – moving with super-human speed – appeared between the two more-than-men. She had an arm outstretched against each one.

"What's the big thing?" whispered Callum Wade to Donny, who was out in the hall, trying to look in. "Neither of 'em got a gun... they 'fraid of a bloody nose?"

"Well, let's just say," laconically observed the trucker, "Them boys get goin' at it, and you gonna need a new house, barn 'n everything, Uncle."

"That's *enough!*" shouted Tanaka, with watering eyes. "Stow it, *both* of you! We can't afford nonsense like this at *any* time, but above and beyond all, not *now!*"

The former science officer turned to stare at Boyd.

"Brent," she counseled, with a trembling, most-unlike-her voice, "That was uncalled-for, in *so* many ways. You *hurt* me and you *know* why... we were both up there, our hearts were breaking... Sam's right – how *dare* you judge us... judge, *me*. You've got nothing to apologize for? Fine, I accept that. But neither do I owe you an explanation... nor does Sam."

Boyd looked down, ran his fist across his mouth and muttered, "Yeah... maybe that *was* a little below-the-belt... didn't mean it, just came out that way, I guess. Sorry. But for Christ's *sake*, Professor – here we are, sitting out in the middle of Hell's Half Acre, off on a futile wild-goose chase to harpoon the Great White Whale of a President, about whose whereabouts we don't have the foggiest idea... and for the sake of *this*, I'm supposed to sit idly by, and watch my family, get kidnapped off to the same kind of monstrous treatment that they did to Bob, Tommy and the rest of those guys from Tucson? You want a stupid idea, that's got to be the great grand-daddy of all of 'em. Besides... it's a done deal now, at least as far as Laura and my kids are concerned. If the Commander wants to use one, I've got two more throw-away phones. He might as well – what's there to lose, at this point?"

Jacobson's shoulders slumped back ever-so-slightly, and, to the immense relief of the rest of them, he backed off, coming to rest with his back to one of the bedroom walls.

"Just get rid of them," he suggested. "As quickly as possible. Even if they're powered down, who knows whether the government's got some secret way of remotely tracing them."

Misha had risen from the bed at the start of the confrontation between the two former Mars mission astronauts; he now positioned himself so as to be able to look through the open slit between the window-curtains.

"Doing so may be wise," he commented, "Because these aircraft – I think they *are* drones, or something similar, perhaps akin to what we fought up on Amchitka – seem to have adopted irregular patterns of movement... they are repeatedly over-flying all the buildings in the area, as far out as I can discern. Even at night, there is little doubt that when they subject this farm to the same scrutiny, they would have sufficient visual resolution to detect some attribute that would identify us – the license-plate on Donny's truck, for example."

He looked downward, doing an immediate double-take.

"What the – *damnation!*" inveighed the Russian.

"What?" came the immediate, concerned response, from several onlookers.

"It is Wolf," advised Misha. "He is heading toward the barn."

"Why'd he – oh, right... the *dogs*," mentioned Donny, from out in the hall. "I'll go get him."

He disappeared down the stairs.

"He's at the barn-door, going in," observed Misha. "Hold on –"

Another one of the flying whatever-they-were's, swooshed overhead.

"I think that pretty much decides it," proposed Jacobson, with a weary sigh. "They'll get a picture of him for *sure*, even if they don't ID the truck or something else about us – we've *got* to get out of here. Let's start packing, and make it fast."

"Yeah... but... to, where?" asked White.

"We implement the plan," stolidly replied the former Mars mission commander, "The one that we jointly agreed upon, previously."

"That really a good idea, when we're already on the run?" pressed White.

"You got a better one?" answered Jacobson.

"When I do, y'all be the first to know," ruefully grunted the former Mars mission navigator.

Suddenly, their ears were accosted by a weird, shrill, high-pitched, siren-like noise, apparently coming from a point over the courtyard, between the house's front door and the entrance to the barn. This was followed, in rapid order, by the exciting, enervating melody of Wolf's now-familiar war-song, and then by a brilliant flash – so bright that it not only lit up the surroundings outside, but was easily-visible even through the curtains – and finally, by a loud explosion that shook the walls of the Wade homestead.

As the sounds of disassembled metal crashing to ground added to the din, Misha quickly glanced outward, then turned inside and explained, "Wolf took a shot at one of them, and evidently, his aim was true... Commander, I will see you downstairs. I would estimate that we have, optimistically, five to ten minutes... before the real, ahh, 'fun' starts."

"*Curse* him, anyway!" complained Tanaka. "All the subtlety of a rogue elephant – we might have evaded them, but now –"

"Recriminations later, Cherie," advised a fast-moving Jacobson, as he headed for the hallway-door. "There'll be plenty to go around. We need to leave here – right *now!*"

"Uncle, Auntie – get whatever you can, family Bible kind of stuff only, into a bag, and follow me," ordered Donny, while the room rapidly emptied. "He ain't kiddin' – we're *out* of here."

"This is my *home*," protested Marie Wade. "I *can't* leave!"

The trucker stepped forward and grabbed his aunt by the shoulders, looking intensely at her.

"Aunt Marie," he said, all the while trying to avoid 'losing it' himself, "I'm sayin' this because I love you... I'm *terrible* sorry, but if you all don't come with us... you and Uncle Callum gonna get *killed*. They're gonna blast this place to bits, and they ain't gonna care who's inside. Now you get your belongin's together, and get ready for a rough ride. I ain't askin' if you approve – I'm askin' if you *understand*."

The farm-wife was utterly flustered and visibly in tears, as Tanaka embraced her.

"I'm very sorry too, Mrs. Wade," consoled the former science officer, "Neither you nor your husband deserve this... just like a *lot* of people, lately, haven't deserved what's been done to them by the government. But Donny's very right – staying here's *far* too dangerous, now that they know we're here."

"H-how's goin' with you all, gonna be any safer?" argued the farm-wife.

Without letting go, but holding the woman a bit further away, Tanaka allowed a momentary surge of the *Fire* to race through her body. With dimly-glowing eyes and a Stentorian voice of confidence, she replied, "Because I'm the meanest daughter-of-a-you-know-what in the valley, Ma'am. When I get going – not to mention my friends here – they won't know what *hit* 'em. You have a group of super-heroes, defending you. *That's* how."

As Tanaka released her grasp and the farm-wife's jaw dropped in wary astonishment, a worried – but level-headed – Callum Wade took her hand and said to her, "Well, my nephew asked if we understand, and that'd be a 'no'... but that's a *different* thing, from bein' caught in the middle of a shoot-out, without bein' on one side or t'other. Come on, Marie... we'd better get ready. I'll let the cat and the horses out – least I can do for 'em. You get us packed."

He led the sobbing woman out of the bedroom and down the stairs.

A short while later – it might have been as few as five minutes, perhaps as many as ten – the Jacobson van had been unloaded from Donny's 18-wheeler, which the trucker had driven to one of the surrounding paddocks, at least a half-mile away, whistling nervously over his breath all the way there and on foot, back.

The Missouri night was uncannily peaceful, for – oddly – since Wolf's unfortunate misunderstanding with the flying-thing (revealed, by the nature of its wreckage, as a drone, although a larger and apparently more sophisticated one, compared to what had been encountered on Amchitka), there had been no more over-flights.

Indeed, the skies seemed to be clear; the flying-things had, apparently, retreated.

They were arrayed under the car-port roof on one side of the barn, which had previously covered most, if not all, of Donny's tractor-trailer.

"Okay, folks," spoke Jacobson. "The following's mostly for Mr. and Mrs. Wade, given that the rest of us have all heard it before. Callum, Marie – you ride in the middle of the van, along with Devon, Brent and Misha; it'll be a tight fit, particularly with all the suitcases and duffel-bags everywhere, but you can manage... right? Wolf and his dogs will be in the back, and don't be surprised if he has to open the rear-doors, to get a clear shot at anything that's stupid enough to follow us. Donny will drive, I'll sit in the passenger seat – I can take a bullet or two... or three... better than anyone else, if one comes from that direction. Cherie is going to sit on top of the van in front of the stuff we've got lashed to the roof-rack, and deal with any threats that come from above. You following me, so far?"

"Uhh... 'deal with' 'em?" mumbled Callum Wade. "How's she gonna do *that?* I offered, but she didn't take old Betsy, the AR I had in th' shed. 'Least the Russkie got the good sense to grab her."

"Moral support only, sir," politely stated Misha. "Or, force of habit."

"*Easy,*" purred Tanaka. "I'm going to power up a force-field, then fly at hundreds of kilometers per hour, as high as the stratosphere if necessary, and blow them to pieces with a barrage of lightening-bolts. I *do* that, you know."

"Oh, *sure* you do, honey," uneasily agreed the farm-wife.

"Y'all bring that Bible, Marie?" sighed Wade. "Wouldn't mind readin' them parts 'bout 'the hereafter', agin... seems like a good time to study up."

"Never a *bad* time, sir," offered White, "But if things get hot... y'all huddle right next to me, and we'll chill down *real* fast – I got my own English on the whole 'force-field' thing. Might be a bit uncomfortable in there, but a damn sight better than gettin' capped by a stray bullet, I reckon. Oh, and one more thing – if y'all hear a lot of strange music startin' to play inside your heads and keyin' y'all up, well, that's just this weird-ass shit that Angel Lady laid on us... sorta like our alien callin' card tellin' 'em 'the boys's back in town', don't you know."

Callum muttered something and shook his head in disbelief.

The side-door to the van self-opened (though this was in fact due to a slight telekinetic push, on the part of Jacobson), and he directed, "Let's get in... get out of here."

"Damn straight," grunted Donny, as he took the driver's seat and started the engine. The rest of them rapidly clambered aboard, but then noticed that Boyd had tarried behind.

"Come *on*, bro'," cajoled White. "*Know* it's tight in here, but y'all can sit on my lap, if you want – and if y'all get excited, I *promise* I won't tell your wife... 'long as y'all don't tell Saquina."

"That's okay, pardner," quipped Wolf, from the back. "I'll make a *point* of doin' that. I'd have made a pass at that little wifey of yours... 'cept for that 'water' shit she's got goin'. Dogs put the kibosh on it, sad to say."

"Yeah, well, she don't like white dudes with long hair," riposted White. "Mutts that burn holes in the carpet, neither."

One of the bounty-hunter's puppies belched out a spark-infused 'yip'.

"*Look*, team –" complained an anxious Jacobson.

"Don't worry," stated the former Mars mission pilot, "I'll be riding on top, with the Professor."

"Brent...?" started Tanaka.

Method to my madness, he sent to her.

When the shooting starts, and you head upwards – I want you to lock on and carry me behind you. When I tell you – let me go.

Don't be insane, she noiselessly protested.

I can't maneuver with you dragging behind – we'd be sitting ducks for the first missile – and you'd be hit by a bunch of them, before you fall to your death!

I know I don't deserve it, he answered. *But do you... trust me?*

For a second or two, while the humans – though not the rest of them – looked perplexedly at the apparent stand-off between the former science officer and the former Mars pilot, Tanaka did not respond. Then, she replied, out loud,

"I trust you... *brother*... with my *life*. How could I... not?"

Boyd wiped a tear, naively hoping the gesture wouldn't be noticed.

"Thank you, Professor," he croaked.

"Listen, everybody... at least, all you, uhh, 'New People'," continued Boyd, regaining his composure as he spoke. "Given that it's dark, and given the nature of my weapon – not to mention the Professor's – I think it would be to everyone's advantage to try to see only in *Um'nàhr'é*, when the bad stuff hits; you could try *Um'b'as'ài*, too... I'll try to suppress energy in both of these, when and if I have to fire – but no guarantees. Wolf, if you see something coming fast toward the van, and it looks like, uhh, a firefly, in the warm-sight... that may be a missile – blast it as soon as you can get a clear shot. Everyone got that?"

"Roger-dodger," grunted the bounty-hunter. "Just don't be anywhere nearby, when I let loose... 'less you got your asbestos undies, on."

"What the hell's he *talkin'* 'bout, this 'oomba' stuff?" whispered Callum Wade to his wife.

"That's Mars-talk for all them funky colors you see, once Her Alien Highness says a 'Hail Mary' over you," advised Wolf. "Don't feel ashamed, if it's all Greek to you... I'm one of 'them', I s'pose... but I don't get three-quarters of this shit, myself."

"I would suggest that you crouch down and close your eyes, when and if Major Boyd unleashes his attack," added Misha. "It is quite, uhh... *spectacular.*"

As White nodded to the two outside, the van side-door closed. Boyd and Tanaka levitated to positions on top of the vehicle, and it began to move rapidly down the long driveway from the Wade place, to the closest side-road.

"Callum... God help us, we're leaving behind our *home...* all those memories..." whimpered the farm-wife.

"It's gonna be okay, Marie," consoled the farmer. "Gonna be... *okay.*"

Most of them were surprised at how far they had gotten, before *it,* happened. The van had gone about a mile and a half down the side-road, when Tanaka raised the alarm, by knocking three times on the van's ceiling.

White stuck his head out of a rolled-down window and asked, "What y'all seein', Professor?"

"Not me," she called back, over the sound of the wind. "It's Little One – she's detecting something, out there... a *lot* of them, whatever they are, over by the Wade place... but there are some coming our way. She's telling me that it's a different, uhh, footprint, compared to the one that Wolf shot down. Stay sharp."

"Damn sure of *that,*" muttered White, as he retracted back inside the van and informed the others.

A few seconds later, there were a series of loud flashes, followed by the now-familiar, deep 'bang' explosion-sounds, off in the distance, corresponding roughly to where Donny had parked his 18-wheeler.

"Good thing we're out of there," commented Jacobson. "None too soon."

"*Shit,*" spat the trucker, as he tried to use the strange new "seeing-the-warm-things" second sight, to scan for threats, out ahead, "Took me seven *years* to save up enough for the down-payment on that thing, and I still got another eight to go, to pay off the loan."

"Don't worry," reassured the former Mars mission commander, "When this is all over with, my friend, we'll make sure that you, as well as your uncle and aunt, are set for life."

"Wish I could believe you, Commander," replied Donny, "But it's been nothin' but fuckin' bad luck, since – *whoa* –"

He had to quickly compensate for the loss of weight on the top of the van, as they perceived dual war-songs instantly powered up nearly to full-bore, then heard Tanaka's entrancing, exciting cry, "***Vìrya Sài'ymë – shield!* Go we now to... *war!*"**

The former Mars mission science officer and pilot, rocketed upward.

The enhanced senses of the more-than-humans detected it first, but in another few seconds, even the farmer and his wife could hear the ominously rhythmic *brap-brap-brap* sound of helicopter-blades, off in the distance, though closing quickly.

"What's... *that?*" nervously inquired Marie Wade.

"Judging from the sound – which I've heard before – they're gunships, I think," answered Jacobson, leaning forward and straining to get the maximum possible range from his "Mars eyes". "Wolf – you seeing anything coming from the rear quarter?"

"Yeah," responded the bounty-hunter, "Damn far away, close to the ground... at least two of the fuckers. Listen, *amigo* – I can take a shot at 'em at long range, but I might miss – the more juice I use, the faster it flies and the bigger the bang, but harder to control... you know? Oh, and Miss Hottie's tellin' me, she can put a wall of fire up behind us – that should melt just about *anything* – but it's gotta be fairly close, if you want it to do its job. Point being, if one of 'em blows at *that* distance –"

He looked down for a second and whispered, "No, you *can't* go off and chomp 'em, girl – they gonna bite you back. Dad'll tell you when it's 'fun-time'."

"Chance we'll have to take," advised Jacobson, while White chuckled.

With now-glowing eyes and a deep, beat-laden war-song beginning to play, he turned to the driver and warned, "Stay on the road, at all costs, we don't need a car-wreck, while being shot at... when things get hot, just believe in yourself, and imagine the impossible – the *Fire's* not let us down, yet; it'll do the same for you. In a few seconds, I'm going to head out the passenger-door, jump forward and knock 'em down, but keep driving – I'll catch up. You got that?"

"But them's *Army* – they're *miles* away – and we're goin' seventy – oh, *forget* it," muttered the trucker. "Uncle Callum, you all got that Bible handy?"

The farmer grimly nodded.

There was an explosion, followed in quick order by two or three more, far overhead.

"Fuckin' bad hair day," complained Donny, as they heard the war-songs of Wolf, White and Misha begin to simultaneously play, albeit at subdued volume compared to those of the just-departed Tanaka, and of Jacobson. The effect, even upon the two humans, was simultaneously inspirational and empowering; which was fortunate, considering that Marie Wade, in particular, was frightened half to death.

At that point, completely without warning, Wolf threw back his head and let out a weird, ululating, wailing howl, one whose lonely, haunting, wilderness music reverberated back and forth, not only through the inside of the van and the very bodies of those therein, but also, over the countryside for a substantial distance, in every direction.

Owoooooooooo...

"What the hell was *that?*" called Donny, over his shoulder. "Felt damn good – like whole fifth of Bourbon, all at once – but next time, a little advance notice'd be nice."

"That, pardner," purred the bounty-hunter, who took his red-glowing eyes off the road and sky behind the vehicle, only long enough to cast a glance forward, "Was a *boost*."

"You just earned your pay," congratulated a satisfied Jacobson, one second before his body became encased in a dimly-visible, translucent, quartz-like suit of ethereal armor, and he sprang out of the van like some impossible kangaroo.

I feel so *much more powerful compared to how I was, up at Amchitka,* reflected Tanaka, as she streaked almost vertically-upward, with her war-song echoing across the Prairie, reaching a few thousand feet in scant seconds.

And God knows... I'll probably need it.

The Missouri night sky was almost completely clear, with only scattered clouds, here and there; and partly because of this, Tanaka could easily see that she had already gone far above the military aircraft, closing in both on the Wade house, and on Jacobson's van.

Get a commanding height and superior speed – preserve maneuvering energy, she mused. *Well, Cherie Teruko... you spent a lot of time studying those NeoNet documents on "air combat tactics"... let's hope you'll pass the test, because you likely won't get a second chance.*

Don't worry, Professor, sent Boyd, who was trailing in the slip-stream, with his dull-glowing eyes – both the former pilot and science officer were trying to suppress this attribute, but it was impossible to do completely while using enough *Amaiish* to go into battle – staring up at her.

Remember what the Commander, Devon and I told you, a few nights ago. The Air Force is trained to fight opponents who are like... them. Don't play to their strengths – do the unexpected, it'll give them fits.

All I ask is, "be merciful". They're just doing their jobs.

Thanks, she answered. *And I'm doing mine.*

Despite systematic use of the "special sight", it was difficult for Boyd to judge the altitude, so he sent another mental message to his former Mars mission co-worker.

When we hit 1,700 meters, let this baby bird go, if you don't mind.

Are you sure? she replied. *I'm afraid for you...*

Corn in the field's already pretty high, he reassured. *If it doesn't break my fall... well, I'll make a pretty good scarecrow, with a stalk or two up my butt.*

Please, she protested. *I'm trying to concentrate, here!*

And I'll glow, he maliciously added. *You can sell tickets.*

Dear that Mother high are now we, advised *Vîrya Sài'ymë.*

With an inaudible gulp, Tanaka counted down,

Three... two... one... Godspeed, Major!

He's not even trying *to stay aloft,* realized a frightened Tanaka. Sensei, *if you can hear me – make him worthy... make him, strong.*

The ex-pilot plummeted downward, his eyes almost disappearing in the inky blackness below.

After bounding forward to the tune of about another half-mile, Jacobson could see his quarry as clear as day, despite the fact that the only illumination here – except for the van's headlights, which Donny had unsuccessfully tried to turn off (it appeared that they were interlocked with the ignition) – was starlight and a half-moon.

Well, he thought, as his feet momentarily made contact with the road-surface, *IR countermeasures or none, you stand out like a blowtorch in Antarctica.*

No longer even surprised at how routine doing so seemed, he propelled himself in another long, forward arc, reaching an apogee of at least three hundred feet, before – with his close-fitting, protective shielding fully-energized – Jacobson came down on the first of the helicopters like the proverbial ton-of-bricks.

Dodged the rotors, he realized. *Probably could have tangled with them, and they'd be the ones to get pulped – not me. I* believe... *maybe...*

Well, Karéin, I'm starting to understand what you said back on the Eagle, *about "jumping off a cliff and not hoping you can fly"...*

To the astonished dismay of the U.S. Army pilot and weapons officer in their armored-glass "front-office", Jacobson struck the gunship just behind its cockpit, the momentum of his *Fire*-enhanced arrival sending it earthward even before his fist smashed into the reduction-gear-cowling and pulped the war-machine's transmission and propulsion machinery.

With the sounds of ripping, tearing metal accosting their ears, the two nonplussed soldiers tried to eject; but since the rotor-assembly was still attached, the gambit failed, and they rode the gunship all the way to a spinning, out-of-control crash, which their assailant evaded with another, much less powerful leap, just before impact.

The pilot's bloody body was likely dead, when the former Mars mission commander showed up at the crash-site and, with only a perfunctory effort, tore away enough of the twisted wreckage to allow the gunner to get out.

"Tell your C.O.," he snarled, from inside his mobile, pseudo-crystalline fortress. "To back off, before he gets you all fucking *killed.*"

Before the dazed, astonished survivor could reply, Jacobson had reversed direction, and was careening toward the other two gunships, which were all-too-rapidly closing the distance with the van.

Consumed by fear and worry for her fellow ex-astronaut – but trying as hard as she could, to concentrate on the mission-at-hand – Tanaka soared further and further upward, until she was (as so informed by her weirding "child", whose mind bombarded her own with an endless stream of situational facts and enhanced-sensory inputs; the effect was distracting, if necessarily so) at least ten thousand feet high.

Military tactic books, not to mention Brent, Devon and Sam, said that in an operation like this, there'd be top-cover, she reflected, while trying not to spend too much time marveling at the translucent, ethereal skull-cap and scale-mail (complete with arm-shield), which had suddenly appeared over her body.

Like her angelic mentor had done before, Tanaka came to a stop, restraining the use of her protective powers as much as possible, and then rotated in all directions, scanning as she went.

And there they are, she ruefully noted. Six fighters – a bit higher than where I'm at, coming in formation from the north-east.

Do they see me? Let's find out.

The exhilarating roar of her war-song – along with another, less familiar, war-cry, from far below – enhanced the adrenaline in her bloodstream, as the energy poured into her shield and she raced upward, straight at the vanguard of the U.S. Air Force.

Well, this is it, realized Boyd, as he fell downward at a quickening velocity that would have utterly terrified a normal human.

If I calculated right – 55 meters per second, or thereabouts – I got about 30 seconds, he ruefully considered.

Time seemed to be slowing down, in a most peculiar way; the seconds lazily floated by, as if he'd been put in the grasp of some funky new drug.

Funny, but I'm not seeing my life flash before my eyes, thought the ex-astronaut.

That's a good sign... right?

As much as he could, Boyd twisted and turned in an attempt to survey the situation, hoping that concentrating on something other than his own, impending demise, would help him calm down.

Far above him – and receding rapidly – he could just detect Tanaka's protective 'bubble', as it streaked toward a gaggle of F-32E's approaching on an intercept course.

Below, as he looked to the right and left while pushing his 'Mars eyes' to the limit, it was immediately apparent that the Wades had been wise to accompany Jacobson And Company : their farm-house was burning brightly, and was being methodically reduced to rubble by repeated rocket-attacks on the part of the six or seven gunships encircling it; meanwhile, three helicopters (no – two – to the ex-astronaut's satisfaction, he witnessed the middle one being stomped into junk, by the former Mars mission commander's alien-tapdanceact) were coming up the road at the tiny-looking van, while another three were approaching from behind the vehicle.

Hmm... falling a bit to the left of the road and of where the van will be in another few seconds... well, at least they'll know where to retrieve my body... wish I had time to experiment with that "light-shield" she mentioned back on the island, but too much new alien-crap to learn right now, as it is...

To Boyd's dismay, not only was he now getting uncomfortably close to the ground, but he also saw the tell-tale flashes of anti-tank missile booster-engines being ignited, two rounds coming from the gunships of the forward group and three coming from the aft pursuit-group.

Shit, he mentally cursed, *One hit, or even a near-miss, by those things will certainly blow the van to bits... and at* this *range, even with the extra time I seem to have, they're flying too fast for me to aim accurately at both volleys – the Commander's too far behind those two gunships, to stop them –*

Aim at the ATGMs coming from the front, and pray that the bounty-hunter's on the ball...

As he forced the *Fire* close to its luxurious, thrilling maximum power, Boyd tried to steady his hands, to target a spot just in front of the emergent missiles; given the air-buffeting that assailed him on his downward plunge, this would have been impossible for a human being, but – somehow – *something* unfamiliar, was stabilizing him.

Shine! he cried, his voice ringing across the Missouri night sky.

Boyd's dazzling, photon-beam attack, traveling at the speed of light, hit home; the two ATGMs prematurely detonated very close to the gunships that had unleashed them, causing crippling damage to both helicopters, which came crashing to ground, encased in flames. Their wreckage was strewn all over the road, forming an impenetrable barrier, with secondary ammunition- and fuel-explosions making the crash-site even more dangerous.

He was momentarily sickened by the carnage.

Except for an accident of history, came an anguished realization, *It could have been* me, *flying one of those 'copters.*

Fuck you, *Mr. President – you* sent *those guys, to a needless death – four more reasons for me to grease your sleazy hide, the minute I get a shot at you!*

But Boyd had no chance to mourn, for he was now only a couple hundred feet over the cornfield, with at most three or four seconds to spare.

Now or never, Brent... come on, fuckin' come ***on****, how do I turn it* ***on****...*

He had been devoting almost all of his attention to his impending impact with the ground and with the situation in front of the van, and in so doing, had almost lost track of the fact that two more ATGMs had just been fired at the back of that vehicle.

But then the former Mars pilot, saw a vivid demonstration of what Wolf was capable of doing, with his own, unique 'gift' : the bounty-hunter had opened up against the oncoming missiles with a spectacular discharge of multiple, small-sized fireballs, each of which flew a winding, interleaving path relative to the others, forming a smoke-and-spark-imbued, Roman Candle-like conflagration, in the path of the ATGMs. And forming behind this – at a distance of no more than ten to fifteen feet from the back-end of the van – was a blazing, circular wall of elemental fire, whose hellish heat was perceptible even as far out as where the plummeting ex-astronaut, now found himself.

One of the missiles was hit by Wolf's fireball-barrage; it pre-detonated at a point about halfway from the launching gunship, but the others somehow evaded his first attack. The two remaining ATGMs reached the fire-wall and simultaneously exploded, perilously-close to the van – which, to Boyd's stunned horror, rocketed upward off the road toward him, as the blast's shock-wave struck the vehicle's rear-end.

Jesus – it's sent them fifteen feet into the air – if they land on top of what's left of the 'copters that I knocked down –

Jacobson was bounding forward, but he had begun his leap before the van was propelled off-course. He tried to change direction, though, it appeared, not sufficiently to intercept the stricken vehicle.

For a split-second, Boyd felt sickeningly helpless, but then, his mind perceived a singing, familiar, friendly, young woman's voice.

You are ready, noble First-To-Touch; now go, and rescue them!

The former Mars mission pilot was overtaken by a different feeling, one of purpose and power; and without really understanding how – maybe it was a childhood memory of the first time he had learned to propel himself through water, or maybe it was intuitive knowledge, accessed in an unforgettable incident, on a trip back from the Red Planet – Boyd made himself effortlessly dive downward, like a cormorant targeting its next meal.

His war-song took on a new, thrilling timbre, like the echo of rapidly-played electric-piano chords off in the distance, as Boyd – his whole *body* now shining yellow-white, only slightly less brilliantly than his sinister-looking eyes – rocketed downward.

In a half-second or less, he had landed on top of the careening, perilously-airborne van; and in the next split-second, the vehicle's forward motion was retarded by the impact of Jacobson's hurtling body, which hit at the junction of the forward windshield and the roof.

The determined, newly-potent look on his former subordinate's glowing face told the Mars mission commander all he had to know; Jacobson did a back-flip, disappearing below the front of the van, as Boyd locked his telekinesis to the vehicle's frame, invoked the *Fire* and pulled the vehicle upward and forward.

Only slightly to his amazement – but none the less, to his relief – the former Mars mission pilot saw a dark-skinned arm and head pop out from the passenger-side window. Boyd felt rush of friendly *Amaiish* and a bone-chilling surge of cold from that location. He saw a ramp of ice, high-end nearest them, cover the area of the two crashed helicopters; this provided a welcome landing-pad for Jacobson, who had positioned himself under the van, carrying it on his back, while it skidded to a gradual stop.

Boyd, still on top of the van and all too well-aware that more gunships were still coming up from behind, wheeled in place, just in time to see one of the war-machines break to the left, while the other went to the right.

Donny leaned out of the driver's-side window, and yelled, "Almost fuckin' *bought* it, man! Uncle 'n Aunt – scared shitless but they're okay, Russian did some kind of green thing, stopped the shrapnel – but don't know if I can get her goin', it's –"

"No *time!*" shouted Jacobson, who had lowered the front of the van as gently as he could, and scurried out from underneath, almost in sync with Wolf, who had tumbled awkwardly out the back-doors. "They'll come back for another pass," warned the former Mars commander, "Catch us in the cross-fire!"

His advice was prescient : each gunship, after having gone off to a distance of about a mile, had turned and was now beginning to come toward the damaged, stationary van.

"Try to draw 'em off, Brent!" demanded Jacobson. "Devon – take the right! Wolf – left!"

Fearful in more than one way, but knowing there was no time to argue, Boyd tensed his knees into a half-squat, felt the thrill of the *Fire* pulsing through his veins, and flew straight upward, though at much less than maximum speed.

If their ATGMs are IR-homers, he mused, *maybe they'll follow me.*

WTF? What am I saying*?*

If they are, *and if they* do, *and I* can't *outfly them – I'm, uhh, SOL...*

He was half-correct. Two missiles were launched from the gunship on the van's right flank, while the helicopter on the left raised its auto-cannon and began to fire – but, thankfully, a half-second before, Wolf's infernal flame-barrier had been raised quite far out, on that side.

As it set the prairie grass ablaze, those few who had the time to notice were amazed to see the thirty-millimeter rounds tumbling (albeit, still with dangerous velocity) to plough furrows in the earth, as they traversed the fire-wall; this had, evidently, either ruined their ballistics or had melted the cannon-shells, outright.

"Fuck, *yeah!"* several heard a triumphant Wolf yell.

Even at his current height – some hundred feet from the ground, ascending slowly and drifting to the right of the van, so as to stay in the battle – Boyd could feel the supernatural chill of White's attack, as a jet of super-Antarctic cold suddenly streaked across the Missouri night sky, striking the left-flank gunship on its underside, immediately freezing its engines and sending the unfortunate machine crashing down. This also sent one of the missiles that the helicopter had launched, harmlessly off-course, but the other one changed direction.

There's the one with the IR seeker, realized Boyd.

And it's seeking – me!

Uh-oh...

He had less than a second to decide whether to stand and fight or evade, and the effort wasn't made any easier by the distraction of a flash, followed by several loud explosions, from a long way overhead.

Coming head-on, small target, and if I miss – no second shot –

Fly, Brent – ***fly!***

Upward he rocketed, his body glowing like a human signal-flare, with his war-song echoing over the heads of those below.

To say that she was "eternally grateful" for the presence of the weirding demi-child that adorned her torso, would have been the understatement of Cherie Tanaka's life, as she increased speed and raced into the troposphere, while becoming ever-more cognizant of what she was up against.

Though she had pushed her "Mars senses" – especially the "special sight", in the near infra-red – to what she believed to be their limit, the imagery that she could discern in the night sky, was indistinct and hard-to-track; some of the onrushing fighter-planes were easy to see, but others, perhaps further away, flickered in and out, and Tanaka feared that she'd be at a heavy disadvantage in simply being able to see the enemy.

Little One, thou are Mother's Great Equalizer, communicated the more-than-a-woman. *Can thou help me to see them? Show me the 'lectro-shine!*

Along eyes see now thine through me, noble with Mother it, came the enthusiastic reply.

Speak warrior 'lectro-voices bad sky-fortress to, east north far and. 'Man-Big' say they orders us kill to. Hate so us why they, Mother?

I don't know, honey, fumbled Tanaka, while almost forgetting how to fly, as her mind was instantly flooded with a bewildering array of non-visual, yet, easily-comprehensible, inputs. *All I* do *know... is, thou and I, against all of them.*

Like that... old sci-fi movie, where they show you what the man-eating alien's seeing, she realized.

Switch it this *way, view the warm-stuff, glow from the engines, friction heating up their forward-sections... switch it* that *way, there are the radio-pulses... ahh, the star-shine, now* that *illuminates them decently... what if I do all of 'em at once – omigod, sensory overload, especially with this crazy near-360-degree awareness – but if I tamp down this one, and that one –* yeah*!*

Couldn't miss *'em if I tried, now!*

Which is good... because if I'm calculating their speed correctly, they're flying faster than I ever have...

Out of the corner of one eye, she noticed mayhem, and substantial-sized explosions, underway at ground-level, although at this altitude it was impossible to tell who was winning or losing; so she continued to close the distance with the fighter-planes.

Mother noble dear, warily alerted *Vîrya Sài'ymë, 'lectro-particle-shine feel the I. Prepare evil fire war-birds kill-arrows us at.*

Jam – uhh, fake – uhh, deceive them, if thou can! responded a worried Tanaka.

I try will, Mother beloved, answered the child-like, weirding mind-voice. *'lectro-beams but many us on shine. All once at hard deceive be will.*

I trust thee, dear one, replied the more-than-a-woman, as she hurtled forward and upward.

In perhaps ten seconds, Tanaka was close enough to see the shapes of her assailants, which, a second or two later, broke formation, with two flying a highly-inclined course upward, two breaking left, two breaking right and the remaining two, diving.

Classic tactics, she mused. *One F-32 and his wing-man in each group, surround us, then...*

Okay – classic response... You two, off to the left – you're the "lucky ones", today. Go ahead and fire your missiles... you'll only hit your friends!

Little One – we attack!

Tanaka abruptly changed course, executing a sharp turn that could have been followed by only a very few denizens of the air. She went head-first toward the left-hand fighter-group, and in another two or three seconds, had streaked right by both of the F-32s, which, evidently sensing that something was wrong, immediately began to double back. But the more-than-a-woman came to a momentary dead stop and then reversed direction.

She was now on the tail of her two adversaries, who promptly lit afterburners in an attempt to escape; and even though the former Mars mission science officer had arranged her force-shield to deflect almost all outside-noise and other hazards, the roar and heat of the military turbofan engines was immediately, unpleasantly apparent.

So, she savagely pondered, *You're faster than me?*

See if you can outrun – this... **sword!**

Dual discharges of scintillating, *Fire*-born energy, raced from the claw-like fingers of both of Tanaka's hands, washing over a broad area of sky, like some lethal search-light; and, given the clarity with which the afterburners were visible, in the "warm-seeing" mode, it wasn't much of an accomplishment, to have struck home.

Which it did. One F-32 had its right wing and stabilizer blown off, and, as it careened downward in a spiral, its pilot ejected, popping his chute a few seconds later; but the second fighter wasn't so lucky : struck dead-on, it exploded in a huge fireball that no human being could have survived.

Sorry, Brent, she thought, while her guts churned.

More real-time sensory warnings from *Vîrya Sài'ymë* snapped Tanaka out of her guilt-ridden reverie.

Them or us – no time for sentimentality, Little One... what's that *– 'bang-arrows'? I see them – damn, they're coming fast – probably can't outrun 'em, and they'd likely intercept us before we get high enough to exhaust their fuel – okay, fly them into the ground!*

Pouring *Amaiish* into both her force-field and downward velocity, Tanaka initiated a crash-dive; she didn't dare look backward, but such a gesture wasn't necessary, as her weirding 'child' supplied the necessary, and unnerving, information, that the missiles – four or five of them – were gaining on her.

As the Missouri corn-fields loomed ever-nearer, three of the deadly projectiles unexpectedly began to tumble aimlessly off-course.

Brains their mixed I up! exulted *Vîrya Sài'ymë.*

Cannot but grab I others on to –

I love thee, thankfully sent Tanaka. *Leave the rest to –*

There was a huge explosion near to ground-level; but her attention was distracted by something else that registered with her special senses, in front of and to the left.

What the H – well, congratulations, Major! But why's he... uh-oh...

As she plummeted past the brilliant-glowing, upward-streaking Brent Boyd, there was just enough time – probably, a tiny fraction-of-a-second – for Tanaka to receive a fleeting broadcast, from her former Mars mission colleague.

Shut your eyes, as I... shine!

The second military helicopter might have been climbing to get a clear shot over Wolf's fire-screen; or, it might have heard the distress-call from its wing-man, which – in the form of frozen junk – had just crashed into the ground, on the other side of Jacobson's van.

But whatever the cause, when the gunship appeared above the flame-barrier, it was close enough to present a good target for the bounty-hunter, who took no chances. Using a "crossed-arms" gesture, a crimson-eyed, fire-and-*Fire*-enveloped, snarling Wolf somehow elevated himself at least five feet in the air, and then unleashed a devastating barrage of soccer-ball-sized fire-missiles, blanketing every direction where the helicopter's pilot could have evaded. Three or four of these struck home (though one would undoubtedly have been lethal, all by itself), and the gunship, along with its two hapless crew-members, was blown to pieces, in a roaring, concussive explosion whose violence temporarily stunned even the hardened members of the Jacobson team.

They could see that there had been a jet of flame lifting the bounty-hunter, as he skidded to a stop alongside the front of the van.

"Smoked that mother –" he started; but all of a sudden, the Missouri night became... *day,* as an incredibly-bright light-pulse from a point somewhere overhead, brilliant enough to rival the noon-day sun, illuminated everything for miles around. Its insanely-intense, supernatural glow was degraded only slightly by the van's tinted-glass windows, and would have blinded Callum and Marie

Wade, had it not been for quick-thinking on the part of the Russian, whose telekinesis forced their heads into a downward position, then covered them with an odd-looking, greenish energy-shroud.

The glow lasted only a couple of seconds, but that was more than enough for all of those inside or in the vicinity of the van. As each of them gingerly removed hands from faces, blinking to degrade the after-effects of the visual overload, Wolf complained, “Not another fuckin' nuke, *please* –”

“No... that was Major Boyd... I *think*,” muttered Jacobson, shaking his head and wiping the tears from his cheeks. “Got to speak to him, about how he uses that skill of his. Let's discuss it later – anyone see any more 'hostiles'?”

“Negative, Commander,” came the voice of Devon White. “Brent's little light-show prolly fucked up them a lot worse than us... but won't be long 'till they send for reinforcements. Can't be sure 'till him and the Professor get back – *whoa* –”

The ex-astronaut pointed to a new series of explosions – two larger ones, which had occurred as a result of something striking the ground, a good distance away from them, and one smaller one, overhead, but at relatively low-altitude. A second or two later, they heard the familiar war-song of Cherie Tanaka. The former Mars mission science officer landed alongside the van, and the translucent battle-gear that had previously adorned her frame, flickered and faded into nothingness.

She was followed by a triumphant, glowing-from-every-molecule Brent Boyd, who flew over the area, scouting for threats, and then came to a stop on the roof of the van.

“Congratulations, Major,” enviously commented Jacobson, addressing Boyd. “I guess the Alien Air Force just recruited a new pilot... right?”

“Guess so,” proudly replied Boyd, as he gradually reduced his shining presence to a soft glow. “Immediate threats have been dealt with, and I saw the rest of the gunships around the Wade place, retreat to the north – but, Professor – what about the rest of the fighters? There were more of them, than the two that you, uhh, 'neutralized' –”

“About that... in between whimpers about 'where did that scary big flash come from, Mommy'... *Vìrya Sài'ymë*'s also hearing some pretty interesting chatter on the military bands,” announced the more-than-a-woman. “Pilots are now basically blind... looks like they can barely keep their planes flying, and they had to use a standard-grade-encryption channel to communicate with the ACT, who's trying to talk them back to base, right now. They're heading away, too. And there's something else –”

“We probably don't have a lot of time, before we've got to get going again,” interrupted Jacobson. “What is it?”

“Little One heard something like, 'the President himself, commands you to press on with the attack, and kill that, uhh, effing bunch of traitors, at all costs',” explained Tanaka. “The pilots actually refused the order... on grounds that it would be suicide. They're being threatened with court-martial, when and if they land back at their base."

"Well, I'd say them boys got a point," noted White, with a rueful grimace. "Based on what we all been doin' to 'em lately... better a jail-cell than a tombstone, don't you know."

"I'm trying not to *think* about it, frankly," quietly remarked a haunted Boyd.

"Yeah, no kidding... I almost feel sorry for them," said the former Mars science officer, "But that's not the most important thing that *Vìrya Sài'ymë*'s intercepted. She's telling me that there were five, uhh, 'hoo-man' voices distinguishable on the other end of the command-channel – three of them seem to have been mid-rank military officers, one was a 'Gen-ral Blah-shard', and the last one, she recognized from having heard him on one of those TV speeches that we watched while back at the hotel. Guess who?"

Jacobson, who was nervously scouting hither and yon, warned, "Good intelligence, Cherie – but that guy who survived the 'copter that I brought down, is undoubtedly calling for Medevac. Can we get out of here, please?"

"We may not *want* to," argued Tanaka. "Because that last voice, was our son-of-a-bitch President, himself. Which means, he's *up* there, somewhere –"

"'Bout fuckin' *time* we had some luck," grunted White.

One of Wolf's puppies belched a puff of cinders and bayed at the moon, as Wolf eagerly commented, with a dramatic arm-gesture, "Well then... what you *waitin'* for? Like Boob says – get Captain Flashbulb there to go along, then fly up and smoke his *ass!* Get this whole fuckin' thing over with, I mean."

After saying a few words to console the cowering two humans under his care, the Russian had escaped the van and joined the discussion.

"As much as that would be desirable, my friend," he observed, "It is unlikely to be practical. Such a command-signal would undoubtedly be obfuscated in multiple ways, for example there would be multiple –"

"Tube's tellin' me, if you keep usin' them damn big words, he's gonna take a chunk out of your butt, pardner," interrupted the bounty-hunter. "What the hell's an 'obfuscate'?"

"It means, 'hidden', or 'intentionally made difficult to understand'," explained an exasperated Tanaka. "But save Misha the hot-seat, please... because Little One *also* said, the signal was low-grade, direct, easy-to-trace – it was coming in a straight line, from a point far off to the north-east. When I was way up there, I thought I got a glimpse of an aircraft – must have been a *big* one, judging from the range – in *Um'nàhr'é*, in that direction; but I was, uhh, 'preoccupied' with staying alive against the fighters, so I didn't hang around and pay it much attention. Of course, it was only one of a bunch of such signatures off in the distance, all over the place; those are probably commercial aircraft."

"This is *ridiculous*," complained Jacobson. "DoD would *never* use anything other than a mil-spec, fully-diverse C3 channel for a high-priority operation like the one we're the target of – *if* any of this is true, I'd lay you 99 to

1 odds that they're simply setting a trap for us – excuse me, *you* – to fly into. Donny – get the car started. We've got to leave here, immediately."

The trucker re-engaged the van's engine, which – much to his surprise and relief – started up with only a little extra coaxing.

"Hmm," added Boyd, as he stood and scanned for signs of danger, "As much as I'd like us to have an easy way to track down our asshole President... I'd have to concur with the Commander, on this one. A mistake like *that* would be made by a corporal on his first tour of duty... not a general, surrounded by experienced senior officers. It's just not plausible, in my opinion."

"But, *Brent*," persisted the former Mars mission science officer, "Don't you think it's worth a *try?* With *Vìrya Sài'ymë* to guide us, we could simply ride the signal all the way back to its originating point... sort of like Karéin did in finding us in the *Eagle*, after her trip to ISS2. How fast can you fly, these days? How many Gs can you safely pull?"

"God only knows, Professor," countered Boyd, "And even if we actually trace the signal correctly, which we *might*, and even if we get the right plane, which we probably *won't*, and even if it *isn't* a trap, which it probably *is*... what are we supposed to *do* – shoot down a large aircraft, possibly with hundreds of marginally-involved personnel aboard, just on the off chance, that the President's there, too? Sorry – I've already slaughtered far too many good people, as it is. I'm not really 'into' the mass murder thing... anything unclear about that?"

"Ouch," sympathetically offered White.

A crestfallen Tanaka looked at her feet, planted on the van-top.

"Yeah... you're right," she acknowledged. "We'll have to figure out a, uhh, 'humane' way to isolate the guilty from the innocent, I suppose. Ahh, *forget* it – it was a long-shot, anyway. We'd probably get jumped by a big fighter-escort, even if it *was* Mr. Big on that plane. Maybe when we've both 'progressed', a little more..."

Her voice trailed off.

"Hey, Jacobson!" called Donny. "Ready to go... I think. But where we goin', exactly?"

"First of all, out of here," indicated Jacobson, as his fists methodically smashed all of the exterior lights on the van, rendering these completely inoperative. Everyone except Boyd and Tanaka (who had elected to remain on top of the vehicle), clambered back into the van.

"Then," added the former Mars mission commander, "We hope to hell that we can get out of this area, without being tracked –"

The side-door slammed shut.

"For what it's worth," mentioned Tanaka, "*Vìrya Sài'ymë* is telling me that she doesn't see any more of those drones... and neither do I. Brent – can you confirm?"

"Confirmed," stated the former Mars mission pilot. "Perhaps my little light-show up there screwed up their sensors, too... but it's SOP for them to back off a little from the engagement area, when the ordnance starts flying. They might show up again, at any time, and that's bound to be a problem. Want to take turns, knocking 'em down?"

The van was now moving down the road, with its inhabitants at battle-stations, and Jacobson hanging half-out of the passenger-side window, both looking out for threats and listening to the conversation between his two former Mars mission subordinates.

"Guess we'll *have* to," declared Tanaka. "Since we're out in the boonies and it's pitch-dark most everywhere, for the time being, why don't we also take turns popping up, say, a hundred feet or so, over the van, every few minutes, to get advance warning of anything coming at us. We'll have to get back in and hope for the best, when we get to a major road, of course."

"Agreed," concurred Boyd. "But on first sight of a 'hostile' – combat-capable or otherwise – we'll need to take it out, *fast*... and then change course, evade into traffic if possible. I got no idea how we're going to *do* that, without ending up on the 8 a.m. news everywhere, of course. Commander – we'd better start thinking of some way to change vehicles. I know we've gotten attached to this one, but its make and license are probably all over the LEA nets, by now. The longer we stay in her, the faster they'll find us."

"Understood," nodded Jacobson, his voice easily audible despite the Prairie wind rushing by. "There are risks to everything, but look at the *good* side of it – even if they catch up to us, which they might well do – President's probably asking himself right now, 'what's it going to *take*, to bring these guys down'? After this last encounter, he's got to know, it isn't going to be enough, just to send in the police, *et cetera*. Maybe we can use that uncertainty, to keep the government off-balance."

"*Bonnie and Clyde*, on the run, except we're out-gunning the posse, at least so far," smiled the former Mars mission pilot. "I can handle that... we might just *survive* this, you know?"

"Let's 'survive', as far as Kentucky, first," coolly responded Jacobson, as the van, with its two ever-watchful, super-human guardians on top, headed east.

You Need Me, Sir

There was a very slight 'bump' – for, the pilots flying this most important of aircraft, prided themselves on making the trip as comfortable as possible – and the unmarked double of Air Force One, touched down on the runway, gradually slowing down with minimal use of thrust-reversers.

"Where *are* we?" asked the former Vice-President, as the aircraft rolled to a slow stop, parking itself at the far end of a runway. "I see a terminal building off in the distance, but no sign... it's pitch-dark out there. Couldn't we have done this earlier?"

"Sorry, sir," responded Bezomorton, with his usual, detached tone of voice, "But apart from that protracted conversation with the Agency, NSC thought it wise to leave this landing until the wee hours... fewer nosy reporters or airplane-watchers, you know. We're in Syracuse, New York – Hancock Airport."

"Well, let's get it over with," grumbled the *faux*-President.

"Affirmative, sir," answered the National Security Adviser. "They've already been carefully searched, and we've confiscated anything that could be used as a weapon; they've only got personal effects and credentials left on them. The woman complained no end when we put on the handcuffs, but she relented when we told her it was 'cuffs or no meeting'. They should be here any minute."

"Fine... I'll meet them at the door, then," stated the U.S. leader.

Bezomorton nodded, and, accompanied by his boss and two tough-looking, heavily-armed Marine guards, he proceeded forward through the labyrinthine Air Force one passage-ways, until the President had arrived at the aircraft's forward entrance-hatch, which was already open.

The U.S. leader took a step forward into the cool night air and looked outward and downward over the runway. A convoy of shiny-jet-black SUVs, with camouflaged, armored cars in front and back, had just arrived at the bottom of the mobile stairway that connected Air Force one with the tarmac.

The *nouveau*-President's beady, suspicious eyes washed over the scene unfolding at the stair-bottom. The doors on the middle-convoy SUV opened, and out stepped a number of uniformed and plain-clothes bodyguards; shortly thereafter, came the three FBI agents in which Crowford had taken such a sudden interest.

The first of these was a slim, attractive-looking, Asian-American woman in her mid-30s, with mid-length black hair. She was wearing a conservative, tight-fitting, dark blue, professional pant-suit with a navy-blue jacket and white blouse. The second was a red-headed, clean-cut, close-cropped, Caucasian sort, also probably thirty-something and much taller than the woman, dressed in a lighter-gray, Bureau regulation business-suit, with a greenish-white shirt and green tie; in front of this – almost-invisible in the darkness – was a small amulet-like thing, attached to a thin gold chain around the man's neck. The last of the agents was an older, big, African-American guy about the same height as the second man (but heavier of frame), with an almost completely-shaved head, wearing a darker business-suit, a white shirt and a brown tie.

All three of the newcomers had polished black shoes, although those on the woman seemed somewhat more casual and comfortable than the lace-ups worn by the two men; and all three had their hands bound awkwardly behind their backs, by silver handcuffs.

"We'll escort you aboard," barked a senior Marine guard, to the woman. "But remember – we have 'shoot-to-kill, on first false move' orders. Do you understand?"

"We certainly do," said the female FBI agent.

She glanced upward, following the stairs, her stare falling momentarily on the former Vice-President; and for a second or two, he felt, well, *weird*, in a way he couldn't really describe. But the feeling quickly passed, and eventually, he called out, "You're this 'Chu' person I keep hearing about?"

"Yes, sir. It's, uhh, a great honor, sir," she politely answered. "I'm Minnie Chu of Project Red Rover. Along with me are my two partners, Otis Boatman and Will Hendricks. May we come aboard, sir?"

"Yeah, you'd better," he grunted. "Advisers are telling me we're not supposed to hang around here, too long. The *alien*, you know."

"Ahh," evenly responded Chu, as her two compatriots gave her a knowing look. "The 'alien'. Indeed. Will – Otis – let's go."

Both the *faux*-President and Bezomorton noted, with mild interest, that even though their hands were bound, the three FBI agents – with Marine guards in front and behind – seemed to have no trouble in rapidly stepping up the mobile stairway, even though its incline was quite steep.

As the three newcomers stepped off the staircase, then into the aircraft, the U.S. leader noticed that the African-American agent was whispering something to his Asian-American superior.

"You got something to say? Then say it out loud," irritably commented the *nouveau*-President. "Secrets are for me to keep, and you to tell me about."

"Oh, sorry, sir," hastily replied Boatman. "I was just tellin' Minnie here, that I can't believe I'm actually gettin' to see Air Force One... or Two, as the case may be. Momma back in St. Louis gonna be *mighty* proud."

"Maybe," came back the off-hand remark. The former Vice-President made a "come-hither" gesture with one hand, adding, "Follow me. We'll meet in the board-room."

As they complied with the order, Chu noticed that Hendricks' facial-expression, after reflexively touching his neck-amulet, had become strangely blank; it was as if he was being distracted by something unseen, like the stare of a person watching a TV-screen that you can't see.

Fortunately, this issue was solved by a sub-vocal whisper by the more-than-a-woman. Then, with her voice calm and restrained as the third agent came back to his senses, Chu spoke up.

"Sir," she said, "Is there a reason why our arms have to be restrained, like this? We're unarmed, you know."

"So I'm told," coolly answered the *faux*-President, over his shoulder.

The walk to the aircraft's largest internal conference-room was a relatively short one, and the enhanced hearing of the three FBI agents detected the sound of revving high-bypass turbofans, before those around them did. The 747-derivative began to slowly move, as they arrived in the room.

"Have a seat," directed the U.S. leader.

There were anxious-looking glances from all three of the newcomers, as, upon sitting down, they were tightly restrained, with latched belts fastened across torsos and waists.

"Standard take-off protocol," said Bezomorton. "When we're airborne, you can get up and walk around, if you want."

"That's, uhh, *great*, sir," politely responded Chu. "Thank you."

Chu had been seated between Boatman and Hendricks; the FBI agents were across a glass-and-chrome table from the *nouveau*-President, his balding, portly, picture-of-a-bureaucrat Security Adviser, some generously-medaled, crew-cut, bull-necked, late-50s Caucasian military guy, as well as another white man – clean-shaven and leather-faced, tight-muscled, middle-aged, with Brylcreemed, black hair and a conservative, almost-black business-suit and red tie, with a very small cross-symbol in the middle of the latter – who they didn't recognize. Two Marine guards were stationed at the entrances on either side of the room (which was in the middle of the fuselage), and there were two dark-suited, plain-clothes government agents, standing with backs to the wall, behind the *faux*-President and his entourage.

The waxing noise of the engines was now obvious to everyone, as was the steadily-increasing, forward motion of the airborne command post. The nose of the aircraft tilted gently upward, as the U.S. leader addressed the newcomers.

"You already know me, I suppose," he said. "Let me introduce the others – this is National Security Adviser John Bezomorton, accompanied by General Blanshard, in charge of the Joint Chiefs of the military, and my, uhh, Spiritual Adviser, the Reverend Brother Harold Crowford, of the Hallelujah Tabernacle. Gentlemen?"

There were perfunctory "how'd you do's" from all three, but as Chu looked at the third man, a momentary flash of panic raced through her mind.

What the H? she thought. *He's a threat, a danger... huh? The Bible guy?*

Damn you, Karéin... why couldn't it give me an explanation... not just a warning?

"I'm sure you're aware of what an... *unusual*, privilege, has been extended to you, Ms. Chu, in this matter," slowly offered the U.S. leader, with his face twisted into a half-sneer that was all too familiar to his courtiers. "What you may *not* know, is, how I've had to over-rule the objections of some agencies of the government, who felt that it would be... *inadvisable*, for me to meet with you, like this, given your previous interaction with the alien, and given that you're going way over the heads of your superiors, within the Bureau. I'll be frank : the *only* reason why I've agreed to this discussion, is on the assumption that you can provide us with intelligence on the alien, which will allow us to effectively fight her... or, should I say... 'it'. It would not be in your interest to disappoint me... do you understand?"

"Definitely, sir," replied Chu, her almond eyes meeting his stare with equal, though entirely mortal, steadfastness. "And as I said to the, uhh, last people with whom I had this type of conversation, I'm now prepared to provide you with a great deal of information that I wasn't comfortable in divulging to anyone else. I'd prefer this just to be for your ears... are Mr. Bezomorton,

General Blanshard and the Reverend Crowford, authorized to be included in the conversation?"

"Yes," he stated. "Proceed."

"Okay," said the FBI team-leader. "First off... you've read my written report, sir?"

"Yeah," indifferently mentioned the *nouveau*-President. "The summary, at least. A few things there that were of some interest to the military, particularly about this, uhh, 'magic' gear, that she's apparently wearing. But not a lot that's 'net new', if you know what I mean. I'm a busy man, Ms. Chu; what you got for me, that would justify me taking a detour from my schedule, landing wherever the hell it was, and picking you up? I don't do social calls, you know."

"I... *see*," she replied. "Well, Mr. President, sir, in the interests of time, I'll get right to the point. You *are* aware, are you not, that your life is under threat, right now?"

"Again," he responded, with coldly pursed lips, "Not new... not at all. If you mean the alien – or that insubordinate prick named 'Jacobson' and his crew of traitors – yeah, I'm very *well* aware that they're all gunning for me, along with the Muslims, various other terrorists, a long list of subversives, and the Democrats, I guess. So what?"

The FBI agents noted that the military guy was now looking away from the conversation; he seemed to be regarding something being displayed on his wrist-communicator, which he was holding below table-level.

"*What?*" they heard him whisper, after abruptly getting up and heading out into the hallway.

It was difficult concentrating on the conversation with her 'Mars ears', but somehow, Chu managed, while never taking her eyes off those left in the room.

"How the hell can those fucking hackers be screwing up the path-diversity of the mil-grade C3 channels?" complained Blanshard. "They're supposed to be on an isolated *network*, for God's sake! Okay... yeah, down all of 'em, until you're sure it's been purged... we'll manage the show from here, over the direct, general-purpose link – air assets already have their orders, anyway. Let me know immediately if you get a clear target ID. Right."

"Sir," remarked Minnie Chu, her stare deliberate and forceful, "What I've come to tell you, today, is : no matter *what* you do – no matter *how* carefully the military and the various intelligence agencies try to protect you, it's only a matter of time, until either Jacobson and his followers, possibly Jerry Kaysten and Sylvia Abruzzio – or perhaps Karéin-Mayréij herself, if the government further antagonizes her – finally catch up to you; and when they do, I'm afraid you're quite right about their intentions... Jacobson, at least, intends to *kill* you, sir, and based on first-hand observations of their intent and capabilities, I have absolutely no doubt, that they *will* eventually succeed in doing that. *Unless...*"

Blanshard re-joined the group and sat down.

With a haughty, quizzical look, the U.S. leader asked, "Unless... *what?*"

"Unless, sir," evenly stated Chu, "Will, Otis and I, are assigned to protect you, '24 by 7 by 365". We are the *only* people under your command, who have the technical knowledge and tactical ability to give the military and Secret Service, a fighting chance, to resist and defeat these plots. This is why I wanted to meet you in person, Mr. President. It's *essential* that we stay by your side, until the disputes between yourself, Jacobson and Karéin, can be peacefully resolved."

The U.S. leader leaned back in his chair and burst out in an openly-contemptuous bout of laughter.

"Oh, for *God's* sake," he half-chuckled, with exasperated mirth, "Ms. – do I have this right – Field Team-Leader, Chu – I'm given to understand that your rank's one or two levels above rookie-agent – you're suggesting that you, and your two gumshoe friends here, are going to keep the big, bad alien boogie-man – excuse me, boogie-*girl* – off my back, where the entire U.S. Army, Navy, Marine Corps and Air Force, not to mention the Secret Service, the Agency and the Bureau – can't?"

"Essentially... 'yes', sir," answered the more-than-a-woman. "You see –"

"*Right,*" sighed the *faux*-President. "And *that's* what you came here, to tell me? Jesus... what a fucking waste of *time*. Okay, we're done –"

"Mr. President, sir," spoke up the man with the crucifix-tie, "If you don't mind me sayin' so, I think you're perhaps being a bit hasty. Now the little lady sittin' across the table from us, has made a pretty sweepin' claim... which it's up to her to substantiate, if she *can*. If not, well... I'd say, we *are* done, in that case."

"Go ahead," sourly muttered the U.S. leader, as he turned to listen to something being whispered in one ear, by the military guy.

Chu tried to keep a straight face, while multi-tasking.

Good work, Mars ears, she mused.

What's this about, 'critical situation over Missouri, TACINT failing'? He sure sounds *concerned, though... which, maybe, is leverage...*

"What I mean, sir," clarified Chu, "Is, Will, Otis and I know enough about the specifics of the, uhh, alien-powers, and battle-tactics, of the Storied Watcher, also those of the members of the Jacobson team, to be able to advise the military and intelligence agencies, about how to optimally defeat these opponents. Let me give you an example, which to the best of my knowledge, has not, up to this time, been made available to the government."

"Go ahead, Ma'am," unctuously cajoled the Reverend Brother. "We're all ears."

"Now take Sam Jacobson, the former Mars mission commander," elaborated the team-leader. "Mr. Jacobson's abilities are formidable : he's immensely strong – far beyond what would be possible for an ordinary human being – and he has a highly-developed ability to rapidly heal wounds that might otherwise be fatal. But, unlike some of the others upon whom Karéin-Mayréij has bestowed these 'alien-powers', he does not, to the best of my knowledge, have any kind of ranged attack – he can only damage items that are within swinging-distance of his arms and fists. So if you engage him, you'd want to do so, from a distance. Furthermore –"

"Just a minute," ordered the *faux*-President. "Excuse me – I've got to take this outside. Crowford, you keep them busy until I get back."

With no more warning, he raced through one of the entrance-doors, with Blanshard and Bezomorton, in tow.

"Uhh... what's that all about?" uneasily asked Boatman.

"Prolly just business," offered the Spiritual Adviser, with an insincere smile. "The Old Man ain't kiddin' you all about bein' busy... happens to me all the time. Now... how 'bout you just tell me, what you were goin' to say, particularly 'bout all this 'alien' stuff. I'll pass it on to him, when we have our next 'one-on-one'."

"*Love* to, sir," demurred Chu, "But I'd prefer to tell that straight to the President, with yourself listening, if appropriate. However... perhaps there *is* something that you can fill Otis, Will and myself, in on, while we're waiting."

"Yeah... what?" he inquired.

"What we're at a loss to understand," noted the team-leader, "Is why the government's been so relentlessly hostile to Karéin, not to mention Jacobson and the rest of them. I'm obviously willing to help the President fight, and, if necessary, defeat the Storied Watcher and the former Mars mission group... but it would be far preferable, and much easier, to just negotiate a cease-fire. Honestly, sir... the government's approach to this matter, just makes no *sense*. Is there anything you can do to enlighten us about what's going on, here, sir?"

For an over-long moment, Crowford just stared impassively forward.

Should I get inside his head? pondered Chu.

No... if anyone, it would be the guy who's pretending to be the President, when, really, we've got no good idea of what happened to the last one. And something tells me... he'd be hard to dominate. What did Karéin say, about 'a disciplined mind, can resist you'? Better save it for the big fish...

"Well," slowly offered the Spiritual Adviser, "Apart from the obvious fact that the alien's made numerous, direct threats against the government generally, and the President specifically, there are those of us who believe that... *larger* forces, are at work, here."

"I'm afraid I'm not following you, sir," politely responded Chu.

"Yeah... who's bigger than the President?" incredulously added Hendricks.

"What I'm referrin' to, my dear, is the eternal battle between God Almighty, and the D –"

His voice was cut off by the sudden re-entry of the *nouveau*-President and his two understudies, into the conference-room. Both Blanshard and Bezomorton wore worried, 'at-a-loss' expressions on their faces.

"Okay, Ms. Chu," interrupted the U.S. leader, "You said you were the only one who could show us how to fight this asshole 'Jacobson', as well as the alien?"

"That's correct, sir," confirmed the team-leader.

"Now you may have a chance – one chance, only – to *prove* it," requested the *faux*-President.

"What do you mean, sir?" asked Chu, trying to sound innocent.

"We have a... *situation*, underway, in the Midwest," he grimly stated.

It's Been A Slice, Moira

Moira Ann Sullivan woke up with the first rays of the sun over her modest, single-level house on Kenridge Drive in Villa Hills, Kentucky; and in so doing, she beat the alarm-clock, by a good six minutes.

Good thing, she mused, while throwing on a night-shirt and slippers, stumbling to the en-suite, dousing her face (*damn – another wrinkle,* she realized) and trying to brush a semblance of order into her graying, off-brown hair.

Haven't seen Sylvia in years *– talked to her a million times on the phone, of course – and she sure looked like she needed a rest, when she arrived at my door-step, last night,* considered the forty-something, "depressingly average-looking", Irish-American.

Odd, though, that she insisted on sleeping apart from that good-looking young fellow that she had tagging along with her... well, after all, maybe she's still keeping up with the vows we both learned, as good little Catholic girls in the same school, "way back when".

No business of mine, I guess... but if she's *not interested in him, well...*

Taking care not to make unnecessary noise, she went to the kitchen and was almost ready to get the coffee going, when Abruzzio wandered in, as well.

"Mornin'," said Sullivan. "You get enough sleep, Sylvia? Pretty late, when you showed up here. Sorry if I woke you up."

"Sleep... huh?" responded the former JPL scientist. "Oh... yeah. No problem. And anyway, I've already been up for a half-hour... Rainbow had to go outside."

"You clean it up?" asked the woman. "I don't care, but that guy I pay to do the lawns... he gets mad if he gets dog-shit in his mower."

The puppy, which had somehow appeared as if from nowhere, let out a friendly "yip", which was awarded by a pat on the head from Sullivan, as she added some water to the cereal-bowl that was acting as a doggie-dish.

"Um-hmm," confirmed Abruzzio. "Amazing what you can get used to, when you're a, uhh, 'parent', you know."

She smiled at the puppy, which cocked its head and returned a gesture that sure could have been mistaken for a dog's version of a grin.

"Bacon and eggs?" asked Sullivan. "Oh, and pancakes. Got the instant-mix already goin'."

“Oh, not for me... just corn flakes, if you've got any,” demurred Abruzzio. “But Jerry might want some, and I'm sure that Rainbow will deal with any left-overs.”

“I'm sure she will,” smiled the woman. “Well, don't mind me, if I go for it. Missed lunch yesterday, we were busy at work, so I'm ahead of the calorie-count for this week. And while we're on the subject, girl... don't you look just *great* – I'd swear you haven't aged a *day* in ten years. No, better than that... you get one of them fancy new face-lifts, or something?”

“Nothing like that,” politely answered Abruzzio. “I guess I've just been hanging around the right people, and getting some, uhh, exercise... it's *amazing* what a little, ahem, fresh air, can do for you.”

“Just wish I had your figure,” pouted Sullivan. “You always *did* have the looks, you know.”

“So... what's your schedule today, Moira?” inquired the scientist. “Just so Jerry and I can plan around it, of course.”

“Gotta get goin' for work, in another hour or so – be back for six-thirty p.m.,” replied Sullivan. “Bridge to Cincinnati gets backed up bad, if I leave too late; and like I told you last night, job's pretty shaky, these days, what with all the crazy economic stuff goin' around. We've had three layoffs, just in my department – I gotta watch my step. If I end up without an income... don't know *what* I'll do. All on my own since Dave split, you know.”

Abruzzio's countenance took on an odd, serenely determined look, as she stated, “Don't worry about that... I'll make sure you're looked after. Least I can do, after we showed up completely unannounced, and you took Jerry and I in, last night... it felt *wonderful*, having a shower and getting cleaned up, after, uhh, being on the road. Oh, and thank you *so* much for giving Jerry and I those old clothes from the basement.”

“Ha... well, no loss to *me*, honey... I haven't fit in 'em for fifteen years, and I got no use for Dave's stuff... just never got around to holdin' a garage sale,” ruefully offered Sullivan, while cracking three eggs into a fry-pan. “Feel free to grab anything else you want from down there – ninety per cent of it, I don't use any more, anyway. But here I thought they weren't payin' you NASA folks the big bucks. You get a raise? Or win the lottery?”

“Oh, no... nothing like that,” said the JPL scientist. “Just that I've, uhh, acquired some pretty powerful friends... unfortunately, some equally-powerful enemies, lately. Same goes for Jerry, incidentally. Listen – if anybody, especially, someone from the government – comes here looking for us... just tell them that you haven't seen me since before the 'comet' thing... okay?”

“Hey,” asked the woman, wheeling in place with a spatula in hand, “You in... *trouble*, or something?”

The former JPL scientist fell silent for a second or two.

“Sorry,” apologized Sullivan. “None of my business. If it's *private* –”

“Moira, we've always been the best of friends,” quietly explained Abruzzio, “I've never lied to you before, and I won't start now. Yes, I *am* in 'trouble', *big*-time. Both Jerry and I are being hunted by the government, which has already tried to kill us, many times. Before we arrived here, we had been imprisoned by the Agency – the CIA, that is – in some upscale jail that they had in downtown Pittsburgh; I only escaped from there by the skin of my teeth... same for Jerry. Since then, we've been on the run for a day and a half, hiding in the backs of trucks and so on, because we don't dare show our faces in public. If we're recognized, they'll call in the SWAT team, with 'shoot to kill' orders. *That's* where it's all at, right now."

"*Jesus, Mary and Joseph!*" gasped Sullivan. "That's, uhh... *serious*. Why'd they want to do *that*? You're just a scientist... what they got against *you?*"

She stopped and pondered for a bit, and then added, "Oh... wait a minute... *I* get it. The *alien*... right?"

Abruzzio nodded affirmatively.

"Look, Sylvia," pleaded the woman, "*Please* tell me that whole thing was faked, like the TV talk-show guys've been tellin' us. I seen all the videos on Neo, before they yanked 'em, but, well, it *can't* be real... can it? Besides – last time we talked, you told me that you and that Ramirez guy, were just in that building down in Texas, talkin' to the astronauts, you never went into space, even though you really wanted to... how could you have possibly been caught up in all that?"

"It's a long story," explained the former JPL scientist, "But, briefly – Karéin is *very* real – be of no doubt about that. She's alive, and is here, on Earth. Hector, Jerry and I have all met her… and it's an experience that one never forgets."

"Some people say she's an 'angel'," stated the woman.

"Yeah," said Abruzzio.

"Well... *is* she?" pressed Sullivan.

"That's... *complicated*, Moira," replied the former scientist. "Some of us certainly think so... others don't. But what I *can* tell you for sure is, being in her presence, also *changes* you... irreversibly."

"Changes you... *how?*" suspiciously inquired Sullivan. "Like those astronauts I saw on TV, a little while ago? The ones with the super –"

"You *bet*," confirmed Abruzzio. "I also know Commander Jacobson and his team, on a first-name basis, and not just from the Mars mission : they were all with Karéin for a time down here on Earth, along with Jerry, Rainbow and myself, as well as a lot of other people who you've never heard of. Along with the Storied Watcher herself, we're all being hunted by the U.S. government."

"So... *you're* a 'super-hero', now?" nervously joked the woman.

"Yeah... I am," evenly replied the former JPL scientist. "Funny, you know... no matter how many times I say that – it always sounds weird to admit."

"Well why don't you, just, uhh, fly off somewhere... get away from the Feds, I mean?" prodded an incredulous Sullivan.

"That's not how it works... at least, not yet," said Abruzzio.

"What can you do, then?" persisted the woman, turning back and forth to avoid burning the pancakes. "*Show* me!"

"I'd prefer not to, Moira," evaded Abruzzio.

"Why not?" complained Sullivan.

"First, because several of my abilities are, uhh... *lethal,*" warned the more-than-human. "Just being anywhere *near* me, when I activate them, could badly hurt you, or... worse. Second, the less you know, the less reason the government has to come after you, on account of me; and, frankly, the less they can get out of you, if they do catch you. All you *do* need to know, is two things : one, we're going to win, real soon now, and in so doing, bring those responsible, to justice. The second is – and make sure you remember to say this, to anyone who comes knocking on your door – is that there will be *hell* to pay, for anyone who hurts a friend of ours. Like... *you*."

"You mean like how that one astronaut guy down on I-22, I forget his name, said he'd do, if anybody touched his –" started Sullivan.

"Major Brent Boyd," interrupted Abruzzio. "That's his name, and I can assure you – he's very capable of making good on his threats. It's basically the same message from me, if they lay a hand on you."

"And Sylvia Abruzzio, nice Catholic choir-girl who got herself a degree from, where was it, is going to –" the woman went on.

"Cornell, undergrad. Caltech, doctorate," patiently answered the scientist.

"Okay, from some expensive university somewhere... point is, you and this 'Kaysten' dude, are going to fight the whole *government*, if they do something bad to me?" chided the woman. "Come *on*, girl... you expect me to believe something like *that*? This whole thing's made-up. It *has* to be!"

"Moira," calmly stated Abruzzio, "Want your pancakes sliced in half, before you douse 'em with corn-syrup, like I remember you always doing?"

"Quarters, actually," said the woman, with a shrug. "Soaks up the butter, better. What's this got to do with anything?"

"When I tell you... stack the pancakes all together, then throw them a foot in the air, please," instructed the former JPL scientist.

"I can't possibly catch all of 'em when they come down!" protested Sullivan. "*You* want to waste food, go ahead, but –"

There was the briefest hint of a chromatic twinkle in Abruzzio's eyes, accompanied with the very muted, subconscious hum of her delicate, multi-tonal war-song, as she half-whispered, apparently to no-one,

"*Vîrya I'ëà'b'*... thou know what to do, for thy Auntie Sylvia?"

A second passed by, and the JPL scientist demanded, "Okay, Moira – do it... *now*."

"Fine... hope your dog likes pancakes," muttered Sullivan, as she put each cake on top of the other, lowered the skillet, then propelled its contents upward. "And who's a 'veer' – what the – *omigod!*"

As if from nowhere, the Storied Watcher's buzzing, singing, *Fire*-imbued buckler streaked across the room, its supernaturally-sharp edge neatly dividing the food into the previously-specified portions, before catching these morsels in its concave side, flipping upside-down above a serving-platter and depositing the sliced pancakes on to the surface of the plate. It then flew back to land on Abruzzio's left arm.

While a stunned Sullivan warily gaped, the former JPL scientist momentarily flinched, with a far-off look in her eyes, and then turned to cast a glance at *Vìrya I'ëà'b'*.

"Thou did good, honey," came the more-than-a-woman's appreciative comment. "What's that? Oh, well, thou see... 'Auntie' Moira didn't believe me, when I informed her about thy mother. Umm-hmm? Yes… I know she's just a 'hoo-man'... but maybe we can fix that."

At this point, Kaysten's trim, delicate-but-still-masculine figure, dressed only in a pair of pajama-pants and slippers, appeared in the doorway.

"Oh – so you've told her?" he said, with a shrug. "Great. What's for breakfast?"

The Team-Leader, Alone

"So what's the latest, uhh –" requested the *nouveau*-President, turning to the bull-headed, tough-faced Army general, within the duplicate Air Force One's computer-bedecked, dimly-lit command-center.

"TACEVAL, sir," stated Blanshard. "That's the term we use to describe 'what's going on, down on the battlefield'. And to put it bluntly, Mr. President... as you know, it doesn't appear that things have been going very well."

"*Fuck!*" cursed the U.S. leader, loudly enough to raise a few eyebrows even among the normally heads-down military personnel who were hunkered over the various hi-tech computer, communications and surveillance systems, all around. "What's it *take*, to 'terminate' a few traitors, these days, General? I thought you *told* me, we had them, dead cold. You got a trace on them, yet?"

"Checking," said the general, as he stepped backward, conferred with a uniformed subordinate, and then responded, "I'm afraid that's still a negative, sir. The, uhh, enemy countermeasures have proved to be a bit more effective than we had counted on; local CAP is non-operational – we'll be very lucky if all of them make it safely back to base – and that burst of high-intensity light seems to have seriously degraded most of the drones' visual sensors. We're redeploying assets, of course, but that'll take several hours, at a minimum. Local LEA has been informed, and they'll be setting up roadblocks as soon as they can. We'll get them, sir... we just have to be a little *patient*."

"You'd damn well *better*," growled the *faux*-President, "Or we'll be having a few more 're-orgs' within the Pentagon... *understand?* And, by the way, I want every one of those effing cowardly pilots, put up on court-martial, for disobeying a direct order from their Commander-In-Chief –"

"Yes, I do," countered the general, "And I've ordered them confined to quarters when and if they make it back to base, subject to investigation by the military courts – but, sir, I think we have to take into account, they had been reduced to a combat-ineffective state, and –"

"Excuses, *excuses!*" angrily retorted the U.S. leader. "They'll be the death of *all* of us, General, if we don't get the lower ranks to do their fucking *jobs*, whether or not doing so happens to appeal to them, at the time. Do I make myself clear?"

"*Very* clear, Mr. President, sir," stolidly replied Blanshard, with his characteristic, cold, impassive stare.

"Alright," spoke the *nouveau*-President, his tone and body language backing off slightly. "Let's go and have our little chat with that Chinese dame."

The general silently nodded, and the two – accompanied by the usual Secret Service protection, with one hulking, black-suited bodyguard in front, and another behind – walked at a brisk pace out of the command-center, through the aircraft's labyrinthine internal passage-ways, until finally arriving at the conference-room that they had rapidly exited, when the Missouri fiasco had first come to their attention.

Without knocking, the U.S. leader and the general entered the chamber, looked around and demanded, "Where's Crowford?"

"He left this area shortly after you both did, sir," remarked a handcuffed – but otherwise unrestrained – Minnie Chu, who had, like her two FBI co-workers, stood upright, upon noting the *faux*-President's presence. "He mentioned something about 'needing to consult with Scripture and do some quick praying'. He *did* say that he'd be back, later."

"Thanks," perfunctorily replied the *nouveau*-President. "You may sit down. Oh... and since you haven't assaulted me yet, after having been allowed to get up from your chairs... I don't see any further purpose to the handcuffs, as long as you understand that it's a privilege which can be withdrawn, any time I so desire. *You*, there – remove the cuffs, please."

One of the bodyguards half-whispered, "Yes, Mr. President, sir," and proceeded to use a pen-like computer-device to un-engage the locking-mechanism on the FBI agents' hand-restraints.

"Thank you very much, sir," said Chu. "We certainly do appreciate it."

"Okay," started the U.S. leader, his voice feigning weariness and hurt. "I'll get right to the point. As you're already aware, there's just been an... *incident*, in and over, south-central Missouri, in which – so General Blanshard informs me – there's a high probability that one or more of your 'alien-powered' friends, were involved. We asked for your help in this matter, and you claimed you'd coöperate; as I understand it, your advice was requested, at several key points during the battle. Would you like to know what transpired, as a result?"

"Oh, *definitely*, sir," politely responded the FBI team-leader.

"General?" shrugged the *faux*-President.

"The bottom line is," spoke Blanshard, his voice flat and expressionless, "As far as we know, the enemy is either still in command of the field of battle, or has exited from it, without us being able to follow his movements. As for our in-area assets, they've been seriously depleted. We lost two F-32E fighters and several helicopter gunships during the engagement, with some other air assets suffering various amounts of damage; two pilots are confirmed dead, with at least eight others wounded or missing and presumed dead. Post-engagement reports are still coming in, but it appears that the enemy deployed weapons and tactics that are, as yet, almost impossible for us to effectively defeat."

"My *God*," breathed the big, African-American agent, while looking down at the table.

"You have something to say, Mr... uhh... 'Boatman'... yes, that's it... right?" sourly inquired the U.S. leader.

"Well I'm not sure exactly *what* I should say at this point, Mr. President, sir," offered Boatman, "'Cept... I sure don't like hearin' about all them casualties... personal opinion, I think that Jacobson fella's stepped over a line... I thought better of him. It's a terrible shame, sir... guess *that's* what I mean."

"Your concern is... *touching*, Agent Boatman," coldly replied the *nouveau*-President, "But it would have been a lot more convincing, if you and your friends here, had given us some information that had really let us get the upper hand on Jacobson and his little crew of traitors; but what my military friends here are telling me, is that all we got was –"

"Mr. President sir, with all due respect, I don't think that's *fair*," interrupted Chu. "We were dictating a suggested plan of action to the DoD people who showed up in this room, right after you left to take charge of the, uhh, engagement... then they left, halfway through, saying something about 'needed back on deck'. We wanted to follow them down to the control-room so we could assist in real-time, but were told that it wouldn't be possible, and that we had to remain here. If we had just been trusted a bit more –"

"'Trust', is a rare commodity, in my business," countered the U.S. leader. "General... how would you describe the usefulness and accuracy of the briefings that you've so far received from Ms. Chu and her two team-mates, here?"

"I'd sum it up as... *incomplete*, sir," stated Blanshard. "The descriptions of the Jacobson party were useful, but of course, we had much of that information, already. While I can confirm that some of what we've been told – for example, Major Boyd's, uhh, 'high-power light-based' ability – is accurate, I'd note that what was significant by its absence, is advice on how to effectively fight these 'alien-powers', using the weaponry currently at our disposal; for example, at one point in the most recent encounter, we sustained attacks which rendered many of our sensors and communication systems, combat-inoperative. We'd sure have liked to have known some way to counter that. Also, some of the TACEVAL that's coming in, is at odds with what we've been led to believe."

A startled Chu immediately asked, "What? Sir, *everything* that I've told you, has been completely true."

“For example, Madam,” said the general, “We've got pretty well-confirmed reports coming from some of the real-time video-links, of *two* members of the Jacobson party – one who we didn't get a good picture of, probably this 'Tanaka' woman, and another, who we have to assume was Major Boyd – becoming airborne, and thereby engaging our local air assets. Didn't you state that only *Tanaka,* among them, had the ability to fly?”

The team-leader shared a perplexed look with Boatman and Hendricks, then replied, “That's, uhh... *correct,* sir. I'm honestly at a loss to explain this, assuming for the moment that your evidence is accurate. All I *can* say is, to the best of my knowledge, Major Boyd never demonstrated any such ability, during the period in which both he and I were in close proximity... and, he certainly had ample incentive and opportunity to do it. As to what's going on now... your guess is as good as mine.”

There was a knock on the door. A Secret Service bodyguard answered it, and, after a short conversation, Harold Crowford's slick-haired, leather-faced figure entered the room, whispering, “Sorry I'm late... thank you, Mr. President.”

The Spiritual Adviser took a seat on the side of the U.S. leader, opposite that of Blanshard.

“Well, Ms. Chu,” sighed the U.S. leader, with mock exasperation, “'Your guess is as good as mine', doesn't seem to be much of a value proposition, for us keeping you hanging around here... wouldn't you say?”

I wonder if I can make him dance for me? pondered Chu.

Maybe... but didn't she say, “it wears off, as time passes, and if he goes too far out of your sight”?

That happens, and my – excuse me, our *– ass is grass. Too risky.*

Gotta save it for one key moment... a “change of mind”, that can be explained away...

“Mr. President, I'll of course defer to your judgment in this matter, both out of respect to yourself and to the office that you hold,” cajoled the FBI team-leader, “But in our defense, I'd note two things. One, I don't believe I *ever* stated that conventional military measures, alone, would be likely to defeat either the Jacobson party, or, even more so, Karéin herself. This is the precise reason why I suggested that the government should try to negotiate with Commander Jacobson and the Storied Watcher, if at all possible. Two – and this is the main thing – it really comes down to, 'do you feel safer with, or without, us, here at your side'? We may not be able to give you one hundred per cent complete advice on all potential abilities of the Jacobson party at all times... let alone, for Karéin-Mayréij, who's supposedly thousands of years old, 'Vanquisher of Demons', *et cetera...* but we *can* provide, and *have* provided, a lot more intelligence than you'd have had, otherwise. That's *my* 'value proposition'... *sir.*”

“Even if that's true,” commented the *faux*-President, “Why do you have to be up here? Why can't we just put you in a nice, safe military base, and then ask for all this wonderful advice you claim to have, via this fancy-dancy video-thing that I'm always using, anyway?"

Now Hendricks, who had been unusually quiet and withdrawn, spoke up.

"Sir, don't want to speak out of turn, here," he offered, "But didn't the General mention something about, 'your communication systems got knocked out'? Yeah, you *can* stick Minnie, Otis and I, down there on the ground somewhere... but what if, when you most need to hear from us... the phone's 'on the Fritz'? That'd be, uhh, kind of too bad... right?"

The U.S. leader let out a contemptuous-sounding "harrumph", but his countenance suggested that he wasn't dismissing the idea out of hand.

There was a long pause.

"Stay here until we get back," he demanded, motioning to the FBI agents, while using a hand-gesture to request Blanchard's and Crowford's presence, outside the room. The three senior U.S. officials rapidly exited, apparently moving to a spot down the hall.

The location was further away than Blanshard had been during his earlier absence, and it was that much more difficult for even the agents' enhanced hearing, to pick up. Chu was able to make out comments like "this is an undue risk, sir – I have *every* confidence that our systems will stay fully operational, this time" and "so what – they step out of line, they get a bullet in the head and a kick out the door at 30,000 feet".

As near as she could determine, the religious-nut-guy was arguing for their continued presence, although Chu was at a loss to figure out why.

After a delay of about five minutes, the *nouveau*-President, Blanshard and Crowford re-entered the conference-room.

"A decision has been made," announced the U.S. leader. "While I'm still skeptical, to say the least, that all this 'inside information' you claim to have about our adversaries, has any appreciable value... I'm not willing to rule out that possibility, altogether. That having been said, we don't need all *three* of you hanging around, to accomplish this goal. So *you* – Chu – you stay here on the aircraft; we'll assign you a place to sleep, nothing fancy of course, but we're already over our staff quota... at least you won't have to hot-share a chair, the way that many of the rest of 'em, have to. The other two will be dropped off at our next landing; we'll arrange to have you put up in a nice hotel, with a suitable communications-link, in the unlikely case that you know something that Ms. Chu can't tell us, herself. Is that clear?"

An immediately flustered and upset Chu stammered, "But – but – *sir* – we've always worked as a *team*, we watch each others' backs – sir, I don't think this is advisable, not at *all!* If, uhh, it's not convenient for Will and Otis to stay up here with me... perhaps it *would* be better, if all three of us were to disembark at the next stop, and take our chances with providing intelligence to the military, over the remote link –"

"Oh, yeah," chimed in Hendricks. "Look, maybe I *was* a bit hasty there – I'm not really that 'up' on the comms stuff – can you just forget the part about the 'phone home' thing, if you don't mind, sir?"

The *faux*-President yawned, got up, cracked his knuckles and dismissively sneered, "Funny... the intel reports, if I recall correctly, said your hearing was perfectly up to snuff, Ms. Chu. Was there something *unclear*, about these orders? As I understand it, we've got about twenty minutes until our next refueling-stop, so you've got that long to say any tearful 'good-byes'. I'd advise you to make good use of the time. Okay... Blanshard – Crowford – we're done here. I need a drink. By the way, Ms. Chu, that last comment's off the record... you understand?"

"Yes... sir... I... *understand,*" softly replied the team-leader, with her head hanging down.

"Air Force orderly will drop by in a few minutes, to show you to your quarters," remarked Blanshard, as he accompanied the U.S. leader, his Spiritual Adviser and the Secret Service guards, to the doorway. "I'll arrange to have your personal effects and luggage sent there, and for those of Mr. Boatman and Mr. Hendricks, to be made ready for unloading. And... welcome aboard, Ms. Chu. I'm expecting great things from you."

"Great... *things,*" dejectedly repeated a crestfallen Chu. "Yeah... well, sir... I have a feeling that you won't be disappointed, in that department."

He reflexively nodded, walked at a brisk place over to the portal, exited and closed the door behind him.

The other two agents had rarely seen the usually-well-composed Minnie Chu cry; but *this* time, she made little to no effort to conceal her heartbreak.

"Listen, guys..." she started, while trying to wipe her eyes.

"Hey, hey... it's *okay,*" consoled Hendricks, as he gave his boss a strong hug, "It's not like we – or you – are *dying,* Minnie; we're just getting holed up in some hotel... all *I* hope is, that they've got the Sports Channel down there, you know?"

"Ha, ha... you... *would*... wouldn't you?" miserably giggled the more-than-a-woman. "Chance to catch up on those damn college games you keep talking about. Just wish I could be there with you, watching them. I'd even learn to love basketball, if I could just..."

She started sobbing again.

"It's just... all of what we've been through, as a team... as, *friends,*" whimpered Chu. "We've done so much... *grown* so much, together. You two are *brothers* to me, now... no, much more than that. I can't *stand* the idea of not having you around."

"Minnie," added Boatman, while taking Hendricks' place in the embracing department, "You don't worry – we'll be alright... and anyway, this whole thing's gonna be over with, in a few days to weeks... right? But we better use this time good... get our act together. When we set out on this-here journey, yours truly *did* consider the possibility that Jerry 'n Sylvia, wouldn't be stayin' with us; but *this* thing, with young Will 'n me, bein' apart from yourself, well now, *that's* somethin' I *hadn't* thought through. You understand what I'm sayin'?"

"Yeah," she half-whispered, trying desperately to regain her composure, "But remember – even though we're alone... this place isn't, uhh, *secure...*"

Hendricks gently released his hold on the team-leader.

"Well, unlike some folks we know, it sucks to have to, uhh, say what I'm thinkin', out loud," he cannily offered, "But if the shit hits the fan, at your end or ours... shouldn't we have a way of warning each other that we need help?"

"Any ideas?" mumbled Chu. "Sorry... I'm not thinking straight, right now."

They stood, silently, for a few moments, and then the third agent proposed, "How about what happened, when you went for that ride with Her Alien Highness... you know, over L.A.?"

"Well, for God's sake, Will – I hardly think my personal life –" protested a startled Chu.

"No, no, for *Christ's* sake, Minnie, not *that,*" back-pedaled Hendricks. "I mean, the thing about, 'open a hole in this thing, because I'm about to'... *you* know?"

"Oh... right," breathed a relieved Chu. "Yeah, *that'd* do. Not something I really like remembering, but, uhh, hard to forget, and I don't think Jacobson and Company were told about it... so a good choice, I suppose."

"Good... we're set on the danger-signal," commented Boatman. "But about the, uhh, *mission* – what 'bout *that?* The idea was always that the three of us was gonna stand in that Jacobson dude's way, and that was gonna be hard enough, as it was – but what if he shows up, and it's just you –"

"I'll be okay," whispered the FBI team-leader. "I... *promise.*"

"Wish I could b'lieve that, Minnie," countered the big, African-American FBI agent, "But I s'pose, times bein' what they are... I'll *have* to, one way or the other."

There was a knock, and the vapid, clean-cut face of a low-level, Caucasian, male Air Force orderly, appeared through a crack in the doorway.

"Ms. Chu – that *you?*" he asked. "General's saying it's time to go. Got your reclinin'-chair and locker, all set up. He asked me to mention, 'hope you don't mind bein' with the galley-crew'... but it isn't *all* bad – you get first crack at the food, before even Mr. Bezomorton has his. Best cut of the prime rib 'n such. If I had the chance, I'd swap with you –"

"That's, uhh, *wonderful,*" ruefully acknowledged Chu, "But can you give us a bit more time? Just one more minute, with the three of us, alone... please?"

"Well, okay, lady," he replied, in an uncertain tone, "But no more than that... General Blanshard runs a tight ship up here – he don't like missin' deadlines. I'll wait outside."

The door closed, and again, they were relatively alone.

"I guess this is 'it', guys," offered a quavering Chu, her eyes welling, as she spoke. "Funny... I can't seem to stop tearing up... and just when I've figured how *not* to, when doing that, uhh, *other* thing... you know?"

"Well now, I guess we've all been learnin' our lessons, thanks to each other, Minnie," said Boatman, as he again extended his big arms; the gesture was immediately accepted.

"It's damn hard on this side of the tracks, too," he whispered. "Take care."

"Listen, Minnie," commented Hendricks, his normally-glib voice laden with emotion, "There's one more thing."

"What?" she forced.

The third agent reached into a jacket-pocket and lifted out a woman's necklace. Its more-robust-than-normal chain-links were of interlocking silver- and gold-tinted metals, connecting at the front with a decent-sized, translucent-cerulean-colored, faceted gemstone; and, well-nigh-invisible to the human eye – though just discernible to the gaze of these three – were a panoply of obscure inscriptions, somehow melted into the ornament's silver-metal setting.

Chu noted the similarities – and the differences – compared to the small locket that her under-study was fingering, underneath his dress-shirt.

Hendricks ceremoniously and carefully draped the thing over Chu's neck.

In an odd, "off-somewhere" tone, he spoke directly at the jewel in it.

"Keep her *safe*, Dad... keep her *safe*... Mr. New Kid," he breathed, too softly for human ears to make out. "My sister will give you a name. Defend her with your life, and mine... never let her out of your sight... you *hear?*"

I hear something, thought both of the others.

No... two of them...

Like Karéin's 'children'... but different somehow...

Fainter, more... human-sounding... what the H?

Hendricks stood, glassy-eyed, for a long second, and then whispered to Chu, "Pure aquamarine – asked for him to be, uhh, 'picked up' for me. Put my own English on him, with a little help from my friends... including her old lady, if you know what I mean. Your birthday's in March, isn't it?"

"Yeah," managed Chu, hiding her emotions with a weak cough.

"I want to see *both* of you back in one piece," inscrutably continued the third agent. "When this is all over with. Got that, boss?"

With the same miserable laugh as she had previously used, Chu responded, "Who *needs* that old 'chain-of-command' thing, anyway? That's *one* order that this 'boss' is happy to follow, dear friend... dear... *brother*."

The knocking sound, re-occurred.

"Ma'am," politely came the orderly's voice, although the door remained closed, "We really *got* to get goin', now."

"Coming!" called the FBI team-leader, while straightening her suit-jacket and fumbling for a tissue; she was assisted by both Boatman and Hendricks, who fussed over her face, cleaning it of tear-tracks, while they took turns shaking her hand and giving her a final hug. The effort was only just finished, when the door swung open.

In the outside corridor, was the orderly – a thin, pimply-faced, bottom-rank kid who couldn't have been more than twenty years old – along with four big, tough-looking Marine guards.

"Duty Officer says these two guys are going to escort Mr. Boatman and Mr. Hendricks toward the aft of the aircraft, so they can disembark," explained the orderly, pointing at one pair of the Marines. "PFCs Walker and Moulos will come forward, with you and me, Ms. Chu. You ready?"

"As I'll *ever* be," she answered, her voice rising to its customary professional poise.

The three FBI agents walked out of the conference-room in single-file, with Chu in the lead, followed by Hendricks and then Boatman; they mustered into separate groups, in the corridor. Two of the guards –with automatic-rifles very obviously at the ready – surrounded the male agents, while the other two joined the team-leader and her young military guide.

"Good luck, Minnie," said Hendricks, with a wave and a smile, as the two groups began to go in opposite directions. "Remember : 'back in one piece'!"

To the annoyance of the Marines, just as they were about to go out of each other's presence, the team-leader stopped for a second, turned around and softly called to her friends,

"Will... Otis... *I love you*."

Boatman and Hendricks also turned to face behind them. They both silently nodded, and then disappeared out of view.

Though in the midst of possibly the most busy and consequential place on Earth, Minnie Chu was now...

Alone.

A stiff-faced Air Force orderly in an impeccably-pressed dress uniform, knocked on the door of the nouveau-President's airborne luxury suite.

After an interval of perhaps six seconds, there was no answer, so the junior officer gave it another rap, this time, with a bit more force.

"Yeah... what *is* it?" came the Old Man's slurred, slightly-inebriated voice, from inside the suite. The door remained shut.

"Circling at 10,000 feet, per your instructions, sir," remarked the orderly. "As high as was recommended to avoid undue interior depressurization, although the compartment will be sealed and isolated beforehand, in any event."

"Where?" requested the voice.

"West Virginia... southern end of the Seneca State Forest, sir," came the answer. "Appalachians... pretty rugged territory. A few moonshiners up there, but little else. If anyone finds the bodies, it'll likely be years from now."

"Well, that'll do, I suppose," pedantically offered the *faux*-President. "Get it over with... and don't forget to clear that part of the plane, before you do it; I don't want any rumors going back and forth. Secret Service told me they don't have any guns with a silencer – and anyway, they didn't want to take the chance of a shot going off-target and putting a hole in the fuselage – so you'll just have to cuff 'em and shove 'em. You got that?"

"Yes, Mr. President, sir," responded the orderly. "Bureau has already been informed of the obits, all details redacted, of course. We'll execute in the next fifteen minutes, with your permission. Any other instructions, sir?"

"No... that'll be all," said the U.S. leader, with a muffled cough. "You may proceed."

"Yes, sir... I'll go now, sir," stated the orderly.

He had taken a step or two, but then he heard the *faux*-President's voice calling, from behind the closed door.

"Yes, sir?" inquired the Air Force officer.

"Before you do it," the *nouveau*-President said, "Tell them... 'did you think I wasn't *on* to you?' Oh... and mention... 'compared to what I'm going to do to that Jacobson S.O.B... well, you're getting off easy'."

"Yes, sir," affirmed the orderly. "I'll make sure your message is relayed."

"Dismissed," commanded the U.S. leader.

The junior officer reflexively saluted, turned and walked aftward.

We Don't Do, "Mercy"

Qusay al-Sabah, in an act of defiance unusual for him, had again let his beard grow out.

Only a few days – maybe just hours – before Paradise, anyway, he reasoned.

I have enough rose-water, at least for my own body, in the little vial... and I have retained a proper men's kameez, *to replace these ugly street-clothes – let us hope there is time to change, in the final minutes! Now, I can only pray that my jaw and cheeks will be fully-covered. Almighty Allah will not look kindly upon one who disobeys such a fundamental rule of the Holy Qu'ran... even if someone said it was "necessary to blend in with the crowd".*

Darkness was falling over the seedier parts of Perris, California, in suburban Los Angeles; and that was a *good* thing. They needed all the cover that they could get.

Al-Sabah and his little band of ten remaining believers hadn't had an easy time, over the past few days. They had already gone through two different vehicles – first, a SUV that was shot to pieces in an initial encounter with some Latino "Piru" gang (several of the faithful had achieved martyrdom, in *that* fight), then, a commandeered delivery-van, whose tires went flat after driving over a hidden spike-barrier – and, despite the weight of the guns, ammo and other accessories – they had decided it would be more practical to go forward on foot.

To make matters worse, they had heard the sounds of army-helicopters, along with heavy-caliber gun- and rocket-fire, somewhere far off, to the north and east; and the radio-snooping-devices – though their abilities were limited, as they could only intercept channels that weren't protected with high-grade encryption – had overheard conversations indicating that the hated American President's military was making a determined effort to push into the city.

Time is limited, he mused.

We must get there before the infidel!

"Any indication of it yet, Brother?" inquired the short, shaven-headed figure of Waqas-al-Nusri, as he tried to clear a pathway through the trash covering the floor of the looted, smashed-window barber-shop, at the back of which the believers had decided to bed down for the night.

Nusri's efforts were largely futile; not only was there far too much in the way of broken glass and general garbage, on the floor, but also, it was all but pitch-dark, in here. Earlier in the quest-trip, they had learned not to use the flashlights anywhere, except in a window-less basement.

Two more dead martyrs could attest to the necessity of *that* precaution.

"Unfortunately, no," replied the average-sized, but lean and intense-eyed leader of the South California *Shaheed* Strike Group, attached to the North American wing of Allah's Muslim Salvation League. "I think we are still out of range. Ai! At this rate... we might *never* find the device!"

"Well then, perhaps we should –" started the *shaheed* lieutenant; but his voice was cut off by a rapid, cautionary gesture, and "shh" sound, coming from al-Sabah's lips.

The Muslim leader's finger pointed outside, through a broken picture-window.

"*Infidels – degenerates!*" he softly inveighed. "Armed. Do you see?"

They could make out three figures – big, hulking Caucasians dressed in biker-garb, each one considerably taller and better-muscled than the spare, lean Islamic warriors themselves – striding down the middle of the street, outside. Two of the intruders each carried an automatic rifle, while the third, who was in the middle, appeared to have only a pistol.

"Yes," confirmed the other man.

"Have you your gun?" whispered the *shaheed* commander.

"Yes – of course," quietly spoke al-Nusri. "But there are three of them. Shall I go to the basement and summon our brothers?"

"No," countermanded al-Sabah, "If you trip over something in the dark, the noise will alert them, and we do not know if more are coming. I will shoot the one on the left – you do the man on the right."

"But what of the middle infidel?" complained the lieutenant.

"You do him, after our respective targets," indicated al-Sabah. "As, your weapon fires faster. I will back you up, in case you miss. Ready? On the count of two and the call of the mujaheddin."

"Allah be with us!" breathed al-Nusri, as he released the safety on his Brazilian-manufactured AK-74M copy, while al-Sabah readied his semi-auto, scope-equipped sniper-rifle.

"One... two..." counted the Muslim leader...

"*Allahu Akbarr!*" he shouted, opening fire.

And his aim was true; the unfortunate interloper on the left – taken completely by surprise and struck multiple times by high-powered rifle-bullets, both in the upper-body and the head – collapsed in a blood-splattered mess; a similar fate befell the man on the left, as Waqas' dum-dum rounds hit him below the belt and in the lower chest, nearly slicing him in half.

But then, matters did not go entirely according to plan. Al-Sabah momentarily hesitated, believing that his compatriot would finish the job; but instead, he heard a frantic warning.

"Brother – *the gun jams!*" exclaimed al-Nusri.

Not missing a second, the Muslim leader again raised his rifle and began to fire, this time at the lone survivor of the ambush. But the man was already running, and al-Sabah's rounds hit him only in the lower left leg. Moaning, he rapidly retreated.

"After him!" shouted al-Sabah. "If he gets away and calls for reinforcements –"

Both men dashed out of the barber-shop, ignoring alarmed inquiries from the several *mujaheddin* who, having heard the commotion, were now charging up the stairs from the basement.

Al-Nusri, fumbling all the way to clear the jam, tripped over something-or-other, and tumbled helplessly to an unceremonious crash-landing on the concrete; but his senior officer was more deliberate, taking a stable, crouching position as soon as he had a clear shot, enabling the low-light function of his scope, and rapidly squeezing off two rounds. One of these impacted with the fugitive just above the hip – probably shattering his pelvis, or causing equally-serious damage – and he fell instantly.

"Allah be *praised!*" intoned the junior *mujaheddin*, seeing that the third white-man was bleeding profusely and was barely able to crawl. "Brother, my weapon is again functional. I will finish him –"

"No!" quickly countermanded al-Sabah. "Cover me, while I examine and disarm him – there may be others of his kind, in the vicinity. We take him back with us."

In a low voice, while scanning the surroundings for any sign of enemies and fortunately seeing none, al-Nusri requested, "Why show mercy, to such an infidel dog?"

The Muslim leader whispered back, "Mercy? Not what I had in mind, brother."

"I do not follow," persisted al-Nusri.

"Well," calmly explained the senior Islamic warrior, "First, we interrogate him... *forcefully*. He may know where those dogs and whores are keeping the... *objective*. Or, at least, where we would go, to obtain the necessary information."

"Ah," knowingly responded the junior mujaheddin.

"Then," elaborated al-Sabah, matter-of-factually like reciting a cookbook recipe, "We... *skin* him."

A Step Into The Void

"Now what's the point of you cuffin' us all over again?" argued Boatman, his voice still genteel and restrained, as he and the third agent shuffled down the exquisitely-carpeted corridor, near the end of the airborne command post that would have, in earlier days, accommodated members of the press corps. "We haven't done nothin'... and ain't about to."

And I wonder why I felt the plane slowin' down, and why all those folks was avertin' their eyes from young Will and me, while we walked by? he mused.

Somethin' don't feel right, *here...*

"Standard procedure for ingress or egress of an untrusted individual, on or off this aircraft," brusquely stated one of the six heavily-armed Marine guards – including the four that had joined the first two, after the tearful "goodbyes" said to the FBI agents' former team-leader – who were accompanying the big black man, and Hendricks, toward the aft of the plane.

As they traversed the last section of Air Force One, Hendricks looked at all the empty seats, and uneasily remarked, "Wow... didn't know you had all this space, around here."

His comment was met with a stone-faced silence on the part of the guards, who, upon reaching the aft bulkhead, entered a combination into a keypad-lock next to a pressure-door, which opened, ushering the group into a confined area, with a sealed portal leading to the outside. There was barely enough room to accommodate the eight of them, within the aft compartment.

The pressure-door to the interior of the rest of the airplane swung shut, and the Marine guards – with pistols obviously at the ready – ordered, "Line up. You – Agent Hendricks – first, then Agent Boatman. Face the door."

The two FBI agents reluctantly complied, with Hendricks muttering something about, "Yeah, well I'll be glad to see the last of *this* place, man."

"I have been told to relay a message to you," spoke one of the Marine guards, a big, brush-cut Caucasian, apparently their leader.

"And what would *that* be?" patiently asked Boatman.

"This is from the President of the United States, himself," the guard went on. "The message is as follows : "Did you think that I wasn't *on* to you? Compared to what will be done to that Jacobson S.O.B., and those around him... you should consider yourselves, as getting off easy'."

A chill went through both of the more-than-human men, as suspicion raced through their minds.

"I don't want to get off easy, man," incautiously cracked Hendricks. "I'll settle for just gettin' off this fuckin' plane, in the first place."

"I believe," coldly replied the Marine leader, "That you'll get your wish, in that respect. Corporal – open the door."

"But we ain't yet *landed* –" protested Boatman.

There was a rush of pressurized interior air and the howl of frigid, high-speed wind, as the portal slid to the side, revealing a vast expanse of night-time sky, with wisps of cloud barely visible here and there.

"You are now to exit the aircraft," shouted the Marine-guard leader.

"What the *fuck?*" yelled the third agent, who was struggling under the tight grasp of two big, tough Marines. "What about a *parachute,* man – we're still *miles* up in the air! We'll be –"

"Resist, and we'll have to shoot you first," answered the leader. "Go voluntarily, and at least you'll have a few minutes on the way down, to prepare to meet your Maker."

A panicked Boatman now got into the conversation.

"Listen, you boys – you all's makin' a *big* mistake, here – we're on *your* side... remember? We ain't done nothin', 'cept to put our lives on the line, for the Bureau, and the government! I'm beggin' you, *please* –" he stammered.

"Aim weapons," directed the leader.

"Okay – *okay!*" interjected Hendricks. "We *get* it. We'll go... we'll do it *your* way. All I ask is... can I turn around, hold my bro's hands, as we go down? Kinda better to say a prayer together than apart, you know? *Please,* man!"

"I'll allow that," shouted the Marine leader. "Then it's a three-count, and we fire."

The third agent swiveled in place, grasping tightly on to Boatman's big fingers.

"Damn, Will," he blubbered, "This just ain't *happenin' – can't* be –"

"One," counted the Marine leader.

"Brother," answered the third agent, his voice strangely calm and reassuring, "It's gonna be *alright.* You believe in God... don't you?"

"Shore do," gasped the black FBI agent, "'Specially, now!"

"Two!" came the loud warning.

"Good," offered Hendricks. "Because *I,* believe in..."

"*Angels!*"

It took most of the effort that the third agent could muster, to carry Boatman's much larger, heavier and, above all else, *unwilling,* body forward, through the portal.

Downward they hurtled, through the cold night sky.

Lay-Over In Paducah

Much to their surprise and relief, the Jacobson group found the job of safely exiting the scene of the recent battle, considerably easier than had been anticipated.

A few drones *were* seen hovering over the road, at long range, by both Tanaka and Boyd; but some highly useful (though only 2-dimensional, and limited-size) “bending-the-starlight-above-us” tricks by *Vîrya Sài'ymë*, plus quick thinking by the former Mars mission commander (who exited the van and then carried it in an off-road eastward detour across the Peck Ranch Conservation Area), allowed them to evade the pursuing air-robots.

The trip across this seldom-traveled region didn't take long, although by the time they had exited the Peck Ranch region, Jacobson reluctantly admitted to being “mightily tired”.

After traveling the back-roads and avoiding the highways wherever possible, the group realized that retaining their current vehicle for more than a few hours, would be far too risky, even though they had managed to escape at least two near-encounters with approaching police-cars, simply by pulling over and having *Vîrya Sài'ymë* “darken the shadows” around the van.

A first attempt at a vehicle-switch at Poplar Bluff had to be called off after the three scouts on top of the van, detected police roadblocks at every normal entrance to that town; so the Jacobson team did another detour, with their hapless leader huffing and puffing as he again played pack-mule, with a van weighing several thousand pounds, on his back.

More challenges awaited further to the east, because the fugitives, figuring on LEA roadblocks at such a choke-point, did not dare try the Great River Road Bridge at the confluence of the Ohio and Mississippi Rivers. Instead, they elected to go across the Mississippi at a narrow point, landing at the end of side-road overlooking the river, just south of Wicksville, Kentucky.

This feat was accomplished with consummate ease, partly due to the Mississippi being relatively calm in the wee hours of this morning but mainly because of the ice-boat – large enough to easily accommodate the Jacobson van and complete with admirably-high sides and a rudder – that was crafted on the spot, by the resourceful Devon White. After they had arrived on the eastern bank and after the vessel's hull was perforated by a few flame-puffs from the bounty-hunter's two pet mutts, it was sent back into the river to sink gently below the waves, while the group clambered back into the van and went on.

By just before dawn, the Jacobson team had reached the outskirts of Paducah, which, mercifully, seemed to be free of law enforcement roadblocks.

They were deterred by a visibly-present night watchman at a first car-lot, which was then bypassed; but the next one was only protected by a ten-foot-tall, barb-wire, metal fence, and it was short work for Jacobson to hop over, do a little quick license-plate-swapping between five of the cars parked in the lot (appropriating a set of plates for himself, while sticking the plates from their current vehicle, on a "junker" sitting behind the garage), and finally, selecting a suitably-sized, dark-green, high-end, max-size Patriotic SUV from the back of the lot, carrying it triumphantly over the fence. The vehicle's ignition interlock and "always-on" tracking devices proved easy for *Vìrya Sài'ymë* to disable, and away the group went.

There were genuine tears of regret when, just before the break of dawn, the van which had steadfastly carried them all the way from Florida – its cargo unloaded, its fuel siphoned and its electronics and ID markings melted into uselessness – was sunk into the Ohio River.

As the first rays of the sun appeared in the east, the tightly-packed group (even for a vehicle of *this* size, interior space was at a premium, and they now couldn't take the chance of Boyd and Tanaka riding on the roof), stopped in the far end of the parking lot at the dilapidated, low-cost Super 9 Motel, off Kentucky Route 62, near the Kentucky Dam Village State Park.

Jacobson and several of the others had wanted just to pull over and sleep in the car; but the thoroughly-exhausted Wades, Donny included, had had enough, and insisted on taking a room.

Reluctantly, the Mars mission commander consented, on the conditions that the transaction be conducted for cash, using assumed names, and that there would be no use of computer networks or telephones.

Callum Wade, posing as a "Mr. Brad Kammler", rented two units, side-by-side, with the explanation that "the missus and me, we ain't gettin' along that well, so she's gonna take her own room with mah son"; given that nocturnal comings-and-goings were par for the course in this low-end motel, the subterfuge worked quite well, and, apparently, no eyebrows were raised when the Wades all ended up in Room 211, while the four former Mars astronauts decamped in Room 212.

The bounty-hunter and the Russian drew the short end of the stick, and ended up having to share the SUV with Wolf's two fire-dogs, but Misha was philosophical about the whole thing : "Whatever else one can say," he smilingly offered, "These accommodations, even with my friend's snoring, are superior to SVR Training Camp."

As the morning sunshine came through the window-curtains of Room 212, Tanaka turned to address her former commander and one-time, furtive, lover.

"Funny thing *is,* Sam," she observed, "I *should* be completely, uhh... zonked... but I'm... *not.* I could really use the sleep... but I don't *need* it. Any of this making sense?"

"Yeah," agreed Jacobson. "But – sleep we shall, none the less."

"Synchronize with the Wades, maybe?" inquired the former science officer. "God knows... they've been through far too much over the past half-day. I feel *terribly* guilty about what we – excuse me, the government – have subjected them to. They're probably hoping that this is all a bad dream, from which they'll wake up..."

"Good guess," said the Mars mission commander, "But just a fringe-benefit, actually."

Tanaka did a poor job of suppressing a yawn.

"Umm-hmm?" she mumbled.

"What I've learned, lately, is," explained Jacobson, as he pulled the bed-covers up over his body, "The night, is our friend."

Bad Karma Broadcast

Though the settings – one, separate bedrooms in a small, working-class house in Villa Hills, Kentucky; two, the same, in a cheap motel in the same state, three, in a cramped reclining-chair on board Air Force One, and finally, in a force-field-protected environment, hurling through the stratosphere at hyper-sonic speed, over the South Atlantic ocean – were different... the feeling, and the reactions, were quite similar.

Jerry Kaysten woke suddenly up in a cold sweat, and was sort of comforted by the immediate appearance of *Vîrya I'ëà'b'*, who – as near as this could be done, by a creature of her ilk – nuzzled him and communicated her shared concern, in the usual inscrutable way. He was joined a second later by an equally-upset Sylvia Abruzzio, who mumbled something about "a bad dream, in which I was falling, and I couldn't stop".

The weirding war-shield also sent a message to (as far as the former Chief of Staff or JPL scientist could make out) to the effect of "to little me oh-kay but is you cousin met never have call"; but both of the more-than-humans were perplexed, not understanding what, or who, *Vîrya I'ëà'b'* could be referring to.

With nothing more that could be done, they both tried, with varying degrees of success, to go back to sleep.

Minnie Chu's reaction was even more panicked. She woke up in something akin to a night-terror, rushing, sick to the stomach, to the closest washroom, and only just making it in time.

Yet, after the unpleasantness was done, a strange sense of peace and calm came to her, along with an odd, non-verbal idea – from she knew not where – similar to the meaning of "alright".

Wishing that sleeping-pills would still work on her, but knowing that they wouldn't, Chu went back to the chair, consumed with inchoate worry.

In the Paducah, Kentucky, Super 9 motel, Tanaka was the first to be involuntarily propelled out of slumber, knocking frantically on the doors to where the others were resting, stammering all the while, "*Vîrya Sài'ymë* woke me up, she's screaming a warning about 'my kin-cousin cries fear for his master, whose life is in peril'".

She was rapidly joined by the others – even Wolf, who complained about "damn voices in my head, worse than a bad synth trip" – but none of them could figure out exactly what was happening.

"Bad feeling about this, though," offered Boyd. "Reminds me a lot of what we were getting from Bob, Whitney, Melissa, Curtis and Tommy, a few weeks ago... you know?" This brought knowing glances from the other three members of the Jacobson team, as they tried to make sense of the event, before realizing that there was little they could do to investigate or rescue. They, like their comrades and competitors elsewhere, eventually went uneasily back to bed.

The Storied Watcher, for her part, had been returning from a shopping- and -"borrowing"-expedition in and around the cities of the South American coast, with a huge, shipping-container-sized, steel-mesh-bound bag of gifts and supplies for the Bouvet refuge inhabitants in tow behind the equally-packed-full *Mailànkh Express*, both of these delicately balanced in the slipstream and hidden from military sensors by a potent combination of force-fields, telekinesis and light-bending-arts.

And there was something – some*one* – else, also being carried, on this trip.

The Storied Watcher allowed a tear to escape her gravity-bending powers; it moistened the dirty, disheveled hair of the deeply-somnolent little Brazilian girl whose slight, under-fed body was compressed tightly against the flaming recesses of *Vîrya Ahn'jë*.

Sleep well, beautiful little one, came the silent invocation. *You shall wake to a new and glorious life; and the lowest of the low, shall be raised most high.*

The alien-girl was on the upward end of one of her climbs-and-dives (up to ten thousand meters for a few hundred kilometers, down under the waves for several tens more, then up again), when a shock of panic and worry reverberated not only through her own psyche, but also, those of her war-children (at least, all excepting the absent, and sorely-missed, "Daughter Diamond-Curtain Tornado").

A cry for help – far away, in the direction of that benighted 'America' empire – from the kin of Will Hendricks, brought to life by mine hand, that of kind Hector, and Will's own, she quickly realized.

I can hurry thither, ruminated Karéin-Mayréij,

But even as my speed through the atmosphere of this world waxes, since only a few days past... that empire is still hours away, still more if I take precautions against detection. I cannot go full-tilt – this precious daughter who slumbers at my breast... even with the kiss of my teeth, she is not ready... she would not survive.

And I have only a single call – he chants not my name, as he knows well how to do... it is a chance that I took, understanding the risk, when I made for Bouvet, along with the little ones from Compton.

And did I not vow, not to intervene?

Yet... the blood of my brother and faithful disciple, eff-bee-ai Will!

How can I forbear?

Then the combined, half-biological, half-techno-voices of her war-children, spoke up.

Mother beloved, they informed, *Be oh-kay will it.*

Thus afar from cousin us informs.

How can it be so? she replied.

Such a cry comes only with mortal peril!

Us thou trust do, Mother beloved? came the answer.

Survives that he assured for are we.

Of course, responded the gratified Storied Watcher.

I trust ye with my very life, little ones, and never have ye failed; therefore, I must equally do, with the safety of my former-human brothers and sisters.

As she began a dive toward the cold, gray waters of the southern ocean, she thought,

But all the same... when those who stay deep within Bouvet have what they need, and when again my path leads north, to the Dark Empire of America...

To the next call, will swiftly come, the Destroying Angel.

As the alien-girl raced toward the wave-tops at a speed that would have terrified any other inhabitant of this planet, she murmured a prayer of thanks and vicarious good-will.

Far from the eyes or ears of any save the denizens of the deep, a towering geyser of displaced sea exploded nosily upward, as the mighty and confident Karéin-Mayréij plunged into the South Atlantic.

O Ye Of Little Faith

"Sylvia," complained Kaysten, as he reclined in the living-room easy-chair and sipped on his imitation Chablis, "This is *almost* as effin' stupid an idea, as it was for you and I to tag along with Minnie, Otis and Will, in the first place."

By now, both he and Abruzzio had almost recovered from the bad dreams.

"Got a *better* one, Jerry?" countered the former JPL scientist, while multi-tasking between working the virtual keyboard and mouse of her friend's flat-screen computer terminal, consulting something on Sullivan's mobile communicator and watching the TV (which was showing the local weather), out of the corner of her eye. "We might as well have something to do, while as we're holed up in here. And anyway... I *told* you – we're not going anywhere, until I have a good fix on where he's being held... that is, as long as Moira lets us stay."

"Oh... don't be silly, girl," remarked the house-owner, "You *know* you're welcome here, as long as you want to hang out. But I still don't get, why on Earth you want to *try* something like this. It's *crazy,* Sylvia... you'll never get *away* with it! By the way... you get enough to eat?"

"O ye of little faith," patiently deflected Abruzzio, while continuing to write notes on an old-school paper pad, to her right. "Remember *that* one, from Catechism Class?"

Her dog let out a "yip", which, somehow, sounded like an affirmation.

"You *tell* 'em, honey," added the former scientist. "And... absolutely. Get me some ripe tomatoes and garlic, and I'll whip you up some of Mama's special spaghetti, tomorrow – you know, you used to come over to our place, just to eat it. I'd do it myself... but not a good idea to show my face too much, you know?"

"Yeah, I guess," admitted Sullivan. "But... tomorrow. Been a long day at work today... don't feel like going out again, tonight."

"Look, Sylvia," persisted Kaysten, "The thing *I* don't understand is... even if we track him down – and even if that's somewhere we have a snowball's chance in Hades, of actually getting to – how the H are we going to *spring* him? Not that I don't want to, of course : I owe that man my whole *career*. Just bullshit, what they did to him! The whole thing was a set-up... I'm sure of that."

"So... Jerry," inquired the house-owner, "I could hardly get a word out edgewise from that choir-girl over there, on the subject... but you never *did* tell me what *your*, uhh, 'thing' is... is it real 'super-duper' stuff? To get you right in there, and fly off with him, like what's-her-face would, I mean –"

"Ha... you mean like her Angel Highness?" chuckled the former Chief of Staff. "Hardly. As for me, well... I run fast... *real* fast. Oh, and I guess I've got kind of a silver tongue, especially for telling jokes, is how you'd say it."

"Tellin' *jokes?*" incredulously guffawed Sullivan. "What kind of a lame 'super-power' is *that?*"

"Doubles 'em up with laughter... or so I'm told," evaded Kaysten, "But only when I, uhh, 'turn it on'. Kind of hard to describe – tell you the truth, I really don't have a *clue* how it works... I'm still at the 'newbie' stage in being a super-hero. Now, that Jacobson guy and his crew, *they're* something completely –"

"Just a second," interrupted Abruzzio. "National news is coming on."

After the re-worked, even more cheerful Disney News Network theme-song (a kind of shotgun marriage between the 'Mouseketeers' theme and an electro-pop rendition of 'Clementine'), some 3-D logo art involving a black skull-cap with two little, circular ears, and an introductory voice-over indicating, "And now... Tom Sabonis, reporting", the announcer – a late-fiftyish, fatherly-looking guy – got right into it.

"Good evening, ladies and gentlemen," he greeted, "Our lead story tonight is a major shoot-out in the Midwest, between public safety forces and an as-yet-unapprehended group of criminals. Our man on the scene, Charles Ludlow, reports. Charles?"

The image on the screen shifted to a scene near a police roadblock, with the broad expanses of the Corn Belt beyond, and the streets and mid-height buildings of a small city, on either side.

"Hi, Tom," spoke the young, business-suited, Caucasian field-reporter. "I'm here at the outskirts of Farmington, Missouri, and as you can see," – he swiveled his torso, so as to draw attention to the road leading out of town, which was backed up as far as the eye could see, with a huge traffic-jam, leading to a series of vehicle-barriers, each with massive police presence – "Local and federal law enforcement agencies have imposed strict restrictions on comings and goings, over, it appears, most of southern Missouri and northern Arkansas, resulting from a serious altercation that took place in the early hours of this morning, somewhere near the town of West Plains. Police have been fanning out all over the state, and have been interdicting traffic on the Interstates. Some routes have been shut down entirely, while long delays are being reported going in to major population centers, for example St. Louis and Kansas City."

"What kind of 'altercation'?" requested the anchorman. "And who are they looking for?"

"Law enforcement authorities have very close-mouthed about the nature of the investigation, Tom," responded the reporter, "But we *have* been able to learn that a 'shoot-to-kill' order has been circulated with respect to the suspects in this case, who are described as 'very heavily armed and extremely dangerous'. What's unusual about the order, of which Disney News has obtained a redacted copy, is that the names and identities of the suspects have been blacked out; and, local police forces are being instructed not to attempt a take-down on their own, but to instead escalate immediately to national-level agencies. Police are also informing the public that deadly force may be needed to apprehend this group of criminals, and that therefore, citizens should immediately remove themselves from the vicinity of the fugitives... something that might be difficult, given that there's no way to know who is being sought. When asked why this is the case, the spokesman involved had no further comment."

The reporter continued, "Furthermore, we've been getting as-yet unconfirmed eye-witness reports from the south-central parts of the state, of loud explosions followed by a series of brilliant flashes, which, according to those nearby, quote, 'lit the sky up as if it was mid-day', unquote. It's been impossible for Disney News to verify any of this, since the entire region in which the confrontation allegedly took place, is now under very strict lock-down by the government, with no unauthorized traffic being allowed anywhere near the site. That's all for now... Tom?"

"Well – certainly something interesting going on, in the 'Show Me State', Charles," opined the anchorman. "Turning now to overseas news, we have a report of a potential leadership crisis in the Kremlin, as..."

Sullivan used the remote-control to mute the set's audio volume to below the level of human audibility, though, in fact, both of the other two, could still just make it out.

"Either of you want to see the rest of this?" she asked. "I always watch *Who Wants The Big Box of Booby Prizes*, this time of the night... kind of lets me relax, you know?"

"Oh... no problem," politely responded Abruzzio, as she handed the remote-control to Sullivan, who switched the channel to a game show where people competed to win gifts like "a ton of last year's moldy bread, plus ten thousand bucks", and so on.

How can she watch *that kind of nonsense?* secretly mused the former JPL scientist, who was momentarily staring at her hostess.

Something that Karéin can fix, maybe?

Oh, look *at yourself, Sylvia... she's your* friend.

What right do you have, to get her mixed up in all of this?

But still... it's a 'blessing'... isn't it? How could you deny it to her?

What would God want me to do?

Kaysten's voice snapped her out of her reverie.

“Hey Sylvia,” he commented, “You think it's *them*?”

“Who?” absent-mindedly replied the scientist. “Oh... *them*... Jacobson and Company, you mean. Well, I certainly wouldn't want to bet against it. Odd, though – what would Sam and his people have to gain, by getting into a shoot-out with the law, especially when he got all that good press, down with the tornado? All I can really say is, 'I hope they're all okay'. 'Brothers and sisters', you know.”

“Yeah,” he quietly agreed. “If this means anything... the Old Man – I mean, the *real* one, before that scheming, “sell your Mom for two bucks son-of-a-bitch” V-P took over – I just have a hard time imagining that he'd ever have authorized anything like what we've seen going on. I talked to him after he got back from his little chat with the astronauts, you know, while they were being held who knows where... he didn't tell me too much, and he was miffed that Jacobson didn't spill the beans earlier, but he still respected Sam, Devon, Cherie and Brent – there's no *way* he'd have knowingly agreed to them being subjected to the bullshit we've seen. There's something else going on... there's *got* to be.”

“Only way we'll find out,” spoke Abruzzio, as she tried to tune out the klaxons, bells and general, mindless din of the game-show and turned to again face the computer-screen, “Is to ask him, to his face. Let's see if this search... *hmm*. Now... *that's* interesting.”

The former Chief of Staff arose from his chair and went to stand over the more-than-a-woman's shoulder, regarding the display along with Sullivan, who muted the game-show and also joined Abruzzio at the computer-screen.

“There's 'standard' NeoNet – the kind that everybody knows about – and then there's 'special' NeoNet,” explained the scientist. “To get access to the latter, which bypasses most of the controls that the government applies to the publicly-known part of the network, you have to know a lot of IPv8 data protocol, and have a credential that lets you get past the firewalls. So –”

“Well, for God's *sake*, Sylvia... why didn't you tell me that, earlier?” complained Kaysten. “I had a special, uhh, 'user name' and password, for the White House system – I could've just given it to you, and –”

“Thought of that already,” noted Abruzzio. “But they've probably already disabled it – after all, they'd have to assume that it has already been compromised by Karéin – and if you used it now, either successfully or unsuccessfully, they might track down the network address here, put two plus two together and conclude that 'Jerry Kaysten is hiding out in Moira Sullivan's house, in Villa Hills, Kentucky'. Same thing would be the case, if I used my own, personal, 'special' Neo credentials. I don't have to explain why the consequences of something like *that*, could be, uhh, 'unpleasant', for all of us."

"'Scuse my French – but you're not just fuckin' whistlin' 'Dixie' there, sister," ruefully admitted the former Chief of Staff. "So how'd you get access?"

"At JPL, we were all supposed to always use our own user names and passwords," elaborated Abruzzio, "But, because of the constant budget cuts, they were never able to tie the various authentication systems together, so just to make the whole darn thing work, they issued us 'generic' credentials that anyone could use... keep in mind, we're talking about a group of at least 10,000 people, across the entire NASA organization, who had access to these. And... hooray! They seem to work anywhere on Neo, at least from where we're now at. We always used to use our generic, privileged accounts, so we could surf to places – for example, the BBC – that were heavily censored here in the U.S., and we learned how to cover our tracks... like, by deleting the firewall-logs that record 'who logged on from where, and what sites they accessed'. Which, I did, about a half-hour ago... so, I basically have unfiltered access to all of NeoNet. Oh, and I used a few protocol-routing tricks, to make it look like I'm located in the JPL headquarters. They should have no way whatsoever, to trace me."

"Well, that's great... I suppose," sniffed Kaysten. "So we can get all the good stuff, that is, porno – even *my* kind of it – and Muslim propaganda about how nasty a guy, poor old Uncle Sam is, that is. I could do the same at the White House, but I got bored by it, after about a week. So what?"

"If I just wanted to watch dirty movies, Jerry, that *would* be it," patiently replied the scientist, "But I've, uhh, got bigger fish to fry – and there's a ton of information on 'hidden' NeoNet that I've been able to download, and which may be relevant to what we're doing... I'll need more time to review all of it, but in the short run –"

"You *found* him?" excitedly interrupted the former bureaucrat.

"Not, uhh... *exactly*," deflected Abruzzio. "But there are some promising leads. For example, I'm pretty sure he's not being kept in a real jail – one of the underground hacker sites have some documents which talk about 'house arrest on-grounds of the 'Kenneth Lay FPDCF', with 24/7 personal medical service, video-on-demand and no-charge access to the lodge and the green'... whatever *that* is. And I'm pretty sure that he has to be somewhere in the continental United States, since the same source indicates, 'ETA from Anderson AFB to destination facility ARN, approximately 1.75 hours, assuming standard en-route evasives'. Even the fastest Air Force transport plane, couldn't make it too far, with that amount of travel time. We just have to figure out what, and where, 'destination facility ARN', is."

"I'll have to leave that kind of thing to the brains of the operation," glumly responded an obviously-disappointed Kaysten.

"Oh... and after 'we' figure that out, Jerry," added the scientist, with a subtly-multi-chromatic wink that was weirdly, immediately mimicked by her puppy, "All we have to do is sneak into what's probably one of the best-hidden and best-guarded secret facilities of the U.S. government, find the former President and get him out and away, without any of us being discovered or being caught. Sound good?"

Kaysten rolled his eyes, groaned, and said, "I have a question, Moira."

"Sure, Jerry," answered Sullivan. "What is it?"

"If she goes off and tries this," he asked, "Do I get to stay here?"

Even Grander Theft Auto

By now, the "Mars Gang" – as White had flippantly named the group of fugitives – had become well-accomplished at the car-theft business.

After a long and tedious day cooling their heels at the Super 9 Motel, with Tanaka and her weirding "child" pumping NeoNet for all they could, and with the elder Wades running food-and-supply-fetching errands back and forth to and from the local Wal-Target and Waffle House Restaurant, Jacobson and Company set out just after nightfall, waiting for the last salesman to close up shop, then expertly relieving the Select Fine Pre-Owned Auto Sales lot on Estes Lane, Paducah, Kentucky, of both a long-cab, full-size, off-red, Ford General pickup-truck, and a gold-colored U.S. Patriotic van, similar to the one that had been ditched in the Ohio River, a short time beforehand.

Jacobson's combination of *Amaiish*-based telekinesis and physical strength had allowed him to loosen scores of retaining-bolts and tie-down chains, with consummate ease; he swapped license-plates between the two automobiles that the gang had "appropriated", not to mention betwixt and between all the remaining ones on the lot, thereby to make the authorities' job of sorting out the truth, all the more difficult.

To assuage his conscience, he had left a scrawled "I.O.U." in place of each of the two missing vehicles, along with an insouciant advisory to the effect of "send all notes of appreciation to my former employer, the President of the United States – while you still can, while he's still in one piece".

The only unpleasantness had occurred when the former Mars mission commander jumped over the man-height steel-lattice fence surrounding the car-lot, and was then immediately attacked by the two thoroughly vicious dogs (apparently, the breed of both of these was a Rottweiler-Husky cross, or something equally large and dangerous), which had been left to guard the place.

The resulting scene was bizarre : the animals latched on to Jacobson's arms and legs, one on each appendage; but his *Fire*-fueled, translucent body-shield effortlessly resisted the otherwise-bone-crushing bites, and Jacobson simply dragged the snarling, drooling dogs into the dealership's garage, levitated slightly, and methodically threw them, one by one, into a pickup-truck that was on the hoist, then shut the truck's side-doors. While inside the facility, he also managed to locate the keys needed to operate the group's two new prizes.

"The thing is," philosophically remarked the former lead astronaut, "I still like dogs... I've even grown a little fond of Wolf's two mutts... I just wish they'd stop setting fire to the car-upholstery."

After *Vîrya Sài'ymë* did her now-well-practiced job of neutering the known, and secret, government tracking-systems within the two new vehicles' on-board electronic systems, the Mars Gang had to decide on driving arrangements.

The bounty-hunter demanded being put in charge of the pickup-truck, and the Russian elected to accompany him; there was some grumbling about the flame-dogs being left in the back of this vehicle, but Wolf assured everyone, "it's cool – no, *hot*, I mean – but what I *really* mean is... I told 'em, 'no supper for pups that jump out of the truck, and none for two days, if they that set things on fire without Dad tellin' em to, first'".

More than a few of the Jacobson party found this less than convincing, but they were not inclined to argue the point.

Since Donny insisted on being in the same vehicle as his aunt and uncle, the three Wades remained in the SUV, along with Jacobson in the passenger-seat; White and Tanaka took possession of the van, while Boyd decided to ride in the back of the pickup-truck, along with Wolf's two dogs.

With the seating-and-driving-arrangements thus resolved, the Jacobson team – with White's vehicle as the vanguard, followed by the Donny Wade SUV and, finally, Wolf's pickup-truck bringing up the rear – set out to the east and north on U.S. Route 60, heading first to Owensboro, on the way to the objective.

Where The Gold Is

Even though they could have made the trip faster on a more direct route, the three vehicles of the Mars Gang – traveling far enough apart so as not to obviously be a convoy, but close enough to always be within enhanced eyesight – left Paducah well after noon, and then took their own sweet time in heading across Kentucky, stopping at several locations to send Donny in to the local stores, to buy provisions and tools of various types.

They studiously avoided the Interstates, and instead followed Route 41A and then Route 60 through Henderson and Owensboro, twice offering to drop the Wades off, along the way. But the farmer, on the advice of his nephew, demurred, saying, "Well, I always *did* wonder what it'd be like to drive a getaway car for that-there Dillinger fella... now, I 'spose I'll find out."

He had then asked Jacobson, "But why *here*, Mr. Space Man?"; to which the former Mars mission commander blandly replied, "Because... it's where the gold, is. Oh, and if we take it hostage... at least we don't have to feed it, or let it call the relatives and tell 'em it's safe."

By about five in the afternoon, they had arrived in the outskirts of Fort Knox, and, taking advantage of the lengthening shadows as well as the rush-hour traffic, proceeded to drive up and down the Dixie Highway, turning to the east on Bullion Boulevard and probing as far as they could go, before seeing the road-side signs warning "NO ACCESS, 1 HALF MILE AHEAD" and discreetly reversing their path. They then proceeded south, and after a stop at a drive-in burger-joint in Radcliff – at which time-keeping-equipment was carefully synchronized and the plans were reviewed for the umpteenth revision – there was no longer an excuse to procrastinate.

The van, SUV and pickup-truck were stationed alongside each other in a far corner of the restaurant's parking-lot, but each one had not gone all the way up to the embankment surrounding the place, so there was ample room for the group to congregate in front of the parked automobiles, and yet be afforded a measure of privacy from those coming and going.

Due to off-road mobility issues and the need for those left behind to have a car, they had decided to leave the van, and thus to undertake their mission only with the other two vehicles.

"So... this is 'it', I reckon," laconically observed the Missouri farmer, as he leaned back against the front of the pickup. "You all sure you're up to this, Jacobson? That-there place's locked down tighter than, well, than *anythin'*, maybe exceptin' the White House."

"Callum," calmly responded the former Mars mission leader, "If you knew some of the places that we've had to force our way in to – not to mention, *out of* – up to this point... let's just say, 'that's not going to be a problem'."

"Yeah, well," sourly commented White, "That may be, Captain – but y'all *know* how eager I am to get my ass stuck down in some hole under the ground, all over again."

"Yeah... no kidding," echoed Boyd. "And *this* time, we don't even have Bob to make fun of. Nor Her Alien Highness, to lend a helping hand."

"Well," observed Jacobson, "Hopefully we won't have to do too much retreating, either up or down. Anyway, we're approaching G-Hour; press releases running off those 'smart picture frames' are all set to go off in another hour, and there's enough of them distributed so one or two for sure, ought to get through to the media. Plus I sent the text to those 'NRA' hackers... we should be able to use them as a back-channel, although I'd prefer not to do so, for obvious reasons. Does everybody know what to do?"

"Yeah... *we* do," answered Tanaka. "*Vìrya Sài'ymë*'s passively monitoring as much of the wireless traffic as she can handle without tiring herself out, and she's got the key-codes to call up those hacker-guys, 'when and if', as long as we can find an open link to NeoNet. She's already got the locations of the drones mapped out; I should be able to drop them just with my telekinesis, so there shouldn't be a lot of warning, except of course for a few video-consoles going dead. And as I mentioned in the car, Little One was able to, uhh, 'sniff' some of the Air Force's IFF codes while we were going against those fighters a while ago... hopefully she can spoof them reasonably well; that might help me avoid some missiles."

"Fewer missiles comin' my way... that's a *good* thing," grunted Wolf.

"Hate to rain on your parade, there," mentioned Boyd, "But it would probably work only for Cherie herself, and the ATGMs don't use it anyway."

"Honestly," continued the former science officer, "The only thing I'm a little unsure of, is the tanks... the gunships at Godman Airfield won't survive more than five seconds against me, assuming that I catch 'em all on the ground, but I don't know how effective my lightening-bolts will be against a heavily-armored target like a Westmoreland tank. To say nothing of taking a direct hit from one of those big guns... that's a *lot* of kilo-joules potentially impacting my shield."

"Well... that 'bubble' of yours *did* take a hit from a nuke up there on the Island, not to mention everythin' a tornado could throw at it," insouciantly remarked White.

"Don't *remind* me," ruefully muttered Tanaka. "Still hurts to remember."

"If you can't actually penetrate their front armor, Professor," tutored Boyd, "Try a rear flank attack – it's typically thinner from that angle. Failing even that, see if you can neutralize their thermal imagers, laser range-finders and other sensors – they're typically on top of the turrets. Doing that should make their return fire very inaccurate. Maybe they'll retreat. That would be good. Fewer people will be, uhh..."

"I understand, Brent," softly replied the former Mars science officer.

"I got to admit to bein' more than a little scared of you, Miss Cherie," carefully stated Marie Wade. "Anybody who can shoot it out with a fighter-plane, or a tank, or one of them bombs, and live to tell about it –"

Tanaka walked over and gave the farm-wife a generous hug.

"Marie," she counseled, "I know exactly how you feel... because it's how *I* felt, when I first met Karéin. We had a conversation something like this with her, on the way back from Mars, and she acknowledged how we might be a little, uhh, *afraid* of her. It's a continuum – some of us are stronger, some less so. But we all have a place... and it all makes sense. At least, that's what I believe."

"Philosophy class later," grunted Jacobson. "Wolf? Brent? Any questions about the marching-orders?"

"Nope," said the bounty-hunter, shaking his head. "Got 'em wrote down, like you asked me to. Glad to be on my own, for a while... no 'civilians' too close, if I have to let 'er fly, you know? Pups's good to go, too. Just wanted to say to *mi Russkie amigo* here, that I'll miss havin' him alongside – though I *do* know the reason for it. You two dirt-farmers... you're in good hands. Oh, yeah... and you, too, Mister Truck Drivin' Man."

"Much obliged," grinned Donny, with a tip of his baseball-cap.

"I will do my best to protect them," vowed Misha. "And to teach my new friend here, a few of the Storied Watcher's martial-arts maneuvers... assuming that we have time."

"I mostly don't go for that fancy-dancy kung-fu fightin' stuff... I prefer just deckin' 'em," joked the trucker, "But maybe *this* time, I'll make an exception."

"Remember," continued Jacobson, "If you don't hear back from the rest of the group in more than eight hours, except in the unlikely event that the government caves to all our demands, or is negotiating with us – head out to the *rendez-vous* point, and wait; even with *our* abilities, we can't allow ourselves to be pinned down in a siege : we have to break out and re-group... understood?"

"Perfectly, Commander," replied the Russian. "Though one part of me sort of wishes that I could be more, ahh, 'in on the action'. A conceit, perhaps; hopefully, a forgivable one."

"Very," allowed a smiling Boyd. "Anyway, Commander... yeah, I'm as ready as I'll ever be. With the usual caveats about fighting the Air Force, of course. But, given that I seem to have been drafted into the *Alien* Air Force, I'll show for duty. No guarantees that I can get one of 'em going without a little help from your, err, kid, though, Professor; most of those aircraft have interlock systems to prevent 'joyrides'. I know a few tricks, but I may well need a jump-start. You know the signals... right?"

"Yeppers," confirmed Tanaka. "One quick flash, or irregular, 'engagement underway'; two fast flashes, 'need help, pronto'; three long ones, 'area secure', and / or, 'proceed with plan'. Four flashes of any duration, 'something's gone wrong, the unexpected happening, shit hits the fan', *et cetera*. Five, and it means 'the Big One's on its way, get out while you still can'. Copy?"

"Copy", replied the former Mars mission pilot. "Beats Morse Code, for sure."

"Tried to learn that, once... gave up with the code for 'C', as I recall," sniffed Wolf. "But I think I can remember this one, good enough."

Misha let out a well-rehearsed sigh.

"Are we ready, then?" requested Jacobson. "We should keep to the schedule... and time's-a-wastin'."

Several of the team mutely nodded and began to file back into their respective vehicles.

"Use your war-songs, if you need to signal your positions to the rest of the group," advised the former Mars mission commander, "And don't forget... we stick to the plan – and timing's *critical*. The provocation's got to be so serious that he *has* to show his face – then, it's up to Cherie's, err, kid, and those hackers, to do the rest – but we have to finesse it so we've still got a safe way out. If we're to have a *hope* of pulling this off, everything's got to go by the book, and a few cards have to flip the right way for us."

"Cards, Cap'n?" joked White, as he climbed into the SUV, along with everyone who was going on the raid, except for Wolf, who now sat in the driver's seat of the pickup-truck. "Piece of cake, compared to playin' poker with Bob in the dark, don't you know. Could barely tell when he was hidin' an ace."

"Good luck, you space gangstas," called Donny, his voice incautiously loud. "Bring me back a bar or two... or three or four – I got *bills* to pay!"

"Do you one better," quipped Tanaka, "I know somebody who can whip up as many as you want."

The SUV and pickup slowly backed out of their parking-spots, then changed direction, facing the highway.

Both Wolf and Jacobson gave a determined "thumbs-up" to Misha, Donny and the two elder Wades, as the Mars Gang drove out on Route 31, heading for Fort Knox.

Eastward We March

Finally got it down, exulted Sebastiàn, as he strode confidently forward, leading his rag-tag – yet, rapidly-growing – army of the gutter, through the streets of Los Angeles.

Since the sun rose on this day, it had been victory after victory, against not only the hated Aryan Brotherhood, but also elements of the Mexican Mafia, the Crips, the Bloods, the 18th-Streeters, the El-Rukns and various other urban gang-bangers.

Each encounter had gone the same way : a few initial skirmishes, some mostly-off-the-mark shooting (and the casualties had proven surprisingly light, because the ex-*Mara* had discovered that he had a limited ability to heal his foot-soldiers, by 'laying on hands' and saying a few curse-words; a shot through the head or heart *was* beyond his skill, but he could fix up many other types of wounds, with the nice side-effect that the "patient" seemed to develop an unnatural loyalty to his *jéfé*), and then a full-scale assault by Sebastiàn's followers, with him in the lead.

The sight of him, with his sinister, rhythmic war-song accentuated by green-glowing eyes and a miasmal cloud of biting, stinging vermin ready to unleash at the first available target, completely unnerved most opponents – at least the ones who had a clear look, before being attacked, poisoned and slowly eaten alive. Despite this (or possibly because they had nowhere safe to retreat), some of the black and Aryan gangs had fought back viciously, sustaining terrible losses as a result. But the *Pirus* and other Latino ones hadn't resisted very much, and indeed, many of their members had simply bolted and taken the pledge of fealty demanded by "*El Nuevo Rey De Los Angeles*".

In one of these battles, Sebastiàn had taken two pistol-rounds – one in the thigh and another just below the shoulder – yet had simply stopped and sat down, taken a good-portion snort of *señor yayo*, concentrated hard for a few minutes while his sinister-sweet war-song reverberated all around, and then again arisen, saying, with an insouciant half-smirk, "*¿Ven ustedes? ¡No pueden matar al Diablo!*"

His reputation – a potent combination of fear, charisma, awe and admiration – had grown apace. And, thanks to a convoy of "volunteered", hot-wired and otherwise-scrounged private automobiles, taxi-cabs, school-buses, tractor-trailer trucks, panel-vans, transit buses, golf-carts and miscellaneous other vehicles, they had covered many miles.

Guided by the "voices" in Sebastiàn's head – which urged him ever to a direction, slightly north of due east – "*El Ejército del Diablo*", numbering well over a thousand gang-bangers and miscellaneous camp-followers, complete with a hierarchy of subalterns and lieutenants under the faithful Ramòn (who, the *jéfé* noted with pleasure, had the severed ears of six personally-killed Bloods and Crips, hanging from his belt), stood on the eastern outskirts of Pomona, California, in the parking-lot of a looted, half-trashed gas station just north of and below the wreck-strewn, otherwise-quiet, San Bernardino Freeway.

Ramòn's victories had also been hard-earned; in his second engagement, he had taken a mushroom-head-bullet in the left lung, leaving him prone, helplessly gasping for air and spitting up profuse quantities of blood.

He likely would have perished then and there, but as he lay underneath Sebastiàn's hands, the ex-*Mara's* "cure" – applied, this time, with fevered, almost obsessive diligence, over the space of almost a full hour – had worked its magic. After a prolonged convalescence in the back of a stolen Disney Mail van, Ramòn had arisen, better than new. More than that : to his amazement and satisfaction, *El Nuevo Rey* noticed a dull, green glow deep within his side-kick's eyes, likely invisible to any except his own kind.

"*Ahora... tú me perteneces, al cien por cien, muchacho,*" offered Sebastiàn.

"Always did, *jéfé,*" replied Ramòn. "*Pero ahora... estos pequeños* you got, all 'round you... I'm hearin' 'em *talkin'* to you... *muy extraño, señor.* But this here's *mi vida loca* – ain't turnin' back, not no way, *jéfé... segundo al mando al Diablo... me encantaría aceptar eso. Finalmente* – I'm *somebody,* boss."

Sebastiàn surveyed the upscale neighborhood, which, in an earlier life, he could only have dreamed of controlling.

En los viejos tiempos, si yo hubiera estado aquí, la policía habría meterme en la cárcel, el momento en que mostré mi cara, he reflected.

Bueno... come and get me now, putos!

Small groups of his entourage had fanned out over the neighborhood, with scouts out in every direction.

One of the chief-lieutenants – a fat, massive, sweaty-faced, goatee-bearded thug named "Rodrigo" – approached him, calling, "*¡Hola, jéfé!* There's *mucho gaz* in them pumps... we fill up now?"

"*Sì,*" confirmed Sebastiàn. "But you spread it out – not too much for one car, *me entiendes?* We got to keep 'em all goin'."

"*Sì señor,*" agreed Rodrigo. "As it is now, we doin' shuttles to get all the *muchachos* from the back of the line, up front, when we makin' it some hot. Need more *coches, por supuesto*."

A squint-eyed, imperious nod from Sebastiàn was all that was needed to send the understudy on his way, and for about a half-hour, his army ceased its advance, taking the opportunity to clean faces and aching feet in the car-wash (after ensuring that canteens and water-bottles were first filled) and to otherwise relax. Eventually, their sinister *jéfé*, having searched through the surroundings and, to his disappointment, not found any more of the precious *yayo*, appeared in the street, giving the "move forward" hand-sign.

But a second later, he abruptly stopped, sniffing with his nose high in the air, as if having detected a warning scent. Immediately, the rest of his army followed suit.

Ramòn double-timed it, to stand at what he knew was the minimum safe distance from his boss.

"*¿Que tal, jéfé?*" he inquired. "Ain't none of them Crip *putos* nowhere *por aquí*... scoutin' parties said *este barrio* is clean as a 13-year-old's butt."

"*Espera aquí,*" ordered Sebastiàn. "I'm goin' up on the *carretera*... got to check somethin' out."

"*Sì señor,*" respectfully repeated the chief-lieutenant. He watched his boss head toward the freeway, but something appeared wrong : Sebastiàn wasn't going to either of the off-ramps, but was instead on a track for the underpass.

"Hey, *jéfé,*" asked Ramon, "Where you goin'? The ramp's –"

With his back turned, Sebastiàn held up a cautionary left hand; then, those around perceived the hum of his ominous – yet, exciting, enervating, stirring war-song – and then they saw the gang-leader being surrounded by the now-familiar insect-cloud. Which, in short order, effortlessly levitated the more-than-human *jéfé*, the twenty-or-more-foot vertical distance, right up to the surface of the San Bernardino Freeway, above.

Gasps of amazement issued from the crowd, as the buzzing shroud seemingly dispersed and the former *Mara* strode purposefully forward on the elevated roadway. He advanced a distance of perhaps fifty feet, and then again gave the "halt" hand-signal.

Those with more sensitive ears – including, particularly, Ramòn – perceived the faint, percussive sounds of something big going on, far away in the eastern distance; and the ones below the highway saw their *lider máximo* staring off in that direction. His gaze was steady and it washed over the horizon several times, before he slowly walked to the side of the motorway, standing before the throng like a *caudillo* about to give a speech.

"*Oyeme muchachos y chicas,*" announced Sebastiàn, with the ominous green glow in his eyes, with his entrancing war-song, as well as the authority in his voice, waxing with every syllable, "Ever since I set this thing up... *ha habido un propósito a ella, ustedes lo saben?* Well... now it's in sight. Over there, down *la autopista*. That's where we're goin' – *that's* where them AB fuckers hidin' *el regalo!*"

One of the braver of them – a fetching, raven-haired, young camp-follower, who had been trading her favors with several of the ex-*Mara's* lieutenants, in exchange for a few sniffs of the white stuff and for being put in charge of the rest of the *prostitutas* – spoke up.

"*Querido jéfé*," she carefully inquired, "How you know that?"

"*Las voces en mi cabeza me dice sobre él. ¿Es lo bastante para ti?*" he replied.

"*Segura*," she said, with a smile. "*¡Cómo no!*"

For a few long seconds, except for the far-off echoes of a battle, there was near-complete silence, as Sebastiàn impassively reviewed the crowd. Then he gave an order :

"Rodrigo – *en cinco minutos*, you takin' *la izquierda, al lado de la carretera*; Vincente – *a la derecha*. Ramòn, mi *hermano* – next to me. Third of you *cholos* in each *grupo*, best *vatos* reportin' to Ramòn, an' as many as can ride *en cada vehiculo*... no *coches* up here, though... too easy a target. Things gettin' off the gate, park 'em somewhere safe, *y bailamos a pie. Me entienden ustedes?*"

The two lieutenant-thugs rapidly complied, barking out commands of their own to understudies and arranging the now-well-armed, battle-toughened Latino gangsters into groups of about three hundred each.

Ramòn, for his part, began to high-tail it up the nearest off-ramp, but was quickly stopped in his tracks by a withering glance and shout from the *jéfé*.

"*¿Adónde crees que vas?*" dismissively accosted Sebastiàn.

"Uhh... up *con usted, señor*," haltingly answered the second-in-command.

"*Claro que sì*," said the former *Mara*, "But you ain't takin' that ramp."

"*¿Pero... cómo?*" nervously asked Ramòn.

"*Cierra los ojos... call* 'em," instructed *El Nuevo Diablo*.

For a second or two, Ramòn stood befuddled; but then – with wide-eyed terror – he realized what was being demanded of him.

"*Señor, no puede posiblemente –*" gasped the understudy.

"*No se preocupe, cholo – no te harán daño*," reassured Sebastiàn. "*Do* it!"

His mind racing with apprehension, his gut churning, Ramòn knew that the proverbial jig was up. So he closed his eyes, held his nostrils and ears shut with the spread fingers of his hands, tightened his sphincter as much as possible, murmured what he feared would be a final prayer, and then whispered,

"*Ven a mí, hermanos y hermanas pequeñas del Diablo... me levantas allí.*"

Before he could make so much as a whimper of protest... *they*, were upon him, all over him, buzzing, crawling, *touching* him, absolutely everywhere, including in his pants and in the folds of his shirt.

The sensation was unbelievably unpleasant, though, not really painful. Somehow, he knew that one false move could easily get him stung or nibbled to death; and for a second, Ramòn's primal reflexes triggered, as he felt an overpowering urge to dive, to slap, to crush... to *run*, in whatever direction. But – just as total, fear-induced insanity was about to overtake him – his mind perceived something else : a wild, barely-comprehensible babble of tens of thousands of individually-faint, but collectively-clear, half-voices, each sounding only one, simple, robot-like, thought...

¡Arriba!

There was a pronounced buzzing sound – undoubtedly, made by thousands of tiny wings – and with no more warning, Ramòn (his eyes, ears and butt-hole still sealed tight, with only the smallest opening allowed in one nostril, to allow for minimal life-support), realized that he had left the ground.

He felt the rush of air all around, and heard a chorus of astonished, wary exclamations from human voices below him. The movement ceased in the vertical but continued in the horizontal for what seemed like an eternity, though it actually took only a couple more seconds. Then, he was again standing on something solid; and in the next half-second, his body was completely clean of the crawling, itching, tickling insect-plague that had recently enveloped him.

Slowly, Ramòn opened his eyes.

Jesús, María y José, he thought. *I'm up here... with him. In one piece!*

And what are all estos nuevos colores *– the dark* rojo *an' the weirdo* violeta *– that I'm seein'? What they do... shoot me with some funky* nuevas drogas?

An exultant Sebastiàn strode over and put one hand on the shoulder of his chief-lieutenant, ushering Ramòn over to look at the crowd below the highway.

"*Escúchame*," demanded *El Nuevo Rey De Los Angeles*. "This *vato* here... *el tiene la cosa real*. You take orders from him, just like you take 'em from me, *si yo no estoy aquí*. And if somethin' happen to me... he's in charge... *él es el jéfé. ¿Entienden?*"

A murmur of approval – or, at least, compliance – reverberated through the crowd, as a still-uneasy Ramòn reflected on his new-found status.

Now, Sebastiàn wheeled in place, turning his attention to the horizon, staring silently forward. In the direction of Ontario and Rancho Cucamonga, Ramòn could just make out shapes of something moving in the air; and his newly-empowered ears, clearly heard the sounds of battle.

"*Y ahora*," he called, with his voice echoing impossibly loud, over a subtle, rapid-beat martial tune which seemed to issue from everywhere and nowhere, "*¡Que vamos... a la última batalla!*"

Like a latter-day parody Lionheart, the green-glowing-eyed *Nuevo Diablo* marched eastward down the Santa Bernardino Freeway, with his army following at his heels.

Two To Sniff Him Out

"This is *crazy*, you know," morosely complained Kaysten, speaking to Abruzzio in the back of Sullivan's used, '28 Ford General compact SUV, while the afternoon shadows lengthened on the sides of the Wattendorf Memorial Highway. "The place is *miles* across, and yeah, of course I can scoot up and down it in no time... but what am I supposed to *do* – go knocking on doors, asking, 'you got any ex-Presidents, in here?' And on top of that... we have no evidence that he's even *in* there."

"*Sure* we do, Jerry," patiently countered the former JPL scientist. "Once we parsed all the meanings of 'ARN', along with the distance factor, and then ran it through the probability matrix, both *Vîrya I'ëà'b'* and Rainbow agreed that it had to be... here. It's not *my* problem if you didn't check out what was on Moira's computer –"

"Sorry to interrupt you two little love-birds," interjected Sullivan, "But it's just up there, at the intersection... right-hand turn. Want me to take it?"

"Not yet," instructed Abruzzio. "Cruise by as slowly as you can do, without drawing undue attention. I'm going to roll down the window beside me, enough so I can get a good, specially-enhanced look at the gate. Oh, and by the way... don't be surprised if you hear some, uhh, 'music', when I do that."

"'Music'?" unsteadily replied the human woman. "On the car stereo, you mean?"

"No... she means, in your *head*," commented Kaysten. "Seems to happen when we get that ol' 'alien' thingamajig, going. I take off at top speed, you'll hear it from me, too... for a half-second."

"Whatever," sighed Sullivan.

"*Vîrya I'ëà'b'*," called Abruzzio, apparently to no-one, "Thou know what we ask of thee?"

There was an odd, chiming, tinkling sound, after which the scientist added, "Excellent... although, I have to admit, I'm *awfully* worried about letting you out of my sight, little lady – you *sure* you'll be okay, flying around with 'Daughter Tornado Diamond-Curtain'?"

The puppy let out an affectionate "yip", which they took as a "yes".

As they passed the short stretch of road heading north of west, off the highway in the direction of Arnold Air Force Base, Abruzzio implemented her plan, slightly rolling down the window and stretching upward in her seat, so her eyes could see out without having a tempered-glass barrier in the way.

Immediately, both Kaysten and, to her amazement, Sullivan, heard the former JPL scientist's delicate, intricate war-song – a melody with the same rhythmic, mesmerizing beat common to most users of the *Fire*, but one carrying subtle notes and themes, reminiscent of what electro-pop would sound like, if composed by someone with a Mozart-like genius.

It was all that Abruzzio's old school-compatriot could do, to keep the vehicle on the road, as Sullivan marveled at the reality of what she was now involved in... and of who – or what – her childhood friend, had become.

The car passed the base-turnoff and proceeded southwest to the junction of the Wattendorf Highway and the Pumping Station Road, at which point, Abruzzio tapped Sullivan on the shoulder, requesting, “Moira... *this* is 'where'. Take a left down this road and then a fast right, so we're next to that stand of trees... then pull over, please.”

The driver complied, bringing the Ford General to a slow stop on the right-hand side of a short connector-driveway between the two major streets. Fortunately, there appeared to be no traffic coming or going in any direction.

Abruzzio continued, “I'll take Rainbow out to the trees on her leash, like she, uhh, has to do her business. Anybody – particularly military police et cetera – comes by... there's our explanation. You two hang out in the car, if you don't mind.”

“Oh, I certainly don't mind, Sylvia,” muttered Kaysten. “It's the 'breaking into heavily-guarded military bases and getting shot', part of it, that I, 'mind'.”

“Oh, come *on*,” pleasantly countered Abruzzio, as she exited the car with the puppy tagging along behind her, “It's not so bad; and besides... you get off on this 'adventure' stuff... just like me.”

“How you figure *that?*” he shouted, through a window.

As the scientist headed off toward the glade, she replied, “True by definition, Jerry : you're where you want to be – because if you didn't want to be here... you'd be somewhere else.”

“Ponder *that* one,” offered Sullivan, turning to smile at the frustrated former Chief of Staff.

They saw Abruzzio, with the dog in tow, calmly walk around to the back-side of the first tree of the stand. She knelt, released the leash from the animal's neck-collar, and – for quite a long time, perhaps as much as a minute or more – spoke to little “Rainbow” in hushed, inscrutable tones.

In the blink of an eye, or less, the Storied Watcher's war-shield appeared at the scientist's side; there was more (apparently) one-way conversation, and then, the puppy did a short jump, ending on the inside, concave side of *Vîrya I'ëà'b*"s shape. She sat down, with legs crossed underneath, while the living-buckler shuddered a bit and self-levitated to shoulder-height.

Vîrya I'ëà'b', along with her canine co-pilot, then shimmered out of sight like a mirage approached too closely.

Though gamely trying to keep a stiff upper lip, Abruzzio's mother-like concern for her pet's well-being was obvious to both Kaysten and Sullivan.

Kaysten opened car-side-door nearest to his friend, but she hesitated, turning and looking to the north-eastern sky.

“I think I know how Karéin felt,” she offered, “When *she* first let her 'daughter', out of her sight.”

Sam J. Knocks At Fort Knox

Former Mars mission commander Sam Jacobson had outfitted himself with the best-fitting, dark-gray business dress suit – complete with black lace-up shoes, a conservative red-patterned tie secured with a brass tie-clip, a convincing imitation Swiss watch and a smart-looking black leather belt – that he could acquire. He had cleaned up in every way (after his turn in the roadside restaurant washroom, he had even put on some after-shave), and had done a double-take in the mirror, silently musing,

Hey there, Mr. Sharp-Looking... you belong on a magazine-cover...

In another time, place and context, he (like Boyd or even Devon White) might have been taken for an insurance salesman, or, perhaps... a bank executive. But an entirely different type of banking-visit, was contemplated, on *this* evening.

Having parked the SUV about thirty feet away, Jacobson adjusted his Mars ears to tune out the night-time chirps of the crickets in the grass, and walked calmly through the alternating lights and shadows, up to the guard-post at the end of the long driveway leading to the United States Bullion Depository.

He got within a distance of about eight feet from the guard-post – which was sealed, with its inhabitants protected behind a thick pane of armor-glass – when he was suddenly illuminated by several bright floodlights.

"Halt!" bellowed a voice from a nearby loudspeaker. "You are trespassing on property of the United States Treasury Department! You are ordered to reverse course and exit the grounds!"

"Good evening," insouciantly responded Jacobson, his face showing an insincere smile. "Actually, I have business here. May I speak to the Director of the Mint, responsible for management of this facility, please?"

"Look, Mister," irritably countered the invisible voice, "We don't take visitors here... and even if we *did*, you're way past visiting hours. If you want to talk to the Director, send him a letter or an e-mail."

"Do you one better," argued the former Mars mission commander. "You've got me on the surveillance-cameras, isn't that right?"

"Definitely," confirmed the guardpost-attendant.

"I've got a letter for the Director, here with me," said Jacobson, as he pulled a piece of paper covered with single-spaced type, from his inside-jacket-pocket. "Do you have somewhere that I can give it to you?"

"This is against procedures," complained the invisible voice, "But just to get your ass out of here... why don't you hand-deliver it to me – I'll come out and take it from you, then put it in our internal mail to the Director... but no funny business, you understand? I'm armed, and we got more than one other guys with a bead on you. Stay where you are."

"Certainly," pleasantly replied Jacobson. "It's just a short note, anyway."

He smiled, looked up and away, and hummed a cute little tune, as a camouflaged, twenty-something, Caucasian soldier, dressed in battle-fatigues, army-boots and a military cap, and equipped prominently with a side-arm, opened a locked door in the rear of the guard-post and walked briskly up to the former Mars astronaut.

"Hi there, Private, uhh... let me see... ah, yes, Private 'Zansky'," greeted Jacobson, as he peered at the ID tag sewn to the soldier's fatigues. "Here it is... oh, and you'll want to get this to whoever's in charge – whether that's the Director, or the night watchman, or... whoever – ASAP."

The guard took a step backward so as to be illuminated by a flood-light and then had a quick look at the document.

"So what's so damn *important*," he muttered, alternating between looking down at the paper and keeping Jacobson within his eyesight, "Press Release... from the 'Mars Gang'? What the hell's *that... whoa!* Look, Mister – maybe you think this kind of thing's *funny*, but I can assure you, it's anything *but*... were you aware that it's a federal offense, to make threats against a facility like this one? I oughtta put you under arrest right here and now... but since it's almost the end of my shift, I don't feel like workin' overtime, so if you'll get your ass out of here in the next minute, I'll be the 'nice guy', and rip this piece of shit up and chuck it in the recycle bin. So if I were you, I'd be moving – *now!*"

"Son," answered Jacobson in his most soft and sympathetic, paternal voice, "Hear me out for a second, before you or your buddies in those three watch-posts – the two on either side of the road, plus the one that you thought you had hidden a way out in the field to the right – do anything *rash*. It's no joke; we're giving you, and all the other grunts who're guarding this facility, some advance warning, precisely because our dispute is with the sonofabitch who's pretending to be the President... not with any of you. We know you're just trying to do your jobs, and we don't want any of you to get hurt – but, be so advised... you have no chance – zero, none – of resisting us. Neither, actually, does the Federal government, itself, not even with all the resources it can call on, from the army base. Am I making myself clear, here?"

The private let out an amused chuckle.

"Oh, I *see*, Mister... you're some kind of *terrorist*... I got that right?" he taunted. "One guy, in a business suit... and you ain't got a suicide-vest on, nor are you packin'... because the sensors would have tripped if you had or were. Get moving!"

"A 'terrorist'?" riposted Jacobson. "No, no, son... I'm much, *much* worse than *that*. Tell you what. You said you've got me on the surveillance-cameras... right?"

"Damn straight," sneered the soldier. "And you're on *file* now, Mister."

"*Excellent*," parried the former Mars commander. "Why don't you ask your friends back in the guard-post, to run a match on the, ahem, rather extensive file that the government's already got on me? Try the Federal Integrated Enemies Of The State system first... that'll probably give you a good match."

"Sure," shrugged the private. "Nothin' better to do, I guess."

He touched his hand to a hidden button on the wireless contraption inserted into his left ear.

"Hey, Brad," he half-whispered, "Mind running a check on this wise-ass I got out here? What's that? Yeah, man, I know I *should* take him in... but humor me, will you, might as well know if he's got a record, before I do... sure. I'm holding."

There was a delay, and after a few seconds, Jacobson looked at his watch and mentioned, "Don't be too long with it."

"Why's *that*, Mister, you got a hot date or something – wait –" quipped the private.

For a second or two, he held his hand to his ear and stared past Jacobson, as if contemplating something; then, the soldier again turned his attention to the former Mars mission commander and, with wide-eyed astonishment, exclaimed, "Holy... *shit!* You're... you're... that... *Mars* guy? The one that was on TV, down south, on the highway?"

A wicked smile was all that came back; though, it was accompanied by the half-suppressed, background sounds of a determined, bass-beat war-song.

"I'm... I'm... gonna have to take you in, Mister," stammered the soldier. "Hands up!"

Just then, his head and eyes swept left to right, looking over both shoulders, in an involuntary reaction to the sounds of massive explosions – a large number of them, from further away, and a big, powerful one, much closer, which momentarily lit up the evening sky with a sinister, orange-red glow – all coming from behind the above-ground, concrete-encased citadel of the Bullion Depository.

"Oops... my timing's a bit 'off', tonight," called Jacobson, as his war-song started to wax, as his eyes began to glow and as his diamond-mimicking force-field, encased his entire body. "Do yourself a favor, son... get your ass out of here, while you still can."

The private fumbled frantically for his side-arm, but was not able to unholster it, before two of the guard-posts opened fire at the former Mars mission commander.

With machine-gun rounds bouncing uselessly off him, Jacobson's legs half-compressed and he hurtled into the air in the direction of the Fort Knox citadel, easily clearing the ten-foot-tall fence that formed the first of many barriers around the most sacred horde of U.S. lucre.

The Almost-Was Bouvet Nudist Colony

Despite a few moments-worth of remotely-triggered hesitation *en route* – and the need to constrain her airborne velocity to account for human weaknesses – the Storied Watcher had actually completed her "shopping-and-borrowing" trip to São Paulo and Buenos Aires, rather quickly.

True, there *had* been a few awkward incidents, for example when the Portuguese that she had been learning on the way in, was found to be rather lacking in vocabulary; but fortunately, even just before closing-time in the late afternoon, the merchants of Brazil's largest city quickly responded in Spanish at the sight of pure gold coins, and they were only too happy to detail all Karéin-Mayréij needed to know about the local supply-chain (including, particularly, the locations of warehouses).

So many poor people, she grimly noted, while briefly touring the *favelas, And the rich ones are happy to sit comfortably by, watching the poverty and misery their brothers and sisters unfold, right in front of their eyes.*

So much work for me to do... a thousand lifetimes would not be enough time... I cannot save them all...

But that is no excuse not to save one of them... like, this *precious little one.*

Sleep, beautiful child... may the mother's milk of my breasts fortify and transform you, as we race to a noble, happy, new life!

Her gaze momentarily looked tenderly on the somnolent, bedraggled figure tightly compressed to, and by, *Vìrya Ahn'jë*'s infernal presence, as the two flesh-and-blood beings – accompanied by five other, sentient ones – raced through the South Atlantic early-morning skies.

The Storied Watcher was, in fact, considerably ahead of schedule when – in typically dramatic fashion – slightly before seven in the morning, local time, she erupted, with her war-song and a shower of sea-spray issuing from the central pool-and-dock area of the Bouvet Island refuge. A huge, double-shipping-container-sized package of "goodies", trailed behind the alien-girl and the the *Mailànkh Express*.

However Billings had tried to reassure the Compton refugees, the alien-girl's timeliness had not prevented the usual grumbling about "where *is* she?" and "ah don' think that-there 'angel' girl, gonna show... mah Gawd, we's gonna *die* here"; the ex-salesman was almost at his wits-end in trying to reason with these people, when, mercifully, the sudden return of Karéin-Mayréij simultaneously woke them up and put paid to the complaining.

"Damn... she look even more scary than befo'," whispered one of the inner-city children, to another.

"Forget not, little brother Durian," gently reminded the fire-enveloped, awe-inspiring figure of the Storied Watcher, while she hovered above and lowered both the vehicle and the gigantic, tightly-bound goods-package, to the Bouvet Island interior floor.

As she began a glide to land right before the youngster, she continued, "That my ears hear many things... even those meant to be private. And yes... I *am,* 'scary'... am I not? But so shall *you* be, sooner than you think – and you will then need to learn what I do now : namely, to say," – the alien-girl got down on one knee in front of the boy – "That though I am mighty... I love you as your servant... your... *friend*."

He felt his arm involuntarily extending under the pull of her mind, and upon the outstretched hand of the abashed but thrilled nine-year-old, Karéin-Mayréij bestowed an affectionate kiss.

"Uhh... Ma'am," hesitantly remarked Durian, pointing at the fire-shrouded, emaciated, unresponsive child's figure who seemed glued to the Storied Watcher's breast, "Who's *that?*"

Karéin-Mayréij came quickly to her feet. She caressed the hair (which was, despite being licked by the flames coming from *Vîrya Ahn'jë*, not burning) of the clinging girl-creature, and whispered,

"Minha nova filha querida, é hora de você acordar."

Slowly, the child awoke. She was deep-brown-skinned, and her face showed a mulatto mixture of Caucasian and Negro characteristics, with large, lambent brown eyes. Dressed in nothing more than a long T-shirt replete with holes and bearing cheap plastic sandals on her feet, she had a petite, skinny figure and appeared to be about six or seven years of age.

Still dazed and evidently unaware that she was clinging on to the equivalent of a brazier, the new arrival murmured something back to the Storied Watcher.

"Oh, claro que eu entendo que você ainda está sonolento... mas é hora de você conhecer a sua família!" responded Karéin-Mayréij, planting a kiss on the child's head.

Now the little girl turned her head to face the crowd. She blinked, pointed to Elissha and asked, "Ela é minha irmã? Aquele que você me falou, Mãe nova?"

"Hi," came back the enthusiastic response, from the Storied Watcher's other adopted daughter. "My name's Elissha... what's yours?"

"Meu nome é Sayuri," said the girl-in-flames. "Isso é estranho. Eu só falo um pouco de Inglês ... mas eu posso entender o que você está dizendo."

"I don't speak, uhh, whatever you're speaking, either," offered Elissha, "But I can understand what you're saying, perfectly, Sayuri. You're right... it's *crazy!*"

Tommy had pushed his way to the front of the throng. Standing beside Elissha, he added, "Me too. Kinda like the mind-talking, but with words. Totally neat, Mom!"

As the Storied Watcher beamed benevolently, Elissha took a step forward.

"Mommy," solemnly stated the golden-haired child, "Before you went off on your trip... you told me to look deep down and talk to Korey... so I did. Did he send Sayuri to be a sister for Tommy and me?"

"Even so," tearfully replied Karéin-Mayréij, "But not *only* that. I went to the poorer parts of a big city on the 'South America' continent, and saw many, who had very little... though sorely tempted to, I knew that I could not tarry there, to help all of them. Then, I noticed Sayuri... she wanted to sell me a something-or-other, as the natives of that country are wont to do with foreigners, but she was too small to reach me, and the other, larger and more aggressive street-urchins pushed her back. I then used my hiding-arts – which mystified the throng no end – and as I did... the voices spoke; they said, "this dear little one is yours to love, yours to protect... *go* to her". So I did, and discovered that she made the alley-ways her home, as no family would call her their own. Moreover, the 'gang' to which she had belonged, had recently been broken up by the local police, and Sayuri was now completely on her own. She had not eaten even a half-meal, in three weeks! How could I *leave* her there, so tender in years? I humbled myself and begged her to call me, 'Mommy'... or, 'Mãe', in her native tongue. Thanks be to the Gods, she accepted, saying, 'I am tired, I am hungry, and no-one loves me'. Well – now, she has at least *one* person on this world, who *will* love her, with all her heart. It was the right thing to do."

"Yeah, I reckon it was, Karéin," commented Saquina White. "Y'all sure got a knack for findin' the down-and-out, and bringin' 'em back with you. But you better dial it back a bit there, girl, or you're gonna end up with one *big* family."

"Ha!" chirped the alien-girl, "Then... so be it. Many worse things have befallen me, lately and before. *So* much love lies within this breast... I would share it with all the people of this Earth, if they would have me."

She turned to the fire-child.

"Você concorda?" asked the Storied Watcher.

"Foi certamente, nova Mãe!", giggled Sayuri. "Agora eu tenho uma família ... um irmão e uma irmã!"

"Not only your brother Tommy and your sister Elissha, have you," beamed Karéin-Mayréij. "Bob... Bob? Where are you, Bob?"

Billings shuffled to the front of the crowd and then approached the alien-girl. He did not seem at all fazed by her infernal aura, as he took hold of Sayuri's delicate hand and gave it a friendly kiss.

"Hey, there, kiddo," offered the salesman. "I'm Bob... and since I'm hanging around with Her Alien-ness there, I guess that kind of makes me your honorary Daddy. Hope I'm up to it... what you say?"

"Eu nunca tive um Pai antes, mas é bom ter um agora. Você vai me levar para a praia no fim de semana, Bob?" coquettishly responded the little girl.

Billings turned his head to remark to Elissha, "You're right... this *is* weird... I don't speak, uhh, 'Brazilian'... but I get what she's saying."

Addressing Sayuri, he added, "Well, kid... I'm afraid the 'beaches' around here, such as they are, are a bit chilly... even for post-human types like me... like, *you*. Next time I get down to Florida, though... you're on."

The fire-enveloped child giggled.

"It will feel much less, ahh, comfortable," noted the Storied Watcher, "But I should let you descend from my grasp and meet your – our – family. Are you ready, dear?"

"Mas é tão agradável e acolhedor, com você, a nova Mãe!" protested the new girl.

"'Warm' is hardly the word, kid," grunted Billings. "Probably a few hundred degrees next to her... can't figure out why it doesn't bother me, or you... or our clothes. But come on... Uncle Bob will show you around."

He offered his hand to the Brazilian girl, while shaking his other index finger at the Storied Watcher and half-whispering, "She's sure cute, Sari, and I don't mind you palming her off on Tommy, Elissha and myself... but let's make her the last one for a while, if you don't mind? I'm starting to have trouble keeping count."

Now it was the turn of Karéin-Mayréij to laugh.

"If that is the case," she answered, "Then I *am*, ahh, 'doing my job'. You should be glad that I did not return with another hundred, akin to our beautiful new little daughter. Oh, Bob... if could only *see* – if you could only *smell* – how dirty, hard and poor, life is like, for Sayuri and the untold millions of others so unfortunate as to have been born into such mean estate! You and I are *called* to love and rescue those such as she! So *many* need our help!"

"We can't change the world, you know," wearily sighed the salesman.

"Wait and see, my love... wait and *see*," came back the immediate answer. "I am greater than you suspect... and so are you, if only you *believe*."

Billings wisely did not try to argue the point, and by now, the Brazilian child had left the Storied Watcher's immediate vicinity. Upon being fully exposed to Bouvet's clammy chill, she whined,

"Oh, Mãe nova ... é tão frio! Eu não posso voltar para você?"

"Of *course*, darling," reassured Karéin-Mayréij. "But in a few minutes. Fear not... the cold-feeling will go away, as your new arts begin to compensate. Tommy – Elissha, dear – would you, uhh, 'show Sayuri around', and then, the both of you prepare to lie down and finish your sleeping? This will help her to become familiar with you."

The two junior adoptees enthusiastically agreed, and ushered the little Brazilian girl away from the crowd; the three children chattered back and forth, without apparently paying attention to the fact that there were two different languages being spoken.

"Now, as to the del-i-ver-ee," announced the alien-girl, taking a step forward and bidding her war-children to their invisible hiding-places.

The rest of them noticed that she had evidently done a little clothes-shopping (or, clothes-crafting) on her recent expedition, as, underneath the incandescent folds of *Vîrya Ahn'jë*, the Storied Watcher had garbed herself in a slate-gray T-shirt inscribed with the same odd-looking, silver-and-gold runes as had been noticed on *Vîrya Ahn'jë*'s skull-cap, a deliciously-tight, dark-gray pair of girl's athletic-shorts and a pair of leg-socks that reached almost to her knees, in the same color. The edges of all three pieces were outlined in silver and the garments were made out of looked like silk or satin, but couldn't have been exactly that, given the heat which they had withstood.

Szabo couldn't help letting out a wolf-whistle.

"Bob," he joked, "Any chance I could get her to play receptionist again?"

Karéin-Mayréij posed and demurely batted her eyes, blowing the envious sales-manager a mock kiss.

"Dressed like *that?*" deadpanned Billings. "We wouldn't get much work done, you know."

It depends, she silently sent to the salesman's eager receipt, *on what kind of 'work' that you had in mind, Bob.*

I long for your touch, my love – and I thank and honor you, for so generously giving of yourself, in welcoming our dear new daughter... let it not be too long, until again, we lie together in the embrace of pleasure!

It is still 'bedtime' around here... is it not?

While Billings' imagination ran uncomfortably wild, his spoken comment was outwardly acknowledged only by a mischievous smile, and then the alien-girl turned her attentions to the huge, two-shipping-containers-sized conglomeration, which she had transported from South America and Africa.

Her telekinesis, triggered or signaled by a slight head-toss, undid the intricate mesh of steel bands and cables that had bound the package; but before the items on top and on the sides could fall, they were individually grasped by the tractor-beams of her mind and were deposited on the floor, being arranged in neat piles according to function and type. It was very noticeable that the contents had been extremely tightly-packed; the onlookers were amazed by the volume and variety of the tools and provisions which lay on the ground.

"I have only, ahh, 'unpacked', a small measure of what I brought," remarked Karéin-Mayréij. "More lies within the *Mailànkh Express*, and the fine details and contents of all this, I will leave for you to discover and apportion, as best you see fit. But briefly – my war-children and I researched the com-pu-ter networks about the 'survivalism' idea that many Americans seem to be enamored of, and, taking this, ahh, 'wisdom' into account, along with the knowledge that I have accumulated over many years, I was guided in what things would be most useful, for a permanent stay, here. So... behold."

She darted through the air to deposit herself in the midst of the delivered-goods.

"Many of the instruction-manuals seem to only be in the Spanish language... I hope that this will not prove to be too much of a problem," explained the alien-girl. "And for most essential items – for example, piz-ee-oh and kin-etic electric generators and batteries, field-toilets and waste re-cyclers, fam-i-lee-size camping-tents, sleeping-cots, fishing-nets, seeds and hai-dro-ponic lights, pots-plates-and-pans, freeze-dried ray-shuns, breakfast-cereal, sacks-of-rice, tee-vee-dinners, beer for Hugo, bum-wiping-paper, washing-soap, shower-and-bath assemblies, cooking-stoves, ree-fridg-er-ay-tors, machines which remove impurities from water and the air, ray-dee-ay-shun meters, clothes-washers and dryers, and the like – I have provided multiples of each, lest one break down and thus leave you without that service or function. I also brought modest qualities of raw building-materials – metal-pipes, wood, hammer-and-nails, drying-wall, painting-things, plastic hoses, steel-cable, faucets, valves, *et cetera* – and I estimated as best I could regarding the sizes of clothing and foot-gear applicable to everyone. I attempted to acquire at least two full 'changes' for each individual, but if adjustments are needed, perhaps Hector can help you in making the materials more, ahh, 'malleable'."

"Yeah... but what 'bout TV, Angel Lady?" demanded one of the Compton kids. "Ah only seen a couple'a shows in, like, *weeks!*"

"Never fear," smiled the Storied Watcher. "As regards entertainment... I have done the best that I can; many mov-ees and vid-ee-oh-games, along with the devices needed to enjoy these, lie within yonder cargo-pile... and yes, Bob, I *did* find your 'sports' shows, although only a few with American foot-ball... I first acquired the South American type, only to find out, too late, that what they call 'football' is a different game than the one you play, in your home country."

"Why don't they just call it 'soccer', so you wouldn't make a mistake like that?" complained Billings.

"Why do not *you*, call *your* game, by some other name?" proposed Karéin-Mayréij. "Who 'owns' the word, 'football'?"

"Y'all better punt on *that* one, Bob," quipped Atasha Jones.

The crowd had a chuckle at the salesman's expense (although he got a congratulatory pat on the back from Szabo), as the alien-girl continued, "The situation having to do with tee-vee and the com-pu-ter networks, is more involved. Just before I plunged into the ocean so as to re-emerge from the center-lake within our refuge, I deposited a very fine-crafted spider's-web of antenna-cables – so thin, that they should not be visible to any overhead spying-eyes – just underneath the surface-ice of this island's frozen shroud; I then connected these to a long metal line, which has been dropped down one of the ventilation-holes, thus to be accessible in the upper reaches of this chamber. I believe – but am not completely sure – that this infrastructure, when connected to the vid-ee-oh devices that I have also brought, should allow you to receive some of the stronger tee-vee signals, at least when the satellites involved are overhead... though as you are aware, there *was* a little, ahem, 'incident', recently, which did result in fewer of these being available."

"No *kidding*," offered Ramirez.

"Indeed," agreed Karéin-Mayréij, with a wry smile. "As to the com-pu-ter networks... you may be able to receive some signals from them via the satellites, but I do not believe that you will be able to transmit any... nor should you. Friends, brothers, sisters – it is *crucial* that you not broadcast anything from here, that would give away your location! Doing so might make you subject to a surprise-attack, perhaps launched from one of the American President's submarines... or, perhaps, one from some other empire. Needless to say, a swift, cruel death will quickly come to anyone who harms you... but by the time when I take revenge, that may be too late. Remember : your safety is not primarily from these thick walls of stone, but rather, from simply being hidden; and once the latter is lost, it likely can never be regained."

"But I got *family* back State-side," protested one of the Latino parents, "Can't I send 'em at least an e-mail, or give 'em a phone-call, just to let 'em know that I'm okay?"

A murmur of support issued from several in the crowd.

"Not from here," countered the Storied Watcher. "At least, not without risking your life, not to mention those of everyone else around you, Enriqué. But if it is essential that you so communicate, I *can* – later on – transport you to somewhere like, for example, the 'Asia' or 'Australia' continents, from which you can send such a message, and also make arrangements to receive replies. Such an arrangement should keep our hiding-place a secret. Perhaps, in the fullness of time – when cowardly treachery, empowered by terrible weapons like these 'atom-smashing bombs', is no longer an everyday tactic of human leaders – *then*, we can consider letting down our guard and revealing ourselves. But for now and the immediate future, it would be far too risky... I will *not* thus imperil the lives of my children... and neither should you. Is this clear?"

"Yeah," he muttered. "You know, Mister Billings... why you all have to hook up with a *chica* who always argue so good?"

"Well, I win as many as I lose, with her," insincerely replied the salesman.

"Look, Karéin," spoke up Saquina White, "All this stuff's great, but as for me... I wanna go *home*. Please don't take this the wrong way – your place is damn impressive, and we're all grateful 'bout what y'all done for us – but we don't *belong* here,... 'least, not permanently. *'Specially* not my kids 'n me, what with Devon off by himself. I'm worried *sick*."

The Storied Watcher now deposited herself on one of the park-bench-alike stone-outcroppings (quite a few of which had an accompanying table, inlaid with dark-and-light squares, thereby composing a convenient chessboard), which had been fashioned hither and yon, in a hasty attempt to make the surroundings more welcoming.

"Oh-kay... to tell you the truth," she quietly admitted, looking down at the marble-like, polished rock-floor, "I had anticipated that you might say something akin to this... and I have been... *thinking*."

The crowd closed in, as the alien-girl elaborated, "Her mother, great-aunt, brothers and sister, miss our little war-daughter, *Vîrya I'ëà'b'*, terribly – she is of *such* tender years – too young to be thus off by herself, but she insisted on 'keeping Jerr-ee safe'. I fear for the safety of both Minn-ee and Commander Sam Jacobson, and their respective followers, as well... but after the Council of the Woods, I could not gainsay their quests, since these both forthcame from earnest revenge and duty. I should not overtly intervene in this affair, though sorely tempted am I, to at least know the status of it."

"Well then," quipped Billings, "There's my ticket back to Tucson."

"Yet it would be *folly* for me to transport all of you, back to this 'America', empire!" forcefully protested Karéin-Mayréij. "You would be at the mercy of the President... and there are so many here, that I could not *possibly* protect all of you, all of the time. Help me out, friends – suggest something that would work. I am, uhh, sort of 'at a loss'."

"Well now," smugly opined Atasha Jones, "Ain't we got a *humble* little 'Destroyin' Angel', all of a sudden... you all at least got the sense to ask for help, when you need it. Listen, Karéin – I ain't too hot on this-here cave you dumped us in, and I don't want to hang out here for the rest of my life, *that's* for sure – but it's a 'learnin' experience', and I s'pose we done been through so much lately, that we're kind of spoiled on the whole 'alien' thing... you know? I can put up with this place for a while, *if* you all's willin' to set a definite date and time when you comin' back to fetch us. I bet there'd be a few others who I could convince to stay 'round and keep me company."

She turned to address the rest of the crowd.

"That right?" inquired the former schoolteacher.

There was a smattering of applause within the group, and most of the Compton parents and children indicated agreement, although several of them seemed to be doing so reluctantly, largely out of peer-pressure.

"But not *all* of you are willing to stay here?" asked the alien-girl.

"Like I said, Karéin," mentioned Saquina White, "I want to go home, see how Devon's doin'. If he's okay, then, yeah, kids 'n me, we'll drag my husband back here, help y'all decorate – maybe get Devon to whip up some ice-cubes for your Daiquiri or somethin', too."

"I do not benefit from alcohol," sniffed the Storied Watcher, "But... your *children*, too, Saquina? That is a great risk."

"Mom," spoke Martin White, "I sure do 'preciate what y'all askin', and I sure do want to come with y'all, but I don't think Dad would want that... if y'all okay with it, I'll hang here with Miz Jones... look after Francelle."

"Honey," asked the wife, "Y'all willin' to stay here with your brother?"

"Yes'm," replied the little girl, "'Long as y'all 'n Daddy comin' back, real soon."

"We are, darlin'... we *are*," softly pledged Saquina White.

Again, the alien-girl looked pensively down at the floor.

"I could not have countenanced such a venture, earlier on, when there was not a, uhh, 'safe hide-out', for those of you who wisely would withdraw from this conflict," she declared, "I can protect only a few – perhaps, up to five – and then, only those whose powers and skills-at-war, have matured enough, to be able to fight on their own. The others, I propose, should remain here, for the interim."

Karéin-Mayréij came quickly to her feet and propelled herself on top of a nearby rock-outcrop-cum-chess-table.

"Who, then, considers themselves to be thus prepared?" she accosted. "Before you answer, mark this : though my war-children and I will do our utmost to defend you... it may come to pass that you will stand alone, or near-so, against all the evils that this 'President' can array; these may include gun-bullets, tank-cannon-shells, rocket-missiles, or even a death-ray, a weak simile of mine own, deadly *Gaze of the Khùl-Algrenàthi'i*. So consider well, and err on the side of caution... if err you must. What say you? Stand forward!"

First, Ramirez complied.

"I'm ready, Karéin," he stated. "I'm going back to help Sylvia, if I can. Been feeling *awful* about leaving her and that yappy little dog, back there."

She nodded gravely at him, as Tommy rushed over to stand below the alien-girl.

"I'm going with you, Mom," he said.

The Storied Watcher tried to respond noiselessly, but her narrow-cast was somehow intercepted by a few within the crowd, notably Billings and Whitney Claremont.

Son, silently cautioned Karéin-Mayréij, *you know that I will not refuse your request, and, furthermore, that your battle-skills are now more than adequate; but is this advisable? For I may need to maneuver by myself, and leave you for a short while, if war come to us. Will you fight alone, if needs be?*

"Yes... I'm not afraid of them... of *anyone*," he growled, with that familiar, unnerving, red glow coming momentarily to his eyes.

"I'll *bet* you aren't," half-whistled Billings. "Well, idiot that I am, I guess I'd better tag along, just to keep the kid in line... and I got a few knuckles to rap, if you know what I mean... but did you want to take Elissha? I don't think this is really the kind of trip for her, sweetheart."

"Aye," agreed the Storied Watcher.

"Dear little one," she spoke, "Uncle Bob, Brother Tommy and I must shortly go on a very, uhh, 'scary' trip... one in which there might be a lot of those loud noises that you said that you did not appreciate hearing. Are you willing to stay here and teach Sayuri how to be your big sister? I believe that Auntie Whitney would be willing to look after you."

Claremont's tongue had not yet fully grown back, so she just sighed and gave an affirmative wave.

"*Wellll,*" coquettishly responded Elissha, "I don't *knowww*... what do I get, if I say 'yes'?"

"A big hug and kiss from your mother," answered the alien-girl, "As well as the toy of your choice, from anywhere in the world... when I return, that is."

"Did you get me my 'Blaine Maine The Brat' dolly?" interrogated the child.

"Oh, that fine thing is in yonder heap of items, somewhere," confirmed Karéin-Mayréij. "You have no idea of how difficult that it was to find, young lady... I had to, uhh, 'enter', six different department-stores."

"Then," offered Elissha, "Just a hug will be fine, Mommy."

As the alien-girl embraced the child, they could all see – but refrained from openly talking about – the fact that the Storied Watcher's face was streaked with fresh-falling tears.

"'*Mommy*'," she breathed, as she kissed the little girl on the cheek. "How fine a word, is that? Live I ten times ten thousand human lifetimes... still will it be the sweetest thing that ever shall I hear."

She looked up.

"Sayuri," commanded the Storied Watcher, "Come here, dear one."

The Brazilian girl complied and was immediately embraced along with Elissha.

"Querida filha... devo sair daqui logo," requested Karéin-Mayréij. "Mas eu vou voltar, quando o meu trabalho é feito. Nesse meio tempo, você vai guardá Elissha, e brincar com ela?"

"Mas a Mãe – temos apenas algumas horas juntos, até agora!" complained the Brazilian child.

"I know it... I know it," softly cajoled the Storied Watcher. "I will stay here for a few more hours, regardless, and I swear – the day will soon come, when no more, will I leave your side. But it is not safe for you to accompany me on this quest, Sayuri... do you remember those evil men with the guns, who had chased your gang down the street in the city, and who killed your three clan-elders?"

"*Sim*," she responded, looking down at her dirty, sandal-clad feet, "Mas eu não quero lembrar."

"I do not blame you, darling," reassured Karéin-Mayréij, "For such memories, though they should never be forgotten entirely, are best left in a secret hiding-place in the deep vaults of our minds, to be retrieved only when we must consider the difference between good and evil. Many of your family and friends know this, only too well."

"You can say *that* again, honey," ruefully muttered Billings, while Tommy nodded gravely.

"It plagues me to have to leave you – even for a short while – after so little time together, blessed Sayuri," continued the Storied Watcher, "But we are going to a place, where there are many, many of these malign men-with-guns; and we may have to do mortal battle with them. Do not worry for my safety, nor that of Bob, Tommy or the others : I am more powerful than all the American President's army-men put together... as he shall shortly re-discover. Will you trust me to return, if I leave you in the care of Auntie Whitney? And will you help her look after your little sister?"

"She can only 'look after' me," pouted Elissha, "If she plays 'dollies' with me."

"Eu tive uma boneca de uma vez... mas os policiais levaram para longe de mim," quietly observed the Brazilian girl.

The Storied Watcher's telekinesis pulled her new daughter close, and as she again warmly embraced the child, she softly promised, "When this all settles down, little one... you will have everything that you need or want, and then some. But in the meantime, you must teach Elissha how to share her toys with you. Will you try?"

And... be gentle with your new, little sister, silently sent the alien-girl.

Terrible things, has she lately suffered... just like your brother, Tommy; both of them show a brave face, but both are hurting, inside... such wounds of the spirit do not easily heal, darling Sayuri. It falls to you, who are no stranger to awful memories, to having cried in fear and pain, all alone, never knowing when deliverance will come, to teach them to live again... to be there, when their tears must fall. Will you love them with all your soul, if I beg you so to do?

"Sim, a nova Mãe... vou tentar," came back the answer, which was in turn responded to with another tearful hug.

"Miz Sari," spoke up Melissa Claremont, "Ah'm goin', too."

The request was met with a flurry of upset croaks and head-shakes from the elder Claremont.

"Momma," explained the teenager, with a dignity that had rarely been previously seen, "Them 'voices' been tellin' me that ah *gots* to. Don' know how, or why... but ah *knows* it. Y'all do any prayin' – y'all be knowin' it, too. Mah mind's made up, an' that's all there is to it."

"Whitney," added the Storied Watcher, "She speaks the truth... as you know it, too. The voices of the Gods... or of your One God... am I not right?"

The Claremont woman hung her head and sobbed, while waving her finger at her son, who was about to chime in, but who then thought better of it.

There were a few seconds of silence, after which Karéin-Mayréij called to the audience, "Do any others among you, wish to voyage with us, to an uncertain future... possibly, to war? Oh, and one other thing : since our path to this redoubt carried us out over Canada, to the east, it seems prudent not to re-trace that route, on the way back. Therefore, when we approach the American Empire, it will be from the south... that is, from over the big 'Atlantic' ocean, thence over the bight called 'Gulf of Mexico', and then due north. We may also stop along the way, to gain additional intelligence on what is going on, within the United States. Hopefully, none of this will be anticipated by the President."

Kevin McGregor was about to speak up, was then un-volunteered by his two parents, but was consoled by Tommy, who went over to the Canadian boy and confided in him, "Listen, Kev... Mom's right, this trip's not gonna be a joke, but when I get back, I'll teach you some of my skills... deal?"

"Deal," happily replied the younger McGregor.

"Hugo," said Billings, "I know this place is a rat-ho – I mean, it needs a little *work* – but you want to stick around and, uhh, figure out what kind of floors and so on, would go where? I can probably get her to drop you off in Tucson if you want... but that might not be such a great idea, you know?"

"Oh, 'your wish is my command', Bob dear," chirped the alien-girl, with a pleasant smile, an eye-roll and diffident half-curtsy.

"Already workin' on it," grunted Szabo. "Any of these jokers stuck in the cave with yours truly, want to lend a hand, I'll even pay 'em union wage... 'long as they'll accept an I.O.U.... no bankin' machines 'round here, you know?"

"Half the time back home, you do work, you don' get paid at all," ruefully commented one of the Latino parents.

"Atasha," asked Karéin-Mayréij, "Will you help Hugo organize such operations as may be necessary, to make this refuge, more livable and comfortable? And... do any of the rest of you, wish to accompany us?"

Jones turned to address the crowd.

"'Yes' to that... and you all *heard* her," she prodded. "As for me, well, I seen way too much shootin', lately... damp 'n cold as this place is, I reckon it beats what we were up 'gainst, back in L.A... I'm stayin' here, 'till things settle, back home. Any of you want to try your luck, with Miss Angel Lady, there?"

It was plain to see that many of the Compton refugees – as well as the McGregors, the two GrayWar mercs and other hangers-on – did not relish the prospect of remaining in this refuge-cum-prison; but, all the same, none of them were willing to test their still-nascent alien-powers, against the dangers that the Storied Watcher had described. So, an unenthusiastic murmur of grudging assent, was the answer to Jones' query.

"Then, it is decided," declared the Storied Watcher. "After you finish your repose for this night, let us all to work, in unpacking what remains of the goods and provisions; and Hector and I now have an especial, personal task, to complete, in the remaining time. For to do this, it will be necessary for himself, plus Melissa, Tommy, Bob and Saquina to undress and hand over their best-fitting clothes, including particularly underwear and foot-gear, to myself; we will then begin the process of –"

"Wait a minute – *wait* a minute, girl," protested Saquina White. "I ain't doin' no strip-tease, 'leastaways for nobody 'cept Devon, and last I looked, *he* ain't nowhere 'round here... and top of that... this 'alien' stuff you got us on, somehow I know that the cold can't hurt me, but it still *feels* chilly – ain't no *way* I'm walkin' 'round here in my birthday suit!"

"'Birthday-suit'?" repeated the perplexed Storied Watcher. "Oh, I, uhh, 'get it'... that means, 'what you wore on the day when you were born'... right?"

"Yeah," confirmed White.

"But everyone around here *knows* exactly what a naked man or woman, boy or girl, looks like, female breasts, furry-sex-parts and all," innocently countered the alien-girl. "What is the *problem?* Would you like me to go first, to make you more comfortable, in so doing?"

"Yeah, *yeah!*" enthusiastically shouted most of the men in the crowd.

"Look, Sari," interjected Billings, "As much as turning this place into a kind of Antarctic nudist colony appeals to the pervert in me... I'm kinda like Saquina – I'd like *that* part of you to only be, between you and me. What's the point of it, anyway?"

"Quando vou nadar para baixo na praia, não vestir roupas," noted Sayuri, to which the Storied Watcher patiently replied, "Yes, I *know* it... but these 'Americans' *do* have many odd beliefs... do they not?"

The little Brazilian girl giggled and shuffled her feet.

“Momma sayin', 'ah ain't old 'nuf to be in no 'nudie thang', neither, Miz Sari,” unhelpfully added Melissa Claremont.

“Hector and I must, ahh, 'transform' these vestments, into something more compatible with the *Fire*,” explained Karéin-Mayréij. “If we start with the clothes that our fellow-travelers are already wearing, at least we will know ahead of time, that these will fit properly.”

“Y'all can 'transform' all you like,” firmly stated Saquina White, “'Long as I can keep my clothes on.”

“That is not advisable,” argued the Storied Watcher. “The arts which Hector and I will employ, would likely affect your skin, as well as the garments... it would be painful, harmful, and – possibly – fatal, even accounting for your new, innate, healing-powers. Oh... and even if you survived, you would have silver-colored, diamond-hard, *Amaiish*-storing skin, from head to toe.”

“Thanks, but I think it'd be hard to find makeup for a look like that,” joked the astronaut's wife.

“I could bend the light-waves to obscure the, ahh, 'private' parts of your body... or to make you disappear altogether,” offered the alien-girl. “Of course, it would be difficult and error-prone to do so, unless you stood alongside Hector, Tommy and Bob... and you would likely all be able to observe each other, at least in the warm-seeing types of ray-dee-ay-shun. Especially those parts of your body which are, ahem, 'hotter'.”

“Like I said,” wryly persisted the more-than-an-African-America-woman, “Only man who gets to see them 'hot' parts, is my Devon.”

Even Karéin-Mayréij laughed at this comment, and eventually, she proposed, “Oh-kay... to accommodate the silly modesty that you humans seem to believe in... I *did* bring many extra garments, in yonder vehicle and goods-packages. You may rummage through what is available, and temporarily don anything that can be worn, in the interim between now and when the work is complete. Would that, uhh, 'work for you'?”

“Have to,” said Saquina White. “Where's it all at?”

“Over there,” indicated the alien-girl, pointing at the as-yet-not-completely-disassembled package-of-goods from South America. “A few vestments are also in the *Mailànkh Express*, in which you can have some privacy for removing the old and donning the new.”

“Come on, all you who's taggin' along with her,” instructed Saquina White, “We might as well get a change of clothes... hope there's somethin' that fits.”

Karéin-Mayréij began to levitate until her feet were about at a normal person's shoulder-height, and called out to the crowd.

“I know that many of you are weary, as my late-coming has prematurely awakened you... for that, I apologize,” she announced. “There will be adequate time in which to fully unpack what I have brought, but now I will hasten to the goods-pile and retrieve things which may be immediately useful for your nightly repose : sleeping-bags, pillows, fold-up-cots, tents, and the like. At least one such will be provided for each family... you can set them up in rapid order, slumber for a few hours... and then, we will set about to the final preparations, ere my companions and I, depart for the Empire of America. While you rest, Hector and I will begin preparations on the trans-sub-stantiated clothing... he need only attend the first-part of this, then he, too, can, ahh, 'get some sleep'. Does this meet with your approval?"

"Yo," responded one of the Compton parents, "Shore would beat tryin' to sleep on mah jacket over a stone floor!"

"Again... I am sorry for having been so late," mentioned the alien-girl. "It was difficult finding all that was needful, within the few hours available on the 'South America' continent... and it did not help that my Spanish and Por-tu-gees is not, ahh, as good as my Eng-lish –"

"Seu Português é bom, a nova Mãe... quanto tempo foi necessário para aprender? Será que você vai para a escola?" interjected Sayuri.

"I learned it while flying toward Brazil, dear one," answered the Storied Watcher. "From tee-vee and ray-dee-oh programs, and the like... some day, I would indeed like to go to school, to learn some words that do not refer to 'futbol' or the latest 'mixed drink for parties on the beach'."

Sayuri giggled, while her adoptive mother beamed and gave a hug.

Karéin-Mayréij turned to address Ramirez.

"Hector, my brother," she stated, "Do you remember those garments, upon which we both worked, for Sam Jacobson and his brave crew?"

"Yeah," he confirmed. "Two days' work, and I had the mother of all headaches, afterwards."

"Verily," she directed, "Again we go to it... except, this time, all must be complete, in a few hours. Are you ready?"

"Oh, come *on*, Karéin," he complained, "You can't be *serious!* There's no *way* – I'll be so drained that –"

"Few goals that are worth the effort, require only a *small* effort," she tutored. "And there is one other thing."

"What?" he peevishly asked.

"Find some clothes which would fit Minn-ee, Otis, Will, Sylvia, Sebastiãn... and several others, whose acquaintance we know not yet," serenely requested the alien-girl.

"Hey, Ramirez," interrupted Billings. "You know what?"

"*What*, Bob?" he demanded, exasperation in his voice.

"I'm glad she didn't give me, *your* abilities," maliciously offered the salesman.

How's The Beef?

The aircraft was undertaking a wide turn, and the slightly-disoriented White House Spiritual Adviser almost missed the chair as he searched for a place, across the dinner-table from the *nouveau*-President.

"You all said grace without me, I'm assumin'?" ventured Harold Crowford.

"Uhh... something like that," muttered the former Vice-President, between mouthfuls of exquisitely-aged prime rib, horse-radish and gravy-soaked mashed potatoes, washed down with a generous mouthful of Scotch-on-the-rocks. "Sit down... dig in. We got some stuff to go over – namely, I need your advice on potential choices for a new Vice-President... to fill my old job. Gotta keep all those 'believers', happy... right? And I'm in a *good* mood today – my orders got executed properly, for once."

"Don't mind if I do, Mr. President," cheerily responded the Spiritual Adviser, taking a place beside Bezomorton, who was the only other man in the Air Force One executive dining-room, aside from the ever-present, dark-suited, stern-faced Secret Service guard. He motioned with one finger to the Secret Service man, who served up a black cup of coffee.

"And I'd be glad to mention some righteous Christian men, all of whom I can personally attest, would be a good fit for that very high office," he added. "By the way... it's a bit late to be sittin' down to eat, ain't it? 'Spose your schedule was especially busy today?"

"Umm-hmm," confirmed the *nouveau*-President, a half-smirk visible on his face. "We got rid of some 'problem-causers'... that's how *I'd* put it."

Brother Harold did a slight double-take, while carefully slicing his roast beef into precisely equal smaller-parts, and then ventured, "Ah, I *see*... we finally get to that 'Jacobson' fella? 'Bout *time*, I'd reckon."

"No... but *he's* next on the list," noted the U.S. leader, his voice calm and routine, as if going over budget numbers. "Actually... I just had a few Marine friends of mine, kick two of those smart-ass FBI agents – you know, the ones who were cavorting with that little 'alien' slut – out the door."

Crowford almost choked on the prime rib, but managed to get a serviette to his mouth, just in time.

"Mr... President," he stammered, "You all did... *what?* We didn't land, not that I noticed... uhh... which two?"

"Oh, the two male ones," diffidently answered the *faux*-President, with a casual shrug. "The Chinese broad's still here... figured we might still be able to pump her for some info on Jacobson's band of traitors, but we didn't need all three of them... right? We'll dispose of *her*, too, when the time's right. Pass the salt, if you don't mind?"

Brother Harold's visage wore an ashen, thunderstruck look, and this was immediately noticed by both the other men.

"What's the matter, Mr. Crowford?" offered Bezomorton. "You had no special attachment to those two... what were their names again? Oh, yeah... 'Boatman' and 'Hendricks', if I recall, correctly. *Surely* you know that these are, ahh... 'trying' times. Sometimes the government has to resort to tough measures, to guard the security of the state... am I right?"

"Oh... yeah... no doubt 'bout *that*," replied the Spiritual Adviser. There was an odd, 'off-there-somewhere', look on his face.

"Even gave 'em some time to say their prayers," insouciantly mentioned the *nouveau*-President. "Can't say we didn't cover all the bases... you know?"

Crowford stood up, though his dinner was, as yet, only half-finished.

"Mr President... Mr. Security Adviser... may I be excused?" he requested.

"No problem – but it's not like you, not to finish your meal," observed the U.S. leader. "Something eating you?"

"Oh, no," prevaricated the Christian man, "Just that I, uhh, got some bases of my own, to cover. Be back in a few minutes, if that'd be okay."

"Don't be late," said the *faux*-President, with a wry eye-wink. "Beef's damn – 'scuse me, *darn* – good. You snooze, you lose... might just not be any left, by the time you get back."

As Crowford hurried out the door, the U.S. leader got the attention of the Secret Service guard.

"We're out of booze... *do* something about that, would you?" he demanded.

Without A Para-Choot

The inchoate terror racking his primitive brain was locked in a fateful struggle with his rational mind, as the fast-plummeting Will Hendricks screamed a plea to his friend, Otis Boatman.

"*Otis!*" he yelled, his voice almost inaudible – despite the "Mars ears" – against the howl of the air rushing by the two, seemingly-doomed companions, from below. "Come back, and this time, don't push me away!"

Though the sky was pitch-black he could easily see the other FBI agent, whose distance was gradually increasing, likely because of greater wind-drag on Boatman's massive body.

Well... at least the Mars eyes are working, grimly mused Hendricks. *I can see Otis clear as day, and I can see that fucking plane climbing away...*

Don't want to look down – not yet – wish I knew how long till we hit –

A response came back from the other more-than-human, and though Boatman's lips were moving, somehow, the third agent could tell that it wasn't sound waves, which were transmitting what the big black guy was trying to say.

Can't do that, Will... you all might survive this... but you auger in with me on top, we're both in that cold, cold ground... need some time to make my peace with the Lord, anyways!

"Don't be an *ass,* Otis!" shrieked a frustrated Hendricks. "We got no time to argue – ground's coming up *fast!*"

But Boatman just shook his head and refused the demand.

Okay, then, resolved the third agent.

Angel Lady – send me the power – not for me... for him.

His friend's astonished visage confirmed that Hendricks' eyes were now glowing, as he reached deep down and tried to remember the trick that unlocked the "mind-push-pull" gift.

Come on, come on, Otis – don't resist, help me to lock on – wait a sec – there you are – gotcha!

Damn, realized Hendricks, *I feel it... surging, through me.*

Thanks, Karéin – better fuckin', late than never!

Like an angler reeling in a prize catch, the third agent's nascent telekinesis began to narrow the distance between himself and Boatman; although, judging from the frantic head-shaking and pained expression on the latter's face, the operation was completely one-sided.

In another two seconds or so, the black agent was close enough to be grabbed by hand.

"Will, blast you," he inveighed, "We's both 'bout to *die!* Okay, do it *your* way – you all know any prayers?"

Only too well-aware that there was little time for smart-talk, Hendricks shouted back, "I thought that was *your* department, man – weren't you in the choir or something?"

"I was, I was... but given the circumstances, I just can't think straight, can't remember the words!" yelled Boatman. "How long we got, before –"

"Almost halfway down!" warned the third agent. "Forty-five seconds, max! Grab my hands!"

"Yeah... yeah... okay," blubbered the big, black agent, as they now fell face-to-face, with hands interlocked in classic sky-diving fashion. "Will... just wanted to say... been great knowin' you..."

"Stow it, man!" countered Hendricks. "We're gettin' *out* of this, dammit!"

"How we gonna do *that?*" cried the panicked FBI agent.

"Otis – remember that 'vow' she made us recite?" prodded the third agent.

"Sort of," evaded Boatman. "She made me say it ten times. Why?"

"Then I'll start, you fill in every other line – and when you *do*, think of *her*," demanded Hendricks. "Call deep down, brother, deep *down* – call on the *Fire*, brother, full *power*, like Rudolph on Christmas *Eve*, man! This one's for the *money!*"

"Goin' to meet my maker, chatterin' some damn alien poem," complained the black agent. "Saint Pete's gonna –"

"She's an *angel*, man," argued Hendricks. "Big Guy will *understand!* Here *goes!*"

His eyes momentarily closed, but then quickly re-opened; and when they did, Boatman was shocked at the brilliant, bright-as-day shine coming from deep within. He heard the third agent begin to chant, and his voice, empowered and amplified by his exciting, staccato war-song, began to echo far and wide.

"Upon my most sacred honor, I will use my power, to love, not to hate," chanted Hendricks, his voice oddly melodic.

Boatman closed his eyes.

Lord, he silently prayed, *I place my soul, in your care.*

Forgive this fool for usin' his last seconds on this Earth, to say these words,

"To heal, not to wound, to rescue, not to endanger," he bellowed; but Boatman's opened, glowing eyes were unprepared for what came next, as his own voice and rhythmic, booming war-song, took on a Stentorian, powerful volume, and he felt the luxurious surge of energy race throughout every molecule of his being.

"To serve, not to rule; ever to follow the Holy Light, not the Dark," sang Hendricks.

Something – coming from they knew not where – started them spinning in the horizontal plane, around an axis equidistant from their four interlocked hands, as if they had become a human helicopter-rotor.

We're slowin' down! realized an amazed Boatman, as he repeated,

"Until I pass from this life..."

Wish she hadn't put that part of it in, mused the black agent.

They were still going down uncomfortably fast, and though neither one dared look straight down, it was now clear what lay below : they were falling into a forested range of low, rolling mountains, with the tree-tops now no more than five or six seconds away.

"With this oath, I bind myself," called the spinning, glowing Hendricks.

"I swear unto eternity!" concluded Boatman.

"Otis – we're gonna *make* it, man – keep on top – let me hit first!" demanded Hendricks, as his telekinesis arrested the spinning-motion and tipped the two men so that he would be lower than Boatman.

With the ground hurtling at them, they streaked past and snapped off several of the highest branches of the trees – only the pines and spruces were still verdant, as the birches and aspens hadn't yet fully-bloomed – toward the forest-floor.

"*Jaysuuussss!*" groaned Boatman, whose ashen face wore that "one second before the Promised Land" look. He closed his eyes, as much to protect them from the oncoming hurricane of pine-needles, wood-chips and tree-bark, as to avoid observing what he feared was an imminent demise.

But in the next instant, the big, African-American FBI agent found himself awkwardly sitting behind Hendricks' head, on top of the latter's pained shoulders. His skydiving-companion had come to a precarious stop about ten feet above the ground on a tree's lowest branch, although this was precariously sagging and seemed likely to snap at any moment.

The third agent spat a distasteful potpourri of tree-debris out of his mouth, looked up at Boatman and then phlegmatically announced, "You know... after *that*... well, this will be a piece of *cake*."

Before his compatriot could complain about the still-potentially-dangerous drop, Hendricks slid off the tree-branch and then floated to a gentle, fully-in-control, upright landing, with his feet resting on the pine-needles of the

Appalachian wilderness. There was no more impact than if he had jumped off a low step-ladder.

"Otis," complained Hendricks, as he stared up with dimly-glowing eyes at the huge black man burdening his collar-bone, "Didn't you say that you'd been losing weight?"

Like An Old Friend

They had been parked off the side of the road in the woods surrounding Arnold Air Force Base for an hour, now; and despite the presence of three adult humans (well, one human and two who were something more) in the vehicle, to Sullivan, at least, things were feeling cold.

"Can't we at least turn the damn car on?" she complained. "I didn't bring my sweater... I'm catching a chill."

"Just a few minutes more, Moira," argued Abruzzio, who had moved to the passenger-side front seat. "It's probably hard for you to notice from your vantage point here inside the car, but I'm using my, uhh, 'arts', to make it difficult for passing Army vehicles to detect us, and if we restart the engine –"

"Whaddya *mean*... your 'arts'?" interjected the woman. "I can see just fine, out the windows. Well, okay... I *could* see fine, if it wasn't so dark out there. Sun will be completely set, any moment now."

Abruzzio allowed a momentary, multi-colored twinkle to shine within her eyes, as she turned to explain, "Ah... welcome to the mysteries of *Amaiish*, Moira; if you were looking from the outside in, even if it were in broad daylight, what you'd see is only the dim shape of a car – kind of like it would appear, if inside a really big beer-bottle. We should be next to invisible to anybody looking for us in the dark, however... except, that is, for *Vîrya* –"

"Am... *what?*" replied the perplexed woman. "And how's startin' the car going to screw up this, uhh, whatever-you're-doing?"

"*Amaiish,*" related the former JPL scientist. "Otherwise known of as 'The *Fire*'... the amazing, apparently-supernatural power of the Storied Watcher, bestowed on the likes of Jerry and me, by Karéin-Mayréij herself, shortly after we first met her. No point in asking me to tell you how it works, or why one person can do 'this' and the other person can do 'that', or anything... because the truth is... I really don't know, myself. All I *do* know, is that when this nonsense is all over... I mean to find out. I suspect I'll have some help in that project, from Cherie Tanaka, and – oh, *look!* Thank God, there they *are!*"

"Where?" demanded the schoolgirl-friend. "I don't see anything –"

Faster than Sullivan believed any human being able to do, Abruzzio flung open the door and dashed forward, toward the road.

In less than a full second, she stopped and was being inundated by puppy-licks from little 'Rainbow', who had jumped into Abruzzio's welcoming arms, while the alien-girl's weirding shield hovered nearby with its odd, warbling, humming drone evident even to the one human member of the expedition. Then, in the blink-of-an-eye, *Vîrya I'ëà'b'* assumed a position on the JPL scientist's arm; but this lasted only until the three entered Sullivan's vehicle, at which point, the living-shield parted company with the scientist and darted over to a resting-position on Kaysten's lap.

"Hey there, honey," purred the former Chief of Staff, "Great to see you – uhh, excuse me, *thou* – back here, safe and sound. What's that? Oh, yeah... of *course* I missed thee, too! Just hell to be away from thee, even for an hour or two... honest! Listen – hate to be so pushy, we're in a big hurry, so did thou – umm-hmm. I *see*... three places where he might be? Well, that's a *start*, anyway. Here's a pat on the back! Darn good job, sweetheart!"

Something akin to a subliminal giggle reached the consciousnesses of all four of the car's flesh-and-blood inhabitants, and it was responded to by a little 'yip' on the part of the puppy-dog.

Kaysten leaned forward to address Abruzzio.

"I don't *know*," he muttered. "Maybe it wasn't such a good idea after all, to send them out near dark... if it'd been in the daylight, maybe one or the other of 'em would have seen him out on the golf-course or something. As it is, if I'm reading her right... we got a *lot* of doors to knock on, and no guarantee that he's gonna be behind any one of 'em. On top of that, even if we *do* find him, he's got to want to go, and then, we've got to find some way to smuggle him out, not to mention hiding him afterwards. Still want to go ahead with it?"

For a few long seconds, the former JPL scientist just stared forward through the windshield; then she looked backward and said, "You're right, Jerry; this is a quest with many perils, any one of which, might be our undoing. But we must have *faith*... for without that, we are defeated, before we even start."

The Chief of Staff hung his head and nervously laughed.

"You know, Sylvia," he offered, "You sound damn like *her*, when you say things like that. Were you practicing?"

Softly, Abruzzio replied, "Nope... just *came* to me, somehow. That ol' 'voices-in-your-head' thing, I guess."

"Riight," uneasily commented Sullivan. "Like... from God, you mean?"

"Or from one of His angels," absent-mindedly responded the scientist. "Who among us, can know the 'wherefores and the whys' of it?"

She turned to look at her childhood friend.

"Moira," asked Abruzzio, "You know what to do, then?"

"Yeah," said Sullivan. "But I'll be worrying myself *sick* every minute that you're off on this nutzoid adventure – don't *do* it, Sylvia... *please!* I don't want to see you get *hurt*, kiddo... I'm even gettin' a little fond of Miss Mutt, there; what happens if she ends up without a master?"

"She won't," firmly vowed Abruzzio. "Like I said... 'faith'. Believed in it when I was in the choir with you... sort of lost it when I took up science; but lately, after seeing – after meeting – Karéin... it's come back to me."

She sent a kindly stare at her childhood, Catholic-school companion.
"Kind of like an old friend... you know?" softly spoke the scientist.
Sullivan bent over and breathlessly embraced Abruzzio.
"You keep out of trouble – you hear?" mock-ordered the woman.
Abruzzio, her eyes welling, soundlessly nodded. Then she ordered, "Okay, all you post-humans... let's go get him."

Red-Hot White Trash, Comin' To Call

Darryl D. Bennington – otherwise known of, as "Wolf" – parked his pickup truck as discreetly as he could, behind a stand of trees on the north-west side of Vine Grove Road, just to the south of being parallel with the target – namely, the United States Bullion Depository – beckoning in the not-too-far-distance.

With his "Mars senses" ramping up and the two fire-dogs maintaining stations behind him on either side, he locked the vehicle and strode forward.

Hmm, mused the former bounty-hunter, *Would've thought that jumpin' that ditch between this road and the highway, and ploughin' right through the fence between the two, would've got somebody's attention.*

Well, he resolved, behind red-glowing eyes, *We'll make sure we get noticed... real soon now.*

Wolf took several more long steps toward the squat, white-stone-and-marble building off to the southeast, coming up almost to the ten-foot-tall barbed-wire fence that completely surrounded the facility. Using abilities that he couldn't possibly have imagined even a few weeks ago, he looked it over.

Fuckin' weird, Darryl my man, he thought. *I can see – no,* feel – *the voltage flowin' through that thing... enough to fry a horse, I'd wager. And out there in the field – though all this damn electric current's kinda gettin' in the way of the Mars eyes – little metal plates, every five feet or so, checkerboard-pattern, just under the topsoil.*

Remind me not to step on any of them things.

Now, if I were that cute little 'Tanaka' popsy (can't blame Jacobson from boppin' her once in a while – he may be Mars, but he's still a man, *right?) – I'd probably get off on pullin' them... what are they... oh, yeah, 'electrons'... into me.*

But as it turns out... high voltage, ain't my thing.

High heat... now, that, *I do.*

Okay, darlin' – you know what to – what's that?

Fuck... yeah. Come on, *you assholes... what's* takin' *you?*

He stood motionless in front of the fence for what seemed to be an eternity, although a quick look at his watch revealed that the delay was, in fact precisely fifty-three seconds. But finally, the "thump, thump, *thump*" sounds of explosions to the northwest, in the direction of the airbase, accosted his ears.

'Bout fuckin' time, *you space-boys and space-girls. Go git 'em!*

A quick glance to the north-east, up Vine Grove Road, meanwhile, warned of approaching vehicles; and their appearance in the warm-seeing revealed that they were considerably larger than even a good-sized SUV.

Humvees, he considered. *Maybe some of them APCs, or even tanks?*

Whatever. They melt fast, they melt slow... it's all good.

Pups – you know what to do... stay with Daddy, and no steppin' on those plates in the ground!

Growling, barking-sounds issued simultaneously from 'Boob' and 'Tube', and the appreciative bounty-hunter saw that the eyes of his two pets had begun to mimic his own; there was smoke coming from their nostrils and mouths, along with a shimmering envelope of heat that encased both of the hell-hounds.

Now, Wolf repeated those words of power that he had come to so know and appreciate, as the war-song-boosted confidence and energy surged through his body, lighting the glow in his eyes to a sinister, infernal zenith.

"*Baby,*" he cried, "*Light my fire!*"

At a distance of perhaps a foot from his body, there appeared a dazzling, incandescent shroud of pure elemental flame, protecting him from almost every angle except directly below. Concentrating on a six-foot-wide section of the electrified fence directly in front of him, he opened his arms in mock-embrace-fashion.

Instantly, the structure's steel wire lattice-work started to smoke and spark; a half-second later, it began to glow a bright red; and a half-second after that, it deliquesced into a steaming, smoking pool of molten metal.

Klaxons and sirens screamed loud alarms, as Wolf took a determined leap over the remnants of the fence, on to the grounds of the United States Bullion Depository.

Hey, you fuckin' fancy-ass bankers, came a grimly-satisfied thought, *Here's the white trash you've been sittin' and shittin' on, since before he was born.*

Here's a hot poke in your eye!

The bounty-hunter had advanced perhaps 20 feet into the prohibited grounds-area – carefully avoiding the hidden land-mines, all the while – when he was illuminated in the confluence of at least three brilliant search-lights. A loudspeaker, far off, barked some kind of a demand to halt; but though he could easily have isolated the words, he wasn't in much of a mood to pay attention.

It was at this point that he felt the first bullet-impacts, evidently fired by the group of vehicles coming down the road, against the rear-side of his flame-shield; and while the shots harmed him not, they began to strike with increasing frequency.

Maybe not a good idea to let 'em keep drawin' a bead on me, mused Wolf. *Yeah, they probably can't get past Little Hot-Thighs' floatin' barbecue... but what did she say? 'Probably', don't cut it. Okay –*

At just that moment, something *big* and much more potent than a rifle-bullet, hit the bounty-hunter's flame-shield, with a shockingly powerful impact, throwing him immediately off his feet.

Wolf careened, ass-over-teakettle, wildly through the air; he was thrown at least six feet into the air, and as he fell back to Earth, he fought desperately to miss the land-mines, upon which he would certainly have landed, except for some last-second maneuvers.

Shit, he realized, while coming to his feet, *A few pieces of whatever the fuck* that *was, got through the screen... damn lucky my thick hide stopped 'em.*

The half-stunned bounty-hunter, now looking backward at the fence and the large conglomeration of heavily-armed soldiers and light armored vehicles, that had taken up firing positions, around and through the breach that he had recently opened.

"Boob! Tube!" he cried, concern all over his voice. "You okay?"

Thankfully, two affirmative "yip" sounds came from considerable distances to Wolf's right and left; the dogs had, apparently, been blown side-wise by whatever had hit him, and there was a little blood on "Boob"'s flank, but outwardly, they did not seem seriously harmed.

He saw – along with the many flashes of garden-variety rifle- and machine-gun fire being directed at him – something else, its signature significantly bigger than the rest, being launched. He did a fast dive to the right and evaded what must have been some kind of anti-tank projectile, which streaked past him and exploded noisily halfway to the Bullion Depository, in turn detonating two or three land-mines. The area was showered with jagged metal-shards – certainly lethal to any normal man or woman unlucky to have been around – but *he,* was no normal human being, and the shrapnel melted harmlessly upon striking his flame-shield.

Fuckin' heavy stuff, realized Wolf, as he commanded the infernal heat within him, to build for an attack of his own. *Lot of 'em, and them APC's is shootin' from behind the road –*

He felt the impacts of machine-gun-bullets, this time coming from the direction of the Repository.

Crossfire, grimly considered the bounty-hunter. *This is gettin' bad – whether I move backward or forward, I get hit, and I don't fancy takin' any more of them bazookas, 'specially not from both directions at once – I can put up the fire-wall, but not front and back at the same time... damn...*

An elfin voice sent a thought to his mind.

Master Blessed, it chirped, *Upward go instead why not?*

We can do that? he answered, thinking quickly, while fending off an increasing fusillade of high-velocity gunshots, which were becoming increasingly hard to avoid by dodging to and fro.

Word just give, compliantly offered the Little Burning One. *Rocket a like! Easier much than bus-ship push sky through!*

One of the dogs yelped in pain and distress.

"Tube! Boob! Jump to Daddy's arms!" shouted a worried Wolf.

In the next instant, he had two flaming mongrels under his armpits; and he noticed, to his dismay, that the female one had a severely-bleeding wound in the hind-quarters.

"There, there, girl," he stammered. "Yer gonna be alright..."

I hope.

Okay, honey – got no idea how this's gonna work... but anywhere's, probably better than where we're at, at this current time – do *it!*

"*Whoaaaaa!*" exclaimed the bounty-hunter, as, like a sinister parody of a Roman candle, he unexpectedly streaked into the Kentucky night sky. The thrust produced by his extra-dimensional alter-ego was greatly more than what would have been needed just to send him aloft, and a half-petrified Wolf hung on to the equally-frightened, squirming puppies for dear life, as he zoomed up, then down, then east, then west, then, seemingly, all almost at once, in a mostly-out-of-control, corkscrew pattern.

Despite a very apt fear of a sudden, catastrophic impact with the ground (and, possibly, the land-mines buried underneath it), as he frantically tried to synchronize his mental commands about direction and thrust with those of the Little Burning One, the bounty-hunter *did* notice one perverse benefit of what was going on : after a chorus of stunned gasps, his assailants came to their senses and again begun firing at him, but the *ersatz* evasive maneuvers made doing so next to impossible, and Wolf's fire-shield was hit only by a few stray rounds.

After six or seven gut-wrenching seconds of being out of control, however, he was able to come to an unsteady hovering position, perhaps two hundred feet above ground-level, drawing the obligatory hail of rifle- and machine-gun fire.

Like his alien mentor had tutored him to do back at the sylvan camp, the crimson-eyed, flame-shrouded bounty-hunter brought his inner *Fire* and hissing, beat-pounding, sweetly-ominous-war-song to near-full-tilt, forced the fingers and thumbs of both is hands in claw-fashion, pushed back his elbows and tensed his arm-muscles as if preparing to throw a couple of solid projectiles (the dogs wailed nervously at this, since they almost fell out of Wolf's grasp), then thrust his arms forward, while releasing the power and defiantly bellowing,

"Okay, fuckers – eat *this!*"

Instantly, a pair of meteor-like projectiles, their Faustian energy illuminating everything for hundreds of yards in every direction, rocketed downward at a steep angle, striking the ground near Wolf's hapless enemies after less than a full seconds-worth of flight.

A huge, double explosion – its blast at least the equal of what would have been done, by two large anti-tank missiles – followed; the soldiers standing nearest-by were literally disintegrated, while those further away suffered either instant death or terrible injuries.

Even Wolf, hardened as he was from recent events and from years of rough justice on the streets of Tucson, couldn't help but do a double-take at the extent of the carnage.

Jaysus, he thought, *It really* is *like shootin' fish in a barrel. Actually... more like dynamitin' fish in a barrel...*

Well... like I said to Mr. Space Man, back on that island... "sucks to be them", I reckon... and if I didn't have a price on my head before, I can be sure of it, now.

I can finish 'em off easy, he mused. *Less witnesses...*

What did she say, though? Oh, yeah... "the measure which separates a savage warrior of the Light, from one of the Dark... is what happens, after the foe is vanquished"... or some-such shit.

Okay, Angel Lady... we'll do it your *way.*

A subconscious mental command to his infernal alter ego caused the bounty-hunter's head to tip toward the Repository; a half-second later, a jet of flame issued from below his feet, and off he went, streaking at the building at a speed that brought him into immediate panic mode. With his mind fumbling for the correct, reflex-like message to his symbiotic partner and bullets from previously-hidden gun-turrets ricocheting from his fire-shield, Wolf almost collided head-first with the building's marble-and-granite outside wall, but at the last opportunity, he was able to rotate his feet downward, resulting in him streaking high up, far past the Repository's top-peak.

Looking down from high above as he figured out how to make just enough thrust to offset gravity, he felt like a god.

The bounty-hunter noticed mayhem – multiple explosions and the sounds of gunfire – to the northwest, and then saw an ant-sized, glistening figure, leap all the way from the guard-posts to the north-east of the building, right on top of it; the distance had to be several hundred feet, if it was an inch. A second later, there was a rumbling, echoing sound from where this super-human being had landed; a large hole had opened in the top-side of the Repository, just under him.

Oh no, you don't, Jacobson, realized the more-than-human. *You ain't gettin' at all that nice shiny gold, before yours truly – worked all my life for fuckin' minimum wage, or close to it...* this *time, I'm cashin' in!*

With contempt, Wolf ignored the feeble machine-gun rounds being fired at him, as he rotated until his feet faced upward and to the north-west, re-ignited his living-rocket and fell upon the Fort Knox Bullion Repository like an avenging meteor.

A Song In The Appalachians

The first rays of morning were breaking across the eastern mountain-tops, providing a welcome respite from the near-freezing cold of the previous night; and for added benefit, the two realized that they could now use their eyes like a normal human being. It had been awkward and treacherous navigating in the 'warm-sight', since the trees gave off only the weakest of emissions. This was a fact that Boatman had discovered "the hard way" at least twice, to the disadvantage of his forehead.

"Darn it all," muttered the sweating, disheveled agent, as he stumbled down the winter-transitioning-to-spring, half-forested, gently-sloping, mountain-side, "Why couldn't she have taught us to fly, like that 'Tanaka' lady? We been goin' for *miles* now, and we ain't seen *nobody!*"

Hendricks seemed to be taking their long trek – hours stretching into a day or more (and that was without a bite to eat, though there was plenty of water in the form of late snow) – more in stride than his FBI co-agent, and as he lithely skipped over a fallen tree-trunk, he replied, "Well, I wouldn't want to be cruisin' up there, without that force-field that she's got going... what with how the Air Force's shooting first and askin' questions later. Besides... I had my fill of being ten thousand feet up and then quickly way down, if you know what I mean."

"Yeah," ruefully grunted the black agent. "Hold up a minute, would you?"

"What's it now?" sighed the third agent.

"Stone in my shoe," said Boatman, as he removed the double-size foot-gear, shook it and took his time putting it back on. "Ain't meant for hikin', you know?"

"Mine neither," offered Hendricks. "But come on, Otis... we gotta make better *time,* walking. We're completely out of the picture, and stuff's probably happening to Minnie... top of that, I don't want to spend any more time up here, than I have to. Somehow I *know* I'm not gonna die from exposure – that 'alien' shit, I mean – but it might still be damn unpleasant, being stuck in the woods, over another night. One was more than enough for yours truly."

"You all mean, '*lost* in the woods', don't you?" sourly answered the black agent. "We ain't got the slightest idea where we's goin'... could be in circles, for all I know."

"Thought I saw some lights, in the direction I think we're heading," noted Hendricks. "While we were, uhh, on the way down, that is. Although as you can imagine, I wasn't paying that much attention to it, considering what else was on my mind."

"Yeah," shrugged Boatman, shaking his head as he spoke. "Okay... lead on, son – just don't get ahead of us'ns who never ran no marathons, you hear?"

So on they walked through the lower slopes of the Appalachian hills, for hour after hour, until, finally, an elated Hendricks saw something encouraging at the far limits of his vision.

"Hey, Otis!" he called. "See that?"

"No," replied the big black man. He did a double-take, and then corrected himself. "Oh... wait a minute... yeah, shore *do!* Hmm... looks big enough to get a truck up and down, too. Well, thank the Lord, it's 'bout *time,* I'd say. Question is, which way you want to take it?"

Hendricks was now racing ahead and he slid down an embankment, not worrying about adding to the considerable splotches of muck which already marred his slacks, and positioned himself in the middle of a backwoods dirt road, winding narrowly through the woodlands with trees lined up almost to its edges on each side.

The third agent looked around in all directions, including downward.

"Tire-tracks," he observed. "Can't tell what direction, but they look sort of fresh to me. I'd say take the left."

"Why's that?" inquired Boatman. "'Less my eyes deceive me, road's slopin' a bit upward, in that direction. Maybe we'd get back to civilization faster, by takin' the right."

"But we got no real idea either way, and maybe there's a farm-house or somethin' up the hill," argued the third agent.

For a second or two, they stood mutely waiting for the other one to make the first move. Eventually, the big black agent proposed, "Tell you what... I got a quarter in my pocket... lucky one. Flip you for it?"

Hendricks nodded. "Heads," he said.

"Makes me 'tails', I guess," stated Boatman. "Ass-end of everythin', as usual. Here goes – and none of that-there 'mind-pushin' stuff, you hear?"

"Oh, certainly not," demurred the third agent. "But only 'cause I haven't figured how to get it to work with craps yet... you know? I figure *that* out, and this bullshit gets sorted... I'm off to Vegas next day."

The black agent nodded in wry acknowledgment and sent the quarter into the air, catching it on the back of his massive hand.

"Consistent, if nothin' else, young man," he grumbled. "Heads."

"Well then, let's go," enthusiastically replied Hendricks.

They had walked about another hour, and Boatman's assessment had proven correct : the road was taking them back upward, something about which the black agent did not hesitate to complain, on a minute-by-minute basis. Hendricks was almost ready to throw in the towel and agree to a reversal-of-course, when the path suddenly entered a partially-cleared area, with what looked very much like the prototype hillbilly-shack a few hundred feet further up the mountainside, at road's-end. There was some kind of other structure, from which a thin wisp of steam or smoke was issuing, behind the first building.

Hendricks froze.

"Otis," he whispered, "Mars senses warning me of something... movement in the trees –"

"Where?" asked an initially-perplexed Boatman. "I don't – oh, wait a minute. Yeah, that's weird, alright... not sure if I'm seein' the heat off their bodies, or the air movin', or –"

A gruff, mountain-man voice from behind them, to the left, shouted a warning. "Don' y'all move a *muscle*," it advised. "'Cept to put them hands in th' air. I got y'all covered... 'n two other triggers on y'all, 'sides. What y'all *doin'* up here, boy?"

Now that's just fuckin' great, mused the third agent. *I don't even drink moonshine... not since I tried it back in college, and puked for two days...*

"We're, uhh, lost," loudly answered Hendricks, as he slowly and reluctantly raised his arms. "Lookin' for help... ride back to town. We don't want any trouble, man, and we didn't mean to, uhh, intrude on anything. We can pay you good, if you can give us a lift."

A surprised Boatman whispered, "What? We only got a few hundred –"

"What y'all think we should do with 'em, Billy-Ray?" came a voice from behind and to the right. The two FBI agents noted with mild interest that the speaker couldn't be far from the steep side of the mountain; whoever it was, certainly knew his surroundings. "Plug 'em an' dump 'em?"

"Well, mah hogs's a mite hon-gry," ominously mentioned the first voice. "But check em *out*, Dorsie," he added. "City-boys, judgin' from them fancy-ass clothes they got on. Somethin' here don' add up... ain't *nobody* goes hikin' in these-here woods lookin' like that, 'specially not *this* early in th' season. Hey, Mister Fancy-Pants! Y'all got an explanation fer what yer wearin'? How y'all git here, in th' first place? Y'all miles from nowhere, if'n y'all hadn't noticed. That's for a *reason* – we don' like nosy city folk, 'round these parts."

"Will," softly growled Boatman, as he unsubtly flexed his hands into and out of fists, "If you want to use whatever tricks you got... I'm ready to rock and roll, guns on me or none – somethin's tellin' me, it's them that's gonna –"

"Wait," countered Hendricks. "Let's see if we can talk our way out, here."

He slowly turned his head, enough to see a tall, thin, bearded, Caucasian guy dressed in hiking-gear, with an assault-rifle pointed squarely at the third agent and his companion.

"I telled y'all not to move!" spat the mountain-man.

"Hey, *hey,*" stammered the third agent, "It's cool... if you want us to turn around and get our asses out of here, we're good with doin' that, lickedy-split... and we won't tell anybody about you, or this place. But listen, man – when I said we could pay... I meant it. If you'll give me a chance to explain, this can work out real good for you."

"And how'd *that* be?" taunted the mountain-man. "I reckon it'd be a lot simpler to just feed y'all to mah hogs, 'n be done with it. An' if y'all got money on y'all, well, we git that whether y'all 'live or daid. Seems to me that y'all ain't got much to bargain with, city-boy."

"Okay, okay," countered Hendricks, "You wanted an explanation about the clothes? And what we got to offer you? Well here it is... and if it isn't good enough, well, I suppose you'll have to shoot us... but if you *do*, be assured, that will be the worst mistake you ever made, man – these woods will be *crawling* with exactly the kind of 'law' you don't want, and somebody far worse, on top of that. They'll be looking for *us*, man, and they won't stop until you're in jail, or dead. Want me to go on?"

"I don' b'lieve a fuckin' word of this," growled the hillbilly, "But I got lots of time 'fore it's feedin' time fer mah pigs. Y'all say your piece, boy."

"Sure," answered the third agent. "Now, I'm gonna give it to you straight, and it's gonna sound crazy, man... but it's true, every word of it. First of all, Otis 'n me, we're FBI – the Bureau, that is –"

"Lord's sake, Will," protested Boatman, *sotto voce*, "Did you *have* to tell 'em that?"

"Well if that's true, boy," hissed the mountain-man, "Y'all just signed your death-papers, I reckon. Go on, an' tell me first – how many more of y'all's wanderin' 'round these-here woods? An' how y'all git here?"

"Nobody," stated Hendricks. "Except us, that is. And as for how we got here... we fell out of a plane, but low enough so we landed in the trees... just about got killed going down, but the branches broke our fall –"

The mountain-man broke out with a cynical laugh.

"Y'all hear *that*, Dorsie?" he guffawed. "'Boy's either the luckiest son of a bitch in his'try... or he's the fuckin' worst liar in his'try. Three guesses an' th' first two don' count which one's more likely. Keep talkin', city-boy... an' while y'all doin' that, y'all might want to 'splain, how come y'all jumped out of this-here 'plane'."

"Fer God's sake, Billy-Ray," came the second voice, "Boy's full of *shit*... cain't y'all see that?"

"Of *course* I know that," retorted the first hillbilly. "But this's gonna make a good story back at th' bar, afore I lets 'em know what happened... next."

"Okay," continued the third agent. "Now like I said... this is gonna sound nuts, but it's the truth. The reason we got kicked out of the plane is, we're kind of on the 'outs' with both the Bureau and the government, on account of being friends with... well, you guys know what went down up there on Mars, just before the comet was about to hit?"

"Yeah," grunted the mountain-man. "Bunch of bull 'bout some kind of 'angel', or some-such horse-shit. Never b'lieved a word of it... just lies we get all th' time from th' guv'ment. All made up. An' even if any of it's true... what's it got to do with y'all?"

"Because," firmly claimed Hendricks, "That 'angel' who you saw – she's one hundred per cent real, man... and we know her *personally*. Maybe you heard of how she did that little ol' face-lift, at Mt. Rushmore? Or the White

House? Don't want to sound *threatening*, man... but if you grease us, she won't stop until everything within fifty miles of here's laid *flat*. She's already done that, more than once – she's very, uhh, 'protective' of people who she likes... such as us. But if you let us go, or, better still, lend us a hand... we'll put in a good word for you, with her, and that'll be the last time you ever have problems with the government hassling you for whatever you're doing up here. Fuckin' *big* return for a fuckin' *small* investment, man."

"You all better believe him," added Boatman. "You boys shore don't want Miss Angel Lady – or 'Karéin' as we know her on a first-name basis – to come lookin' for you. Whole big heap of dead Army 'n Air Force people will attest to that... as will the President himself, real soon now."

The mountain-man let out a cackle, but the heightened senses of the two more-than-human men could tell that there was a tinge of hesitation, or, perhaps, nervousness, in it.

"Well, now, isn't *this* just the grand-daddy of all tall tales," countered the gun-toting mountain-man. "Y'all got any proof of all this shit?"

"Sure," eagerly answered the third agent. "How about these clothes we're wearing? You said yourself, they don't fit the surroundings, and you're damn right about that. You think we'd go hiking, dressed like this?"

"Maybe y'all jus' hid your car back there down th' road somewheres," parried the hillbilly. "That don' prove nothin'. Okay... I think we's 'bout done talkin' –"

"Just a minute, man," desperately protested Hendricks. "Look – if we could do something that no human being could do – something you can't explain at all – would that convince you?"

"Give y'all ten seconds to do whatever yer plannin' to do, city-boy," ominously accosted the hillbilly, "But if I was y'all... I'd be sayin' some prayers."

"Otis," breathed the third agent, "Last chance... I'll power it up, but if I have to move... you move too... got it?"

Boatman knowingly nodded.

"Okay," exclaimed Hendricks, to the mountain-man. "You're gonna hear some music... that's what I call my 'war-song', and as you can see, I don't have any fuckin' loudspeaker strapped on me, so that ought to prove we are who we say we are. And you know what, man?"

"What?" uneasily replied the hillbilly.

"When you hear that, you'd better lower that gun... your friend over there, behind the bushes, too. Didn't think we knew where he is? You're out of your league here, man... but we don't want a fight. Don't give us one, and we'll both be good. Here goes."

Hendricks reached deep down and tried to call upon just enough of the *Fire*, to start his song, without simultaneously lighting up his eyes and body. And the melody came, brought on a sudden breeze with an exciting, staccato, rock-funkadelic, adrenaline-enervating beat that seemed to reverberate from every leaf, branch and tree-trunk.

Bam, wham, thank you Ma'am, wham, bam, thank you Ma'am, it echoed and repeated, through the Appalachian hillside.

"What the *fuck* –" gasped the hillbilly.

"Gotta be a trick!" shouted the other mountain-man. "I'm hearin' it – no, I ain't – yes I is – Billy-Ray, y'all want me to smoke 'em now?"

"What you *say?*" called the third agent. "By the way... pull that trigger, and that's the last thing you'll ever do."

After a very tense two or three seconds, during which Hendricks struggled mightily to avoid his powers running completely away, the first hillbilly slowly lowered his gun, inveighing, "God *damn*... n-no... leave 'em be, Dorsie."

"I'll dial it back," announced the third agent, "And I'm gonna lower my arms... Otis too. Don't worry, we aren't packin'."

"Y'all don't make no moves," warned the first mountain-man, while Hendricks' war-song gradually faded. "How the fuck y'all *do* that, anyways?"

"Long story, man," offered the slightly de-stressed and relieved former FBI agent. "Tell you about it over a coffee or a beer, if you got any."

"Up in th' cabin," directed the hillbilly. "Y'all walk ahead of Dorsie 'n me, and like I said... don' do nothin' stupid, or we's grease y'all, fancy-ass stere-o sound or none. We's gonna have a nice lil' talk 'bout a lot of things, city-boy."

"Gentlemen, now that we're talkin'," offered Boatman, "I *do* have one thing to say, right at the outset."

"Which would be?" asked the mountain-man, prejudice obvious in his demeanor.

"Well, if you all liked my friend Will's little number, which was given to him by Her Destroyin' Angel-ness," smoothly explained the big, black agent, "Just wait until you hear... her own."

A Chat With The Old Man

Despite a few close calls with occasional Army patrols (easily evaded with Abruzzio's light-bending arts, plus woodland foliage in the dark), infiltrating Arnold Air Force Base had proven easier than either the former JPL scientist or the former Chief of Staff, had first anticipated. Sullivan had driven them almost to the dead-end of an unlit Hawkersmith Road, and then the two more-than-humans, along with the puppy and the Storied Watcher's weirding "child"-shield, had decamped to the southeast through a cornfield adjacent to the base-limits.

Abruzzio's childhood friend turned the car and drove away, hoping all the while that the scientist didn't see the tears or feel the fear in Sullivan's stomach.

There had been an eight-foot-high, barb-wire fence, several hundred yards inside the base, but this proved easy for Abruzzio's burgeoning telekinesis to lift Kaysten above and over, while the dog hopped on to the now-familiar *Vìrya I'ëà'b'* and joined the two more-than-humans on the other side. As far as either the shield or Abruzzio could determine, there were no motion-sensors, at least not on this part of the base.

About a mile in, avoiding the runway-area and its military installations (which surely would have been better-guarded than the rest of the base) all the while, they had arrived in the country-club-like residential environs of Arnold AFB. Initially, although there were plenty of non-military personnel strolling around the grounds, Abruzzio and Kaysten elected to remain hidden, dashing from building-side-to-shadow. But they twice had to double back to fetch the tarrying living-shield; *Vìrya I'ëà'b'* seemed fascinated by the vintage aircraft – among them, a F-14, a F-18 and a F-22 – which were positioned as static museum displays, at various places around the airbase.

Upon inquiring, Abruzzio got a mind-message from the buckler to the effect of, "close-up wanted I see them to, them fighting after air up in", and the former JPL scientist had decided that it would be better if *Vìrya I'ëà'b'* were to use her disappearing-skills, while carrying little 'Rainbow'.

The weirding-shield vanished, though both the flesh-and-blood party-leaders were still aware of its presence, as it guided the group to the first location that *Vìrya I'ëà'b*'s initial reconnaissance had scouted out. This was an base apartment-complex, in which the living-shield had detected someone resembling the former President. However, despite a half-hour of careful, fully-'cloaked' searching, this individual – whatever his identity – was nowhere to be found.

So on they went to the next location, which turned out to be bungalow on the grounds of the Arnold AFB golf course, about a half-mile from the apartments. Right away, the place appeared to be an excellent prospect, because the house was well-protected, being watched over by at least two uniformed Marines, plus a civilian watchman; and on top of that, the property was defended by a six-foot-chain-link fence, complete with motion detectors and trip-lights. But when Kaysten got a good look at the man who came to the door to say "goodnight" to the guards, though the resemblance to "The Old Man" was striking, the former Chief of Staff instinctively knew that this must have been a stunt-double.

"Okay, honey," asked Abruzzio, from the group's hidden, cloaked vantage-point, behind a dumpster halfway between the golf-chalet and the fake-President's bungalow, "This is our last chance... where was the third one? Umm-hmm... yeah... really? That far? I mean, that's all the way over to the reservoir... well, no point in hanging around here, I suppose. Come on, folks – let's hoof it."

They headed southeast, avoiding the roads, though as the darkness became complete, the base appeared to be closing down for the night; only one or two jeeps, each with a couple of military police, cruised by in the distance.

The streets in this part of the airbase were now almost deserted, since it was past the dinner-hour; so, in order to save time, Abruzzio dropped the cloak, and she and Kaysten mimicked man-and-wife-out-for-an-evening-stroll, while taking sidewalks leading to the AEDC Retention Reservoir. They had said a few pleasant "good evenings" to one or two passers-by, who, evidently, paid no special attention to the apparently normal pair.

"*Vîrya I'ëà'b',*" spoke the former JPL scientist, apparently to no-one, "We're going in the right direction, are we not?" She stopped to ponder for a second, and then added, "Ahh... okay. Lead thou the way, if thou mind not?"

There was the customary, odd, just-beyond-audibility "chirp", and Abruzzio double-timed it, until they entered a genteel-looking subdivision, with a number of stately, double-story, upper-class residences, each on a spacious lot surrounded by well-manicured lawns and a full tree-line providing privacy. The residences bordered the lakeside, and some had a yacht-dock, or a tennis-court, or other trappings of wealth and authority.

The former scientist abruptly stopped.

"Jerry – there it is," she whispered, demurely pointing at a cream-brick-colored, red-roofed semi-mansion, the third such visible to their left and in front. "Can you use your Mars eyes to give it a look-over? I don't see any guards... which is not what I'd have expected."

"Yeah... sure," complied Kaysten. He scanned what could be seen of the property for about thirty seconds, rubbed his eyes with his hands, blinked, and then offered, "You're right, I think... just looks like a banker's house, or something. Even did the whole 'warm-seeing' thing, and that other one she taught us, you know, with the UV... nothing there, either. Man, it's annoying when I switch back... wish I could run 'em all at the same time, but too much info, you know? Anyway... you want to zip around it once or twice?"

"Better idea," countered the scientist. "*Vîrya I'ëà'b'* – could thou please take Rainbow, and warn us of any perils which might lie, over yonder?"

There was another weird "chirp", as Kaysten remarked, "You got the alien-talk thing down pat, you know, Sylvia."

The flying-shield rapidly disappeared from immediate talking-range, remained so for a minute, and then returned as quickly as it had gone.

"If thou say so," uneasily murmured Abruzzio. "Are thou sure, little one? Ahh... yes. Too bad that all the windows and doors are closed, but thank thee for not, uhh, 'slicing' them open – no, that would *not* have been a good idea. Very well... but please stay close enough for us to call thee... okay?"

"So what's the plan?" inquired Kaysten.

"The plan is," calmly explained the more-than-a-woman, "That you simply go up and knock on the door... see if they can let you in, and if you have to use that silver tongue that she gave you, now would be as good a time as any. *Vîrya I'ëà'b'*, Rainbow and I will hang around under cover, and we'll be there to help if you get into trouble – just yell at the top of your lungs, and we'll come to the rescue."

"And *then* what?" protested the former Chief of Staff. "We got no way to get out of here, other than on foot, I'd remind you. And I'm *not* using, uhh, it – whatever the hell 'it' is – on the Old Man, if we're lucky enough to find him here. He's gotta come *willingly*... understand?"

"Understood," replied Abruzzio. "And remember, we only have to get him, and ourselves, as far as Moira's car... you rode on *Vîrya I'ëà'b*'s back all the way from D.C. to the Canyon, so if we have to get shuttled one by one, so be it. You ready?"

"No," he muttered, "But I guess this would be a bad time to come to my senses, so... here goes."

With a reluctant sigh, Kaysten walked briskly ahead, until he had reached a line of hedges slightly less than shoulder-height, surrounding the property. In the middle of the hedge-row facing the front of the house was a metal gate, which unfortunately was locked shut; however, it was only a little higher than the hedges themselves, so with a little boost from the mind-push-thingie, he did an arm-levered hop-skip-and-jump over the barrier, landing lithely on his feet with consummate agility. He walked down the stone-and-mortar-tiled pathway leading to the front door, when, at about the half-way point, he was illuminated by a confluence of previously-hidden searchlights.

A voice, which Kaysten noted with interest was female, curtly barked out from a loudspeaker, "Halt! Who goes there? This is private property, and you're trespassing! Leave immediately!"

He adjusted his eyes to filter out most of the glare, relying instead on the Storied Watcher's two new vision-modes, as he replied, "I'm not 'trespassing'... I'm here on official business. May I speak to the man of the house, please?"

"He and his family have retired for the night," answered the remote female voice. "Come back tomorrow."

His family, mused the former Chief of Staff. *Shit – never considered that –*

"That's, uhh, not possible," said Kaysten. "I have something very important to tell him, and it's got to be delivered in person – time's of the essence –"

"Sorry," countered the woman behind the loudspeaker, "No visitors after six p.m. – no exceptions. Those are the rules. Now get out of here... or do I have to call the cops? They can be here in one minute, if I just push a button."

Should I call her Slice-And-Dice-ness and just barge my way in there? he considered. *No – he might get hurt, or one of them might... never forgive me...*

"Okay... *okay*," stuttered Kaysten. "Look, this is so important, tell you what... I'll meet you halfway. If you'll meet me in person at the front door, open it up and let me see you, I'll give the message to you, and then you relay it to him. I'm clean – no piece, no nothing. See?"

He spread his arms, opening his jacket and revealing that he had no hidden weapons.

There was a long pause, but eventually, the voice responded, "Fine... but no funny business, you understand? I got a gun, and I'm not afraid to use it."

"Oh, certainly," answered the former Chief of Staff.

He advanced down the stone-path, walked up the three nicely-fashioned polished-granite steps leading to the house's outside deck and stopped about five feet away from the door, which slowly opened, revealing, just beyond the portal, a sumptuously-decorated interior, with a huge picture-window looking out over the lake.

Inside the passageway was a matronly, forty-something Caucasian woman with very average looks, shorter than the former Chief of Staff by at least a full head. Her auburn hair was short and done up in a butch-like twist behind her head, and she was wearing an unfamiliar, un-camouflaged uniform of some sort. She was carrying an un-holstered pistol, which was clearly at the ready, as well as a mobile communicator.

"So what's your name?" she demanded. "And be quick about it. I'm already taking chances by even talking to you."

"Hi," he answered, with an faked smile. "Actually, my name's the most important part of the message. Can you tell the President, that Jerry Kaysten's here to see him?"

A look of intense suspicion immediately appeared on the guard-woman's face. "What makes you think the President's here?" she challenged.

"Oh... let's just say, I've been doing a little research," diffidently responded Kaysten. "He *is* here... right?"

"I wouldn't tell you if he was," sneered the guard-woman. "This is bullshit, and we're done. Turn around and get out of here."

She began to close the door.

Okay, fine, he resolved. *No more Mr. Nice Guy...*

"Look," he protested while gesturing with both hands and stepping forward, "Can't you just –"

"One more step and I'll shoot you between the eyes, asshole," growled the guard. "Now *move!*"

There was a strange, just-visible twinkle in Kaysten's eyes, as he stared directly at the woman. His voice took on a purring, hypnotic quality as he chanted, "You know what, Ma'am? I fully understand where you're coming from... can't just let *anybody* walk in here and see the President, can you? So why don't you tell him, 'Jerry Kaysten's here with the most important news he'll ever get'... I'll head out and wait in the street, until he asks me in. Deal?"

The guard-woman did a half-stunned double-take and mumbled, "Yeah... alright... I'll tell him. Now you back off."

"For sure," replied Kaysten, as he did a polite head-salute, wheeled in place, reversed course down the pathway and jumped back over the gate.

It fucking worked! he exulted, while standing on the sidewalk.

"Jerry?" came Abruzzio's hidden voice. "What's going on?"

"All I can say is, 'I think I'll talk Massachusetts into going Republican, next election," insouciantly answered the former Chief of Staff. "Because if I can get away with what I just –"

At this point, the mansion's front-door opened, revealing a very familiar – though obviously older and grayer – face and figure, dressed in a night-robe.

"Jerry... Jerry *Kaysten?*" came the voice of the former Chief Executive. "That really *you?*"

"You *bet,* Mr. President!" shouted an elated Kaysten, as he again hand-vaulted over the closed gate and hurried up the pathway, stopping just in front of the man who had been his boss and mentor for untold years.

"But... but," uncertainly offered the President, "It *can't* be! You're... *dead!* I *saw* her kill you!"

"Don't believe everything you see on TV, sir," answered Kaysten, his eyes brimming with tears.

"My God... my *God,*" gasped the other. "Come *here,* son!"

At first, it was just a hand-shake; but in an instant, it turned into a heartfelt embrace.

"Man, is it good to see *you* again, sir," blubbered Kaysten.

"You too," mumbled the former President. "You'd... you'd better come inside, I guess."

"Just a sec, sir," requested the former Chief of Staff. "I've brought some friends with me. Sylvia? Oh, and you *too,* kid... but out of sight for now, if you don't mind."

"'Out of sight'?" asked the perplexed Chief Executive.

"Long story, sir," parried Kaysten. "Oh... *there* you are. Sir, let me introduce Sylvia Abruzzio, of the Jet Propulsion Laboratory –"

"Marnie," ordered the President, turning his head to address the guard-woman, "Release the gate, would you?"

Still appearing a bit dazed, the gun-toting door-person complied, and Abruzzio hastened down the path, accepting a handshake as she mounted the porch.

"It's a great honor, sir," she gushed. "To meet you again, I mean."

"Abruzzio... Abruzzio... oh, yeah... you were along with that other scientist, what was his name again, when we were talking with the alien –" he observed.

"Hector Ramirez," interjected the former JPL scientist. "But he's not with us, today... Jerry and I are alone... sort of. Sir, may we come inside? I don't think it's a good idea to be discussing what we have to tell you, here in the open."

"Oh... of course," he replied. "Come on in."

As Abruzzio and Kaysten (as well as the cloaked *Vìrya I'ëà'b'* and her canine co-pilot) followed the ex-President through the door and into the house, they quickly began to appreciate that if the man had been imprisoned, it was in the proverbial golden cage : the place was magnificently decked-out, with a Steinway grand piano, original paintings hung on walls, finely-woven carpets, expert interior decoration and, above all, a panoramic view of the AEDC Retention Reservoir. Down the slope from the lake-side part of the mansion, was a set of concrete steps leading to a jetty, at which was docked both a fast runabout and a large yacht, the latter much too big to have been practical on a body of water as relatively small as this makeshift lake.

A late-fifty-something wife, white-haired but quite pretty for her years, also dressed only in a housecoat, appeared in the entrance to one of the corridors leading from either side of the house's open-concept, central area.

"Clark? Clark!" she called. "What's going on, here? It's awfully late... you'll wake up Matt and Clairie. Whoa... who's *this?*"

"Oh, hi, Mrs. First Lady," politely responded the former Chief of Staff. "Remember me... Jerry Kaysten? White House... President's staff."

The woman did a double-take.

"Absolutely I remember you – but didn't they say you were dead?" she inquired.

"Like I just told the President," he smartly offered, "'Rumors of my demise are greatly exaggerated'. But listen, Ma'am, and Mr. President, sir – we've got a lot of very important information to explain, and we might not have much time in which to do it. I'd like to get to that as soon as possible, if you don't mind."

"You bet," agreed the former President. "You two park yourselves anywhere you want in the living-room, there. Can Marnie get you something to drink?"

I get to slurp the best booze there is, with the Old Man, as a friend... an equal, mused a frustrated Kaysten, *And because of this 'alien' crap, it won't even give me a buzz. One step forward, two steps back...*

"Cappuccino, if you've got any," requested a smiling Abruzzio.

"Same," shrugged Kaysten.

The ex-President motioned to the guard-woman, who, with a suspicious stare at the two newcomers, retreated to the kitchen and set about to brewing on its fine, Italian stainless-steel *barista*-gear. Then he ushered Abruzzio and Kaysten into the spacious, comfortable living-room, with small flickers coming from far-off dock-lights on the opposite side of the Reservoir, lending a peaceful atmosphere to the surroundings.

The President and his wife sat beside each other on one leather-bound couch, opposite the two more-than-humans.

"Well, Jerry," he observed, "This sure *is* an unexpected – but welcome – visit... like I said, I can't imagine how you survived what she did to you, but I'd be very interested to find out. Beforehand, though... I should mention what *I've* been dealing with. Bottom line is, they maneuvered me out... an 'offer I couldn't refuse', ha ha. I gave that son of a bitch at CIA a direct order to put an end to the campaign against the alien, on the hopes – probably futile I realize – that she might reciprocate; he refused outright and then got together with George and John to stage a *putsch*. Basically, it was 'you resign and hand the reigns of power to the VP, or something 'bad' might happen to you'. I might have taken my chances with that, but they threatened Kathy and the kids, too... I still had a lot of support within the Bureau and the military, but what with the damn Muslims and the alien at our doorstep, if I had stood my ground, the government might have ended up in a civil war with itself, when we could least afford it."

"So... here I am," he noted. "I get to do anything I want, as long as neither I nor my family leave these grounds, except for touring around the lake on my nice big yacht. Oh… and I get an escorted trip to the golf course, once per week... they close most of it, so that nobody sees me. Kind of takes the fun off of getting a birdie or a hole-in-one, you know?"

Kaysten hung his head, shook it ruefully and then looked up at his former Commander-In-Chief and replied, "Mr. President, with all due respect... if only Sylvia and I had as easy a time of it. Want to know what *we've* been up to?"

"By all means," answered the ex-President.

"So far," said Kaysten, drawing a breath, "Along with Jacobson, a FBI lady named 'Minnie Chu', the Storied Watcher's 'family' – the one that she was willing to blow up the whole country over – some or all of us have been carried by Her Alien Highness to Los Angeles, to Canada, and then to Amchitka in the Aleutians... that's where the Agency was running a big underground torture chamber, by the way."

"I was there, up on the island, Mr. President," commented Abruzzio. "The government tried repeatedly to kill both Karéin, her family, and us, using everything in its arsenal, up to and including dropping a hydrogen bomb on us. I still can't fathom why she didn't carry through with her threats, at that point. We came within a hair's-breadth of having the whole *country* destroyed, sir."

"Wait a minute... *wait* a minute," interrupted a confused and on-guard ex-President. "Anything that got done at that point, would have been on *George's* orders, not mine... but there's something I'm not getting, here."

"Yes, sir?" innocently replied the former JPL scientist.

"You said that they dropped a H-bomb on you?" he ventured.

"You *bet*, sir," she replied. "It was no more than a few kilometers away when it detonated... and we were caught right in the open."

"Well, excuse me for repeating what I asked of Jerry," he pressed, "But... why aren't you *dead?* After seeing the disaster in Mumbai, I thought that anyone *that* close to –"

Abruzzio turned to regard Kaysten.

"We've got to tell him *sometime*, Jerry," she remarked.

"Yeah, I suppose," he reluctantly agreed. "Listen, Mr. President, sir... before she says what she's going to say... I want you to understand... whatever's happened, I'm still good ol' Jerry Kaysten, the man who owes you his whole career – and I'd *die* for you, sir. As I well may have to, sooner or later."

"*Now* you're worrying me," carefully mentioned the ex-President. "So, Ms. Abruzzio... you were saying?"

"You wanted to know how we survived the terrible heat and radiation of that accursed thing, Mr. President, sir?" forcefully stated the scientist, staring straight at the man. "It was so powerful that those unlucky enough not to be with our group, were all killed instantly... at least, I *hope* they died quickly."

Her eyes began to shine like a kaleidoscope illuminated from behind, as she said, "The truth is... *I* stopped it, with the incredible powers given to me by the mighty Destroying Angel, Karéin-Mayréij... these are a small fraction of her own, but they are far, far beyond the reach or knowledge of mortal men. Jerry, too, has inherited a similar blessing, and it's partly what allowed him to survive Karéin's little, ahh, 'love-bite', which you saw him receive on that recording she left for you. I believe you've seen the TV reports on the activities of Sam Jacobson and the Mars mission team?"

His face blanching, the ex-President stammered, "Look... *look* – if you're here to kill me, for God's sake, just me, *please*, leave my family out of it –"

"Sir," responded Kaysten, leaning forward to speak forthrightly, "I said that I'd die defending you, and I *meant* it... killing you or your family, or allowing them to be hurt in any way, is the *last* thing that Sylvia or I want to do."

"That's, uhh, good to hear," nervously offered the ex-President. "The part about you not wanting to kill us, that is."

He grimaced and then called to the kitchen, "Marnie... can you put something nice and strong in my coffee, if you don't mind? Make it a *double*."

Abruzzio, whose eyes had now returned to normal, couldn't help laughing, and her chuckle was mimicked by another, much less easily-audible one, coming from somewhere near the ceiling.

While the ex-President and ex-First-Lady looked around in confusion, Kaysten continued, "But, sir... larger things are afoot, right now. The reason why we've come, is to get you and your family the hell out of here... and then, to put you back into the White House, while kicking George's ass – oh, and Bezomorton's, too – into next week. Don't mind saying, I never liked him... John, that is. Doesn't surprise me that he'd try to pull a stunt like this."

"Jerry, *Jerry* – I know we've worked together for years, son... but why would I want to do something like that? Like I said... I leave this place, they'll know it in five *minutes*... I won't make it to the outskirts of the airbase! And they've probably got this place bugged – they're listening to everything we're saying, so –"

"Just a minute, sir," interrupted Abruzzio.

She looked up and behind, at a spot just to one side of a finely-cut, modern-style, crystal chandelier.

"*Vîrya I'ëà'b'*," called the more-than-a-woman, "Do thou detect any of these 'spying-things'?"

There was a slight pause, and then Abruzzio added, "Very well... thank thee for being so, ahh, 'ahead-thinking'. Keep them covered with white noise, until the President and we are finished and on our way. Yes, sweetheart... I'll let you have a drink, in a few minutes... hold tight. Mommy loves you."

"With whom are you talking, Ms. Abruzzio?" asked the former First Lady.

"Oh, just the Storied Watcher's arm-shield," answered the scientist, with a diffident shrug. "Her name is '*Vîrya I'ëà'b*", or, in English, 'Daughter Tornado Diamond-Curtain'. Kind of apropos, don't you think? Considering that she can stop cannon-shells and slice army tanks in half, when she goes at 'em."

Again, the ex-President's visage took on a frightened look.

"Isn't that one of the things that she – the alien, I mean – used in that first encounter... down at the hotel, I mean?" he inquired.

"Indeed," insouciantly confirmed Abruzzio. "*Vîrya I'ëà'b*'... it is time thou show thyself. Come and lie on me, if thou please."

The ex-President would have leaped backward out of his chair, but for the fact that there was nowhere to go except right into a priceless Monet, as the weirding-shield blinked into view, rocketing from its ceiling-level vantage-point, to take a position above the scientist's lap, though there was something underneath it, as it was at least a foot off Abruzzio's knees.

"My... God," he stuttered, "That's really... *it*... the one that attacked...?"

As the scientist nodded confirmation, the weirding-shield gave off an annoying, high-pitched whine, but was quickly patted on the back, as one would do with the cute-looking little puppy that shimmered into view, underneath *Vîrya I'ëà'b*'.

"There, *there*, honey," consoled Abruzzio. "The President meant not to demean thee... he is not used to the likes of thee... but we will, uhh, bring him up to speed... will we not?"

The buckler let out a more convivial chirp, which, unfortunately, did not significantly help the ex-President's nervousness.

"How – how is it, that you've got that thing – I thought it was the alien's –" started the former U.S. leader.

Vîrya I'ëà'b' shook back and forth, with the cringe-inducing tone that she had emitted a moment ago.

"Mr. President," cautioned Abruzzio, "Please don't refer to her as an 'it', or a 'thing'... you'll insult her. *Vîrya I'ëà'b*' is, basically, just a child... admittedly, a somewhat, ahh, 'unusual' one. She's *extremely* intelligent, and actually not very hard to get along with, as long as you treat her with respect. Starting with, you've got to use 'thee' and 'thou', as pronouns... apparently, that's how they do it, in the Storied Watcher's native language. Oh, and by the way, the little lady in my lap here, is my companion, named 'Rainbow'. She's much more than a pet."

The dog let out a friendly "yip", lolled its tongue and settled down.

"Oh, and sir," spoke up a grinning Kaysten, "As to why *Vìrya I'ëà'b*'s here with us," – he said with a knowing wink – "She's kind of got a crush on me... decided to stick with me, on this little trip I took to find you." He added, in a whisper, "Don't want to disappoint the kid, you know? Gotta be *nice* to her."

At this point, the living shield darted out of Abruzzio's vicinity, coming to rest on the lap of the former Chief of Staff, just as the gun-woman was approaching with the coffee-service.

The nonplussed guard stopped dead in her tracks.

"What on God's Green Earth is *that?*" she questioned.

"Her name is '*Vìrya I'ëà'b*'," matter-of-factually stated Abruzzio. "She's a flying, lethally-powerful, bio-mechanical, sentient, self-aware, intelligent, non-human life-form. Is the coffee ready? I hope it's decent Cappuccino – like I used to get at Uncle Sal's restaurant back in Jersey, you know? But I guess nothing could quite equal *that.*"

She looked over at Kaysten and giggled. He reciprocated.

"What's that?" he mumbled. "Oh, *sure* thou can, kiddo... but no sudden moves with the lady – she's not used to thee yet, thou know? Man... this 'thee' and 'thou' stuff's hard to get used to!"

"That's just because you never took Latin in grade school, like some of us Catholic girls had to, Jerry," serenely offered Abruzzio, with a wry smile.

The former Chief of Staff looked up. "'Marnie'... that's your name, right?" he said. "Just stand there, and when 'Daughter Tornado Diamond-Curtain' here gets under your serving-tray, let go of it... she'll do the rest."

Before the guard-woman could react, *Vìrya I'ëà'b*' had positioned herself as Kaysten had predicted. The move was timely, because a startled Marnie (more out of alarm than compliance) dropped the exquisitely-decorated, wrought-silver serving-tray, complete with four small demi-tasses, and quickly retreated to what she imagined was a safe vantage-point. The tray, meanwhile, was instantly caught and stabilized by the Storied Watcher's weirding-shield, which then floated over to a spot within the ex-President's easy reach.

For a few seconds, he froze, staring with obvious fear; but then, he relaxed slightly, muttering, "Well... if it's – uhh, sorry, she's – going to slice me in half... I might as well have a last drink, beforehand... right?"

A friendly-sounding "chirp" came from *Vìrya I'ëà'b*' as the ex-President reached for a cup with his initials inscribed; then, the buckler floated to one side to serve the former First Lady, who seemed somewhat more at ease with what was going on. After this, *Vìrya I'ëà'b*' offered the last two demi-tasses to Abruzzio and Kaysten, darted to a nearby dining-table, unloaded the silver serving-tray, and then returned to land on the more-than-a-man's lap.

"That's... that's, quite a 'pet' you've got yourself, there, Jerry," offered the former U.S. leader.

"Ahh... if only she were, a 'pet', that is," replied Kaysten. "More like a kid who follows you home from school, and you kind of know you shouldn't have her tagging along – but you don't want to upset her, by telling her to go away."

“Yeah,” agreed the ex-President, with a forced half-smile. “So, Ms. Abruzzio... what you and Jerry have shown Kathy and I so far is little short of amazing – and there is a lot that I don't yet know about the back-story here, believe you me I want to be filled in on the details, eventually – but what, precisely, do you want of me?”

“The short answer to that question, sir,” requested Abruzzio, her dark eyes staring intensely, “Is, we want you to re-take control of the Presidency – in so doing, wresting it away from the current occupant of your former office, who is currently rapidly leading the country into total ruin. Then, we want you to meet Karéin herself, and explain to her – which I hope you *can* do, with complete honesty – what the hell happened between the government and her, in those crucial few days after she crashed down to Earth after destroying the 'Lucifer' comet. Mr. President, you *must* gain the Storied Watcher's trust, and if that means getting down on your knees and apologizing to her for the misdeeds done to Bob Billings, the Claremonts and, especially, Tommy – not to mention another child about whom you're probably not yet aware – then that's exactly what you're going to have to do! I'm basing this on the assumption that the entire mess was some kind of colossal mistake... because if not...”

“That's, uhh... *complicated*, Ms. Abruzzio,” evaded the ex-President.

“No, it's *not*,” she defiantly countered. “I may not be an expert in the workings of the Executive Branch, but of *this* much, I'm sure : *someone*, gave the order for Karéin's 'family' – not to mention the entire Jacobson team – to be tortured, presumably to the point of death. Was it you? If so, this meeting is over with, our quest will end in failure, God help the United States of America, and... God help *you*.”

The former U.S. leader abruptly put his coffee-cup to one side, got up and began to pace in front of the picture-window, with his back to those in the living-room.

“Are you *sure* you want to know the answer to that?” he challenged. “I can give it to you, on one condition : do whatever you want to me – but leave my family *out* of it! Deal?”

“No – no deal!” loudly protested the former First Lady, who also came to her feet. “Madam, I don't know *who* you think you are, waltzing in here and making threats against my husband, but I won't *stand* for it! Clark, we've *got* to call the police –”

The ex-President took his wife in his arms and whispered something to her, while gently shaking his head. Abruzzio and Kaysten could easily have overheard it, but they chose not to.

“Ma'am, I completely understand why you're upset, and if it reassures you any, if either Jerry or I had come here as assassins, your husband – and anyone who stood in our way – would already be dead,” answered Abruzzio. “Mr. President – I don't have a grudge against you, although I suppose I'm entitled to one... that probably goes for most of those upon whom Karéin has bestowed the formidable powers that Jerry and I, now possess. But we *must* know the truth, before we try to engineer a counter-*coup* to put you back in the White House. We cannot take the chance of doing this and then being, in the eyes of the Storied Watcher, 'accessories after the fact', to the abuse and attempted murder, of her loved ones. In that case, *we* might be at risk, ourselves. What is the truth? The *truth*, sir – *out* with it!"

"Sir," added Kaysten, "I want you to know that whatever the answer, I'll be sticking with you, come hell or high water... Sylvia's damn smart, but neither she – nor almost all the rest of them hanging around Her Nuclear Highness – have ever been in the Executive Branch... no reflection on her, but I don't think any of them understand the trade-offs that we always had to make, just to keep the country from coming completely apart at the seams. I bet it *is*, 'complicated'... and if you tell me to, it'll just stay between you and me. I can't speak for Sylvia, of course."

"No, Jerry… you can't," observed the former JPL scientist. "I have to know, and I can't be bound by that promise... although I *will* be discreet in who I entrust the truth to."

There was a long, tense silence, and then, after turning to face the group, the ex-President again began to speak.

"You want the *truth*, then?" he glowered. "Okay – here it is. I *did* authorize some of the, uhh, 'measures', taken against the alien's so-called 'family' – but not willingly, and so help me God, it was the greatest mistake I could ever have made. The whole rotten idea was cooked up by the CIA director, basically; he had this stupid plan that if we inflicted enough, uhh, 'discomfort' on the alien's loved ones, the feedback would somehow kill her –"

Abruzzio's baleful stare caught him in mid-sentence, and he froze.

"Well, Mr. President," she coldly remarked, "If you ever see that son of a bitch again, you can tell him, his vicious little trick *almost* worked... we were with Karéin on at least one such occasion, and the pain that you vicariously inflicted on her, rendered her unconscious. A bunch of us came to her rescue, or she might have died, right there. But you can *also* tell him, that it won't work any more, although it *will* probably get her attention in a way you wouldn't want to. Like any goddess, she evolves – she learns how to defend. She's had hundreds of thousands of years, in which to learn how to defeat this kind of crude attack. So these atrocities were to absolutely *no* purpose; all they did was needlessly antagonize and enrage the most powerful being in this Solar System. I hope you're *happy* with yourself!"

"No, Ms. Abruzzio – I'm *not!*" angrily shouted the ex-President. "Do you think I *wanted* things to turn out this way? It was all a *monumental* fuck-up, from beginning to end! I only found out about it after the Agency had gone off and started it without my knowledge or consent, which I only reluctantly gave, *ex post facto*, when this 'Storied Watcher' you seem so enamored of, threatened to kill me, and then destroy the entire *country!* After I saw what a disaster had come of it, I tried to rescind the order, and was then ushered out of office by that weasel CIA director, who, I think, had been conspiring with George, right from Day One. Call me weak – call me stupid – if you must... but I was *not* the one behind the plan to hurt the alien... at least not at first. If I must be judged, then those are your facts."

Kaysten sent a long, declarative stare at his distaff companion.

"See, Sylvia? *See?*" he argued. "What did I *tell* you? When you're in a job like his, none of the decisions – none of the trade-offs – are simple ones! Mr. President, sir... I can't speak for *her*, but there's no doubt in *my* mind, that you're telling the truth. And that my trust in you, was one hundred per cent, justified. I'm with you, sir... whatever may come."

With a tear in his eye, the ex-U.S. leader looked down at the finest-Afghan-carpeted floor and quietly replied, "Thank you, son... thank you *so* much."

Now Abruzzio got up, allowing her puppy to roam hither and yon, not caring if a little tinkle or two ended up on the beautiful short-shag. The former JPL scientist joined the ex-President by the picture-window.

"Sir," she inquired, in a subdued tone, "Is that *really* the truth? You're not leaving anything out? If it's of any interest... within Karéin's circle of friends, we have several people with a supernatural ability to detect lies. So if I were you..."

"Yeah... God help me... it *is*," he confirmed, with a sad sigh. "And you know what the *funny* thing is, Ms. Abruzzio? I was actually looking forward to meeting the alien, in person... after the comet business, that is. After all, I had spoken to her, while she was with Jacobson and the other astronauts, on the way back from Mars. I thought she was a fascinating being, who might have been able to lead us into... I don't know... something, 'better', I guess. If *only* I had this one to do over."

"You know, sir," she quietly offered, "I have no idea whatsoever, how Karéin would react, if she knew what Jerry and I have just heard. There was a time, I'm sure, when if she *had* heard, she'd have disintegrated you – or worse, and yes, there *is* 'worse' – on the spot. But since we have rescued most of those who she loves and cares for... she's, uhh, 'mellowed' a bit, is how I'd describe it. Whether that would get you off with just a warning... I honestly can't say."

"That's not much of an incentive to camp on to your project, Ms. Abruzzio," noted the ex-President. "If the alien's planning to kill me, I might as well spend as much time as remains, with Kathy and my family."

"Oh, *Clark!*" sobbed the former First Lady, as she buried her head in his shoulder.

Kaysten had now joined them by the window. He stated, "I won't let her do anything to you, sir. That's a *promise*."

The ex-President shook a finger at his former Chief of Staff.

"Jerry," he admonished, "I don't want to hear anything more like that... most of this occurred while you were either out of the loop, or physically under the control of the alien – it's between her and me… not her and you."

"But –" he stammered.

"Look, Mr. President," interjected Abruzzio, "I'll admit that this wasn't the greatest of news, but there's no way that you can change what's already been done; and hanging around here just waiting for the Storied Watcher to show up with blood in her eye – as certainly she will, at some point – isn't going to *improve* your chances. I don't personally believe that she means to harm you anymore... but I can't be so sanguine about some of the rest of them – Tommy George and possibly Bob Billings, in particular –"

"Tommy... George?" confusedly replied the ex-President. "Wasn't he just a kid? I remember seeing a briefing saying that he was a native Indian, who she claimed to have 'adopted' –"

"Check those assumptions at the door, Mr. President, sir," commented Kaysten. "That little bugger's *dangerous* – and not just because he'll key your car or something."

"What do you mean?" asked the former U.S. leader.

"Sir," demanded Abruzzio, "Now, we must entrust *you* with a secret of our own... one that you and your wife should reveal only if *absolutely* necessary. Especially, it should not be divulged to anyone within the military or the intelligence agencies. Do we have your word?"

"Yes, I suppose," he replied.

"And you, Ma'am?" pressed Abruzzio.

"Of course," stated the former First Lady.

"Sir," elaborated the scientist, "What Jerry refers to is, simply being in the close physical proximity of Karéin-Mayréij – if she regards you as her friend or loved-one, that is – *changes* a person. You become something more than a human being, yet less than Karéin herself. Every one of us who have traveled with her, has undergone this transformation, though its exact effects differ dramatically from person to person –"

"Wait a minute," he interrupted. "Is this, that '*Fire*' thing, that I found out about, from Jacobson and the other three astronauts?"

"Yes," she confirmed. "The 'change' gives you the ability to use the Storied Watcher's primary power, called '*Amaiish*' or '*The Fire*'... there are many other effects, all beneficial as far as we've so far been able to tell. The point is, sir, that everyone within Karéin's party – including Tommy George, who's very close to the Storied Watcher and who has therefore inherited a lot of her native abilities – has their own 'alien-powers'. Tommy could *easily* kill you, or any ordinary human being for that matter, if he wanted to... and, having been cruelly tortured for days on end, he certainly has a motive to do so. Same goes for Bob Billings, and potentially a few others as well. See where I'm going with this?"

"Could he kill *you?* Or... Jerry?" carefully inquired the ex-President.

Abruzzio looked away, and then shot a kaleidoscopic stare at the former U.S. leader, with a hint of her war-song playing from everywhere and nowhere.

"I honestly don't know," she admitted. "My own abilities are... *formidable*, and Jerry's – while I think he's somewhat behind me – are catching up fast."

"Fast," exulted Kaysten, flexing his muscles. "Yeah. *Fast*. Like the sound of that!"

"What's that music?" asked the former First Lady. "It's like I'm hearing it in my head – stirring, exciting –"

"My 'war-song', Ma'am," replied the scientist. "A warning to evil-doers, a blessing to those of us, who follow the Light... not sure what else, on top of that. We each have our own. You should hear Karéin's one... it sort of communicates, 'you'd have to be *nuts*, to try and fight me'. And how very true that is."

"Air Force reported something like that," observed the ex-President.

"You have to understand, Mr. President," continued Abruzzio, as the ethereal music was diminishing, "That while she ordered us never to fight one another, she never addressed the question of what might happen if one or more of us, tried to harm, someone like you. All I can say is, Jerry's not kidding : I've seen Tommy's powers in action, before – Bob's, too – and I sure wouldn't want them aimed at me. I might take them down with me... cold comfort if I'm dead."

"Just out of interest, Ms. Abruzzio," inquired the ex-President, "What exactly are these 'powers' of yours? If you don't mind my asking."

"Oh, I do 'radiation'," she *faux*-innocently mentioned. "All *kinds* of it, from below visible wavelengths to X-Rays and beyond. And as I'm sure you're aware, ionizing radiation with enough energy poured into it... is *extremely* dangerous. Since it's mostly invisible, it can cripple and kill you before you're even aware that anything's amiss… you know?"

"I'll *bet*," he nervously agreed. "Jerry?"

"I run fast... *real* fast," proudly responded the former Chief of Staff. "Faster than even Sylvia yet knows. And I got a few other tricks up my sleeve, as well."

"Is this, uhh, 'transformation', affecting Kathy and I, right now?" asked the ex-President. "Does it affect your judgment? Because I want no part of it –"

"I don't believe so, sir," stated the scientist. "It doesn't seem to be transmissible past the first generation... that is, you have to be directly exposed to Karéin herself, and for more than a few minutes, before it takes hold. Whether it would pass, for example, to the biological children of one or more of us 'more-than-humans', is anyone's guess – it's something that I plan to research, when and if the present crisis is properly dealt with. And I can personally attest that becoming a 'super-human' has no effect on one's free will... except, maybe, to see things as they really are, as opposed to what one's been told."

"Well, *that's* nice to know," he ruefully attested. "Listen... can you give Kathy and I a few minutes alone? We need to discuss this."

"Certainly," politely responded Abruzzio. "Just as long as you understand that calling the police – or anyone – while our back is turned, would be a *terrible* mistake. We'd have to, uhh, 'shoot our way out', and that would likely be very hazardous for everyone in the vicinity... you know?"

"You have my word that I'll do no such thing – nor will anyone here," he quickly answered. "I appreciate you having been so, uhh, frank with me, Ms.

Abruzzio... and I won't put Jerry's safety at risk, especially after seeing him again, after I thought he'd bought the farm."

"Neither will I allow you to be hurt, sir," firmly vowed Kaysten, to an appreciative nod from his former Commander-In-Chief.

"I trust you, sir," acknowledged the more-than-a-woman, as she motioned to Rainbow, *Vîrya I'ëà'b'* and Kaysten.

"Come on," she requested. "Let's wait outside, on the front porch."

The two (plus puppy-dog and weirding-shield) had waited out front for an unusually long amount of time, so much in fact that as a precautionary measure, Abruzzio had sent *Vîrya I'ëà'b'* around to the lakeside-facing part of the house to verify that the ex-President hadn't reneged on his promise; but thankfully, the cause of the delay was apparently nothing more than a drawn-out argument between the former U.S. leader and his wife. 'Daughter Tornado Diamond-Curtain' also reported that there were two more "hoo-mans" in the living-room, but that these did not appear to be armed or in uniform.

Abruzzio knocked on the door, calling, "Sir, it's been enough time... may we come in?" This entreaty went initially unanswered, but presently, the guard-woman opened the portal and the scientist, accompanied by Kaysten, Rainbow and the again-uncloaked *Vîrya I'ëà'b'*, re-entered the mansion.

They stood at the threshold of the living-room, and noticed that the ex-President and First Lady had been joined by a handsome, dark-haired, clean-cut Caucasian man, probably in his early twenties, as well as a somewhat younger, light-brown-haired teenage girl.

"Oh... I guess you didn't yet meet Matt – my son, and Clarisse – my daughter," remarked the former President. "The commotion got them out of bed, I'm afraid. Matt, Clairie... this is Ms. Sylvia Abruzzio, of the Jet Propulsion Laboratory, and Jerry Kaysten, who I think you may have met in earlier days, back at the White House. The dog belongs to Ms. Abruzzio, and that thing hovering by him – uhh, excuse me, I meant, 'that little *girl* – is called 'veer-ya ee-ab'... hope I pronounced it correctly?"

Vîrya I'ëà'b' let out a friendly-sounding "chirp".

"*Neaattt,*" gushed the amazed and curious teenage girl. "Is that the one that belongs to –"

"Umm-hmm," confirmed Abruzzio. "She's a real sweetheart – just like little Rainbow, here – but I wouldn't want to get on the *bad* side of her. Nice to meet you, Clarisse... Matt. Mr. President? Do you have a decision for us?"

There was a pained look on the former U.S. leader's face, but eventually he forced out, "Kathy and I have thought about this very carefully, but I'm afraid the answer has to be 'no', Ms. Abruzzio."

The crestfallen ex-scientist hung her head and slumped into a nearby chair.

"That's... *very* disappointing, sir," she managed. "Any particular reason?"

“A lot of them,” he carefully replied. “Starting with, 'I go with you two – you *four* – and my family's likely to be the first thing that George and the Agency go after. In case you hadn't noticed, when it comes to 'matters of national security', CIA *doesn't* play by Marquis of Queensbury rules. Add to that, the fact that you appear to have no way to get me somewhere, like the White House or Air Force One, for example, where I could try to take charge of the government – and even *then*, to put it mildly, there'd be no more than a 50-50 chance that the Secret Service and the military would support me, especially if George was still there, calling the shots.”

“But, *sir*,” implored the scientist, “I'm *sure* that we could –”

“Look, Madam,” interrupted the ex-President, “Above and beyond all that, the risks to an initiative of this type are *enormous* – like, possibly causing a civil war with one wing of the government fighting another – and the only potential 'winner', as far as I can tell, seems to be this 'alien'-friend of yours. I'm sure she'd like nothing better than to have the military completely paralyzed by internal in-fighting, when she picks her next landmark to topple. What's in it for *me*... for America? Sorry, Ms. Abruzzio; as little as I like what George and the Agency director have done to me, I'm *not* willing to risk the stability of the government, leaving it at the mercy of the Muslims, or your 'Storied Watcher'... or both of them. I know you may not agree with my reasoning... but there it is.”

“Sylvia,” consoled Kaysten, “He's *right*, you know. What the V-P's done stinks on eighteen levels, but the one thing that he *is* doing, is... governing. The Old Man shows up there out of the blue and tries to take over, the first thing they'll say is, 'he's just under the control of Miss Nuclear Goddess, we can't trust anything he says', and *that'll* be *that*. The most that we'll accomplish is to get a lot of people killed, and not change a damn *thing* about who runs this country.”

The President's son stepped back and into a hallway. Abruzzio and her entourage could tell this was because some kind of an alert-light had begun to blink, on his mobile communicator.

“Pretty much bang-on,” offered the ex-President. “Jerry, I should have promoted you... while I still could.”

Abruzzio stood up, muttering, “Gee, thanks for the *support*, Jerry.”

“Mr. President, sir,” she quietly demanded, “There's a great deal about Karéin – and us – that you don't yet know. I think – I *hope* – that if you did hear the whole story, you might change your mind... or, at least, work with us, to figure out some alternate plan of action. Sir, although the Storied Watcher's off the warpath for now, in my opinion, it's only a matter of time until the current Administration undertakes some other stupid, provocative move, which sets us back to Square One; in which case, this country will be in for something much worse than an intra-agency dispute. We *need* you, sir!”

They heard a peevish complaint from the hallway, to the effect of, “Come on, come *on* – why isn't it *working!*”

“Matt,” remonstrated the ex-President, “Could you keep it down a bit, please? We're talking *business*, in here.”

"Oh, yeah... sorry, Dad," apologized the twenty-something. "It's just that the 'Ultra-Emergency-News' beacon on my mobile's going apeshit... but I can't get the actual video or audio on it – all I'm seeing is a bunch of interference. Just got it brand-new, two weeks ago, too!"

"Well," sighed Abruzzio, "We can accomplish at least *one* thing tonight, I guess. *Vîrya I'ëà'b'*... would thou be nice enough to un-jam that young man's techno-box?"

An elated look on Matt's face, upon seeing the high-quality video appear immediately on his mobile communicator, quickly changed to one of awe and consternation.

"Dad," he called, "You'd better come see this."

The daughter hurried over to regard what was displayed on the communicator. She, too, did an astonished, wary, double-take.

"Later," countered the ex-President. "Son, I don't think you understand how important this conversation really is. Now, Ms. Abruzzio... like I was saying –"

"Dad," interrupted the son, "I *really* think you need to see this."

"*Look*, young man," retorted an irritated former U.S. leader, "Anything on that damn thing, will have to wait until –"

Now it was Clairie's turn to take a chance with her father's patience.

"Daddy," announced the wide-eyed teenager, "The astronauts have taken over Fort Knox."

Here's Our "Ask", Major

The sounds of mayhem – repeated gunfire and explosions, as well as a spreading pall of smoke – to the north-west, were still very much evident, during a temporary lull in the fighting around the Repository. Though the walls of the stoutly-constructed, squat building were now riddled with bullet-impressions and scorch-marks, there hadn't been a lot of shooting for about the last twenty minutes.

Admittedly, there was a very good reason, for that : advance parties of Special Ops forces who had tried to approach the Repository from the north and west, were met with a hail of blazing, intensely-hot fireballs from some unknown opponent, firing from a protected, inside position. Those trying to infiltrate from the south and east, received a similarly unpleasant welcome; only in this case, the attack – no less lethal, though it appeared to be deliberately aimed low on the first few volleys, perhaps as a warning-shot – was a spinning, icicle-spewing, dimly-blue jet of agonizingly-cold, something-or-other-energy. Army snipers cursed their inability to get a good imaging infra-red scope fix on whomever was firing at them; there were veritable clouds of blazing heat and Stygian cold floating randomly around the facility, and these – possibly something else, as well – were playing havoc with all the fancy electronic targeting systems.

Wisely, the siege force had backed off to build entrenchments, while waiting for a vertical envelopment force from the airbase to drop from above and clear out the strange terrorist gang that had invaded this temple of lucre.

A wary semi-calm had descended over the area, when, to the surprise of the encamped, encircling U.S. Army Fort Knox Recapture Force, as well as to the small contingent of local media who had somehow managed to sneak into a position far enough forward to have a good look at the front of the Repository, its huge, metal-bound door opened.

The soldiers (as well as those of the media with the forethought to have brought a long-distance, parabolic microphone) were astonished, at what came next, through the portal : a lone figure of a pretty big guy, who was encased from head to toe in a weird-looking, dimly-glowing thing that resembled a crystal matrix, sort of like a body-suit made up from parts of a chandelier. This strange being's appearance was accompanied by an announcement blaring over the Repository's obviously-commandeered loudspeaker system.

"Attention, soldiers of the U.S. Army, and you GrayWar peeps!" it called, in a voice that they could just tell sounded, African-American. "Please don't shoot – we'd like to deliver a message, not get any more of y'all killed... y'all can't hurt any of us... but there's still some human folks with us in here, and we don't want them to end up like 'collateral damage'."

"Cease fire!" shouted the field-commander. "But be ready to resume on my mark!"

Despite the government's most diligent efforts, this was front-page news, everywhere; and it was being covered in real-time – even by the Disney Network, which was delighted to see that for some hard-to-understand reason, the government's insta-censorship tools seemed to be either turned off, or were, perhaps, malfunctioning.

The crystal-man proceeded forward, slowly and deliberately, until he was about ten feet outside the door.

"Send one or two guys forward, so we can deliver our message," announced the loudspeaker. "We give y'all our word that they won't be hurt."

There was almost a minute of confused, back-and-forth discussion within the Army camp; then, the local second-in-command, along with a bodyguard of two MPs, walked past the now-wrecked guard-posts, to a point just on the outside of the Repository's outermost protective fence; the barrier had a number of bullet-holes, but was otherwise still closed and intact.

"I am Major Benjamin Tauk, First Armored Division," spoke the military-man. "I'll agree to a ten-minute cessation of hostilities so we can communicate... but you – whoever you are – need to know, that I have orders to re-take this facility, forthwith, regardless of casualties – including several deaths and serious injuries among my personnel – for which you will be held criminally liable. I have massive military force at my disposal, and I will not hesitate to use it, to achieve my objective. Now if you have something to say... I'd get it over with."

There was a short pause, and then the crystal-man replied, although those present could not figure out how the sound of his words was passing through the pseudo-armor that enveloped him.

"First of all, Major Tauk," he said, "My name is Commander Sam Jacobson, formerly of the Mars exploration mission, and on behalf both of myself and my crew-members, we sincerely regret any loss of life, which, I will attest, occurred when members of my force were attacked; we returned fire only in self-defense. We can't do anything about that, but we'd greatly prefer not to run up the casualty count any more than has already happened. You speak of 'massive military force'; well, sir, I can assure you, that neither you, nor anyone in the government, has a *chance* of defeating the forces that I have under my personal control. Please don't make us demonstrate this superiority."

"I'm not going to debate that, here," growled Tauk. "I'll only state that I am completely confident of my forces' ability to successfully complete our mission. You said you had a 'message'? Now would be the time to relate that."

"Very well," evenly replied Jacobson, from inside his shimmering, crystalline fortress. "Here it is, and it's meant both for the American people, and the man falsely calling himself 'President'... *especially*, him. First of all, my crew and I – all of whom have inherited a variety of extremely powerful supernatural abilities from the being called 'Karéin-Mayréij', who you also know of as the 'Storied Watcher' – are now in complete control of the United States Bullion Repository –"

"Not for long, you're not," interrupted Tauk. "But go on."

"Just *try* to dislodge us, Major!" retorted the more-than-human. "We'll maintain our position here, until we can verify that the President, the Director of the CIA and the entire Cabinet, as well as other officials to be determined on a case-by-case basis, are being tried by the Congress under articles of impeachment for high crimes and misdemeanors, specifically including but not limited to staging an illegal *coup d'etat*, large-scale kidnapping, illegal confinement, torture and murder, war atrocities, criminal use of nuclear weapons against a civilian population, and other flagrant violations of the Constitution, the Bill of Rights, not to mention a wide range of other applicable domestic and international laws. The exact details of the comprehensive and damning evidence against the President, in this matter, are now being provided to the public via a series of NeoNet communiques. We have ensured that no matter how carefully the government tries to suppress this information, any such efforts will be futile."

"Oh, I see," sneered the other man. "And just *how* are you going to get him to do this, might I ask?"

"That's all been thought out, my friend," firmly stated Jacobson. "We'll give the President twenty-four hours to surrender himself to the impeachment proceedings, counting from ten minutes after this discussion between yourself and myself, is completed. If he complies, we will proceed to the Capitol Buildings to provide eyewitness testimony which proves the President's guilt, although we will not surrender to the authority of the courts ourselves, until the impeachment proceedings have come to a satisfactory end."

"There isn't a *chance* he'll do that, you know," curtly offered the army commander. "You're wasting your *time*, mister! And you have no way out of here... we'll cut you down, the second that you step out of that building, again."

"Oh, I don't think that's going to happen, Major," countered Jacobson, "Because we could easily break out any time we wanted to, and heaven help the man who stands in our way; but in the short term, we choose not to do so. You see, for every hour past the deadline that the President fails to show, my team is authorized to destroy – that is, chemically alter, at the atomic and molecular level – one-tenth of the bullion reserves of this Repository. After we're done with each such batch, it will no longer be gold, and therefore, it will be of zero currency value; oh, and by the way, it will also be rendered *intensely* radioactive."

"How you figure you're going to do *that?*" incredulously demanded Tauk.

"Just wait and *see*," growled the crystal-titan, "We have powers you can't even begin to imagine. And when we're done with the last ten per cent, we'll be on our way to attack other economic assets, until we've reduced this country's ability to finance the government, to, precisely... *nothing*. We'll refrain from going after the President personally, within the first twenty-four-hour period; but if he refuses to submit to the impeachment proceedings, after that point, all bets are off; we *will* target the President, as well as anyone directly defending him, for immediate termination with lethal force. It is only a matter of time, until we locate him and bring him to justice. To sum up, sir, however risky such a venture may be for my team and I, we'd far prefer to seek justice through the Constitution, via the legal mechanism of impeachment, and the outcome for the President – and the country – will be far easier, if that's the route taken. If he's stupid enough to defy us... well, you don't want to know, what will happen, in that case. Do I make myself clear?"

"Yeah," muttered Tauk. "Delusional... but, clear enough, that's for sure. Is there anything else?"

"As a matter of fact... there is... there, *are*." confirmed Jacobson. "Two things."

"What?" asked the army-man.

"First... as you know from an earlier discussion we had with the media," calmly explained the former Mars mission commander, "Major Brent Boyd, one of the key members of my team, warned the Administration against threatening or harming any of his family-members or loved-ones. I'd like to amplify that warning, here and now : to everyone in the military or law enforcement, if you hurt or imprison anyone associated with my team, including those members who the government knows about but the public doesn't... we won't stop pursuing you until we've hunted you down and *utterly* destroyed you. If you have to disobey an order and go to jail for so doing, for God's sake, don't hesitate to do that... your own life is at stake."

"I don't think they'll find that very convincing," grunted the army-man.

"If they don't, they'll find out why they should have," riposted Jacobson. "And the second thing is for you, and your troops. Like I said, Major... I'm military, myself, and I know all about following orders – but there's a difference between 'bravery' and 'suicide'. Without getting into details, let me just say, the members of my team have various ways of defending ourselves, and many of them are inherently very destructive. So I'm asking you, soldier-to-soldier – lay back, take it easy, at least until we can see what the President's going to do. It makes me *sick* to think what will, without a shade of a doubt, happen to your troops, if they're ordered to do a frontal assault against my team. I don't want any more deaths on my conscience, Major. Don't make us fire back at you."

"'Don't want any 'more' deaths'... do I have that *right?*" derisively shouted Tauk. "That's r*ich.* Want to explain your tender feelings to the families of the grunts out back, who that, uhh, whoever the hell he is, blew to pieces, a few minutes ago? I have ten dead and at least six more who may not live till tomorrow morning. You're gonna *answer* for that, mister, sooner or later. I mean to make it, 'sooner'. Get it?"

"Yeah," quietly responded the former Mars mission commander. "Maybe I will... after the President's answered for the thousands, who *he* has cruelly tortured and murdered. I think I'll have a much easier time of explaining my actions, than he will have for *his*. Get it?"

There was an icy pause, and then the army-man said,

"Are we done?"

"I think so," agreed Jacobson.

Tauk gave a stiff salute, wheeled in place and began a brisk walk back to his encampment, while the crystal-encased-man, ever facing straight forward, slowly retreated behind the Repository doors, which shut tight behind him.

Not On My Signature

"There it is," evenly remarked the tallish, young, callow, clean-shaven Christian man, reflexively checking his neck for a tie that wasn't there, as he peered out the plain-white, delivery-van window. He was dressed, as were the four others, in a nondescript brown, GrayWar-subsidiary, civilian-contractor uniform.

Far down the runway, a 747-derivative jumbo-jet, replete with windows and dark-green "World Wide Airways" markings like an ordinary civilian airliner (but featuring various, non-standard, bulbous fairings and antennas) had just rolled to a slow stop, not too far from the end of this "just-long-enough" Air National Guard landing-strip, with its left side facing the terminal.

"Yeah... Lord's deliverin' His blessing on La Crosse," grunted an older, shorter, muscular, olive-skinned man. "Sorry for askin' all those questions back there, Brother... just that if we get this *wrong*..."

"It's okay," contemplatively answered the leader. "I checked three hotels there... orders were the same in two, and so what if the third said that they couldn't find the message. Just lucky we got here in time, if only that. Another few minutes... *anyway*. Let's get ready – you all know the drill? We only get one kick at *this* can."

The other men silently nodded confirmation.

"Let's *do* it," said Brother Martin, as he re-started the engine and proceeded through the dark, closed-down streets, to the only checkpoint leading directly from Madison Boulevard to the Volk Field tarmac. They got intermittent glances of the jumbo-jet, which was slowly pivoting on its multi-wheeled under-carriage, evidently in preparation for taxiing to a spot nearer to the military airfield's main control tower.

The Christian man felt reasonably confident; after all, there had already been one check at the front gates to Camp Douglas, and they had gotten past *that*, with little to-do, other than for a perfunctory check of faked ID credentials.

A stern-faced young Caucasian military policeman, coincidentally quite similar in build and complexion to Brother Martin himself, stopped them at the security gateway. This, the Christian strike-force-leader noted with interest, consisted nothing except a small, single-story building and a standard, eight-foot-tall, metal-lattice fence; there wasn't even any barbed-wire, though there were two other uniformed soldiers working at desk-jobs, visible through the picture-windows providing a perspective on the building's interior.

"Halt!" called the soldier. "Who goes there? State your business."

"Supplies," calmly replied the van-driver, offering a pleasant, vapid smile, as he spoke. "Spare parts, repairs that is... for the aircraft."

"Schedule communicated to us was that this was just a refueling stop," challenged the MP. "There's nothing on it, indicating a supply-load... and it's gotta be inspected, beforehand. You got a Secret Service clearance certificate for the cargo? And I need to see your badges. How many in the vehicle with you, mister?"

"Oh, yeah... here's all the paperwork and such," smartly answered Brother Martin, while handing a smart-paper form with an elaborate set of stamps and signatures on it, along with five expertly-falsified identity cards, each complete with a corresponding smart-chip and X.709 encryption code. "See?"

"Just a minute," requested the soldier. He used a computer-device to scan the identity-cards. His expression did not change as he shone a flashlight on the document.

"'Replacement Secondary Galley APU' and sanitary components, eh?" queried the MP. "What's *that* for?"

"Not sure, honestly, sir," coolly responded the Christian man. "Got a requisition from GW Legion Federal Special Projects Branch about 'food prep heaters on the plane are acting up, Old Man's complaining about his steaks being over-cooked, and the dishes aren't getting cleaned spic 'n span', or something like that – we just deliver the goods where we're told and go on to the next one, you know?"

It's not a sin to lie in the service of God, he reassured himself.

"Hmmph," hesitated the soldier. "Well... I don't know. Hold here for a minute."

It was the longest minute that Brother Martin had ever endured; well, okay, the *second*-longest, after once having been given a private dressing-down by his blessed leader, upon the latter having found an "unauthorized" translation of the Good Book, in Brother Martin's seminary sleeping-quarters. But eventually, just as the jumbo-jet rolled to a gradual stop in front of the airfield control-tower, the MP returned. Oddly, he went around to the back of the van, though he was still just visible from the driver's-side of the vehicle.

"Don't like 'surprises'," he grumbled, "But the paperwork seems to be in order, at least. Okay – open her up, I'll have to ride in the back."

"Uhh... *what?*" uneasily replied the startled Christian strike-force-leader.

"Oh, for fuck's *sake*... didn't they give you GrayWar dickheads any training at *all,* on this kind of thing?" complained the MP. "No… I guess not… right? Standard protocol for loading or unloading a Class 3 or higher Federal vessel or aircraft – positive military or Service control over all cargo, at all stages in the process. Just a quick visual inspection, I sign off on the manifest with the aircraft quartermaster down on the runway, and up she goes. Any of that unclear?"

"Oh, no... uhh... very clear," stammered Brother Martin. "Just a second – I'll let 'em know."

Thinking as quickly as possible, he returned his head into the van, turned and whispered, "He gets wise – you know what to do?"

There was grave determination dimly visible on the faces of the four faithful in the darkened rear-part of the vehicle, as they nodded acknowledgment.

A latch was disengaged, and the stone-faced, helmeted military policeman first took a long look at the surroundings, then put one foot up into the van and propelled himself into the confined quarters.

"That the cargo?" he asked, pointing at an elongated crate, surrounded by smaller bundles and packages, in the precise center of the van-floor.

"Yeah," breezily replied Brother Martin. "That one and there's these three on the right, plus the two on the left... just like the bill of lading specified."

The MP stared overlong at the cargo-crate, as he illuminated it with his flashlight.

"Can't see much of it through those slats," he complained, "But it looks damn big to be an oven-heater or something."

"Got no *idea,* man," deadpanned the Christian strike-force-leader. "All these things are, uhh, 'packaged up' so you can't replace just one part... you got to send the whole thing back to the factory for repairs. Just like all those car engines, I guess."

"Yeah," warily stated the MP. "Okay, you monkeys – move over, get me a seat. Name's 'Grassleigh', by the way."

He sat down at the far end of the bench-seat on the driver's side of the van, looking straight at the two 'GrayWar Delivery' staff on the port-half of the vehicle. One of the undercover Christians closed and locked the rear door.

"Okay... can we get going?" asked Brother Martin, from the driver's-seat.

"Just a sec," countermanded the soldier. "You're not going *anywhere*, until I get confirmation from the big rig... unless you want to get dusted by three guys with AR's and a .50 sniper rifle, the minute you get within fifty feet of her."

He obviously wasn't kidding about this, as the Christian man noted that at least four dark-suited, stone-faced Secret Service agents, each equipped with a pistol-at-the-ready, had assumed guarding positions underneath and around the airborne command post.

"You're right," grimaced the Christian man. "We're not moving until I hear an 'okay'."

The MP took out a bulky, military-grade radio from his utility-belt, held it up to his ear, pressed a button on its side, and announced, "One-Eleven Volk Truck, license 817-BTK, Specialist First Class Simon Grassleigh calling Big Daddy Wings. Request clearance to deliver cargo per manifest. Authentication by voice and endpoint ID. Over."

After a short delay, a voice came back.

"One-Eleven Volk Truck, this is Logistics Chief, Big Daddy Wings Group," it began. "Your credentials read good, but this is, uhh... unscheduled? We're not aware of a delivery. Please explain."

"Something about a busted galley heater or shit of that type," answered Grassleigh. "I know, sounds stupid, but the paperwork checks out... requisition's in the system. Look, man, I don't care one way or the other... want me to turn these jokers from GrayWar around?"

Brother Martin's head was spinning, now.

One kick at the can... I cannot fail thee, Lord!

Send me a sign!

"Stand by, soldier," came the message. "We're checking."

After another interminable, breathless, noiseless wait that lasted at least three minutes, the undercover Christians heard,

"One-Eleven Volk Truck and SFC Grassleigh, you're cleared to approach and unload. Sorry for the mix-up – this one was a non-standard, turns out not to have been in the regular queue... got added by special request from the exec team, somebody really high up there pulled rank, that's the bottom line. I got an annotation on the file saying, "the Old Man wants this *fixed*, pronto". But just to set an expectation... you better tell your GrayWar friends that it ain't gonna get installed, in any event, until this bird puts down for IRAN, and that's probably not for a couple of weeks at the earliest. So it's just gonna go in the hold and sit there, until we can get some ground-time. Over."

"You hear that?" said the MP. "Fuckin' waste of *time,* you know."

He spoke into the walkie-talkie. "Roger that... Grassleigh out," he said, disengaging the push-to-talk and re-holstering the communicator.

"Oh, well," philosophically replied Brother Martin, trying as hard as he could not to wipe the perspiration on his brow, "Happens all the time, in our business – we just drop it off where it's supposed to go... 'long as we get paid, we don't care if it just gets thrown in the trash-heap, afterwards... right?"

"Yeah. Whatever," muttered Grassleigh. "Okay... you can proceed forward, but do *not* exceed a speed of six miles per hour, and stop *immediately* when you see a red light on the port side of the plane, flashing on and off. Violate any of those rules and you'll get all of us shot dead... understand?"

"Very definitely," agreed the Christian strike-leader. "Okay... here we go."

At that moment, the soldier happened to look downward, at a small, plastic badge that bedecked his chest. He immediately barked out an order.

"Just a second – *stop!*" he demanded.

"Yeah... what?" asked an irritated Brother Martin. "I haven't even taken off the parking-brake!"

"What the *fu...*" inveighed the confused and suspicious soldier. "I'm getting a *Rad-Haz* reading! Okay, mister – this trip's *over* –"

The Christian strike-leader sent a grave-looking nod to one of his bigger, more muscular compatriots, who lunged at the MP; but the badly-outnumbered Grassleigh fought gamely back, punching and kicking hard and then trying to clamber over the other men. He reached desperately for his service-pistol, but couldn't quite grab it in time.

Bang! came a shot to the back of the head, from a concealed, silenced plastic snub-nose, drawn by one of the other Christian acolytes. The bullet struck the opposite inside-wall and either stayed embedded within it, or bounced off it.

And with that, the life of the unfortunate Specialist First Class came to a grisly end, as half of his brain-matter – not to mention much of his skull – was blown out of his forehead, splattering in a disgusting mess over the inside-wall on the driver's-side of the van.

"Oh, *sh* – uhh, *forgive* me, Lord, but even I forget my vows, at a time like *this!*" exclaimed a frustrated Brother Martin.

"What're we gonna *do?*" shouted a panicked co-adventurer. "If they catch us with him – "

"Just a second... I'm *thinking,*" stammered the Christian strike-leader. "We can't go back now... okay. I've got it. Strip him!"

"Uhh... what'd you say?" asked one of the others.

"I said, 'strip him', and that's exactly what I meant," retorted Brother Martin. "Dark in here... I don't think they got a good look at my face, from either the guard-post or from the aircraft. I'll get into his clothes... he's about my size. All I got to do is fake being him, until we get the thing aboard the plane. Brother Jack, take my place in the driver's seat, and take my ID! Brother Dave, clean up the mess – use the Handy-Wipes under the seat, get the stains off the walls, hide the towels anywhere you can! Put his body behind the front seats, and cover it with the tarp from the ready-locker under the left-side bench! *Do it! Now!*"

Shedding clothes down to the underwear-level, he dashed into the back of the van, fumbling with buttons and belt-catches, while the rest of them hastened to implement the directives.

Luckily – other than for some easily-wiped-off blood on the front inside of the dead man's helmet – Grassleigh's uniform and other equipment showed no obvious signs of the struggle that had led to his untimely demise; even better, his boots did fit Brother Martin's feet, although they were slightly too narrow and were uncomfortable when laced-up.

The Christian leader had just put on the dead MP's trousers, when, to Brother Martin's dismay, the walkie-talkie's "Message" light again began to shine.

"Sir – what do we do –" asked one of the nonplussed acolytes.

"We hope it doesn't have a video-feed," quickly responded Brother Martin, as he grabbed the communicator and pressed the "Talk" button.

"Grassleigh here," he announced, talking with his hand right in front of his mouth.

There was a short pause.

"You *okay* there, Grassleigh?" inquired the remote voice. "Sound funny..."

"Yeah... I'm... uhh... fine," answered the Christian strike-force-leader. "Radio's been acting up lately. Got a requisition in for a replacement. May we proceed to delivery, sir?"

"We were *wondering* when you'd be doing that," said the airman at the other end. "Anything *wrong*, there?"

"No... all okay here," uncomfortably prevaricated Brother Martin. "Sorry for the delay, sir... just trying to get the paperwork done. Noticed that one of the, uhh, forms, hadn't been completely filled out. But we're good to go now."

"Oh... *right*," acknowledged the remote voice. "Understood. Well, get your butts over here – refueling's almost over, and we don't want to keep the Old Man on the ground any longer than we've got to. Logistics Chief standing by."

"Grassleigh out," said the fake-soldier.

He sighed away a bit of the tension and turned to his compatriots.

"Okay," he remarked, "Clearly, the Lord's with us, tonight, Brothers. Is this dead guy put away... good. Now listen – anything goes wrong up there, you turn around and get as far away, as fast as you can – that's an *order*. Don't worry about me... I trust in God. He'll look after me, as only He can. Got it?"

"God be with you," said several of them, in unison.

"*Go*," directed the Christian strike-force-leader, pointing at the aircraft.

They drove slowly up to a point about fifty feet from the looming side of the huge, 747-derivative airborne command-post, when a red beacon near one of its already-opened lower cargo-doors, began to flash rapidly back-and-forth.

The van came to an abrupt stop.

"Prepare for cargo ingress," sounded a hidden loud-speaker. "Local positive control authority approach the aircraft."

"I guess that's me," mumbled Brother Martin. "Get the, uhh, goods, ready for unloading."

Several of them mutely nodded confirmation and set about to unfastening the clasps and catches that had secured the cargo to the van-floor, while the Christian strike-force-leader, adjusting his chin-strap so that the helmet stayed on his head, unlocked the rear access-doors and hopped down to the tarmac.

He walked around to the front of the van and saw a low-to-the-ground, elongated golf-cart-like vehicle, with two armed, camo-suited soldiers and one unarmed, older guy, approaching. In three or four seconds, the newcomers had arrived. They stopped their vehicle, got out and advanced to greet Brother Martin.

"Good evening, Specialist Grassleigh," greeted the leader, a fiftyish, Caucasian guy in a standard, casual Air Force uniform. Unlike the other two, he did not have a helmet on, and was armed only with a pistol in a side-holster. "I'm Logistics Chief Darren Aliotti. Can I see the bill of lading, please?"

"The... oh, right, sir. Just a sec – here it is," answered Brother Martin.

I hope I handed him the right one, he thought.

The older guy scanned the document for about ten seconds, then said, "Okay... where is it? Jenkins, Gruber – get the cart around the back... load 'er up, and be snappy about it – five minute ETA to takeoff, you know."

While the disguised Christian strike-force leader sweated proverbial bricks, the two soldiers implemented their orders.

"Sir, I think they'll need some –" started Brother Martin; but he was cut off by a loud cry from behind the van.

"Hey, Chief!" shouted one of the guards. "Damn thing weighs a *ton!* Can hardly *budge* it!"

"Like I said, sir," smoothly continued the disguised man, "You better get those, uhh, GrayWar guys, to help your boys. To load the main cargo up, I mean. The other ones – the spare parts – they aren't so bad, should be easier."

There was more complaining, but in a minute or two, the precious, crated 'box' appeared on the carrying-cart, which Brother Martin noted, had some kind of elevator-assembly, undoubtedly to help raise its cargo to a level where it could access the aircraft. The other boxes were also on the cart, by now.

"Alright, Grassleigh," mentioned the logistics-chief, "We're almost done here. Just gotta get you to sign off on the manifest, transferring the goods to my ownership, and –"

Another interruption now occurred; there was a call from one of the guards, who had, like his partner, returned to the small seats on either side of the cargo-cart.

"Chief, I think we might have a *problem*, here," warned the soldier.

Lord... help me... silently prayed Brother Martin.

"What?" answered an obviously-irritated Aliotti.

"Scale read-out's showing 427.8 pounds," explained the guard. "Just for that crate. Didn't you say that lift's only meant for 400 at a time? We'll have to off-load the rest of those boxes, before we send 'em up to the cargo-bay."

"427?" incredulously remarked the logistics-chief. "That's not *possible...* bill of lading says it's 150."

He turned to the disguised Christian strike-force-leader.

"You got an *explanation* for that, soldier?" demanded Aliotti.

"Uhh... no, sir," fumbled Brother Martin. "I... uhh... was just relying on the documentation supplied to me by... uhh... GrayWar. I'm sure this is just a minor error, though, sir – if you like, I'll go back there and ask them –"

"Now, *now*, Grassleigh," tut-tutted the logistics-chief, "I'm *disappointed* in you, son; you oughtta *know* that on *this* bird – what with the surprise audits we undergo, all the time – we can't have *that* kind of discrepancy in the paperwork... if we were talkin' about a difference of, say, five pounds, that'd be one thing – but three *hundred?* Sorry, kid, but pun intended, that ain't gonna fly – at least, not on *my* signature. I ain't wearin' an audit exception... that's worth six weeks' pay. I'm afraid there's only one thing we can do, here."

Brother Martin gulped.

O Lord... I have failed thee... strike me down now! he mused.

"No... what, sir?" he managed to answer.

"Bottom line here, kid," continued Aliotti, "Is... you want this thing to get on board... it's on *your* signature, and it's *you*r responsibility, especially if we get a snap-audit."

Thank you, Father God, inwardly gasped a hugely-relieved Brother Martin.

"Oh... well... I... uhh... that'd be fine, sir," he answered. "I'll, uhh, take full ownership, of the... situation, sir."

"Damn *sure* you will, soldier," chuckled the logistics-chief. "Okay... get aboard."

"Get... 'aboard', sir?" warily replied the Christian strike-force-leader.

"Oh, for Christ's *sake,*" muttered Aliotti, rolling his eyes and shaking his head. "Don't tell me, let me *guess* – this your first time in loading the Old Man's Bird, son?"

"Uhh... yeah, sir, I'd have to admit that it is," replied Brother Martin.

"Well, then, let me bring you up to date on the briefing you were supposed to have had, before you ever got given an assignment like this," grumbled the logistics-chief. "Positive control, soldier – since the goods aren't being transferred to *my* control, they stay under *yours* – and anything on board this very special bird, *has* to be owned by somebody who's *also* on-board, at all times, until that control is specifically transferred, in writing, to someone else. Ergo, you're goin' with us, until the paperwork's one hundred per cent straightened out... it's either *that*, or that new galley-oven stays right here, down on the ground I mean... and *you* get the call when somebody has to explain to the Old Man, about why his steaks aren't gettin' cooked proper. *Capiche?*"

"But... but..." stammered the disguised man, "I'm due to report back to the check-point, after I offload the, uhh, cargo, to yourself –"

"You the only MP on base, here?" riposted Aliotti.

"Why, no, of course, sir," answered Brother Martin.

"Easy, then... S.O.P. for this situation," said the logistics-chief. "I'll just message that checkpoint over there, that you're coming with us, I'll tell them to send another MP to relieve you. Hopefully we'll be able to let you off next stop, when the paperwork thing's resolved. Oh, and don't worry about transportation – Air Force'll pay for a first-class plane ticket back here. Besides... don't try to tell me, you didn't want to see the insides of this rig... chance of a *lifetime*, soldier. A lot of guys try their whole lives, and never get anywhere *near* her, you know."

'Chance of a lifetime', mused Brother Martin. *A much shorter one.*

But... nearer, my God to Thee!

Utterly at a loss, the disguised Christian strike-force leader hesitated for a second or two.

"That's... uhh... *great*, sir," he offered. "I, uhh, can't... wait. But listen, sir... I'll have to wave off those GrayWar guys – tell 'em to go right back to the checkpoint, I mean. Can I have a minute, please?"

"Thirty seconds," sternly advised Aliotti. "We're on a schedule here, you know. And if they deviate from a nice straight line away from this plane, well, you better hope they've got a nice insurance-policy, if you get my meaning."

He pulled out his communicator, punched in a code and began speaking into it, saying something about "Big Daddy Wings Group calling Volk checkpoint – requesting immediate relief for SFC Grassleigh".

Brother Martin nodded in acknowledgment and then rapidly proceeded to the back of the van. Looking over his shoulder, he noticed that the crate had been raised on the cart's scissors-like elevator-mechanism, and was being slowly hauled aboard the jumbo-jet by at least three grunting, obviously-unhappy Air Force crewmen, inside the lower cargo-deck.

"I'm going with the aircraft," announced Martin. "Don't ask – I'm making this up as I go. Drive directly back to the gates that we came in, or they'll shoot you. There shouldn't be any trouble at the checkpoint, but if you get questions... keep them talking until at least the plane takes off... understand?"

"But, but, Brother – what will we *do*, without –" came back the anguished response.

"Trust in God... and pray for me," earnestly mentioned the disguised, Christian second-in-command, holding his hand over his heart. "As I'll pray for all of you. These are the Great Days, Brothers; and future generations will remember your names. Now *go!*"

"Grassleigh!" shouted the logistics-chief. "Get your ass *over* here! One minute to engines-on, and you don't want to be behind 'em, unless you want to be well-done on both sides!"

"Coming, sir!" answered Brother Martin, as he cast a long, tearful glance at his compatriots, pushed the rear-doors of the van shut, and dashed over to where Aliotti was standing.

The van turned and slowly began to drive back to the checkpoint.

"No time to go up to the cargo-deck," remarked Aliotti, huffing and puffing as he did a fast trot toward the jumbo-jet; clearly, it had been some time since this man had undergone Basic. "We'll have to take the bottom egress-hatch – you go first. Oh, and by the way, son..."

"Yes, sir?" said Brother Martin, trying to avoid looking the logistics-chief in the face.

"You better think of something to say to the President... just in case," suggested Logistics Chief Darren Aliotti, as a telescoping ladder appeared above the two men.

They Don't Fight Fair, Man

After somewhat more than an hour – since they were, at the time, retreating from the rear-flank of the Bullion Repository battlefield in "ass-thoroughly-kicked" mode – the soldiers of the U.S. Third Brigade Combat-Team, First Infantry Division, were overjoyed to see and hear the arrival of what they took to be long-overdue air-support, in the form of a vectored-thrust, vertical-envelopment V-37 Kingfisher II V/STOL light tactical transport aircraft, roaring overhead.

But the relief had quickly morphed first to wary confusion and then to more panic, as the aircraft, atypically, showed up completely by itself and then disappeared entirely from view – as did most of the scenery, when an inky-black, billowing shroud of *something*, descended on the retreating infantrymen, leaving them groping aimlessly for a way out.

The more intelligent of them ran or crawled in a straight line, away from the sounds of the fighting (though this had subsided, somewhat, lately). Many of the rest just went to ground and waited for developments, alternately shouting for help and cursing their now-useless night-vision gear.

A few of the soldiers who were facing the front- and side-flanks of the Repository caught a glimpse of a V-37 – followed close behind by an almost-invisible, bubble-encased figure – landing directly behind the building's north-west side. A couple of seconds later, an ice-shroud began to extend from the top of the Repository's main level, forming – after several minutes – a kind of *ersatz* wall-extension to the edifice, completely enclosing the now-landed aircraft as well as the ground for several dozens of feet to the north, south and northwest. This was followed, in short order, by multiple jets of the dark-blue weapon seen earlier, striking the open-area outside the new ice-enclosure, in so doing, creating dozens of large, “dragon's-tooth”-like obstacles that blocked a clear line-of-fire from the north and west, against the Repository's new addition.

What the H's going on? wondered those soldiers who watched the spectacle unfolding.

Just ice... won't hold up against a tank-shell... but then again... first, we'd have to get a tank close enough to get a good shot... wouldn't we?

“Well, now *there's* a sight for sore Mars eyes... welcome home!” happily exclaimed Jacobson. “You get it?”

“Parked out back,” exulted a smiling Brent Boyd. “I think the pressure-hull's completely intact, too.”

“How's that dog doin'?” asked White, as he re-entered the Repository's marble-tiled, sparsely-furnished main-floor, having just returned from his icy remodeling job at the building's rear, in the company of the obviously-satisfied Boyd and Tanaka.

“Ahh... not sure,” answered Jacobson. “Poor thing... I tried to have a look at it, but it's still pretty wary of strangers... growled a bit at me, so I backed off, after getting it some water and a few pieces of sausage from one of the refrigerators. And anyway, it's bloody *hot,* when you get too close. Maybe that's its way of healing. We'll just have to hope for the best.”

“Yeah,” agreed the black ex-astronaut. “Too bad – I ain't much on its master, but I ain't got nothin' against the mutt, or its brother, neither.”

“What happened to it?” inquired Boyd. “And I'll echo your comment about Mr. Wolf, up on top of the building – he almost dusted the Professor and I with one of those effin' fireballs, on the way in, until she flashed the code at him.”

“Seems to have taken a round, or maybe shrapnel, in the hind-quarters, during Wolf's first engagement with the military assault force on the north-west,” offered Jacobson. “Listen, Brent, Cherie – before you fill me in on what went on up there... what's the tactical situation, outside the walls? I've been stuck waiting in here, since my little chat with the local commander, out front.”

“I did a circling pass or two around the Repository grounds, using my darkness ability for stealth,” explained Boyd. “Most of the army's falling back in disarray, but they've left a skeleton force encircling this building. I think they're just shocked at the amount of firepower that we were able to throw back at them – but there's always the chance that the retreat is in preparation for a massive, lethal attack, perhaps using heavy-caliber ordinance – and they don't want to dust their own grunts, if they're too close to the target.”

“Yeah... we always knew that was a risk,” agreed the former Mars mission commander. “Alright... Cherie, you and your, uhh, 'kid' had better get up there to do top-cover, as soon as possible. But... how'd it go, at the airbase?”

Tanaka's aura was perceptible, and more than a little intimidating, even to the more-than-humans that she was addressing.

"Piece of cake, really," she insouciantly observed. "Every aircraft and helicopter on the airfield – except for the one that we, uhh, 'borrowed' – has been, shall we say, rendered 'non-operational'... it took some time but I ferreted out everything that could be a threat to us and gave 'em the treatment. Oh, but I didn't blast the ones in the hangars, because there were too many unarmed personnel milling around –"

"Thanks for *that*, Professor," appreciatively interjected Boyd.

"Yeah," she acknowledged. "The few armored-vehicles that I saw there, presumably for base security, they were no trouble... hit 'em with a couple of warning-shots, disabled their auto-cannons, and the crews bailed immediately. Lucky *them*. Only thing I'd warn you about is, I *was* able to see signs of large-scale mobilization, on and around Fort Knox... tanks, large numbers of other armored vehicles, and *lots* of soldiers. My guess is that it will take them an hour or more to get here, in any numbers; when they do, we'd better be ready."

"Agreed. So what condition is the transport in?" asked Jacobson.

"Mint," replied the former Mars mission pilot, "Fully-fueled, and by the way it can take standard Jet-A or -A1. I can fly it with no problem, and it should be just as straightforward for either you or Devon... much easier than a fighter, I'd venture. Even Donny or Wolf should be able to manage it, at least for level flight, with a few minute's instructions. But we'll need the Professor's, uhh, her 'child's, trickery, to get it started... I zapped the entrance-hatch lock, but the anti-joyride interlocks are too complex to bypass, at least without me having a lot of time to re-wire things."

"Understood," said the former Mars mission commander. "We'll have to co-ordinate around that limitation, assuming that we still have the aircraft at our disposal, henceforth. Devon – how's your ice-job holding up?

"Well," commented White, "I've been doin' some tricks of my own, stuff that Her Angel-ness taught me back at the camp – kinda 'face-hardened ice', is how I'd say it... idea is that I compress the shit out of it with that telekinesis, as it shows up from, uhh, I don't know where. Supposedly it's almost as good as mild steel, takes a long time to melt, and you can layer it for depth... but it takes a *shitload* of juice outta me, and I can't just whip it up on the fly... I gotta really concentrate and take my time, you know? I'd wager that the shield I built over the 'plane will hold up for a while against small-arms, maybe a RPG-hit or two, but against anythin' heavier than *that*... don't bet no money on it, y'understand?"

Boyd began laughing, semi-hysterically.

"What's so funny, Brent my man?" inquired the black ex-astronaut.

"'Don't bet any money'... how much do you *want?*" replied Boyd. "Remember where you are?"

A broad grin showed on White's face.

"Got me there, bro'," he ruefully admitted. "All the fuckin' cash in the world, and nowhere to spend it, don't you know."

"Oh, I'm sure that Karéin can get us somewhere that we can spend it, so make sure to stash a couple of ingots before we get out of here," wryly noted Jacobson. "Listen... we have a more immediate issue to deal with, unfortunately; looks like the Army's cut all the telecom links going in here – two points to them – so we're basically isolated from the outside world... no way to find out what the government's reaction is, nor any to get our message out. I tried one of the communicators that we confiscated from the guards who are confined in the third office, over there; but it looks like the siege force is also jamming the wireless... I can't get connected *that* way, either. Any ideas, folks?"

"Way ahead of you, Commander," smugly remarked Boyd. "I figured they'd do something like that – standard EW tactics, of course – so in my copious spare time coming back from the airbase, I set that hacker's communicator to deep-scan all the available frequencies. Turns out that the V-37 has at least two on-board wireless access points, one general-purpose and one that goes back at least part of the way into the military network via SATCOM; and you can route traffic from one to the other. Which is exactly what I did... you should be able to get a call out from the aircraft's systems; but we should do it while we still can – that is, before the Fort Knox garrison wises up to the fact that one of their aircraft's in our possession. They'll isolate the node, the moment they figure out what's going on."

"Good idea," observed Jacobson. "Let's get our butts out to it, ASAP... and since we're going to be outside the relative safety of the Repository walls, Cherie, can you get up there and knock down anything that gets shot our way?"

"Do my best," replied Tanaka, with a determined look on her face. "Though I'm going to need some down-time – pun intended – at some point. Playing 'flying goddess' kind of wears one out, you know?"

"Take your godly word for it," pleasantly teased the former Mars mission commander, as he headed for the rear of the building, with Boyd in tow.

They exited through a small, almost-invisible door recessed into the north-west-side wall of the Repository, being immediately confronted by the looming shape of the V-37 V/STOL transport aircraft, its angular, olive-drab lines softened somewhat by the trickle of moonlight coming from above – plus a brighter, though still subdued glow, on the part of Brent Boyd.

"Wow, Devon," remarked Jacobson, "I'm *impressed*... that's a huge dome you built over this thing... remind me to call you, if I ever need some more living-space... or if I need to cover in a basketball-stadium."

"Sure, 'long as y'all doin' some homesteadin' or shootin' some hoops in Alaska," laconically replied White.

Boyd pulled a release-lever on the side of the airplane, and a combination side-door-and-staircase was lowered in front of the trio. They entered its interior, which had only a few side-portholes and which was big enough to accommodate a good-sized truck, though the pilot-and-navigator area was open to the cargo-bay. The furnishings here were otherwise Spartan, with all emphasis on functionality and none on design, but it was familiar territory to the three former military pilots.

"Okay," started Jacobson, "Let's see if I can get it to associate... hmm... no dice... here, let's try... wait a second... good! Looks like we're patched in, but the signal's weak – having a hard time getting through Mr. White's little igloo here, no doubt."

"So we're on Neo... 'that right, Captain?" asked the black ex-astronaut.

"Yep," confirmed the former Mars mission commander.

"Two cheers for us," grunted White. "What y'all want to do? See if we made the Times, or Disney News?"

"Checking the news-feed headlines, now," said Jacobson, as the other two looked intently on. "Wow. Coast-to-coast – *that's* funny, I would've thought that the government would have this thing completely hushed-up –"

"Maybe they can't," suggested White. "We're big news, after all. I mean... yeah, they *did* tell a lot of lies about Angel Girl herself, but that comet was just *too* big for them to pretend it wasn't there. I'd bet the possibility of losin' all that damn gold's got too many folks' attention."

"Let's hope it *has*," muttered the former Mars commander, "Since our threats are largely bullshit... I wish Hector had come along with us, for obvious reasons. Anyway. You guys want to have a look?"

"Yeah, if you don't mind," requested Boyd. He reviewed a few news-site pages, carefully scanned (and downloaded) a number of detailed maps, did several unexplained searches relating to a small area in West Virginia, and then handed the box to White.

"Wish I knew where Saquina and the kids is," unhappily commented the African-American more-than-human, after he idly checked out some sports scores and tried, with marginal success, to access real-time-satellite imagery of both downtown Los Angeles (which was, mercifully, apparently still there), as well as of the Fort Knox surroundings.

"Lots of local storage... I thought we had already downloaded all we'd need for our tactical uses, but I guess I missed a few," mentioned Jacobson. "I'm pretty disappointed, though, that the news has next to nothing except the usual belligerent posturing, on what the government's position is, relative to our little initiative, here; I mean, I'd have thought that we'd at least get a press-release –"

At that precise moment, the "incoming call" light on the communicator, began to flash on and off.

Jacobson pressed the "answer" icon.

"Who's this?" he challenged. "If you're the right caller... you'll know me."

"They can *target* us with that," warned Boyd. "If they get a trace on it."

"Don't I *know* it," warily acknowledged the former commander.

A faint, metallic voice – unaccompanied by any video-image – came through the communicator's speaker.

“NRA here, man,” it said. “We're showin' Jacobson and Boyd there... anyone else?”

“Yeah... Devon White at your disposal,” mentioned the black ex-astronaut.

“Roger that,” confirmed the hacker. “Your key's showin' good... we should have at least twenty minutes before we gotta ditch the session. My handle's 'Hudson River Pirate' – next in line after Buddha-Boy, we got a strict rule of 'no two successive calls from the same end-point'. Where've you *been,* man? We've been tryin' for a *day* to get through to you.”

“We've been, uhh, *busy,*” evaded Jacobson. “Surely you've seen the news?”

“No *shit,* dude,” replied the hacker. “We're in awe here on this side – we're all takin' bets about when you're gonna melt that gold into, like, yellow plutonium, or whatever; can't be too soon for us, you know, fuck them bankers, get the people back to the land, 'root of all evil', and –”

“Yeah, yeah,” impatiently grumbled the former Mars mission commander, “Can we skip the philosophy-lesson, just this once? You got anything *important* to tell us? Like, for example, intercepts of military communications, in the Fort Knox area –”

“We've been probin' 'em as hard as we dare, without exposin' ourselves too much,” replied 'Hudson River Pirate', “Not a lot of intel we can give you on that front – Army's got the circuits locked down pretty good, we're only gettin' a few bits 'n bites – but if I were you dudes, I'd be ready for a big counter-attack, within the next twelve hours or so. Military traffic that we have been able to crack has got talk like, 'send every drone within the surrounding seven states and Arkansas too' and 'all CONUS Aurora-II and ADVCAP F-32 wings to Fort Knox local deployment stations'... they're strippin' their assets elsewhere, to beat up on you there. There's a lot of bitchin' and moanin' goin' on about it, especially for some reason on the South California front, somethin' about 'you'll cripple our Priority 1 drive to re-take the objective' or some-such shit, not sure what it really means, but there it is. Hope you knowin' that, helps.”

“*Definitely* does,” appreciatively responded Boyd. “Commander – predictable tactics on their part... 'overwhelming concentration of force', of course. That's something we can potentially turn to our advantage... you know, the classic 'mobility versus massed firepower' equation.”

“Yeah,” muttered White, “Assumin' we don't get our asses greased by said 'concentration of force', first. Y'all *know* about 'assumin', don't you?”

“Do I *ever,*” ruefully acknowledged Jacobson. “Okay, well, thanks for the update, but we really should be –”

“Wait, wait, man – there's *more,*” interrupted the hacker. “And you better hang around for it.”

“Fine,” said the former Mars mission commander. “What is it?”

“Not sure how to, uhh, say this to you, man,” offered 'Hudson River Pirate', “But... remember how, uhh, who was it now, oh yeah, both you and that 'Boyd' dude, warned the Feds to leave your folks alone?”

With his gut churning and the blood rushing out of his face, Jacobson replied, "Yeah?"

"Well," continued the hacker, "Ever since before those public statements, on our side, we'd been doin' round-the-clock traces on Fed traffic that mentioned any of your names, like, 'Jacobson', 'Tanaka', and so on, not only those ones but extended family, like, maiden-names and such... originally it was just so we'd have a chance of trackin' you down before the Man got to you, but we forgot to disable the keyword flags and rainbow hashes, after we made contact. Damn good thing we did... because it looks like there's some *heavy* shit goin' down."

"What?" demanded Jacobson, his voice heavy as he returned Boyd's grim stare.

"Near as we can tell, man," carefully recounted 'Hudson River Pirate', "From the time that you dudes first showed your faces – back on the highway with the tornadoes, that is – the Feds had the word out to locate where your families were located. Of course *that's* nothin' new, they do that all the time on anyone and everyone in this fuckin' *country*... but after you pulled this caper at Fort Knox, they went into high gear. I got traces in front of me that are talkin' about 'round up everyone related to Jacobson, Boyd, Tanaka or White, for use as coercive assets'... that don't sound very good to me, man. We're tryin' to keep an ear to the ground about how far they're gettin', but –"

"Jesus H. *Christ!*" atypically cursed the former Mars mission commander. "Listen, you, you, whoever you are – I want you to pull out all the stops, you've *got* to tell me if they've been captured, where they're being held –"

"Hate to say 'I told you so', Commander," quietly commented Boyd, "And if it's any consolation... it gives me no satisfaction to say that."

"I'm just glad Saquina and the kids are, uhh, wherever the hell they are," mordantly added White. "Cherie's just got a mother... isn't that right?"

"Just a second," requested Jacobson, holding up a cautionary finger and speaking into the communicator. "We need *all* the information you've got on that subject. *Immediately!*"

"Hey, hey, man, I know how you *feel*," stammered the hacker, "But don't shoot the messenger, you know? We're workin' on it already, and I'll pass the word along to the rest of my dark-net that this is, like, *important*... but there's limits to what we can get, especially, in a short amount of time –"

"No, son," growled the former astronaut-leader, "You *don't* know how we feel, and you don't *want* to know. Would it help to know that within the Storied Watcher's followers, there are people who can cripple or kill, just by projecting hatred at a target? Anyway... do you have *any* information on our families, above and beyond what you've just told us?"

"Not a lot, man," replied 'Hudson River Pirate'. "But here's what we know now. Apparently the spooks showed up where Boyd's family lived, but they'd already left for parts unknown... the Man's tryin' to track 'em now, but from what we hear, he's still not havin' a lot of success on that front. They're organizin' a bunch of Men In Black for headin' toward the Jacobson place, but they haven't arrived there yet –"

"Why don't they just call the local cops to, uhh, 'arrest' the Commander's family, and so on?" asked Boyd.

"Not sure... but that's never been their style," stated the hacker. "They mostly do this shit all by themselves... I guess they don't like the local LEA to be in the know about it. But so you know, Tanaka's mother got grabbed out of her retirement home apartment, about three hours ago –"

"Oh my *God!*" gasped the horrified former science officer.

"They're real foxed about White's family – odd story there, we're hearin' chatter like, 'we can't safely get agents into Los Angeles, so this one's going to be a challenge'," continued the remote voice. "Oh, and there's stuff we don't really understand... Fed-talk's also goin' on about makin' a friendly little call on the families of somebody named 'Abruzzio', another one named 'Kaysten', and of some guy who, like, used to be with the space program... 'McPherson's his name, I think. They were originally goin' after those of two guys called 'Hendricks' and 'Boatman", too, but they called off the search for some reason... and then there's some guy named 'K. Lee' in New York – software developer, well-known in the underground Open Source community – who they're plannin' to grab. That last one *puzzles* us, man – like, he's not with you dudes, and we thought he might have been one of us, but he's not NRA, maybe a freelance hacker, or something –"

"*Shit,*" spat Boyd. "But why would they be targeting Sylvia and Jerry, or Will and Otis? Those four were with, well, you-know-who, and 'Kaiser's her fiancée. To say nothing of poor old Fred, wherever *he* is. It makes no *sense* –"

"No... unfortunately, it makes about as much sense as anything that we've so far been subjected to," interjected Jacobson, "However enraging and frightening, it is to us. Listen, 'Hudson'... is there any way you can get a message to the people who're being threatened, in this manner?"

"Maybe," hesitated the hacker, "At least for the ones that they ain't grabbed yet... but there's no guarantee that they'll take it seriously, you know, even if we *do* get in touch with them. A lot of folks just think we're, like, some kind of crank caller, even when we tip 'em off that the Man's on the way. And it's gotta be short – these are mostly unencrypted channels, and sayin' more than a few words is like puttin' a big bulls-eye on our backs for the Feds."

"Commander... may I?" requested Boyd.

"Yeah," breathed the former Mars mission commander, as, with his head spinning and his shoulders slumping, he leaned back in the F-37 co-pilot's chair and tried to cope with the situation.

"Send this message to everyone who you can," counseled the former Mars pilot. "If they're in danger, tell them to chant the name, 'Karéin-Mayréij', over and over again, out loud; and if they're captured, they're to keep doing that, silently, in their heads. They're to keep it up twenty-four hours per day, if necessary. And tell whomever captures or imprisons them, that anyone who harms them, will surely be punished, when we show up, as we inevitably will; if they seriously hurt or kill a family-member... we'll *kill* them, slowly and painfully. Tell them that the government's going to lose this war, and that they'd better not be on the wrong side, when that finally happens. Got it?"

"That's, uhh, more than a few words, man," warned 'Hudson River Pirate', "But we'll see what we can do."

"One more thing," requested Jacobson. "Can you please – *please* – carefully monitor whatever channels you can, to detect an impending raid on my family's place of residence, or wherever Brent's family happens to be... or an abduction that's underway? And if you *do* see it happening, can you contact us *immediately?*"

"We can *try*, man," said the hacker. "But we'll have to have names... locations..."

"My wife's Yvonne," replied the former Mars mission commander. "I have two daughters, Jennifer – she's 18, and may be away at school right now – and Jeannie, who's 14. My son's name is Riley; he's 12. Our house is 17104 Saint Therese Road, Manor, Texas, 78653."

"My family won't be at at home," explained Boyd, "And I'd prefer not to give away the exact location of where they're going, just in case the government does manage to compromise this circuit – I'll only say that it's 'north of Charlotte, North Carolina". But I *can* give you their names : my wife is Laura, and I have three kids, too... Wendy, who's 10, Brent Jr., who's 7, and the baby of the family, Nicole... she's 4. Oh, and they'll be traveling with a dog, whose name is 'Roofer'."

"What about White, or Tanaka?" asked 'Hudson River Pirate'.

"Devon's family is as safe as they can get," noted the former Mars pilot, "But make sure the government doesn't know that – the more wasted effort they spend trying to pick up his wife and kids, the better for the rest of us. We'll ask Cherie about her mother and get back to you, but in the meantime, do whatever you can to determine where Mrs. Tanaka's being held. We may also have some others who will need to be protected – that remains to be seen."

"Listen, Mr., uhh, 'Hudson', there," concluded Jacobson, "On behalf both of me and of my team, I'd like to say 'thank you from the bottom of my sinking heart', over this one. Your information's been *invaluable*... I can't stress how much so. Now we've got some decisions to make, and we've *got* to go. We'll turn off the communicator for a while, to make the government's cyber-forensics job as hard as we can, but we'll be back on, as soon as we can. Understood?"

"*Definitely*, man," responded the hacker, and his next comments – distorted though they were, by the multiple layers of encryption and obfuscation being employed by the special link – carried a tone of genuine concern and sympathy.

"And... welcome to fightin' our fuckin' asshole government, man," he said. "Every one of us's been through this... they don't fight fair, you know? They know how to hit you where it *hurts*. But they're dorks – they fuck up all the time – people get tipped off, they do the jet, end up in one of our safe-houses, the whole nine yards. Sometimes, folks get away... *sometimes*. Hold on to that, man. It'll keep you goin'."

"Yeah," agreed Jacobson, his voice almost inaudible. "See you."

"See ya, man... *buena suerte,*" echoed the hacker, as the former Mars mission commander cut the link and powered down his precious, single channel to the world outside.

They were now in the top-level of the Repository building, a place smaller in square-footage than the relatively capacious main-floor (and much smaller still, than the cavernous, largely-unexplored reaches below ground-level : they had heard the rumors of a remotely-triggered flooding-trap, and had, for the most part, avoided the bullion-vaults themselves).

While Tanaka, White and Wolf kept watch through the small vision-slits originally-occupied by base-security snipers, looking for signs of an attack on the building, and while the more-than-a-woman's "war-child" did her best to jam the U.S. military's surveillance-gear, Jacobson, seated on a marble-carved side-bench, led off the discussion.

"So there it is, team," he admitted, "The best-laid plans of mice and men, I suppose. As much as I'd like to stick to the original script, I can't just stand by and watch them kidnap or harm my family. And every passing second that we spend debating this, is one more they've got to go after Yvonne and my kids. I've *got* to go protect them. You *saw* what they did to the Wade place, after all."

"Glad to see you're coming around to my line of thinking," unhelpfully mentioned Boyd, "If however belated."

"My pride on conceding a point isn't worth the safety of my family," quietly remarked Jacobson. "Sorry I was so hard on you, Brent."

"Don't worry about it," consoled the former Mars pilot.

Never taking her eyes or other Mars senses away from the outside, Tanaka spoke up.

"Sam," she said, "I understand what you and Brent are saying, but we've got to think this through – the government's got several hours head-start on us as it is, and it's unlikely we could make it there before they do –"

"We don't know where they're starting *from*," argued the former Mars commander. "And we've got the plane, which they may not yet be aware of."

"Look, Mister Space Man," challenged the bounty-hunter, in his usual, gruff manner, "Much as I get how them doin' this to your folks stinks like three-day-old road-kill... there probably ain't *shit* we can do about it, and that's a fact that's gotta be faced. 'Sides... say we do get down there ahead of them Men In Black, we do find your family, *et cetera, et cetera*... what then?"

"What do you *mean*, 'what then'?" countered Jacobson.

“What I mean is,” offered Wolf, “So you get 'em loaded up in that nice big hover-jet that we got parked back of here – assumin' we don't get our asses blown out of the sky, goin' down there or comin' back –”

“There's that 'assumin' thing again,” muttered White.

He got an appreciative nod from the bounty-hunter, who continued, “Well, what the hell we *do* with 'em, then? I mean, it's been bad enough with Donny's folks, but carryin' a bunch of kids along with us – don't forget, we specifically ruled out anything like *that*, back at the campsite, since they can't protect themselves like we can. And what if we do the same with Mister Sunshine's crew? Thing is... you save *this* bunch, Feds'll just go for your next-of-kin, like, 'aunts, uncles 'n cousins' and so on... it'll *never* stop, man. That's what they *do*. It's what they've *always* done. I thought you *knew* that, when we started out on this whole thing... or didn't you?”

“I took a calculated risk,” evenly responded the former Mars mission commander, “Because the alternative was just sitting idly by and letting the government get away with what it had already done.”

“Well that may *be*,” said Wolf, “But I'd call it more of a bluff... one that just got called.”

“Don't *you* have anyone that they might target?” complained Tanaka.

“Sort of,” he replied. “Girlfriend and her son, back in Tucson. I'll admit I don't want them tied up in all of this... but what with me bein' in the line of business I'm in – that is, the one I *used* to be in – she always knew there might be, uhh, 'trouble', someday. Guess now's that day.”

“Glad to see you're so sanguine about it,” observed the former Mars science officer, with the fury – and the supernatural grandeur – waxing in her voice, body and eyes, as she spoke. “But according to the hackers, they've already got my mother – and if they touch so much as a hair on her head, I *swear*, I'll blast this whole effing *country* to bits, starting with the Agency and everyone in it –”

“Where'd I hear somethin' like that, before, lady?” commented Wolf, with a malevolent, red-tinged half-smile. “All I can say is, 'this time, I ain't lettin' the Russkie talk you out of it'.”

“Okay, look,” forcefully asserted Jacobson, “Here's what I intend to do. I'd like to take the aircraft with me to pick up Yvonne and the family – it should be easily possible to make it to Austin without refueling, which I can do at some local airport, anyway; I doubt anybody will get in my way when I try to gas up. And I want to leave within an hour of now. If, may it so please the Lord, I *am* able to get there first, I'll take them somewhere safe... don't ask me where *that* is, one thing at at time if you don't mind. Brent... where's your family, at the moment?”

“*Assuming* – ha ha, there's that word again, right? – that Laura did what I asked her to, and *assuming* that she didn't get grabbed on the way there, after leaving Charlotte... she should be at a small B&B called the 'Morris Harvey House' in the mountains, near Fayetteville, West Virginia, under an assumed name," explained Boyd. "She already has orders to call for Karéin, in the event that the Feds are closing in... faint hope I know, but better than nothing. The issue for us is obvious, though : it's pretty much the exact opposite direction from where you're going."

"It's okay if you want the plane," said Jacobson. "I'll hop all the way to Texas by myself, if I have to, and besides... our work here is basically done... either the President falls for it, or he doesn't. We can wreck the place before we go, so that the gold's inaccessible, even if we haven't completely enacted our threats to make it into, uhh, glow-in-the-dark slag. Just return when you've picked up your own family, we can arrange to meet at –"

"This is *insane*, Sam!" protested Tanaka. "Splitting up the group is *exactly* what the government would *love* us to do – it was a bad enough idea for us to go separately from Minnie and her team... but doing *this*, is just inviting them to pick each of us off, one by one."

"She's right, you know," voiced White. "I know it's kinda out of turn for me to be sayin' anything about this, given that my family's under the care of Her Nuclear Highness somewhere, but... it'd be *nuts* for half of us to go one place, and the rest another. *If* that's what's bein' proposed, here."

There was a long, tense silence, and then, finally, Boyd again spoke up.

"Alright," he said, his voice as calm and dispassionate as could be expected, under the circumstances. "Here's how I see it... we've got a situation where the Commander's family is under more of a threat than, God willing, is my own... and unlike me, he has no straightforward way to get from here, to there, quickly enough to head off a government kidnap team... nor, has he my kind of tactical mobility. So I think the logical thing is for the rest of you to go with him in the V-37, and for me to fly on my own, to Fayetteville... defend Laura and the kids, until you guys can pick up the Commander's family, then double back and drop in to West Virginia. After that, we call *en masse* for Karéin, and hope she helps us with Cherie's mother and the rest of those being targeted by the government. After all, didn't she offer to do that, at one point?"

"Yeah, I believe so," mentioned Tanaka. "But Brent... you'll be flying by yourself, right? I'd sure feel very, uhh, *vulnerable*, doing that without *Vîrya Sài'ymë* to jam the Air Force's sensors, and so on. And you'd be traveling at night, without a force-field..."

"Leave that to *me*, Professor," defiantly stated Boyd. "It's true that I don't have your little high-tech friend, but on the other hand, I've still got my enhanced senses, as well as *years* of air combat experience under my belt... I know their capabilities and tactics like the back of my hand. On top of that, the terrain between here and there is rough – should be difficult for them, even with a modern look-down SAR – and they're stripping their air defenses everywhere else, to concentrate on the Repository. The only thing, frankly, that I worry about, is simply that you'll have to overfly this area, or go close to it, on the way back from Austin. I'd suggest that you detour well to the north or south, but that would significantly delay your ETA – which may not be a good idea, if I happen to be fighting off the Feds all by myself, at the time."

"As much as I don't like lettin' my man Brent out of my sight for even a minute," quipped White, "It's worth pointin' out that if we head off in one direction and he goes the other, given that we're by far the bigger and more important target... that, by itself, should take their attention off him."

"Don't *that* just give me the warm and fuzzies," muttered the bounty-hunter. "The part about bein' the target of the day, I mean."

"We're *already* 'the target of the day'," observed Jacobson. "It's a wash, threat-wise."

"Well, for the record, I think this whole thing's a load of bull... but say we do it, and everybody 'cept Mister Sunshine here heads west, while he goes east... what about Donny, the Russkie and them two civilians?" said Wolf. "We expect 'em to wait in the car for a couple of days, or somethin'? If I was them, I'd be gettin' a bit *impatient*, about that."

"Yeah... hadn't thought of that," admitted Jacobson. "Logical thing to do would be just to drop by on the way out and pick them up. I'd bet we could even fit one of our vehicles in the back of the V-37."

"Isn't that going to, uhh, draw a little *attention* to us... landing the aircraft in the middle of the restaurant parking-lot, back in town, I mean?" asked Tanaka.

"True, but they can't just drive around to the back of the Repository and load up here, right?" noted Boyd. "I'll go with you that far and show my face there, walk off by myself, hide behind a tree or something, then take off for Fayetteville... it might lead the authorities to conclude that I'm still in Radcliff, or at least in north Kentucky. Might buy Laura, the kids and I, some time."

After another extended period of silence, Jacobson spoke.

"I don't like any of this," he said, "And I'll admit, right up front, that there are many risks, with at best an uncertain chance of success... but we can't just sit here and do nothing. I also have one *other* thing, that I'd like to say."

"Yeah?" asked Tanaka, with a quizzical eyebrow.

"If we get there – and we find out that they've hurt Yvonne, or any of my kids," calmly vowed the former Mars mission commander, "Whether or not he stands trial – the President's going to *die*. I *swear* it."

"*Now* you're talkin', Mister Space Man," hissed Wolf, his infernal aura involuntarily surging.

Jacobson nodded affirmatively, and then addressed the bounty-hunter.

"Think you can melt some gold?" he asked.

"Why, I believe I *can*," said Wolf, with an evil, red-eyed smile. "'Long as I can keep just a few, ahh, *souvenirs*."

"Plenty of those, for everyone," offered Jacobson, with a wry smile. "Though I believe the aircraft *does* have a weight-limit."

He stood up and commanded, "Let's do it."

The Old, "Old Man" And The New, "Old Man"

"Can you get it on the TV?" asked a worried ex-President, calling to his son, who, like his sister, was staring intently at what was unfolding on his mobile communicator.

"I'll help you, Daddy," chirped the teenager.

She managed to tear her eyes away from the small screen and hurried across the room to the comfy-chair, within which her distinguished father had recently been reclining, reached on to a recessed shelf behind the seat and retrieved a remote-control unit. This was pointed at the wall on the opposite side of the living-room.

A subtle whirring-sound was heard, and a dining-table-sized, flexible projection-screen dropped down from a hidden location in the ceiling. With a few more controller-commands, a suitable news-channel had been located.

"There it is," she announced. "Oh, wow – look at *that* –"

"My *God*," gasped the former First Lady, upon seeing the scene, which had a distant image of the Fort Knox Repository in the middle of the screen; suddenly, something looking rather like a spark streaked up from behind the building, then abruptly stopped and hovered for a second or two.

The astonished, frightened onlookers saw several smaller, bright-glowing projectiles issue from this far-off, flying object, and shortly thereafter, the on-scene camera shook from the shock-wave of a series of large, hidden explosions, evidently going on behind the Repository.

A voice-over from the television-broadcast explained,

"Ladies and gentlemen, we're not sure exactly what's been going on, tonight – what you're seeing is footage captured earlier, from a major incident that's apparently still ongoing, at and around the Fort Knox National Bullion Repository. I'm Bill Gowdee from Disney News, reporting from our field-headquarters, on top of a building in Radcliff, Kentucky, several miles from the battlefield. We were escorted away from positions closer to the scene, by the U.S. military, which is in the process of a major push to re-take this very important national asset, from a group of terrorists describing themselves as the 'Mars Gang', led by one 'Samuel Jacobson', formerly – and, ladies and gentlemen, I know how improbable it sounds, but this is the claim – the leader of Earth's space mission to the Red Planet, prior to the 'Lucifer' comet incident."

The ex-President turned an accusatory stare at Abruzzio.

"Madam," he demanded, "What do you know about this?"

The former JPL scientist was about to reply, when the face of the middle-aged, Caucasian on-site reporter showed up in front of the camera, stating,

"Administration sources, which are releasing few other details, confirm that this so-called 'Mars Gang' recently stormed the Repository, overwhelming its small force of on-site guards. So far, accurate information about what's going on to the north and west of us has been extremely difficult to come by, but local sources are speaking of, quote, 'hundreds and hundreds' of casualties suffered by the First Infantry Division, including large numbers of soldiers killed in action. I should caution our viewers, however, that these reports are unconfirmed. Hold on – wait a minute... there's something new –"

He was handed a thin piece of flexible e-Paper, and, after studying it intently for a few seconds, the field-reporter again spoke up.

"Ladies and gentlemen," he nervously repeated, "It has traditionally not been the policy of the Disney News Network to broadcast terrorist propaganda, on the grounds of denying publicity to groups whose only motive is to harm our country. However, in this case, our national editorial staff have agreed to an exception to the policy, given the very unusual circumstances that are ongoing at the current time... therefore, I'll now give our viewers a short summary of the 'Mars Gang Manifesto', which is, apparently, now being widely distributed over Neo-Net and over other media outlets."

"*Well?*" pressed the former President.

"Let's see what he has to say," temporized Abruzzio.

"The statement begins," recounted the field-reporter, "With a claim that the Government of the United States is guilty of, and I quote, 'crimes against humanity', inflicted on a number of named individuals, all of whom, it's said, have some connection with the so-called 'Storied Watcher', that is, the alien being alleged to have returned with the *Eagle / Infinity* Mars mission, some time ago. It also claims that the current President of the United States is – and again I quote – 'an illegitimate usurper of the highest office in the land, installed by means of a violent *coup-d'état*, who has committed numerous, impeachable high crimes and misdemeanors, including but not limited to the illegal removal and imprisonment of the former President, as well as conspiracy to torture, murder, kidnapping, false imprisonment and subversion of the Constitution –"

Kaysten winced, as the reporter continued,

"The 'Mars Gang Manifesto' goes on to provide a long list of 'non-negotiable demands' that, according to it, the Administration must execute within the next twenty-four hours; foremost among these appears to be a demand that the President surrender himself for trial by Congress, per the Constitution's articles of impeachment, but there are many other things, including particularly the elimination of censorship on the television and Neo-Net networks, release of 'political prisoners', the uhh, disbanding of the Central Intelligence Agency, and amnesty and reparations for the members of the Gang and all those associated with it."

"The document," – the Disney News guy briefly looked down at the smart-paper, then again stared into the camera – "Also contains a number of threats, which, it warns, will be enacted in short order, if the Administration does not fully capitulate to the Mars Gang's demands... in addition to a 'promise' to render the gold found in the National Bullion Repository unfit for use as legal tender, there is an explicit threat against the life of the President of the United States, should he, uhh, 'attempt to harm or imprison anyone related to, a family member of, or a friend or acquaintance of, any member of the Mars Gang, or of the Storied Watcher, herself."

"This self-entitled 'Manifesto'," concluded the reporter, "Ends with the statement, 'to the cruel liar who is now posing as 'President'... your only chance of living to see next month, is to surrender to the Congress now, and stand trial; we are far beyond your powers of coercion – you cannot defeat us, and if you want mercy, ask it from the people of America. If you don't get it from them, you can forget about getting it from us. You have 24 hours. Choose wisely.' I should add, by the way, that as of now, the Administration hasn't issued any response to this rather unique communiqué."

While a voice-over, evidently from someone at Disney News headquarters interrogating the field-reporter about the details began to sound on the TV-screen, the ex-President gave his daughter a hand-signal requesting a diminution of volume. He again turned to confront Abruzzio.

"Is this *your* doing, Ms. Abruzzio?" he accused.

"Uhh... no... not *exactly*, sir," she stammered.

"*Really*," he sarcastically countered. "Didn't you tell me that you had been hanging around with this 'Jacobson' guy, along with the three other astronauts that went along with him to Mars? Fred McPherson and I had a meeting with the four of them, just before I got dumped, and I've got tell you, I found them very... *evasive*, about all this 'alien' stuff. At the time, I had doubts about their loyalty to their country – and I think I was entirely right. Wouldn't you say?"

"Sir," replied the scientist. "You're making assumptions about a *very* complex situation, most of which I haven't yet had a chance to brief you about."

"*Do* enlighten me," he sniffed.

"Okay," answered Abruzzio, with an involuntary half-grimace. "You want the truth? Here it is, as best I know it – although I have a feeling that there may be developments afoot, that even *I'm* not privy to. After we all barely managed to get away from the CIA's Amchitka prison-camp with our skins still intact, Karéin took us – and by 'us', I mean not only Jerry, myself and the Jacobson and Billings groups, but also a bunch of others, particularly, Minnie Chu of the FBI and her two fellow-agents, to a secluded foreign location, in which we had a number of extended discussions about 'what to do about the crimes committed against the Storied Watcher's family, by the government of the United States'. You have to understand, sir, that we're talking about a large number of completely-innocent people, who were snatched off the streets and despicably tortured by the Agency, in some cases, for days on end... many of them were furious : they wanted *revenge*. And – crucially – they've now got the superhuman powers needed to enact it."

"*Jesus*," grimly muttered the ex-President, shaking his head. "Just what I needed to hear."

"Mr. President," piped up Kaysten, "Sylvia's telling the truth, but for what it's worth, along with some of them, I stood up for you – for the government, that is. I gotta mention, though, that after listening to what the Agency put these people through – especially the kids, of whom there were several – it was a tough case to make. Sir, somebody's *way* out of line on this file, and if we don't want the whole thing to go up in flames –"

His commentary was interrupted by footage of yet more, brilliant, noisy explosions going on at the north Kentucky battlefield, this time showing an airfield under attack by a dimly-visible, darting, airborne drone of some kind; this strange enemy repeatedly loosed a barrage of scintillating, multi-colored lightening-bolts at the neatly-parked military aircraft, reducing each one to a charred heap of scrap-metal.

"Uhh... any more than it already has," said Kaysten, with a reflexive gulp, "We've got to take charge of the situation... stop it from escalating any more than it already has. That's my opinion, for what it's worth."

"The outcome of these deliberations, sir," continued Abruzzio, "Was that a team made up mostly of the former Mars astronauts, plus a few people who you don't yet know of, set out on a mission – I'll be blunt about it, sir – intended to track down and, 'bring justice to', the current President of the United States... Sam Jacobson was non-committal about what he'd do to your former Vice-President, if and when he was cornered, but I don't think you have to be a rocket-scientist – ha ha, funny choice of words, wouldn't you say? – to figure out that it probably wouldn't go very well for the current owner of the Oval Office."

"You *do* know that you've just described a plot involving criminal conspiracy, treason by a military officer and premeditated murder... don't you?" retorted the ex-President.

"Please hear me *out*, sir!" answered the scientist. "Many of us, including Jerry and myself, felt that such an action would be counter-productive, and far too provocative; so, along with Minnie Chu, Will Hendricks and Otis Boatman of the FBI, we formed a second group, intending to warn the government ahead of time, about what was coming... we hoped that we'd be listened to, but instead, we were treated first with suspicion and indifference, and then had our safety threatened. Jerry and I bolted and only narrowly got away with our lives. As far as I know, Minnie and her two FBI co-workers are still trying to talk sense into the current administration –"

"Wait a minute," requested the former U.S. leader. "How'd your group, and the Jacobson one, get here... to this country, I mean?"

"Oh, *that's* easy," stated Abruzzio. "The Storied Watcher transported both them and us... dropped us off, as it were."

"I don't understand," he pressed. "*Both* of you? Whose side is she – the alien, I mean – on?"

"Neither," noted the scientist. "She's neutral... sort of. As long as nobody's stupid enough to try attacking her or her adoptive family, that is. The same is true of a large number of others, some of whom – for example, my dear friend from the JPL, Hector Ramirez – have also developed their own, very potent alien-powers. The Jacobson and Chu strike-groups are a small subset of the

Storied Watcher's super-powered followers, which at least limits the number of us that the government has to contend with, at least in the short-term."

"Well, it's not *all* bad news today, then," he observed. "But what happens if these two groups, end up fighting each other?"

"I don't know, and we're hoping that doesn't happen," replied Abruzzio. "But what I *can* guarantee you, sir, is that if the current Administration doesn't take Sam Jacobson and his team seriously – there's going to be a *disaster*. I have little doubt that he *will* eventually track down and kill your former Vice-President, but the longer that takes, in the absence of negotiations between himself and the current President, there could be *significant* property-damage and loss of life within the public safety and military organizations –"

"From what I'm seeing on the screen here, Ms. Abruzzio," testily offered the ex-President, "Something like that seems to be well-underway, already. And you want *me*, to put my stamp of approval on this 'Jacobson' guy's violent rebellion against his own country... do I have that right? You've *got* to be kidding!"

"*Sir*," shot back the scientist, trying to control the tone in her voice, "I don't think you fully appreciate the situation, here – just look at what's going on at Fort Knox, for God's sake! Sam Jacobson, Cherie Tanaka – *especially* her – as well as Devon White and Brent Boyd, also two other 'more-than-humans' who are with them... they all have developed alien-powers of *immense* destructive potency. We are talking about a bunch of angry *demigods*, wandering around the United States, figuring that they have nothing left to lose, since, from their perspectives, the government's already tried repeatedly to torture and kill them, and won't stop until either side is dead. What I'm saying, Mr. President, is that only you *might* be able to put a stop to all this, by taking back the reigns of power and suing for peace – your leadership isn't, ahh, as 'tainted' by recent events, as is that of the current administration. Fail to do that, and this country's facing a potential *catastrophe*."

"Sounds very much like what we were hearing about the alien, you know," coolly responded the ex-President. "And if you hadn't noticed... the President of the United States – either this one, or his successor – isn't in the habit of 'suing for peace', especially to a bunch of renegade ex-astronauts. None the less, clearly, this situation *does* deserve my immediate intervention. Will you excuse me for a moment?"

Though instantly suspicious, Abruzzio politely replied, "Of *course*, sir."

The former U.S. leader rapidly exited the scene, disappearing down a side-corridor toward the master bedroom.

For about twenty seconds, the group stood around the high-definition screen, warily observing the goings-on around the Bullion Repository, which appeared to have temporarily died down. Then the ex-President re-entered the living-room. He was carrying a mobile communicator, albeit, one that appeared larger and somewhat different than those in everyday use by ordinary citizens.

“Can you ask, uhh, 'veer-ya' whatshername, to let the signal from this, through, please?”

The scientist shot a glance over her shoulder at the hovering, subtly-reverberating war-shield, and said, “*Vîrya I'ëà'b*'... would thou be so kind as to... ah, oh-kay.”

“Good... getting on the private Mil-Net,” indicated the ex-President.

There was a delay of perhaps five to six seconds, and then he began speaking into the communicator.

“This is the former President, on my dedicated, privileged circuit,” he started. “Get me the President of the United States... immediately!”

“Mr. *President!*” shouted an alarmed Abruzzio. “You've *got* to hang up! If the government finds out what we've been talking about –”

“That's *exactly* what they need to do, Madam,” he countered. “And it's what *I'm* going to do, unless you want to use these high-and-mighty 'alien-powers' of yours, to kill me –”

“Clark, don't *say* things like that!” intervened an anxious former First Lady.

A remote civil servant voice sounded over the communicator's speaker.

“Confirmed old C-In-C, audio-only Class 8A secured link... nice to hear from you again, sir,” it said. “He's busy, but I'll see if I can get him. Should take a minute or so.”

“Good,” answered the former U.S. leader.

He turned to address Abruzzio.

“Out of courtesy to what you've so far done,” he commented, “I won't go off somewhere to do this in private, as I really should.”

The scientist sent an anxious glance at Kaysten.

“Jerry – make him *stop* this!” she pleaded.

The former Chief of Staff nonchalantly shrugged. “Welcome to the Executive Branch,” he replied. “The 'boss' is the 'boss', as we used to say.”

“Jerry!” protested Abruzzio. “This is *insane!* He'll make us a sitting *duck*!”

“More so than we already are, Sylvia?” he taunted. “Give him a *chance*, for God's sake. And, anyway... if they drop a bomb on us, I bet I can run away faster than it can get here.”

The frustrated scientist walked forward to a spot almost within arm's-length of the ex-President.

“Sir,” she quietly stated, “The rational thing for me to do, at this point, is to fry that thing's circuits, with a high-powered burst of ionizing microwaves... give me one reason why I shouldn't do that, right now. Aside, of course, from the fact that it would badly burn your hand, and likely give you cancer.”

“You get *away* from him!” demanded the First Lady.

She took a couple of steps, but was immediately deterred by the ominous presence of *Vîrya I'ëà'b*', who took to a hover-position just over and behind Abruzzio's head.

"I wouldn't do that, if I were you, Ma'am," cautioned the scientist. "I promise I won't hurt you, but I don't have complete control over 'Daughter Tornado Diamond-Curtain' there... think of her sort of as a flying, partly-trained baby Rottweiler."

The buckler let out one of its trademark, inscrutable "chirps".

At this, they noticed that the puppy had joined Abruzzio's side, and was staring intently at the ex-First Lady.

"That goes for Rainbow, too, by the way," warned the scientist. "She has some of my alien-powers, all on her own... and they're *more* than powerful enough to do real damage."

Grimacing and frightened, the First Lady stepped back, to be joined by her two nonplussed children, on either side.

"In answer to your question, Ms. Abruzzio," remarked the ex-President, "You won't do that, not because you care about *me*... but because you care about your *country*. And, because you trust me to make the right decision. Do you?"

There was a tense silence for a second or two, during which several of those in the room thought that they heard the far-off call of the more-than-a-woman's eerily-beautiful war-song, and then she solemnly replied,

"You know, Mr. President... sometimes, I hear *voices*... like Karéin does. She says they're the counsel of the divine, or something like that. Today, they're telling me, that you're a good man... that you're *trying* to be one, at any rate. So yes, sir... I *do* trust you. I sure hope you know what you're doing. Go ahead."

"Thanks, Ms. Abruzzio," he softly acknowledged.

"This is Old Man," sounded a voice over the speaker. "Somebody told me that it's Old, Old Man, on the other end... that *you*, Clark?"

"Yeah, George... it's me," confirmed the ex-President. "Anybody there with you?"

"No... I'm alone in the small conference-room on Air Force One, dodging from rat-hole airfield to crappy airstrip, to stay one step ahead of the fucking alien, the Muslims and the Democrats... but I'm really busy, right now," came back the reply. "You were supposed to only use this channel in an emergency, you know – and I've got a *shitload* of those on my plate, right about now. Can't this *wait?*"

"I'm afraid it can't," countered the ex-President. "It's very important – having to do with what's going on down at Fort Knox, right now."

"Fine, then... for *that*, you've got ten minutes. What's up?" asked the current President.

"Within the last hour," explained the former President, "I've come into personal possession of some extremely valuable intelligence, regarding this 'Mars Gang' that's invaded the Repository... its motives and capabilities. I'd like to brief you in person about it, but as we've got limited time, I can –"

"Wait a minute," interrupted the *nouveau*-President, "How the H would you get *that* kind of 'intelligence'? We've got you squirreled away nice and good, after all."

"I'd prefer not to say, except in person," replied the former President.

"Don't play *games* with me, Clark," growled the *faux*-President. "Remember... you keep your nice little retirement-home, only at my sufferance."

"Okay, *fine*, George... you want more than 'games'? Well, you'll get it, then," shot back the man's predecessor. "The reason why I know what's really going on here – and, by the way, you *don't* – is that I've got both Jerry Kaysten, who you'll recall was my Chief of Staff and who is, contrary to popular belief, still very much alive, and Sylvia Abruzzio, the former JPL scientist, here at my side; and both of them have been in personal contact with the alien. They've filled me in on the whole she-bang, and it's pretty interesting –"

Abruzzio looked sick with concern, as the *faux*-President again interrupted.

"Kaysten... he's supposed to be *dead*, he got a... anyway. So *what?*" he cackled. "I've got one of *those* here with me, on the plane – what's her name again – oh, yeah, the Chinese one, 'Chu', as I recall. All I'm getting out of her's double-talk, though... don't believe a *word* she says. What's this 'Abruzzio' broad got to say that's so different?"

"Jerry," whispered the scientist to the former Chief of Staff, "You hear *that?* Minnie's on Air Force One!"

"Yeah," he answered, *sotto voce,* "But where the hell are Otis and Will, then? Those three always worked together, didn't they?"

Abruzzio sent him a worried-looking nod.

Their attention returned to what was becoming a lively back-and-forth between the two Presidents.

"Well, for starters," explained the former President, "She's confirmed that this 'Jacobson' guy's gunning for you –"

"That's not news," argued the *nouveau*-President. "Everybody with a TV or a communicator knows that, by now. We tried to do the usual hush-hush stuff at first, but apart from this bullshit at Fort Knox being just too *spectacular* to keep quiet, there's something going on, with the computer networks – not sure what, but the security twerps are telling me it's some fucking group of hackers, or something... we'll get around to them, as soon as we deal with Jacobson and his bunch of traitors –"

"Look," interrupted the original President, "What's important is, according to Ms. Abruzzio, as well as according to Jerry Kaysten, who I trust implicitly, Jacobson and his group definitely *do* have the firepower needed to overwhelm the military, the Agency, and so on. Based on what I'm seeing at the Repository, I'm worried that she may be right. Abruzzio and Jerry have briefed me on what this 'Mars Gang' is capable of doing, and it's, uhh... little short of terrifying. The point here is... we need a new strategy, George."

"Not following you there, Clark," evenly replied the *faux*-President. "You say you've got this 'Abruzzio' woman standing, nearby?"

"She's right here," confirmed the other man. "She, Jerry and my wife and kids, are all hearing this."

"Good to know you've forgotten all about 'need-to-know', Clark," snorted the *nouveau*-President. "Well, be that as it may, your alien-loving friend might want to know that we're going to do a little rain on Mr. Jacobson's parade... a rain of bombs, that is. By an hour from now, there's going to be little more than a smoking hole in the ground where that Repository building used to be... then we send our boys in to dig out what's left of the gold. Our problem there was simply insufficient *firepower* – not a mistake I'll make again –"

"Mr. *President,*" spoke up the scientist, "This is Sylvia Abruzzio; as your predecessor indicated, I'm standing beside him. Sir, I'm *begging* you not to proceed with this ill-advised strategy! *Nothing* good will come of it!"

"I don't take orders from the last Administration... or, from smart-ass egghead scientists, who've been cavorting with the greatest single menace to this country, that it's ever seen," he contemptuously retorted. "But *humor* me, Ms. Abruzzio – if I'm *not* to hunt down and destroy a bunch of traitorous terrorists who have already murdered dozens of soldiers and whose stated goal is the violent overthrow of the government, including my own murder... what, exactly, *should* I do? Maybe kiss and make up with them, send them a 'no hard feelings' greeting-card… or something like that?"

"Frankly – *sir* – neither I, nor the Storied Watcher, who is my friend and mentor, as she is for Sam Jacobson and his group, gives a *shit* what you think!" defiantly riposted Abruzzio. "But I *can* tell you this much : like your predecessor said, Jacobson and his group are far beyond your control; if you throw the entire Army, Navy and Air Force at them, add the CIA and other spook departments in for full effect... with good luck, you might hurt or even kill one or two of them. But you *won't* stop them, and they *will* track you down and blow your sorry arse to Kingdom Come!"

"We'll *see* about that," he growled. "You got any more sweet nothings to tell me?"

"Yeah," she persisted. "If you have any brains – to say nothing of the slightest concern for the lives of the soldiers and police who'll be in the way, when the 'Mars Gang' comes looking for you – at the very least, you'll surrender yourself to the oversight of the Congress, and publicly announce that you're returning the Presidency to the man standing next to me. Only that way, can we avoid a fight that might wreck the United States from end to end, until the inevitable happens and Jacobson catches up with you. *Sir*."

There was a long pause, and it was hard for those in the room to discern if it was because the *nouveau*-President was really taken aback from what he had just heard, or if he was taking his time in preparing a response.

At length, it came.

"You know, Ms... 'Abruzzio' – that's your name, right?"

"You bet," she quickly confirmed. "JPL, *Infinity / Eagle* control team."

"That sounded very much like a *threat*, issued from someone who's actively conspiring with Jacobson and his little gang of traitors," he hissed. "Coming on top of reports that I've received from the Secret Service, about the death of an Agency specialist, involving you, down in Pittsburgh. You know what we do with people who violently resist the government, I presume?"

"Oh, I sure *do, sir,*" she countered, with her eyes showing a now-familiar, kaleidoscopic glow. "I found out all *about* it, while I was with Karéin and Sam Jacobson up on Amchitka Island... you know, where you dropped a hydrogen bomb on all of us, after we had the temerity to free the hostages that you'd been torturing, deep underground. And as for the Pittsburgh, uhh, 'incident'... that's something that I can explain, and that I make no apologies for. The man tried to murder *me*, first – seems to be 'Standard Operating Procedure' for those under your command –"

"She *killed* someone?" gasped the former First Lady.

"It was self-defense, Ma'am," whispered Kaysten. "I've personally been shot at, too. Wait 'till you hear the whole story, before you judge us."

The ex-President hit a button on the communicator, and he whispered to the scientist, "Ms. Abruzzio – I understand your feelings on this, but don't let the argument get out of control. We need to keep the dialog going."

She nodded and he re-enabled the link, cutting in on an extended rant on the part of the successor President.

"– lecture *me* about how I should deal with national security –" he was shouting.

"Sir," interrupted Abruzzio, "I don't think we're going to resolve that disagreement here, but I wanted to explain that neither I nor Jerry – nor the Storied Watcher herself, nor any of the rest of us who have lately been in her company, including any of us who you may have now with you – are party to Sam Jacobson's campaign against the government... at least, not so far. The reason why Minnie Chu, Otis Boatman, Will Hendricks, Jerry and I came back to the United States, in the first place, was to warn you of what the 'Mars Gang' was up to – and to plead with you to try to compromise with Sam Jacobson, turn over power to your predecessor and defuse this crisis, before it takes on a life of its own. That point may already be past us, unfortunately... and I regret that."

"Well, Ms. Abruzzio," sourly commented the *nouveau*-President, "I think I know where *you're* coming from. Clark?"

"Yeah... I'm here," indicated the former President.

"You need to tell me, right now, that you're not involved in this fucking ridiculous scheme – and that you'll turn this 'Abruzzio' broad, Kaysten as well, over to the contingent that I've now got on the way, over to your residence... your guard has a gun, right?"

"*Sure* she does – but, George, you don't *understand* – the situation's far more complicated than that," protested the ex-President. "Starting with the fact that I *won't* be a party to Jerry's arrest. He stays here with *me*, until I've got a full picture about what the hell's really been going on with the alien and her camp-followers –"

"You're not in a position to make any such demand!" guffawed the *faux*-President. "I give you my personal guarantee that he won't be harmed, at least as long as he cooperates –"

"Is that *right*, Mr. *Vice*-President?" interjected Kaysten, with an unusual tone of genuine anger in his voice. "Well, I've seen, first-hand, how much a promise like that's worth – like, not a faint whiff of a buffalo-fart. You're not *half* the man of the one who's standing next to me here and now – you never were and you never will be, because you're not a *leader...* you're just an incompetent, power-hungry, money-grubbing asshole. I just hope that Jacobson greases Bezomorton, one second before he kicks your sorry ass to, I don't know, Jupiter or something. Oh, and, like I said to those Agency spooks down in Pittsburgh – you *want* me, Mr. Vice-President? Then fucking come and *get* me! I think you'll find it a bit harder than you'd expected."

"I'll take you up on that," threatened the *faux*-President. "All understanding, that resisting arrest... well, all bets are off, in the 'tender-gloves' department, in that case. Don't say I didn't warn you!"

"Jerry," wearily offered the ex-President, "I'd always *suspected* that you didn't like George... or John. Guess I was right."

"You *think*, sir?" said a grinning Kaysten, with one of his eyebrows raised.

"I gotta go, Clark," came the final commentary from the *nouveau*-President. "Don't do anything stupid – you hear a knock on the door, just stand there with you hands up, until they give you the all-clear. Oh, and... don't bother calling me again... I'm a busy man, these days! Bye-bye..."

The line went dead.

Abruzzio advanced to the ex-President and, with a look of comradeship and sympathy in her multi-colored eyes, took hold of his hand.

"Welcome to the Company of the New People, sir," she said.

Don't F With The *Mossad*

The other half of the Mars Gang had spent no more than a half-hour or so at the Bucko's Burger Joint drive-in restaurant, in the small town of Radcliff, Kentucky, when the sounds of several big explosions, several miles off, east of north, brought surprise and alarm to the ten or so customers who had elected to sit down at a table inside the place. Those nearest the windows, could just make out red-tinted flashes, briefly lighting up the horizon in that part of the sky.

"Holy s*hit!*" gasped the cook. "That's out by the *Repository!*"

Misha, Callum, Donny and Marie silently exchanged knowing glances, as a couple of State Troopers, who had been quietly sipping on coffee at the far end of the lunch-counter, left their half-eaten scrambled-eggs-and-bacon dinners, rushing to their squad-car and roaring out of the parking-lot, with sirens loudly wailing.

"Hey, *Marv!*" called out a local, who had deposited himself several booths down from where the four partners-in-crime had been sitting. "That TV of yours, workin'? Somethin' *big's* goin' on, down th' highway!"

After the initial excitement had died down (though the television stayed on, with only sparse information about the goings-on around the Bullion Repository, while convoy after convoy of LEA and military vehicles roared northward on the highway, past the restaurant), when questioned about why they "and those two nice young guys with you" were staying so long, Callum Wade proved a better liar than he had made himself out to be; the farmer affably answered, "oh, we're just waitin' fer some folks from out of state, and they *said* they might be an hour or two... 'zit okay if we hang 'round here?"

As long as the orders for coffee and beer kept coming, the local proprietors were happy to let the group stay.

It had been at least another two hours, and halfway through, there had been another set of explosion-sounds coming from the direction of the Repository, although these ones were not accompanied by the same visual effects that the first lot had displayed; rather, there was a spectacular, volcano-like plume of fire, which persisted for perhaps thirty seconds, then disappeared.

Meanwhile, the population of automobiles and people passing through the Bucko's parking-lot had completely turned over five or six times. But the place was open twenty-four hours per day, and by now, the local soda-jerk and his two waitresses had gotten to know the three Wades on a first-name basis; although, each time that the conversation wandered into prohibited territory – particularly, about what had gone on, in the last few hours and days – a warning-glance from the Russian had caused a diplomatic, if abrupt, change-of-subject.

Deep into the night, the short-order-cook commented to Callum Wade, "Well, maybe you folks *are* my lucky-charm; usually I don't get *anybody* in here, after dinner-time... but man, we've got, like, twenty cars and trucks lined up... all these, like, 'government' types, they're insistin' on eatin' in their cars but *I* don't care, as long as they order something – best business I've had in *weeks*."

Donny smiled and walked away. He approached Misha, who was sitting by himself at a table on the inboard side of the restaurant, so as to be less visible from the parking-lot, and quietly asked, "Y'all hear that? I seen 'em too. Hangin' round here, off on one side, over there, nearest the street. Think they're on to us? Maybe we better skee-daddle..."

"I do not believe that they recognize us, and as you know, I have, ahh, considerable experience in these matters," offered the Russian, his voice equally subdued. "So I do not think that we should leave right now. But after watching the televised coverage of these developments, I am somewhat worried about the lack of any political response from the U.S. government. I cannot help but think that the situation at the Repository may be degenerating into a long siege... something that we had hoped to avoid. And you have seen how the American military is using this area as a staging-base for what I presume will be an assault on the, ahh, 'objective'."

"Y'all can bet on that," grunted the trucker. "The part about them Army boys throwin' everything they've got at, well, you know... them, uhh, 'terrorists'."

With a thin smile, Misha remarked, "Perhaps you are learning some of my trade-craft, my friend. The point is... the, uhh, 'boss', asked us to wait here for several hours more, but I am concerned that if the entire area is put under military rule – as may well happen – we might be caught in an inspection as we try to exit. I would recommend that we give it another hour or so, but then advise your aunt and uncle that we are heading to the pre-arranged point. Do you agree?"

"Yeah... good a plan as any," confirmed Donny, with a shrug. "I'm goin' outside for a smoke... okay?"

"Doing that is bad for you... oh, *forget* it," grumbled the Russian. "I recall that most of these 'vices', are no longer dangerous to us... you know? But please try to be discreet. Keep your face out of clear view from the parking-lot and the street, if you do not mind."

"Sure thing, boss!" cheerily replied the trucker, as he wandered out one of the side-doors and lit up a cigarette, puffing away aimlessly.

For some time, nothing out of the ordinary occurred, with Misha feeling out of sorts, given the situation and given the fact that unlike most of the rest of the members of the "Mars Gang", though he inwardly knew that his own special abilities were waxing in like measure to those of Tanaka, Jacobson, Wolf, White and Boyd, so far, he'd only been able to exercise a modicum of them.

He noticed that Donny had apparently recognized, and had struck up a conversation, with a slender, very young-looking (she couldn't have been more than twenty, and was probably less than that), winsome female, dressed provocatively in typical woman-of-the-night fashion, with fishnet stockings, an absurdly tight-fitting, polyester mini-skirt, garish make-up and eye-liner, and large, circular, dime-store earrings.

Oddly, she did not approach the side-door from the front-side of the restaurant that faced the parking-lot and the street, but, rather, had appeared suddenly from somewhere behind the building.

After a few minutes of animated conversation, which the Russian tried to ignore, the trucker ushered the girl into the restaurant, sitting opposite her at a booth as far away as possible from both his in-laws and Misha. A waitress came over and Donny ordered a full-course meal with coffee, but when this was delivered, it was given to the girl, who – in between nervous-looking glances right and left, forward and behind – began to consume it with undisguised gusto.

What is going on here? mused Misha. *I hear commentary like, "it's been a while, honey"... they obviously are familiar with each other... but this is not a good time to re-make old acquaintances...*

Finally, either his curiosity, or his wary sense of responsibility over the group, got the better of him, and the Russian walked over to address the trucker and his new companion.

"Donny," he carefully requested, "I take it that you know this young woman? Should you not introduce her to your uncle, your aunt, and I?"

"Oh… it's nothin' too special," evaded the more-than-human man. "Sammie here's just somebody who I – uhh – met, while I was on the road, few years back. We kinda get together for some fun, if y'all know what I mean, when I happen to drive my rig through these parts."

"Well… thanks a *lot*, Donny," whined the girl. "Who's your friend? Hey, mister... ya not from around here? The *accent*, I mean. Not that it's anythin' to me, that is. I mean –"

"Oh – no offense, Madam," smoothly prevaricated the Russian, as he extended a hand to her. "I am, uhh, Israeli, actually – it must be the Hebrew influence... you know, English is not my mother tongue. My name is 'Misha'. I take it yours is – uhh – 'Sammie'?"

Well, he thought, *I actually* did *learn some Hebrew... and since I met 'you-know-who', I have begun to remember it as if it were yesterday.*

So it is not completely a lie...

"Samantha," she answered, with a cute, childish smile. "But everybody just calls me 'Sammie'. Listen, Donny – thanks for the grub, but like I told ya, I gotta get goin' – if I know Ray, he's gonna check out every place in town… and it's only a matter of time until he shows up here. Where's that rig of yours? Just get me *out* of here, man – I'll give ya freebies all the way to wherever yer goin – long as it's too far for Ray to find me there. *Please!*"

Uh-oh, reflected Misha.

This does not sound good.

"It's... uhh... not workin' no more," dodged the trucker. "I got a van, but it's gotta stay here for awhile, 'long with yours truly and my Uncle Callum and Aunt Marie – see them too, over there by the counter? Yeah, there they are – come on, wave to 'em."

"Come *on*, Donny!" pleaded the girl, with tears welling in her eyes. "He catches up with me after I ran with the whole week's earnins', I'm fuckin *done* – ya met him once – ya *know* I'm not shittin' ya! Never should have started workin' for him, but –"

At that moment, a look of sheer panic appeared on her face, as the side-door that they had entered, flew open. Through it strode three very tough-looking, Caucasian guys, dressed in various combinations of denim, black jackets, running-shoes and leather boots, baseball caps and cowboy-hats.

One guy, the largest of the three (a good inch or so taller than both Donny and Misha), was brush-cut, while the other two – including the apparent leader – had long, hippie-like hair and were about the same size as the trucker.

All of them had tattoos, combined with a mean, stone-faced demeanor.

The three tough-guys advanced rapidly toward the table at which the trucker and the girl were sitting. She tried to bolt, but could not get upright in time, and after roughly shoving an alarmed Misha to one side, the three newcomers surrounded the exit from the booth, implicitly daring both Donny and his distaff companion, to force their way out.

"How you *doin'*, Sammie?" snarled the leader, a lean-bodied, stubble-chinned man with a prominent scar on one cheek.

"What you *want*, Ray?" said the obviously-frightened girl.

"I think you know already, you little whore!" he countered. "For starters, all of *my* fuckin' money, that you decided was yours. Then we'll talk about how you're gonna work off the rest of what you owe me. Get up!"

Donny turned to look upward, but did not attempt to stand.

"Hey there, man," he remarked, trying to sound as non-confrontational as possible, "She owes y'all somethin'? I understand, man... understand *totally!* Listen... I got some bread on me, probably more than enough to bail her out. Why don't I settle up for her?"

"This ain't none of your business, boy," snarled the tough-guy-leader. "And I doubt you all got anywhere near enough to pay her bills. 'Sides all that... she's spoken for. Belongs to *me* and me only. Sammie – get your dirty lil' ass off that bench, before I carry it out, sideways!"

The girl began to slowly arise, but was motioned not to by Donny.

"She ain't goin' nowhere," amicably offered the trucker.

Upon seeing this, an increasingly desperate Misha intervened, stepping in front of the visibly angry pimp.

"Sir," he requested, "My friend here is just being a little, ahh, 'obstinate', but what he said *is* true, in one respect – we have lots of money to offer you, far more than a low-class girl like *her*, is really worth! Just name your price... what will it be? Five hundred? A thousand? In cash or gold coins? The metal is nearly one hundred per cent pure, I can assure you –"

"This ain't just about money," hissed the lead-tough-guy, "Bitch has got to be taught a lesson, and in front of the other girls."

"Now *get up!*" he shouted at Sammie.

Strangely, Donny had sort of bowed his head, covering his face with fingertips on his temples.

The voice of the short-order cook sounded from far down the restaurant.

"Hey, you!" he warned. "Keep it down, back there... and you got a problem with one of the customers, you take it outside."

A humming, susurrating back-beat, kind of like a hillbilly banjo version of a Top-40s rock-anthem, began to be heard at the limits of human consciousness.

So that *is what your war-song sounds like*, mused Misha.

It fits you well...

The pimp did a head-toss to one of his buddies, who walked to a position in front of the cook and growled, “Shut your fuckin' *mouth* and mind your *business*, old man!”

Without further warning, the lead-tough-guy grabbed for the girl, but, in a panic, she resisted, moving as quickly as possible down the bench and leaning backward to avoid his grasp; this maneuver succeeded, but he simply took hold of her legs and began to drag her, screaming and kicking, outward.

Suddenly, the trucker lept to his feet.

His eyes were dimly-glowing as, in a weirdly-enhanced voice, he spat,

“*Y'all* fuckin' back ***off – boy!***”

The pimp was astounded at the sight, but it didn't deter him, and as people everywhere – including the girl and Callum and Marie Wade – dove under tables and behind chairs for cover, Ray stepped back and reached for a small pistol, which had been concealed on the inside of his leather-jacket.

His arm was elevating the weapon in an attempt to fire at Donny, but before the man could loose a round, the body-lightening-infused, glowing-eyed trucker had thrust his arms forward in a pushing-motion, though Ray was much too far away for Donny to have made physical contact.

Somehow, the lead-tough-guy – now dazed and gasping, as if he had been struck by a heavy object traveling at high velocity – was sent flying head over heels on top of a table immediately behind him, with his gun discharging into the ceiling as he fell.

Meanwhile, the other two thugs turned on Misha, with one charging forward with a switchblade, while his comrade, who had been threatening the cook at the lunch-counter, retrieved and aimed yet another concealed handgun.

With fighting-instincts both human and super-human instantly activated and his own, thrilling, rapid-fire war-song adding to the adrenaline-rush excitement of Donny's one, the Russian's hands made a perfectly-synchronized, impossibly-fast gesture, feeling the presence of his two throwing-knives after less than a half-second's delay.

With grim professionalism and a single double-throw maneuver, Misha unleashed *Væran Ivan* and *Væran Pyotr* at the gunman; the inerrantly-guided, singing, glittering war-knives struck home first at their target's left arm – the one holding the weapon – precisely at the wrist, while a second later, hit his tarsal-joint, pinning the bleeding, shrieking man both to the lunch-counter by the wrist and to the floor by the foot.

The thug with the switchblade saw only the briefest glimpse of the throwing-knives as they streaked past him, and so he dashed across the floor, brandishing his blade. But to his astonishment, the Russian vanished from his sight for about a second – only to reappear, utterly without warning, within easy grappling-distance.

The man first felt a crippling martial-arts kick to the crotch, but this was, in fact, the least of his worries; in the next split-second, Misha's iron grasp struck the thug's knife-wielding arm about three inches from his wrist, and the limb was overwhelmed with an agonizing rush of numbing pain, as its outer flesh-layers suffered an other-worldly frostbite.

He fell helplessly to his knees, only to receive a rib-cracking kick to the torso that sent him completely out of the battle.

Misha turned to see what had been going on behind him, and was frightened to see that Ray had managed to regain his feet, step forward and re-ready his gun. He fired wildly, with several bullets apparently heading in Donny's direction as well as impacting with and shattering parts of the window looking out over the parking-lot.

The trucker spun in place and kicked the thug-leader's hands upward, resulting in more rounds in the ceiling, about a second before landing a devastating, *Fire*-energized punch on the pimp just below the latter's right collarbone, which shattered in a bloody mess as Ray was knocked back by at least two feet, leaving him coughing blood on the floor.

"*Like that*, motherfucker?" shrieked Donny, as he advanced with clenched fists, toward the crippled, moaning street-thug. "Want *another?*"

"*Enough!*" angrily countermanded Misha. "We already have *enough* of a disaster on our hands – this nonsense is bound to attract the authorities! Callum, Marie – prepare to leave!"

Both war-songs, and other *Fire*-manifestations, rapidly ebbed to nullity; and in a completely self-propelled fashion, the Russian's two throwing-knives detached themselves from their victim, returning to concealed positions somewhere under Misha's upper-garments. The thug who they had transfixed, fell over on his side, bleeding from his savagely-wounded hand and foot-joint.

The streetwalker had, by now, shuffled out from underneath her hiding-table. Wide-eyed, she accosted the trucker.

"Donny – *thanks*, man," she gushed. "Knew ya didn't take any shit from nobody, but... wow, what *was* that ya hit him with? Not that I care, mind ya... but... y'okay, man?"

"Nothin'... nothin', honey," he evaded. "I'm fine."

"Yeah, but you're *bleedin'* – see?" she said, pointing to a blackened, round hole in Donny's jacket, just above the waist.

The trucker looked down at the wound, and, to his dismay, discovered that the observation was accurate : he had, indeed, been shot.

He opened up his jacket and rolled up his shirt, revealing a serious-looking gunshot-wound, with blood splattered all around it.

The two elder Wades had now extracted themselves from hiding-positions, and they stepped gingerly past the crippled tough-guys. Upon seeing their nephew, Marie Wade cried out, "Donny! We gotta get you to a *hospital!*"

"What you *worryin'* about, Auntie?" he mentioned. "Don't hurt none."

He let down his shirt and re-adjusted his jacket.

"Son… you took a bullet to the trunk," warned Callum. "Your aunt's right... somethin' like that'll kill a man slow for sure, if it don't kill him fast. You ever buy any health insurance?"

Misha, who had been studying the mishap closely, offered, "Take another look at it, sir... I think you will find that my friend's disclaimer of harm, is well-justified; and that is only one of a hundred good reasons why a trip to the hospital is, how do you Americans say it, 'out'."

Donny obliged, revealing the wound again. It was still there, but was subtly-glowing, and was half the size it had been, not a full minute before.

"*Told* y'all, Uncle Callum," said the trucker, with a wicked grin. "Reckon I'm one of *them*, now, and man… don't it feel *great!* Hey, there, Misha, buddy – no hard feelins'? Fucker took a grab at Sammie... what was I *supposed* to do, just let them boys drag her out and beat the *shit* outta her?"

"Frankly – yes!" muttered the Russian, "That is *exactly* what you should have done. But there will be time for recriminations later... I *hope*."

"I love you too," sarcastically remarked the girl, in Misha's direction.

He walked over to where the semi-conscious Ray was lying, and, with no smile on his face and in a voice loud enough to be easily-audible throughout the front half of the restaurant, unctuously advised the thug, "Next time, my friend – think twice, before picking a fight, with agents of Israel's *Mossad!*"

Donny was going to say something, but thought better of it at the last minute, and just nodded while commenting, "Oh... *yeah. Oy vey*, man!"

It is so hard to avoid laughing around Americans, mused the Russian, hoping that the trucker's telepathy wasn't yet good enough to read the broadcast.

Misha now stood upright and addressed the crowd, which was beginning to come out of hiding.

"Ladies and gentlemen," he announced, "I apologize for the – uhh – incident, but I must ask you to refrain from using any form of picture-taking or other recording equipment – we will have to confiscate any such item that you deploy, until we have left this place –"

"This-here's a free country," complained a stubble-bearded country-boy. "You got no right!"

"The *Mossad* makes its own 'rights', as you no doubt have seen," countered the Russian. "Keep your communicators and wrist-cameras hidden, unless you would like to lose them. To my fellow-agents... come with me."

Callum whispered something to his wife, and she decided to silently play along, as did Donny. All five headed toward the door that the unfortunate Ray and his two hapless enforcers, had entered; but just as Misha had exited, he noticed that the streetwalker was walking behind the trucker.

"Donny," said the former SVR-man, as he turned his head and stopped in place, "What is going on, here?"

"What you *mean*, 'what's goin' on'?" came back the reply.

"*Her*," clarified the Russian, pointing at Sammie.

"Oh... I invited her," diffidently mentioned the trucker. "To come with us."

"That is out of the *question!*" protested Misha. "You know very well, why."

"Talk about this outside," requested Donny.

They all exited and stood at the side of the restaurant, with Misha's eyes nervously scanning the parking-lot for the possible appearance of local law enforcement.

"Look," claimed the Russian, "We already have two – ahh – civilians, along with us, on this project; the Commander will not be happy in seeing a third. You obviously know little about covert operations –"

"Well, *mi amigo*," observed the smiling trucker, "Judgin' from what's been goin' on up at the Repository earlier this evenin', the word 'covert' don't seem to fit too well, wouldn't y'all say? And anyway... she ain't got nowhere else to go, man. 'Less y'all want to go back there and finish off ol' Ray – somethin' that I'd be happy to help with, by the way – he'll be comin' back for her, sooner rather than later. Y'all want to go ahead without me, be my guest – but I ain't goin' without Sammie comin' along with me!"

"I love you, Donny," whispered the girl, batting her eyes.

It even sounded half-sincere.

Misha, still scanning in all directions, stepped around the Wades, to speak directly to the streetwalker.

"Madam – if that is – ahh – the right thing to call you," he started, "What Donny has not told you of – but what I will, now – is the fact that he and I belong to a gang of what the American government describes as, uhh, 'terrorists'. We have *killed* people, Sammie; we are wanted men and women, with a price on our heads – your government wants us *dead*, and will not *hesitate* to kill us, the moment that they get a shot at us. Come with us now, and your life will be in grave danger; and I will not guarantee your safety, or, even, a competent effort to preserve it. You are in way over your head, traveling with us! Do yourself a favor – get on the next bus out of town and forget that you ever met us."

The Russian's diatribe had obviously made an impression, because Sammie, her visage showing serious worry, hesitated for several seconds, and then asked the trucker, "Donny... that *true?*"

"More or less," he confirmed, briefly looking down at his feet before staring the girl, face-on, and elaborating, "But what Mr. Russkie there left out, is that we ain't just any ordinary bunch of desperadoes... most of us, him 'n me included... we're super-heroes... or super-villains... or some-such shit, dependin' on how y'all look at it. Honey… we're the meanest sons of bitches in the valley, if y'know what I'm sayin'. Ask yourself – could two *normal* men, have done what y'all seen us do, back there?"

A broad smile showed on her face, as she replied, "No... sure couldn't. Ya took a bullet to the gut and yer still talkin' to me, right?"

"Y'all got it, sister... hear *that*, Misha my friend?" remarked Donny. "She's goin'."

"Listen to *reason*, for Heaven's sake!" protested the Russian. "We cannot adequately protect Callum and Marie, as it is – we only made an exception for them, because of the hospitality that they showed us, and because they are your blood relatives. If we pick up every woman-of-the-night with whom you have –"

He stopped talking for a second or two, and then warned, "Aircraft approaching!"

"What?" interjected Callum Wade. "I don't hear *nothin'*."

"Me neither," added the streetwalker.

"But I do," contradicted Donny. "Far-off, but headin' this way fast, that's for sure. Okay then, Mr. Russkie – been a slice. Come on, Sammie... we'll hitch a ride on a rig, or somethin'. I got lots of bread on me –"

"Donny," desperately pleaded Misha, "What am I supposed to *say* to Commander Jacobson, when he and the others –"

And then the former SVR man again fell silent, for a moment.

"Damn!" he cursed. "*Sirens!* This may be an *ambush!* Donny, prepare to call on your *Fire*, full-power!"

"What you talkin' about, mister?" asked a perplexed Sammie. "He ain't got any flamethrower, not even a gun –"

Suddenly, something *large*, at least the size of a commuter-jet, flew overhead and came to a crazily-abrupt stop. As its side-pod-mounted turbofans swiveled to a vertical position and bellowed a deafening din, it began to drop vertically-down to an unoccupied part of the parking-lot, with its under-fuselage search-lights brightly illuminating the area all around (though the aircraft lacked, or had turned off, the running-lights commonly seen elsewhere on its fuselage and wings).

Most of those who had been in the restaurant during the confrontation with Ray and his fellow-thugs, exited the building on the opposite side from where Misha and his party were located, in order to get a better look at this amazing new development.

The airplane – now revealed as a camouflaged, angular military V/STOL transport of some type – came to a full stop, and as its side access-staircase opened up and descended to touch the pavement, a shadowy figure, encased in an almost-invisible 'bubble' of some sort, dropped down from some previously-hidden aerial location, coming to rest on its feet, on the parking-lot-surface, between the aircraft and the Russian's group.

"You are back early, are you not?" called the former SVR agent.

"Misha?" came Tanaka's familiar, friendly-but-dignified voice. "Yeah, we are... necessary change of plans, I'm afraid – fill you in when we get airborne. You got Callum, Marie and Donny there? Good. Listen... Brent and Devon are dropping the rear-ramp on this thing, as we speak. No time to waste – can you please get behind the van and drive it into the cargo-bay, Sam will direct you –"

The sound of sirens, though still far-off, was now perceptible even to human ears.

"Ah, I *see*... yes, well, congratulations, Professor – having such an airlift capability will be very useful for us," observed Misha. "I will get right to it, but you should be aware, there are *complications* at this end –"

"What do you – oh, wait a minute," replied the more-than-a-woman. "Yeah, bullet-holes and one of those restaurant-windows is shot out – what *happened* here? LEA or the Agency show up?"

"Not... *exactly*," grimaced the Russian.

He sent an accusatory stare at the trucker, and gave a parting comment while heading for the van in a rapid trot : "*You* explain it!"

"Donny?" guardedly asked Tanaka.

"Bunch of assholes wandered into the restaurant and tried to grab my, uhh, girlfriend, here... Misha 'n I taught 'em a thing or two."

"Uh-oh," exclaimed the former science officer. She half-stepped, half-flew over to stand directly in front of the three Wades and their new companion. Almost whispering, Tanaka inquired, "You *kill* anyone?"

"Could've, would've, but Mister Russkie gave 'em a bye," casually answered the trucker. "I got shot but how's it go again – I got better. Don't mind sayin'… this 'alien' shit sure grows on a man!"

The sirens now sounded like they could be no more than six or seven blocks away, as Tanaka looked the streetwalker, up and down. The others could see that the van was being carefully backed up into the rear of the aircraft; luckily, the crowd, which was growing with every passing second, was keeping a respectful distance from this spectacle.

"Donny... who's *this?*" she asked.

"My name's 'Samantha'... but everybody calls me 'Sammie'," spoke the girl. "If ya don't mind me askin'... who *are* ya? And, like, where'd ya come from, lady? It was like ya dropped from way up there, without a parachute –"

"I'm *Vîrya* Cherie Tanaka, First Of The *Fire*," haughtily replied the professor. "Sammie – did anyone explain the nature of our group, or of our mission, to you?"

"Sorta," uncertainly responded the girl. "Sounds like fun. Or at least, more fun than what I've been dealin' with, lately."

"We don't have much time," warned the more-than-a-woman. "But there are some things that you *must* know. Donny – get Callum and Marie on the plane, while I talk to your, uhh, 'girlfriend'."

"I told the Russkie, that I ain't –" argued the trucker.

"Donny – get your folks on the damn *plane!*" forcefully insisted Tanaka.

"Okay… *okay!*" grunted a wisely-retreating Donny. "But y'all take off without her, and I'm gonna punch my way right through that door and jump the hell out, no matter *how* high we are... understand?"

Tanaka mutely nodded as the trucker led his aunt and uncle around the side of the aircraft, to its rear access-ramp.

She approached her new acquaintance until she was standing within arm's-reach.

"Sammie," advised the former Mars science officer, her voice kind and sympathetic despite her dimly-glowing eyes and otherwise regal, other-worldly demeanor, "Misha, Donny and the other five of us – Callum and Marie excepted – we're what the press is referring to as the 'Mars Gang'... we all have super-human abilities, and we sure do need them, because we're fighting it out with the most destructive weapons that the government can throw at us. I won't deceive you – going with us, assuming that none of my friends object, is likely to be an *extremely* dangerous adventure. And there's something else."

The sirens were now just a few blocks distant.

"What?" nervously asked the streetwalker.

"Should I assume that the reason why you know Donny, is – uhh – the reason that I *think* it is?" replied Tanaka.

"Ya mean, 'am I a whore'?" sniffed Sammie. "Of *course* I am, lady... ain't got no schoolin', past Grade 8, that is... how ya 'spect me to make money? Donny 'n me, we get together every time he drives through these parts. But he's special... always treats me better than the others. I really *like* him, ya know?"

The super-woman's arms extended quickly and seized the girl by the shoulders.

With an odd, glowing, far-away look, Tanaka counseled, "Sammie... I like *you*, too. Right now, you are so, *so* far beneath us... and I don't mean about what you do for a living. Now listen very carefully; if you get on that aircraft, your life will change *forever*, in ways that you can't understand or appreciate, right now. I won't kid you : there's no going back... but it's worth it, I *promise*. We offer the greatest gift that a human being can receive... in exchange for a lifetime of service. You have about sixty seconds to decide."

The nonplussed girl warily replied, "Why should I believe ya?"

And who's that other voice? she silently considered. *Sounds like a kid... but I'm not hearin' it – talk about 'el weirdo'...*

"Because I'm a *demi-goddess*," serenely and confidently replied Tanaka, "You asked how I showed up, Sammie? Easy – I was *flying*, all by myself, up in the air, surrounded by an invulnerable force-field, just like Superman, or, I guess, like Supergirl... and I decided to land here, in front of you. I could disintegrate everyone and everything in this parking-lot, with nothing more than a wave of my hand... but what I'm all about, is love, freedom and peace... not hate, cruelty and war, and be aware, if you go with us, that's going to be *your* mission, too. We're going to change this country, from top to bottom, starting with our asshole President – then, we'll change the *world!*"

"Holy... *shit!*" gasped the working-girl. "That Israeli agent guy – the one with the knives – said I'd be, uhh, in over my head... maybe he was right..."

"The ever-resourceful Misha's *Russian* – not Israeli," noted the professor, with a wan smile. "Though he definitely *is*, or *was*, an undercover agent. And he *is* right – you're *way* out of your league, honey. Getting on that aircraft will be like jumping from sandlot baseball to the World Series... and you're down by five runs in the bottom of the ninth, last game. But if Donny thinks you're up to it... well, he's my *brother*, Sammie – and I'll take his word for it... on faith."

"Yer related?" replied the confused streetwalker.

"Just a figure of speech," explained Tanaka, as the sounds of the sirens came from just around the block. She released her grasp, turned and walked toward the aircraft, whose rear cargo-door had closed.

As the gravity of the situation began to sink in, the former Mars science officer stopped and called to the working-girl.

"*Coming*, Sammie?" she beckoned.

For a few seconds, the girl hesitated, while considering her options. Then she raced to catch up with Tanaka.

"Life I had up to now, ain't nothin' to write home about," ruefully admitted the streetwalker, as the first of what would ultimately be three police-cars, roared off the street, into the parking-lot. "'Dead by twenty-five' kinda thing, ya know? I hope I'm makin' the right decision."

Tanaka's eyes were welling as she replied, "You sure *are*... oh *God*... thank you... *thank you*, Karéin... now, I know how it *feels*... to extend the hand of nobility..."

"What ya *talkin'* 'bout, lady?" asked a perplexed working-girl.

"You'll find out, my new sister," answered a strangely-elated, effervescent Tanaka. "Now let's get *out* of here!"

As if to reinforce the point, the sounds of far-off military aircraft-engines, followed by a cacophony of loud, percussive explosions in the direction of the Repository, reverberated through the atmosphere and earth.

As they went at a brisk pace toward the folding-stairway leading to the aircraft's cabin, a familiar face appeared in the entrance-hatchway.

Rapidly, Boyd descended the stairs, walked forward and then stopped.

"Already said 'goodbye' to them that's in there, and was going to do the same with yourself, Professor," he offered, "But... who's *this*?"

"Her name's 'Sammie'," replied Tanaka. "Latest member of our team."

"Eh?" he spoke. "How's that?"

The police were pouring out of their squad-cars, and, with the aid of a loudspeaker, were bellowing orders to the effect of "stay in your vehicles, until an officer has told you that you can leave". Several of the cops had entered the restaurant and appeared to be questioning the short-order-cook.

"Long story," said the former science officer. "Listen, Brent – we got to get out of here... I just wanted to wish you 'Godspeed', my brother."

He came up and embraced Tanaka, whispering, "Cherie... I'm sorry for what I said, back there... you know?"

"It's forgotten," she reassured. "Doesn't matter."

With a warm hug of her own, she added, "*This*... is what matters. And, the 'remember-your-vows' thing... I guess *that* does, too. I can *feel* your power surging, Brent. Use it wisely!"

"Deal, as long as you do too... *sister*," he answered, with a smile.

"*Deal*," she echoed, wiping a tear. "Take care of yourself."

He nodded, broke contact and raced off into the shadows behind the restaurant.

"Who was *that?*" inquired Sammie, as the two dashed up the stairway, which immediately retracted behind them.

"*Væran* Brent Boyd, the first man to ever touch minds with an angel," described Tanaka, while directing the streetwalker to a seat within the aircraft and, to the girl's astonishment, using telekinetic skills to accelerate the process of doing up the various buckles and straps needed to secure the girl in place. "He's going to save his family from the government... welcome to our war."

"Next stop, Austin, Texas, folks," came the deep, strong voice of Sam Jacobson, as they heard and felt the power of the V-37's turbofans, propelling them westward into the Kentucky night.

One Poke Too Many

Chu had tried mightily to get herself invited to the President's decision-making circles, and she had dropped tantalizing little tidbits of (mostly false or misleading) information about the Storied Watcher and her hangers-on, as an incentive.

Despite all these efforts, she met with a decided lack of success; receiving only intermittent reports of the goings-on, from the twenty-something, frat-boy-faced Air Force guy who served her meals and occasionally let her do a quick, results-censored search on his personal mobile communicator (he claimed this was "totally safe, because I run all the comms on this ship anyway, and I got it on an unmonitored channel").

The fact that something *big* had lately been going down, however, was obvious – she intercepted a few comments about "heightened threat to the President, keep the Service in close proximity to the C In C" – but beyond that, there was a frustrating lack of information.

Now, in the hours immediately following the very bad episode, Minnie Chu's somnolent mind was being invaded by an onslaught of odd – yet, somehow, familiar-feeling, happy and reassuring – dreams

I made it clear to Kai that I wasn't going to have children, until I made it at least to the Regional Manager level, she half-consciously mused.

That's ignoring that stupid "Women's Place In The Home" law, banning maternity leave and requiring you to quit if you get pregnant, of course...

So how is it, that I get these persistent dreams of a little boy speaking to me... his features obscure, intangible, out-of-focus, just around-the-bend... Tommy, maybe?

But if so... why's he calling, "Mommy, where are *you"?*

It's not right, that I feel such an irrational, gut-level, surge of love for him.

Tommy's her *boy, not* mine. *What right do I have?*

Chu awoke, less sure than ever about the dividing line between the Storied Watcher's oft-quoted “dream-world”, and reality.

Groggily, the team-leader looked down at the locket that she had been given by her fondly-remembered fellow-agent. A tear came to her eye, as she held the aquamarine-centered locket in her hand and said a silent prayer for her brothers Will and Otis.

Protect them, Destroying Angel, she asked. *Wherever they are.*

And while you're at it... protect... me.

Her semi-reverie was interrupted by the appearance of a dour-faced, crew-cut, black-suited, male, Caucasian Secret Service agent, peering through one of the now-opened galley-doors.

“Ms. Chu?” he called. “I'm here to escort you.”

“Well, sure... but where?” she asked, while standing and looking into a mirror, trying to make herself look presentable.

“The President's asked for you presence in the small meeting-room,” explained the agent. We have two minutes to make it there. Let's go.”

“Oh, that's great,” replied the team-leader, “Although I wish I'd had time to really clean myself up –”

“I'm sure that won't be an issue,” he replied. “Please walk between myself and the other agent, who will follow us.”

“Of course,” said Chu, with a polite, vapid smile. She went out to the corridor, turned and proceeded forward through the aircraft, arriving at the destination with at least twenty seconds to spare.

The Secret Service man knocked three times on the door to the meeting-room, received a “come in” acknowledgment, and ushered Chu inside. Crowford, the *nouveau*-President, Bezomorton, Blanshard and a new guy – he was short and squat with flabby, pasty-white skin, had a bald head and beady, shifty eyes, even worse than those of the Security Adviser – who she didn't recognize, were arrayed around the table, and there was a bland, middle-aged, expressionless Caucasian face displayed on a flat-screen display on one wall, within direct view of all participants.

That's the guy from Pittsburgh, mused the team-leader. *The creep who I met up in the penthouse...*

“Have a seat,” directed the *faux*-President. “I'd like to introduce Bill Warnock, Director of the FBI, who's replaced Cesar Ochoa.”

We'll get Cesar out, too... eventually, she inwardly resolved.

With an insincerely pleasant expression, Chu bent over the table and offered her hand to the new guy, who shook in a perfunctory manner.

“It's an honor to meet finally meet you, sir,” she said. “Before this all started, I hadn't personally encountered anyone at the Bureau, above Senior Regional Director.”

“Well… let's hope you can hack it, at this level, Ms. Chu,” he replied.

The team-leader demurely smiled and nodded, then sat down.

"The fellow on the video-feed's the Director of the Agency," matter-of-factually mentioned the nouveau-President. "I believe you've met?"

"Ahh... yes, I believe we *have*, sir," evenly answered Chu.

So that's who he was... figures, she thought.

And I had a clear shot at him.

I could have burned a neat little hole right through his cold, stone heart, then informed Karéin that the bastard responsible for her family's agony, had paid with his life.

Damnit! Don't make that *mistake again, Minnie...*

The man on the video-screen just impassively stared, but did not offer any commentary at this point.

"I'll get right to the point," started the U.S. leader. "What do you know about Jerry Kaysten and Sylvia Abruzzio?"

"Well, Mr. President," slowly recounted Chu, "Sylvia's a former JPL scientist, who, as you may recall, was one of the ground-controllers for the *Eagle / Infinity* Mars exploration mission... Mr. Kaysten was, as I understand it, the Chief of Staff for the President who preceded you in your current office, sir. Both of them traveled along with my fellow FBI agents and the alien known of as the 'Storied Watcher', a.k.a. Karéin-Mayréij, first to a campground in Canada, and then Sylvia and I – but not Jerry – went to the Aleutian island of Amchitka, following after Karéin, who had gone there ahead of us, to free those who she regards as her 'family'. All of this is recorded in my written report, sir."

"*Really*," offered the *faux*-President, with mock-agreeabilty in his voice. "That's *all* of it?"

"Yes, sir," answered the team-leader. "All I know of, that is. Keeping in mind, that Karéin is, to say the least, quite an inscrutable and intimidating being, to deal with, up close. A lot of what goes on with her, I can only guess at... and I'm pretty sure that's true of both Sylvia and Jerry, as well."

"You know," he observed, "Some of us have noticed that you refer to these two individuals by their first names. Do you regard them as friends?"

"'Friends'?" uncertainly responded Chu. "Uhh... not *exactly*, sir. What I mean is, all of us who went with the Storied Watcher during those few days, learned to depend on her, and on each other... sort of like Otis, Will and I have done as a team, since they got put under my command, a couple of years ago. Have I come to personally like Sylvia and Jerry, and wish them well? Yes, I'd say that would be a fair statement."

"I see," commented the U.S. leader. "So would it also be a fair statement, that you wouldn't want to see anything bad, to *happen* to them?"

Chu's heart sank, though she tried as hard as she could not to visibly show her apprehension.

Shit, she mused, *Did the Agency catch them?*

Wait a minute... if they closed in on Ms. Abruzzio while wearing anything other than a lead-lined suit of armor... and Jerry'd just run away...

"I don't want *anyone* to be hurt, sir," replied the FBI team-leader, "Least of all, not them. Are they in some kind of danger, sir? Is there anything I can do to help them get out of it?"

"Oh, I think you might be able to, Ms. Chu," he unctuously confirmed. "Bill?"

Now Warnock leaned forward in his chair, with his corpulent belly spilling part-way over the edge of the table, as he focused his squint-eyed stare on Chu.

"Ms. Chu," he stated, "As you're no doubt aware, I'm at the top of the Bureau's chain of command, and in that capacity, I'm ordering you to truthfully answer everything I ask, to the fullest extent of your knowledge. Do I have your cooperation?"

"Of course, sir," she said.

"That's good," he replied. "Now, based on what I've so far read in your reports, it appears that the alien named 'Karéin-Mayréij' somehow bestowed a bunch of superhuman abilities, on the members of the Mars mission team, who are, incidentally, now calling themselves the 'Mars Gang'... is that right?"

"That's correct," she affirmed.

"Was anyone *else* given these powers, Ms. Chu?" he inquired.

Uh-oh, she thought.

Okay – they would have been able to put two plus two together, just from what went on down at that Agency facility in Pittsburgh.

No point in dissembling, on that front...

"Yes," stated Chu. "Those who I know of, in addition to the Jacobson group, that is, are Sylvia Abruzzio, Hector Ramirez, Darryl Bennington (a.k.a. 'Wolf'), and Jerry Kaysten."

"Is that right?" he disputed. "Considering that a large number of people accompanied the alien all over the place, isn't it a little *odd* that only a few of them ended up being, uhh, 'changed', in this manner?"

"With all due respect, sir... I don't think it's 'odd', at all," evaded the team-leader. "There were, uhh, extenuating circumstances in all of the above cases. For example, along with the Jacobson team, Sylvia and Hector were part of the Mars mission, to whom Karéin felt deeply obliged, simply for having woken her up from her sleep in that tomb up there. Wolf – though he had never met her prior to that point – defended the Storied Watcher by shooting an assassin who was trying to kill her, in the Tucson hotel situation, something for which she was very grateful. With Jerry, I'm less sure of the motivation, but she said something about 'those who I bite, become akin to as me' or something to that effect... I took it to mean that she had injected some kind of venom that transformed him. Like I said in my report, sir – when one is talking about a being like Karéin-Mayréij, there are bound to be a lot of un-answered questions."

"I don't find that very convincing," he persisted. "For example, why would she only –"

At this point, Crawford mumbled something under his breath to the *faux*-President, and though this was clearly meant not to be overheard, Chu's alien-powered ears made it out easily.

"If them FBI boys really *did* have any of these fancy-ass 'alien-powers', Mr. President," he whispered, "Then why didn't they put up a fight, when you took 'em to the back of the plane and –"

The U.S. leader nodded as if to convey agreement, but he motioned the Spiritual Adviser to stop talking.

A horrified Chu was surprised that she was able to keep a poker-face, upon hearing this; perhaps it was something in the back of her head saying "it's alright, Mommy... it's alright", which kept her in control, at that moment.

I should show you motherfuckers what an 'alien-power's all about, she furiously considered.

But if I give you what you deserve, I might slice the tail off this plane... and I want to live to see justice done.

That's just a temporary reprieve, you bastards... not a pardon.

But the tone of her voice still changed, and whatever polite smile that she had previously feigned, disappeared instantly.

"I'll ask you directly, Ms. Chu – did she 'transform' either *you*, or *anyone* else with whom you're familiar, including but not limited to Agents... what're their names again... yeah, Agents Boatman and Hendricks, in this manner?" demanded Warnock.

Coldly, she replied, staring him directly in the face, "No. *Sir,*" she said.

"Are you sure of that?" he pressed. "I'm sure you know that lying to a superior Bureau officer is a dismissal offense, not to mention being a felony."

"Yes, I know that, sir," parried the team-leader. "And as I believe I've mentioned before... at least in my case, as well as with my friends and co-agents Will Hendricks and Otis Boatman, while we *were* on what I'd describe as 'cordial' terms with Karéin, she was well aware of the fact that our primary allegiance was to the government and to the Bureau... which is why we never got the abilities that she bestowed on the others. I should also mention that we specifically asked not to be involved in this 'treatment', as well."

"Okay, well, I think we've beaten *that* one half to death," interrupted the *nouveau*-President. "And – based on some current events with which I believe those with a need to know, are aware of – I'd tend to believe our junior FBI agent friend here. Now let me get to the specific reason we asked you about this 'Abruzzio' dame. We need hard information on her capabilities – those of Kaysten as well. In particular, we need to know how we can best defeat these 'alien-powers' that you're so hot and bothered about."

"Again, with all due respect, sir," dispassionately remarked the inwardly-seething Minnie Chu, "I don't think that's a fair characterization of my feelings on the matter... but what, specifically, did you want to know?"

Blanchard spoke up. "The Agency director here," – he gestured at the screen – "Has informed us that this 'Abruzzio' murdered one of his people, in an incident in Pittsburgh with which you're familiar... but we're still not sure exactly how she did it. Tell us everything you know about this woman, who, as you're no doubt aware, is now an enemy of the state. Go ahead."

"Well, sir," replied Chu, choosing her words slowly and carefully, "Although I didn't directly observe Ms. Abruzzio's alien-powers being used, the Storied Watcher indicated that she – Sylvia, that is – had been given some kind of control over what Karéin referred to as 'the little particle-shine', which I took to mean, some type of radiation. She did warn Sylvia that this power could be very dangerous to human beings, if too much of the *Fire* was used with it."

"Did the alien say anything about a maximum range, or the number of Rads that Abruzzio could emit, or how long she could sustain an attack with this power?" pressed the general.

"No," answered the team-leader. "That isn't how Karéin talks, anyway; she tends to use antiquated-sounding, rather formal language, and she didn't give precise facts or figures about any of these 'alien-powers', including those belonging to Sylvia, or Jerry. For example, with the former Chief of Staff, she said something about 'quicker than the fastest race-steed shall you be, Jerry; and neither shall a dash of several leagues tire you'... that kind of thing."

Although didn't my personal 'Angel' say something back at the camp about, "Soon, Minn-ee, your wide gaze will set a forest-glade afire, and your narrow-stare will cleave even an ar-mee-tank, in twain"? she mused, while trying to keep track of the conversation.

Would that *count as a 'fact or figure'?*

"Sir," continued Chu, "It might help if I knew what the context of this all is. If you don't mind my asking... what's going on, with Ms. Abruzzio?"

America's most privileged power-elite exchanged glances, and then the *faux*-President spoke up.

"Well, I suppose it can't hurt for you to know the situation, at least at a high level," he mentioned. "Briefly – we have reason to believe that Abruzzio and Kaysten are holding the former President hostage –"

"Why would they do *that?*" interjected a genuinely-perplexed Chu.

"You've heard the latest demands of Jacobson's 'Mars Gang', I presume?" he replied.

"I'm afraid not, sir," she said. "I haven't had much access to the communications media, lately; and what I have had, has been, uhh, rather 'locked-down', if you know what I mean."

"Then let me bring you up to speed, Ms. Chu," grunted the U.S. leader. "This traitor 'Jacobson' and his little gang of fellow-terrorists have taken over the Fort Knox Bullion Repository, and one of their self-styled 'non-negotiable demands' – I can hardly bring myself to repeat it, without laughing out loud – is that I, yours truly, that is, hand myself over to an impeachment trial held in Congress. Don't ask me who'd bring the charges, let alone vote to confirm them, since we have a Republican majority in both houses of that institution... but anyway, it appears that Abruzzio's in cahoots with Jacobson, since she demanded, in a call made from the direct line of the former President, not an hour ago, that I 'resign' in his favor. Since he'd never do anything like that voluntarily, the only logical conclusion is that he's being held against his will; and the only way to free him in one piece, is to figure out some way to defeat this 'Abruzzio' dame, not to mention Kaysten, as quickly and effectively as possible. *Capiche?*"

Smart going, Commander, she silently considered.

More power to you.

"That's... *wow,*" temporized the team-leader. "I honestly don't know what to say... except that you should proceed with caution, if you're planning to make a move against Sylvia, Jerry or the Jacobson group, for that matter. Karéin warned us that some of these 'alien-powers' have an inherently wide area of effect, if enough *Amaiish* – that's her word for 'the *Fire*' – is used to energize them. If Sylvia had to defend herself in this manner, being anywhere near her might be very dangerous, both to the former President and to anyone else in the vicinity."

"I *see,*" neutrally offered the current, *faux*-President.

Now, the bland-faced man on the video-screen finally spoke up.

"So," he inquired in his characteristic monotone, "Would it be a fair observation, that our, uhh, 'rescue' teams, can't safely approach Abruzzio closely enough to overpower her?"

"I'd think not, sir," replied Chu.

And I'm not just fucking whistling 'Dixie' there, my friend, she thought.

"Mr. President," he went on, "One more question, and a comment, from this end, if you don't mind."

"Go ahead," said the *nouveau*-President, with a shrug.

"Ms. Chu," asked the CIA director, "I assume that you've had some experience in doing interrogations... on behalf of the Bureau, that is?"

"Yes, I have," she confirmed. "I took the Bureau's training-courses on this subject and have been on a number of criminal cases, during which I employed our standard techniques."

"Excellent!" he smoothly remarked. "Now, regarding this 'Abruzzio' woman, and Kaysten... how resistant do you think they would be, to psychological pressure – a threat to life and limb, that is?

"I'd have to say, 'not very', sir," responded Chu. "While it's true that Sylvia *is* a civilian, like many of the rest of us, she's lately had to deal with a lot of personal risk and stress, and has held up remarkably well. As for Jerry, at first I didn't think very much of him – courage-wise, that is – but eventually I came to understand that he's a very strong person, in his own way. So I don't think that threatening either one of them, at this point, is likely to be much of a deterrent."

"Hmm," idly sounded the Agency man. "Is that right? Let's, for the sake of discussion, assume that it is. Would you say that's the case, if, for example, Ms. Abruzzio – or Mr. Kaysten, not to mention those in this so-called 'Mars Gang' –

were to find out, that the government had one or more of their family-members in, ahh... 'protective custody'?"

"What do you *mean*, 'protective custody'?" coldly riposted Chu.

She struggled, hoping all the while that it wasn't externally visible, to subdue the *Fire* that raged throughout her soul.

"Oh, well... maybe that wasn't exactly the best term for it," he stated. "It's not really that 'protective', after all. The point's the same, either way, though; if we can't directly get to these 'super-beings' that you seem to so admire, Ms. Chu, perhaps we *can* get to them *in*directly, by making it clear that their families –"

Upon hearing this, the famously-under-control Minnie Chu, "lost it". She jumped to her feet and loudly proclaimed, "I'll hear no more of this... *sir!* I've *seen*, first-hand, the kind of treatment that prisoners get from you and the psychopathic thugs that the Agency tolerates within its ranks... and my cooperation with all of you, is over with! You want to disgrace this country any more than it's already done, and in so doing, guarantee your own destruction at the hands of Jacobson And Company, be my guest – but leave me out of it!"

"You'll retract that outburst, Ms. Chu!" growled an angrily red-faced Warnock, "And apologize to all of those here, but especially to the Agency director. *Immediately.* That's an *order!*"

"Order declined… *sir!*" defiantly spat back the team-leader. "And I'll spare you a few words – I resign from the Bureau, as of right now. You can *have* my badge and my pension, for all they're worth! I won't demean myself by associating with a government like this... I was a *fool* to think that I could reason with you, or change you."

"I'd agree with half of that," chuckled the *nouveau*-President, who, evidently, found Chu's spitfire diatribe mildly amusing. "The part about you being a 'fool', my dear."

He turned to address the others. "What'd I *tell* you, about wasting our time on the junior ranks, guys? You never *learn!* Oh, well... 'nothing ventured, nothing gained', I suppose."

"I'd agree, Mr. President," said Crowford. "Pretty disappointin', if you ask me. I really thought this girl had a brain in her head... obviously, I was wrong."

Why does the danger-sense go berserk, every time I look at him? the seething Chu silently pondered.

He's just an effing preacher... *what's he, compared to the cruel and powerful sons of bitches to whom I just mouthed off?*

But didn't it feel good, *doing that?*

Whatever happens... they can't say that they weren't warned.

The U.S. leader tapped a button under the table and the same two hulking, taciturn, black-suited Secret Service agents that had escorted Chu to the meeting, opened the door and leaned through it, into the meeting-room.

“This woman is insubordinate and has resigned her position in the Bureau,” he declared. “She's to be considered an untrustworthy passenger and is to be confined to quarters, until you hear differently from me. Understood?”

“Yes, sir,” spoke the first agent. “*You*, there – follow me outside,” he called to Chu. “You will be restrained to a seat in the Security Section, and be aware that in situations like this, I'm authorized to use lethal force, at the *slightest* sign of resistance or flight... so no funny business.”

The team-leader stepped forward, but just before leaving the room, she stopped momentarily, glanced at the elite group who she had so thoroughly antagonized, and commented, “You know, 'gentlemen'... Karéin informed me, that she had, at one point, told the Agency director, 'for you... all hope is lost'. How right she *was*. What will be... will be.”

“I forgot to mention, Ms. Chu,” came the infuriatingly dispassionate voice of the Agency-director, from the video-screen, “That we've picked up one 'Kaiser Lee', from a software company in New York? I think he's known to you... isn't that right? He's being held in relative comfort... but that situation *could* change at any time. Just thought you should know.”

“Don't you *dare* do anything to him!” she grimaced. “Try it – and I’ll hunt you down, no matter where you try to hide… so help me *God!*”

“I guess the 'empty threats' shtick is getting a little boring, my dear,” sniffed the *faux*-President. “We've got *work* to do.”

He motioned to the Secret Service guy, and said, “Take her away.”

With her head held high and her eyes straight forward, Minnie Chu, formerly of the U.S. Federal Bureau of Investigations, walked out of the room.

Sweet-Talkin' Some Mountain-Men

A visibly-impressed Will Hendricks let out a whistle and offered, “Man, I guess I *see* now, why you guys were so careful with strangers,” upon surveying the country-barn's-worth of combo moonshine-and-synth-making gear, that the hillbillies had accumulated in this secluded spot. “Gotta be a thousand gallons worth, either bottled up or being brewed.”

Bubbling, hissing decanters of various liquids, connected by flexible rubber-and-plastic hoses and glass pipes, appeared in every direction the eye could see, and there were barrels of precursor-ingredients stacked right up to the ceiling on three of the place's four, wood-and-sheet-metal walls.

“We's servin' th' whole county from here, city-boy,” snorted the leader of the mountain-men. “Fifty year or more, man cain't make a livin' no other way, in these parts.”

“I'm surprised that nobody's found you yet,” opined Boatman. “What with those drones and spy-satellites that they're s'posed to have all over the place.”

“Well,” laconically answered the second hillbilly, “We's off th' grid up here – solar, wind 'n diesel – an' we got that shit on th' top of th' roof that's s'posed to block them heat-seekin' thangs. But ev'ry so often, maybe they *do* see us, since we get th' law comin' up that road that y'all stumbled 'cross, or one of them 'copters happens to fly by... they's local LEA boys, ain't never sent none of them Fed-ral buttholes up this way. So we jus' show up with our guns a-ready, 'n then offer 'em some cash 'n all they kin drink, in exchange fer them keepin' their mouths shut an' tellin' them Feds that there ain't nothin' here."

"You've been lucky that you haven't been dealing with the, uhh, 'Fed-rals' who've been after us," ruefully commented the third agent. "I think you'd find 'em a bit more aggressive than the cops from around here."

"What makes y'all think *that*, city-boy?" replied the hillbilly leader. "Tryin' slicker-talk on them deputies down 'n th' valley be a *bad* idea... they don' take nice to bein' sassed... or dissed."

"Oh… I don't know," said the black agent. "But I guess havin' them drop a H-bomb on our head on account of takin' a dislike to us... why, after somethin' like *that*, dealin' with whoever you got 'round here, that's gonna seem like that proverbial walk in the park."

"Y'all talkin' *shit* there, blackie," sneered the second mountain-man. "Ain't *no* man live through somethin' like *that!*"

"You're right," obliquely mentioned Hendricks. "No *human* man..."

He paused for a second or two and continued, "Anyway, guys... thanks for the, uhh, 'hospitality' so far, but there's some stuff we need, and like I said, when this mess is over, we'll pay you back ten to one at the very least –"

"Yeah?" asked the first hillbilly. "Like what?"

"Ride to... I don't know where would be nice," said the third agent. "But first... you got NeoNet here? We've been kind of out of the loop lately... need to catch up with what's been going on."

"Don' be *stupid*, boy!" growled the boss-man. "Ain't got *nothin'* that'd let th' law trace our location, not just that damn networkin'-shit but ain't no mobiles or CB 'lowed, neither. We *do* got TV off th' antenna... only four channels, mind y'all, an' some of 'em don' come through too good sometimes on 'count of th' mountains. Y'all free to try it, fer what it's worth."

"Sure," eagerly replied the third agent. "Where is it?"

"Right over there," said the hillbilly-leader. "Big screen over th' vid-e-o players we got set up to waste some time, while we's guardin' the shack in a brew cycle. Red button on left of th' controller."

"Great, man," said Hendricks. He strode over to the assembly and powered it up, but all that showed on the screen was a blue, "no-signal" flood-fill.

He began rapidly switching channels, noting with interest that there was a junior-league basketball game (thought the signal quality was poor) on one of the available stations; the next one's picture was even worse, but it seemed to be a cooking-show of some sort.

The third channel was so interference-laden as to be unwatchable, but – thankfully – there was a newscast on the last station, and though it was only low-definition, the message that it related came through loud and clear.

"And now, ladies and gentlemen, to recap the top story of the last 24 hours," drawled the clumsily-toupéed male announcer, speaking in front of what had to be the tackiest 1980s-holdover TV news-room backdrop that Hendricks and Boatman had ever seen, "The crisis at the Fort Knox Bullion Depository is still on-going, with the self-styled 'Mars Gang' terrorists apparently in control of that facility, despite a heavy Army and Air Force bombardment and significant loss of life inflicted on the soldiers of the Fort Knox garrison; the Administration has just issued a statement demanding 'calm in this time of national challenge', and has hinted at the re-imposition of full martial law, should the Fort Knox situation not be resolved in the very near future. Meanwhile, Governor Wilmer has reassured West Virginians that the conflict is exclusively centered in Kentucky and poses no threat to our state. WVNS will monitor this important story and bring you bulletins as they occur. Now, we return to our regularly-scheduled programming, the 'Appalachian Stompin' Jamboree', with that good ol' conductor boy, Merle Milton..."

He cut the power.

"Shee-*it!*" exclaimed a warily impressed Boatman. "Looks like that Jacobson fella gone and *done* it. Give him nine out of ten for execution, but... what's his game?"

"Beats *me*," admitted Hendricks. "Sam's just gonna piss the President off even more than he already is. If that's *possible*... which it probably isn't."

"Y'all sure *has* been out of th' loop there, boy," offered the second hillbilly. "Pretty much everybody's heard it by now – them terrorists is demandin' that th' Pres'dent give himself up for some kinda fuckin' trial, in Washington... D.C., that is –"

"'Bout as likely as us folk up here swearin' off moonshine," grinned the first guy, showing the prominent gap where one of his front teeth used to be. "But did I get it right that y'all knows some of them-thar 'terrorists'? Cuz I'm *warnin'* ya, boy – we ain't much up on th' law 'round here, fer obvious reasons... but we's still good, honest Americans... we don' cotton to them Moo-slims, or–"

"Do we know Sam Jacobson, and the rest of them who make up that 'Mars Gang'? Absolutely," stated the third agent. "Are we Muslims or 'terrorists', or are we in on what they're doing? Nope – but I'll *level* with you, man... being shoved out of a plane without a parachute... that kind of hardens your attitude to whoever did it, you know? Anyway... I got a few hundred in cash on me, and I hope you'll accept it as a down-payment on what we need."

"An' what 'zactly would *that* be, city-boy?" asked the hillbilly-leader.

"You can call me 'Will'," said the third agent, trying to be as friendly as possible. "First, if you got a shower or something around here, I wouldn't mind getting cleaned up, and I bet Otis would too –"

"Got *that* right, son," grunted Boatman. "Didn't figure on hikin' when we got on that plane."

"Yeah," agreed Hendricks. "Then, we'd like a ride to the nearest large town... where would that be, by the way?"

"White Sulfur Springs be 'bout 25 miles down Route 92," noted the second hillbilly, "But ain't much more than a fuckin' big golf course an' a big-ass ho-tel. Warm Springs 'cross Virginny state line's closer, though y'all gotta go over th' hills on a back-road, an' it's smaller. If'n y'all want anythin' more than a corner-store, y'all pretty much gotta go to Lewisburg, an' that's a good twenny mile further up I-64 an' Route 60, goin' west. But we ain't no taxi, an' we ain't takin' y'all back up –"

"Just one-way would be fine," reassured the black former-agent.

"Think we'd better pick Lewisburg," declared Hendricks. "Next... you guys got any spare clothes, that'd fit us, I mean... and two pistols, with maybe a couple'a spare clips, each?"

"Y'all got to be funnin' us, boy – give y'all a *gun?*" chuckled the hillbilly-leader. "We got plenny – can't be caught short, we ain't shootin' it out with th' law, of course, but some other fucker from next county show up here meanin' to lift our *product*, that's 'nother matter... an' as fer th' clothes, yeah, same thang there, jus' 'case we get snowed in or somethin' – but why should we do all *that* fer two city-boys like y'all?"

Now, an exasperated Hendricks shut his eyelids, summoned the power and then took a step toward the mountain-man, opening his eyes and allowing the *Fire* to dance and swirl throughout his body in the same instant, while traces of his war-song began to issue from the walls, floor, ceiling and everywhere else.

"Why?" he half-shouted. "I'll *tell* you why! Because you backwoods 'billies are *way* out of your league, in dealing with the likes of Otis and me! Use your *brains* – you *saw* what's going down, at Fort Knox... right? Well, that was six super-heroes, or super-villains, or super-*somethings,* just like the two of us, holding off the whole fuckin' *U.S. Army and Air Force,* man! All we're asking for is a little help in the short-run; and what you get out of it, is being in on the big-times, for the long-run. Having trouble with your neighbors? Well, *that'll* end, for good, when what's going on, gets sorted out. You *get* me, man?"

"I ain't afeared of –" started the hillbilly-leader; but he was interrupted by his compatriot.

"Fuck's *sakes*, Billy-Ray," pleaded the second guy, "Look at the boy's *eyes!* An' there's that damn music, again! Boy's got a swelled head, fer sure, but he's got some kinda voo-doo shit goin' on –"

"Oh… he ain't the *only* one," smiled Boatman, as he, too, energized his alien-power; and in addition to the same external manifestations that had illuminated his fellow former-agent, for the first time, the mountain-men heard the black ex-agent's deep, powerful war-song, its rhythmic beat adding to the adrenaline-rush already-stimulated by Hendricks' psycho-melody.

"Now you all listen up, boys!" added the big black man, "Young Will 'n I, we don't mean you all any harm, – because if we did, well, there wouldn't be much left of this fine liquor-brewin' establishment that you got up here, and there'd be even less left of *you*. Did I mention that I can disintegrate things, just by touchin' them? Here... have a look."

He picked up a piece of copper pipe that had been lying around as a spare part for the distilling-assembly, grasped it with both hands and directed his attack at the tube, which collapsed in a glittering shower of orange-colored dust.

"I don't think I have to explain what might happen if I used this little trick on, say, somebody's neck... and I got a few other ones up my sleeve, as well," confidently observed Boatman, while the two mountain-men gaped in frightened astonishment. "Such as – or so I'm told – bein' close to invulnerable to bullets... that's obviously one that I ain't too eager to try out... but it's there, just in case. Anyway... the reason we want all of what Will's been askin' you for, it isn't for lack of firepower, on our part – it's more that there's a lot of, uhh, *complicated* stuff goin' on these days, and we'd prefer not to make ourselves too conspicuous, until we get a better handle on what the situation out there, is. With that in mind... can we count on your help?"

"Say 'yes', Billy-Ray," stammered the second hillbilly.

"Yeah... I guess," reluctantly complied the leader. "But fer evr'y dollar worth of stuff y'all takes from here, y'all be owin' us five back... understand?"

"Seems fair," insouciantly replied the black ex-agent, as both war-songs and the signs of the *Fire*, abated. "Although I'd bet, what with where he's sittin' now, that Jacobson fella's probably got a bit more at his disposal, to pay you all off with."

"Yeah," opined Hendricks, "But I got no idea how he's gonna carry all that gold with him, or where he's gonna take it, not to mention what the hell *our* next move is, after getting our asses out of here."

"I'd say, 'findin' out what's happened to Minnie', would be a good place to start, young man," replied Boatman. "Maybe Sylvia 'n Jerry, not to mention 'Daughter Tornado Diamond-Curtain', as well. Somethin's tellin' me that there's some mighty big events fixin' to happen in these parts, and I'm not just thinkin' of Mister Jacobson And Company... we gotta get back in the game, you know?"

"'Daughter Tornado'...?" interrupted the leader mountain-man. "What th' hell's *that?*"

"Somethin' – 'scuse me, some*one* – that you all sure don't want to get on the bad side of, my friend," genially explained the big black man. "Unless, of course, you'd like to lose a few pounds of ugly fat, the hard way."

"Y'all talkin' *shit*," argued Billy-Ray.

"If you ever get a chance to say that to her face," diffidently offered Boatman, "It'll only be to spite your nose, which you might soon be missin'."

Hendricks almost cracked up, but he managed, "Come on... let's get showered, dressed, packin', rested... then, outta here."

Odin Speed To Valhalla

Another tough, bloody day lay behind the Aryan warriors, with nothing but more of the same anywhere in sight, as the California sun began to set.

Many others in their current position – specifically, sandwiched between a mysteriously-burgeoning army of Latino gang-bangers and other low-class miscreants, which had appeared out of nowhere, on the west, and the real U.S. Army, which had been slowly pushing forward, from the east – would have taken the easy way out, and just surrendered to the tender mercies of "the authorities".

But the bitter-enders in the Brotherhood were not easily-disposed to do so; and, if truth be told, many of them were already seeking a replay of the glorious *Götterdämmerung*, here in the baking-hot, arid, garbage-strewn streets of suburban Los Angeles.

The South California Lictor General had chosen their headquarters – the lodge of the upscale Empire Lakes golf-course at 6th and Cleveland, with the scenic San Gabriel Mountains looming to the north – very well. The expensively-decorated, three-story (two above, one below-ground) building, though now built into a sand-bag-reinforced fortress, complete with concentric rings of perimeter warning-sensors, machine-gun-nests, land-mines and carefully-cleared fields of fire covering all possible approaches, was still a place of luxury. It had been stocked from basement to ceiling with foodstuffs, liquor, ammunition, spare weapons, fuel, "comfort-captives" (most of whom were young, female and Caucasian, although there were a few Latinos and boys as well, for the discreet enjoyment of those Aryan warriors who played the other side), porno-movies, swastika-flags, Confederate-flags, portraits of Adolf Hitler, of Wesley A. Swift and other necessities, stolen or scrounged from everywhere within miles.

There was also a makeshift prison located in the basement, and at odd hours of the day, those above-ground could hear the screams of those unfortunates with whom the Lictor General and his immediate understudies, decided to "have a little fun". So far, of those who had been dragged or thrown down those dark stairs, precisely "none" had again been seen alive.

It was not a surprise to anyone, of course.

But strategically, the situation was grim. The small cadre of doctors and nurses who had been frog-marched out of local hospitals at gunpoint, had been overwhelmed by the steady stream of severely-wounded Whiteman warriors – particularly from the western front, where an increasing number were showing up covered in strange, abrasive injuries, as if their skin had been literally eaten away by some sinister, unknown new weapon – and the available, jury-rigged medical-facilities were primitive. Crippled Aryan street-fighters (some moaning in pain, most stoically dealing with their predicament) lay on park-benches, cots and lounge-booth-seats throughout the eastern half of the lodge, and more were arriving every hour.

The casualty rate was plainly unsustainable in the long-run, although the warriors took some consolation in the fact that that for every one of their own who had fallen, at least two "wetbacks", and at least three U.S. Army draftees, had suffered a similar or worse fate.

Any ordinary-sized human male would have felt immediately intimidated in the company of the three who were arrayed around the map-table, in the *Führerbunker*-imitating, basement operations-room at the Empire Lakes Lodge.

The Lictor General – an older man with streaks of gray in his shaggy beard, but one whose cruel, cunning survival-instincts and keen judgment had prevailed over uncounted opponents, both internal and external – himself stood over six-foot-three, and the two senior lieutenants who had been summoned before him, though younger, were both either this size or were slightly taller and heavier still. Furthermore, their bulk wasn't just flab; these were guys who could – and frequently *did* – speak with their fists, boots and muscles.

They had the scars – and the kill-count-tattoos – to prove it.

“Okay,” grunted the Lictor General, “I'll start with what you're both gonna ask me... and the answer's, 'not yet'. We got our best minds workin' on it – includin' two of them pansy-ass scientists that we grabbed out of a electronics company warehouse two blocks over, told 'em it's half a toe for every hour we figure they're stallin' us – but we ain't figured it completely out yet. They *think* they can rig it to go off... but they don't know if that's 'right away', or 'six weeks from now'. Obviously we can't take that chance and let the fuckin' thing get captured, then defused. So –”

“Any idea when they'll have the bugs worked out?” interrupted the first of the other Aryan warriors.

“Soon,” replied the General. “They just need some parts... resistors, clock chip, wire, some damn thing called a 'mosfet'... whatever the fuck *that* is. We got a team scroungin' for 'em now. Soon as they show up, I'm bein' told it's a couple of hours... maybe three or four..”

“Well... that's good news,” offered the warrior. “I know this ain't my pay-grade, but... what's the plans, when we *do* get the fucker ready to blow?”

“That's for me to decide and you to be told, Whiteman,” growled the Lictor General, “But I'll let you in on *this* much : I figure the fuckin' thing's our ace-in-the-hole, against the government, at least... we'll see if the wetbacks have the brains to realize what they're up against – probably not, if I know *them*. The Army gets too close – we just tell 'em, 'one step over the line... up goes half of fuckin' Los Angeles'.”

“And if they call us on it?” pressed the second warrior.

“Then they'll get a big fuckin' ol' *surprise*,” evenly stated the commander. “You *afraid* of that?”

Without the slightest hint of hesitation or nervousness, the Aryan soldier replied, “Why *would* I? Up to Valhalla in thunder and fire, just like our Lord and Savior Adolf Hitler did, when the Fates called for him – no better way! We all gotta go *sometime*, after all.”

The other Whiteman warrior grimly nodded confirmation.

After a couple of seconds, the Lictor General changed the subject.

"So... what the fuck's goin' *on* out there, today... any improvements?" he demanded.

"Beat the Army back a bit on that incursion they did past two days, north of the Freeway... took back the Auto Club Speedway and pushed 'em as far east as Beach and Randall," replied the first Whiteman warrior, pointing with his big, hairy index finger at a spot on the paper map. "But we lost some ground on the highway itself – they've made it almost to Valley and Cherry, and they're movin' some heavy stuff down the highway to that area –"

"I thought we were gonna *blow* the fuckin' thing," interrupted the Lictor General. "What's the hold-up?"

"Truck with the nitrate and diesel took a stray round and went off early," replied the lieutenant. "Whole block went *with* it, of course. But we got another on the way. Should be there by midnight. You want us to hide and rig her to blow when they drive by... or just knock out the road?"

"No – just park it under the Cherry Street overpass and bring the fucker down... block it best you can," directed the Aryan leader. "But put a few mines in the rubble, and stick some snipers with a clear shot at the area, just to make 'em take some time tryin' to clear it."

"Done," said the first lieutenant. "You know... we're gettin' reports from the few sleepers we got within the Army Southwest Front H.Q., that morale within that pussy army's damn shitty. They scraped the bottom of the barrel to get enough boots on the ground to make this push, and they're payin' for it – they're only advancin' if they got max firepower deployed, and they stop cold if we pick one or two off. We inflict a few more casualties, we might even get a mutiny out of it. Somethin' to *hope* for, in other words. Wish we'd been able to hook up with our NLR brothers in Beverley Hills, instead of endin' up stuck out here. Sure could use a few more boots on the street."

"Yeah," agreed the Lictor General. "And I haven't ruled out tryin' to break out toward the Hills, either; but we'd have to cross a shitload of hostile turf, carryin' the 'package' along with us would make that even harder... and we gotta make a stand *somewhere,* after all. I'm just glad that we're not seein' too many of them fuckin' drones – waste of a MP-SAM to take 'em out. Make sure you enforce the rule I sent out last week – 'save the missiles for high-priority targets... 'copters, transports, tanks, APCs, and so on'. We got a decent stockpile, after knockin' over that armory – but we gotta make every one count."

The lieutenant nodded affirmatively.

The Lictor General turned his attention to the other man, a huge, hulking guy with a shaved head and tattoos all over his scalp.

"What about the western side?" queried the Whiteman commander. "'No quarter there'; that's the front we *got* to prevail on. What's the status?"

"Hold on," argued the second Aryan warrior., "Even the *spics* ain't crazy enough to go up against a *nuke!* Why don't we just *tell* 'em about it... same as with the government?"

"Even if we *can* negotiate with the Army over the 'package'... which is by no means assured," explained the Lictor General, "Fuckin' wetbacks are too stupid to understand English in the first place. They'd never believe that we even *got* it."

"But didn't we get it off 'em in the first place?" pressed the shaved-head man. "They *must* know that we've got it!"

"Supposedly," confirmed the commander, "But I'm told that we smoked every *one* of 'em that was in the van that we stopped at the check-point. This is second-hand, as we lost a lot of soldiers in that fire-fight, and they didn't get an exact count of how many *tamale*-suckers that they were up against. Point is... the wetbacks got nobody to verify that it fell into our possession. It got sent from Hitler knows where, for Hitler knows what reason... and then it just *vanished*. They're so fuckin' dumb that they probably think the van that had it, got in a car accident or something. And all this is on top of the fact, that I don't 'negotiate' with an inferior race of brown-skinned mongrels and degenerates, in the first place. The Army's bad enough. So we gotta do them Latino fuckers, the old-fashioned way. Now... what's the report, Whiteman?"

"Wish I could give you some good news," ruefully admitted the second under-study, "But I can't. For every one of them scumbag Latinos that we smoke – and it's been *hundreds* now, I bagged three today myself – another two seem to show up out of *nowhere*, to take over for 'em. They're mostly comin' straight down the Freeway, and they've made it as far as North Vineyard, although we've noticed groups of 'em tryin' to infiltrate as far north as 8th Street. Had a few fire-fights up there, sent 'em runnin'... but we're low on boots on the ground in that sector. I'm not sure we can hold the line, if they make another strong push along 8th."

"What *I* don't understand," accusingly commented the Lictor General, "Is why a bunch of fuckin' *tamale-suckers* like them, has managed to push back the finest of the white *race!*"

"General," defensively answered the gigantic, west-front lieutenant, "It's not just numbers... although that's a big part of it. They got some fuckin' new weapon, likes of which I ain't never seen or heard of; only a few of our warriors who ran into it, lived to tell. Apparently, when they're gonna use it, first you hear that damn music that the wetbacks love – but it don't sound exactly the same, it's, like, rock, *mariachi* and an orchestra all together with a real fast beat, and the sound comes from *everywhere*, not from in front of you –"

"What the *fuck?*" exclaimed the Whiteman leader. "*Music?* What's the *point* of somethin' like that? Just gives 'em away!"

"Could be psy-ops," offered the east-front lieutenant. "But for what it's worth, I ain't seen *nothin'* like it on my side... which is a *good* thing."

"You ain't heard the *best* part," continued the frustrated west-front subordinate. "After the music, this cloud of flyin' shit – like an insect-plague or somethin' – it comes rushin' at you, and it don't matter if you open up with an AR or a RPG, rounds go right through it; flamethrower slows it down, but it just goes around the flame and comes right at you. If you don't get the fuck out of there immediately, well... we re-took a strong-point that had been hit by this thing, and the results weren't pretty. Our men had been eaten away almost down to the bone, and there were a bunch of maggots and other such shit all over 'em. Of course, we took what was left for a proper Aryan burial on the funeral-pyre... but the point is, this thing can easily break *any* position we got – however well-fortified."

"Let's say you're right, and I don't fire you on the spot, for not knowin' how to fight a war," growled the Lictor General. "I don't need excuses – I need *plans, ideas*... somethin' that'll *defeat* this thing! Floor's all yours, Whiteman."

Knowing that the penalty for failure within the Brotherhood was usually not a pleasant one, the west-front commander hesitated for a moment, considered his options and then said, "First of all… although the damn thing has showed up in different places at different times, 'far as I know, we never seen it in more than one place at any *one* time. So maybe they only got one of whatever the fuck it is. Secondly – if we're up against a better weapon than we got, basic rule of combat is, 'every gun's gotta have a guy firin' it'; so maybe it'd be smarter to attack the wetback who's *controllin'* this fuckin' thing – side-flank, rear-flank, that is – rather than to go up against it, frontally."

"So how should we *do* that?" patiently asked the Lictor General. It was obvious that he already knew the answer; this was just a test, one that the west-front lieutenant would fail only at his peril.

"Well," he slowly proposed, pointing at the map as he spoke, "Our problem now is, every time that this fuckin' thing's showed up, after the screamin's over, there's nobody left who had a good look at it... or at whoever's aimin' it. To do that – and to pop the wetback with the weapon, maybe even capture it for our own use – we'll need a scout-team, maybe three or four of our toughest guys, to sneak around on foot behind them Latinos' front lines and get some intel, then take the shot. It'd be risky, to say the least, because there's *thousands* of 'em in Upland and Ontario... we'd have to detour north through San Antonio Heights, maybe take Route 210 west and try not to get tied up in any long fire-fights."

"*Now* you're talkin'!" appreciatively responded the Whiteman leader.

"I'd recommend that we turn south on Monte Vista and then hope we hear that damn *mariachi* music," continued the west-front commander. "If so, we'll know we're gettin' close. I'd suggest goin' south – shorter distance – but we had a patrol smoked down there a few days ago, circumstances aren't clear but it looks like a different bunch of gang-bangers done it, and we *know* the Latinos are thin up north."

"Now who, do you suppose, should be on this strike-force?" asked the Lictor General.

"I ain't afraid to lead it," answered the big, tattooed Aryan warrior. "I promise you a *thousand* wetbacks will fall, in exchange for this pure, white body. I'll need Buzz Blackworth and Little Joe Hale – I don't think either of 'em will turn down a glorious mission like this – not sure about the third guy, if any.

I'll let you know my choice by end of day today. We'll need our pick of the best weapons and gear, particularly that body-armor that's in short-supply... okay?"

"You *got* it!" confirmed a satisfied Lictor General.

"Anythin' else?" requested the east-front lieutenant.

"Just one thing," indicated the Aryan Brotherhood leader. "We aren't broadcastin' this to the troops... but as you are both senior leaders, you're entitled to be warned. If we think we got the 'package' rigged and ready, we'll send up two star-shell rockets, one after the other, a safe distance away from the bunker. We'll repeat that once more over the space of an hour, just so you can't miss it."

"And if it's time... *our* time?" stiffly asked the west-front lieutenant.

"Another star-shell... accompanied by *Ride of the Valkyries*, comin' from the biggest speakers we got," explained the Lictor General. "We've also got a radio-transmitter here, we'll do as many channels as we can over-ride, with the power we got. Even just from the speakers, you should be able to hear it at least a mile away... maybe further."

"A mile's still more than close enough to be... *you* know. Or so I've been told," stoically offered the east-front warrior.

"When you hear that sacred song... you'll know you got thirty seconds to a minute, to prepare yourselves," calmly remarked the Aryan leader. "And you'll know that I'll have already started what can't be stopped, and that I'll be standing right on top of the 'package', with sacred white blood dripping from my dagger, as final sacrifice to our Savior, Adolf Hitler. With my last breath, I'll growl your names, as Aryan warriors who died, nobly fighting for the white master-race. Terrible are we... and terrible will be our fate!"

"We'll make you – and our race – proud!" gruffly pledged the west-front lieutenant. The other one just nodded affirmatively, with a stony facial-expression.

As the two big, tough, race-warriors were just about to leave this room in the underground refuge, the Lictor General called out a blessing.

"*Odin speed to Valhalla, Whitemen!*" he bestowed.

– Here ends –

The Race